THE CHEMICAL COCKTAIL

80
Hg
Mercury
200.592

Fiona Erskine

POINT
BLANK

A Point Blank Book

First published in Great Britain, the Republic of Ireland and Australia
by Point Blank, an imprint of Oneworld Publications, 2022

Copyright © Fiona Erskine 2022

The moral right of Fiona Erskine to be identified as the Author of this work has been
asserted by her in accordance with the Copyright, Designs, and Patents Act 1988

ISBN 978-0-86154-033-4
ISBN 978-0-86154-034-1 (ebook)

Typeset by Geethik Technologies
Printed and bound in Great Britain by Clays Ltd, Elcograf S.p.A.

This book is a work of fiction. Names, characters, businesses,
organisations, places, and events are either the product of the author's
imagination or are used fictitiously. Any resemblance to actual
persons, living or dead, events, or locales is entirely coincidental.

Oneworld Publications
10 Bloomsbury Street
London WC1B 3SR
England

MIX
Paper from
responsible sources
FSC® C018072

For Matthew, of course.

Brazil is the country of the future – and always will be.

Guide to chapter headings

 12

Twelve months earlier

Just before midnight, seven days before Christmas

Christmas Eve

Christmas Day

DETONATION MINUS 7

Praia de Moçambique, Florianopolis, Brazil

Seven days before Christmas

The crunch of shoes on gravel jolted her from sleep.

Jaq Silver opened her eyes and raised her head from the pillow. Darkness enveloped her, just a pale sliver of moonlight stealing through the gap between shutter and window. No light inside the beach house. Mercúrio had left her. Had he forgotten something? Returned quietly to avoid disturbing her? Quietly? She dismissed the thought before it even half formed. A human tornado, Mercúrio was more puppy than panther.

They'd argued before. He'd walked out on her before, but this time he wasn't coming back. Things were said that couldn't be unsaid. Honest things. Angry things. The holiday was over. She'd be alone again this Christmas.

The footsteps were closer now, moving from the path to the veranda. A mosquito whined in her ear as she strained to listen. Crepe soles on polished wood, crinkly coagulated latex squeaking against the wide mahogany planks. Slow and stealthy, moving round from the garden to the beach side of the house. Furtive. Up to no good.

A thief? There was little of value here. If she had any common sense, she would lock herself in the bathroom and let him take whatever he wanted.

But when the adrenaline flowed, she tended to follow the

chemical messengers coursing through her body. Which told her not to back herself into a corner, but to face trouble head-on.

Reaching over the side of the bed, she swept her hands just above the floorboards until a fingertip touched the soft fabric of her dress. Short skirt, halter neck, the silk creased and rumpled from the speed at which she'd removed her clothes last night. She pulled it on. Cover enough.

The footsteps halted. Heart thudding, she swivelled her legs until her feet made silent contact with the hardwood floor.

What if it wasn't just a thief outside? What if someone was coming for her? Someone who knew Mercúrio was gone for good? Praia de Moçambique attracted a colourful bunch. Those who needed to put some distance between their surfboards and civilisation. Rich kids escaping controlling parents, poor kids escaping the drudgery and toil of real life, foreign kids playing intrepid explorer.

While Jaq was working, improving the design of a nitrogen propulsion system, the surfers slept through the hottest part of the day in hammocks slung between the palm trees, waking from the long siesta to gather fruit and catch fish. They shared everything round bonfires, smoked weed, played guitar and talked nonsense. Up all night. Watching the tides, the shape of the waves, evaluating the breaks. Waiting for that hint of dawn, the trigger to paddle out to sea again.

Was it one of them creeping around outside? Someone she'd surfed with? Unlikely. Mercúrio's friends were a peaceful crowd.

Someone passing through? A convict on the run from a high-security prison? A rapist? A murderer?

The bathroom was definitely the safest place. A window too small for a man to climb through, a sturdy lock and a bolt too. That's where she should go. Grab her phone, make a dash for it, barricade herself inside and call for help.

She reached out to the bedside table. Her fingers brushed a

water glass, a book, a pair of earrings. No phone. *Xiça!* Where had she left it? Think. She closed her eyes.

She'd last seen it on the dinner table, silver against the white tablecloth, a splatter of garlic and parsley forming a halo all around. Mercúrio had cooked *spaghetti alle vongole*, sweet little clams, *amêijoas*, fresh from the surf. She'd been texting Marina when Mercúrio slammed down the serving spoon, accused her of ignoring him, taking him for granted. This criticism a bit rich from a twenty-something who was never without his phone, driving up the mountain in search of a signal just to update Instagram. But his anger was the trigger they both needed. Time to face the facts. She'd turned her phone off. Laid it down on the dining table. Where it must still be. *Merda.*

A new noise. Leather on brass. A gloved hand turning the outer door handle. She had locked up; she was sure of that. But Mercúrio must have unlocked the front door to leave. Had he locked it behind him? She held her breath. The door rattled but held. *Obrigada, querido.*

Click, click. This was no amateur, no sneak thief hoping for food or drugs, or cash to buy them with. How many people wore shoes and gloves on this beach? How many people used a lock pick?

Jaq sprang to her feet and yanked the bedroom door open. She sprinted across the corridor, racing to get to her phone before whoever was out there broke into her house.

Too late.

As she burst into the *salon*, the outer door swung open. Waves crashed onto the beach outside as a figure moved into the frame, silhouetted against the security light.

She backed away, swallowing hard at the rasp and click of a safety catch being withdrawn. The man in the doorway raised a gun and pointed it at her chest.

'You are Maria Jaqueline Marta Ribeiro da Silva,' he announced in stentorian tones.

Friends called her Jaq. Professional colleagues addressed her as Dr Silver. The child who was Maria Jaqueline Marta Ribeiro da Silva had become Jaq Silver many years ago.

Only one person continued to call her by her birth name. Right up until the day she died.

Y 12

Twelve months earlier

The bright white tower of Hospital São Francisco Xavier rose from a hill above Lisbon, commanding a fine view over the river Tagus to the port of Trafaria. The geriatric medical department was on the third floor, the female wing consisting of several nightingale-style open wards with eight beds in each section.

If this hospital was unfamiliar, it smelt like any other, a mix of bleach, chloroform and despair. Jaq hurried down a long corridor, the rubber soles of her trainers squeaking against the tiled floor, heart beating faster than feet could carry her.

Come quick, they said. She may not have much time left.

Angie lay in a simple hospital bed, one hand resting on the border of a white sheet where it had been folded over a pale-blue blanket. Her eyes were closed.

'Hello, Angie,' Jaq said.

Her mother's eyelids flickered, but there was no other response.

Jaq sank into a chair beside the bed, suddenly deflated. Anxiety gave way to light-headed relief. And something else, something darker, something she wasn't prepared to examine, not yet. She gazed down at her mother.

Angie had been a beautiful woman, and there were still traces of that loveliness as she slept. The delicate bone structure framed a heart-shaped face with high cheekbones and full lips.

A machine beeped and a nurse approached to check the charts at the end of Angie's bed. His aftershave, a scent of pine forest, followed in his wake. It smelt better than triiodomethane or carboxylic acid, more hopeful.

'*Como está minha mãe?* Jaq asked. How's she doing?

'*Muito melhor.*' Much better now. He smiled and continued in Portuguese. 'The consultant is just starting her daily round. Best ask her.'

An elderly woman in the bed opposite began shrieking.

The nurse sighed. 'I wish all my patients were as lovely and easy as your mum.'

She must be seriously ill then. Jaq opened her mouth to explain that her mother was never normally so tranquil, but patients in other beds were shouting for attention now, and the nurse moved briskly away.

The consultant introduced herself and pulled up a chair to sit opposite Jaq.

'Are you the daughter?'

'Yes.'

'Nasty episode. A reaction to the drugs she was on. She's stable now, but you need to steer clear of any more experimental regimes.' The doctor checked her notes. 'Quite the chemical cocktail.' She frowned at Jaq as if to say – what were you thinking?

What indeed? Jaq lowered her eyes. 'What's the outlook?'

'It's hard to say. Physically, there's nothing out of the ordinary for a woman of her age. Good heart and lungs, that's the main thing.'

'And mentally?'

'We haven't been able to do the usual tests. She seems to have checked out, switched off.'

'She's been like that for a long time. Before the new treatment she hadn't spoken for years.'

'With this experimental treatment, was she lucid?'

'Briefly. When we listened to music, she knew the composer, the piece, even the artist.'

'She was a musician herself?'

Ripples of sadness lapped at the edge of memory. Jaq nodded. 'Once upon a time.'

'It's common, even with advanced dementia, for patients to have clear early memories.'

'She complained of being in pain.'

'The admissions team mentioned that. We checked for any undiagnosed fractures or nerve damage. She has a touch of arthritis but nothing that could explain constant physical pain. How did it manifest?'

'She described it as if something was eating her bones from the inside.' *Terrible, terrible pain. Excruciating, unbearable.*

'Any delusions?'

That the convent nursing staff were torturing her. That the matron was the devil. That her son had been killed by her daughter. Not all of those things were true.

'Delusions, yes.'

'Had she been taking strong pain killers?'

'I believe so.'

'Classic symptoms of withdrawal from morphine.' The doctor frowned. 'Pain is difficult to treat correctly. It's the body's alarm signal to alert us that something is wrong. But often, especially with the elderly, the signals get mixed up or triggered for no reason and we can't find any underlying cause to deal with.'

'You mean it's not real? It's all in the mind?'

'All pain is in the mind. It doesn't mean it is not real to the sufferer.'

'But – to use your analogy – you can silence the false alarms?'

'Chemically, we can control it. Muffle rather than silence, and only temporarily. The body builds up tolerance. And wants more. And then you have a whole new set of problems.'

Jaq looked down at her mother. 'What next?'

'There's nothing more we can do for her in hospital. I'm proposing to discharge her. Will she be going home with you?'

The very idea brought panic, sudden and visceral.

'No,' Jaq said.

'So, back to …' the consultant checked her notes, 'the convent nursing home?'

'Yes.'

'Then make sure they don't peddle any more miracle cures.'

Jaq waited until the doctor moved on. She took her mother's hand and stroked the long, thin fingers. The ache in her heart sent tears to her eyes.

'Goodbye, Angie.'

Angie opened one eye and stared at her daughter. The moment of recognition was followed by a glare of pure venom.

'Maria … Jaqueline … Marta.' She drew quick, sharp breaths, separating each word with a hiss. 'Get … away … from … me.'

With a strength that never failed to surprise, Angie gripped her daughter's wrist, digging sharp fingernails into Jaq's skin before snatching her hand away.

'Go!'

It was the last time Jaq ever saw her mother.

Praia de Moçambique, Florianopolis, Brazil

The intruder remained in the doorway of the beach house, his large body filling the entrance, a gun pointing at Jaq. Dazzled by the security light behind him, she couldn't make out his features, but the booming voice was distinctive. Unique. She was certain they hadn't met before; she would remember that bass timbre with its guttural rasp. He had the delivery of a preacher addressing a vast congregation. Or a judge commanding a court of law. He knew who she was, had spoken her birth name aloud. Not posed as a question, pronounced as a statement of fact. What did he want?

Mouth dry, pulse racing, she scanned the room. In the soft glow of fairy lights on the Christmas tree, she could see the phone. Exactly where she'd left it, on the dining-room table at the far end of the room. Even if she could reach it before he did, call for help before he shot her, it would take time for anyone to respond. Praia de Moçambique was one of the least crowded of the forty-two beaches on the island of Santa Catarina. An hour's drive from Floripa with no population centre near the beach, the very remoteness of this cabin was the reason she chose it. To spend time alone with Mercúrio. To celebrate their first Christmas together.

And now he was gone.

No time to think about what was lost. A madman was pointing a gun at her.

'Get out of my house,' she said.

'It's not your house,' he said. 'This is an illegal construction.'

Porra! An armed eco warrior? Come to save the turtles by murdering tourists? Many of the beach houses in the national park were unlicensed, tolerated by the authorities to encourage an influx of tourist wealth. But Marina had helped her to rent this house perfectly legally and her environmental impact was benign, if not positive. But perhaps now was not the time to point this out to a man with a gun.

'The police are on their way,' she lied. 'We can discuss legalities with them.'

'Sit.' The man in the doorway waved the barrel of the gun towards the sofa.

She obeyed.

'Hands where I can see them.' He spoke with a Brazilian accent, educated, more Porto Alegre than São Paulo. She placed her palms on her lap, smoothing the short dress down over her thighs.

He pulled a phone from his shirt pocket and barked something unintelligible into it. Footsteps on the veranda. The slap of flip flops and squeal of bare feet. *Merda*, there were at least two more of him. Two men, faces covered with neckerchiefs, silhouetted by the outside light.

He gave an order. She didn't understand the dialect, but the message was clear – search the house.

Stepping forward, he kicked the door closed with his heel. The rattan creaked and squealed in protest as he slumped into a cane armchair. He reached out a gloved hand and clicked on a side light.

The man with the gun was in his forties, blond hair wisping at his collar, thinning over the crown, clean shaven apart from darker sideburns. His face was angular – square chin, thin mouth, sharp, triangular nose, deep-set eyes and protruding brow. He wore a checked cotton shirt, open at the neck to reveal a smooth chest, denim jeans and tan leather shoes with crepe soles.

A big man, solid rather than athletic, heavy rather than fat. Judging by his laboured movements, she could easily outrun him, but he sat between her and the outside door. He had a gun, but it was the gloves that gave her pause. Guns were not uncommon in Brazil, guns and gloves more sinister. Stay calm.

His two sidekicks were wreaking havoc. Pulling out drawers and throwing the contents to the floor. She could hear one of them in the bedroom and see the other one in the *salon*.

'If it's money you're after,' Jaq said. 'Take my wallet.' She nodded at the beach bag hanging from the dining chair opposite her phone.

'I don't want your money.'

'I don't have much of value.' She reached round to the back of her neck and unclasped the silver chain from Angie's box. 'Here.' The chain snaked into a little coil in her palm, and she stood up, holding it out to him.

He remained sitting, leant slowly forward and smacked it out of her hand. Jaq caught her breath at the casual violence. The silver chain flew into the air, described a glittering figure of eight, and clattered to the floor, skittering along the polished wood before coming to a rest beside the Christmas tree.

'Sit,' he ordered.

She obeyed. 'What do you want?'

'You know what I want.'

'I have no idea.'

'Your inheritance.'

⍙ 7

Teesside, England

Angie died in her sleep, slipping away one night when everyone least expected it.

By the time Jaq received the message, she couldn't get to Lisbon in time for her mother's funeral. Under Portuguese law, a burial or cremation had to take place within 72 hours of any death by natural causes. The nuns took charge of the burial arrangements; all that was left was for Jaq to arrange collection of her mother's personal possessions.

They were pitifully few. Jaq gave instruction for the disposal of everything except the strongbox.

When it arrived in England by courier, Jaq didn't open the parcel straight away. She placed it on Aunt Lettie's piecrust table in front of the high window that looked out over Yarm High Street and went for a run.

She chose a longer route than normal, over the road bridge and then along a muddy footpath that followed the sinuous River Tees up to Preston Park. The river was swollen with summer rain, brown and turbulent. Crossing the river again near Ingleby Barwick she used the cycle path as a running track, increasing her speed on the flat. She slogged up the hill to the prison and then flew back down into Yarm.

Panting, muddy and sweaty, she glanced up at the window as she crossed the road to her flat. The parcel was still there, glowering behind the glass, lurking in wait.

She scrubbed herself clean in the shower, dressed in skinny jeans and a loose shirt, and made a strong coffee, finding other tasks that needed her attention: cooker top to clean, emails to answer, bills to pay.

It wasn't until a shaft of evening sunlight illuminated the cardboard that Jaq finally gave the parcel her full attention. She traced the flowing cursive letters with her finger. One of the nuns must have written delivery instructions on the side of the cardboard packaging. Jaq stared out of the window for a while. Then she went to the kitchen and fetched a sharp knife, sliced through the parcel tape and extracted the strongbox.

Made of steel with a leather covering, the strongbox measured about forty-five centimetres, a foot and a half, on each side. The padded leather handle suggested that it had been used as a travelling safe in the days before luggage sizes were standardised and banks moved money electronically. Inside, the box was lined with quilted red silk that had faded to pink and come away in places, exposing the welded steel plates behind. The handle was secured to the lid by two brass rings, and there was more polished brass on the four sides: a sturdy brass lock on the front, double hinges at the back and latches on either side. The tan leather was in good condition everywhere except the eight corners of the cube. If the sharp edges had been rounded, the strongbox might have passed for a modern vanity case, but it was lumpen and heavy, not a thing of beauty.

Jaq picked up her mother's parting gift and set it on her lap. The sharp metal corners poked through the tan leather, digging into the skin of her thighs through her jeans.

She untied the string that attached the rusty key to the handle of the box. A pulse beat in her throat as she inserted it into the lock. It stuck and snagged, the mechanism stiff from disuse.

There had always been an air of mystery associated with the strongbox. It had been hand-made specially for her grandparents at a time when they were wealthy. The da Silva family fortune was long gone: the farms in Angola confiscated after independence, the properties in Lisbon sold to fund Angie's care. But the contents of this box had come to Jaq's rescue more than once. She'd never been allowed to see inside it before, but it had produced a birth certificate for a new passport when she was on the run and emergency cash that allowed her to disappear for a time.

Abandoning the key in the lock, Jaq fetched some olive oil from the kitchen to lubricate the mechanism.

Now the key turned smoothly. The lock sprang open.

Jaq took a deep breath.

DETONATION MINUS 6

Praia de Moçambique, Florianopolis, Brazil

The sky outside was lightening, the pre-dawn chorus in full throat. Mercúrio and the other surfers would be paddling out now, the milky phosphorescence lighting their hands, guiding their boards, a green, briny tang in the air. Jaq longed to be out there with them, bare feet on cool, damp sand, head cocked to hear the size and shape of the magnificent rollers breaking in the dark, ready to catch the first waves as the sun rose.

She'd often surfed with Mercúrio before breakfast, banishing the dregs of sleep in the cool Southern Atlantic water, catching a few waves before starting a day's work. How she wished she was out there now, stomach down on a rough board, each scratch and dimple on the polyurethane preserving a memory, a story to share. Hands and arms propelling herself through clear water, paddling out towards the sunrise and the swell.

Anything was better than being held at gunpoint by an oaf in gloves, while his goons emptied the drawers and cupboards of the beach house with careless abandon.

'My friend will be back any minute,' she lied.

'Mercúrio?' He shook his head. 'No, Mercúrio won't be coming back.'

Merda. She clenched her fists, digging her nails into the soft palm. How did he know Mercúrio? How could he know they had parted?

'What do you mean?'

'Mercúrio won't be going anywhere.' He laughed, a harsh, guttural sound.

What was he implying? *Amor de Deus.* Had they harmed Mercúrio? Why would anyone wish to harm someone so harmless?

The goons reported back, empty-handed. She couldn't follow the dialect, but she could get the gist of his anger before he turned on her.

'Where is it?' he demanded.

'Where is what?'

'Don't play dumb with me,' he said. 'Your mother's old leather strongbox.'

Jaq swallowed hard. How did he know about her mother? And the box of hateful secrets. 'I have no idea what you are talking about.'

'Call Mercúrio.' He nodded towards her phone on the table.

Jaq gulped. Had Mercúrio spoken to this man? Confided? Or worse, could Mercúrio be in league with these criminals?

She moved slowly to retrieve the phone, aware of three sets of eyes on her. She could call the police. And she would, as soon as she understood Mercúrio's involvement. Her fingers trembled slightly as she found his number and dialled.

An unfamiliar voice answered. 'Wait a moment.' The stranger spoke in heavily accented English, shouting above the chug of an engine.

'Where's Mercúrio?' Jaq demanded.

The lap of water was followed by the sound of bare feet on wood. Then a slap and a shout. *Acorde!* Followed by a groan and a rattle of metal chains.

'Jaq? *Graças a Deus!* No doubt about the voice this time, Mercúrio. 'I'm so sorry …'

Xiça! Where was he. 'Are you OK?'

'God, I've been such a fool.' She caught the sob in his voice. 'Just do as they say.'

'What's going on?'

'Jaq, listen to me. You're my only hope. If you give them what they want, they say they'll let me go.'

Jaq could hear the sea in the background. *Crash, swirl, gush and splash.* Vaguely familiar. 'Where are you?'

'I have no idea.'

'Who are they?'

'I don't know, but they mean business.' More noises. 'Jaq, be careful—'

A thud, a cry and then the line went dead.

Y 6

Teesside, England

The sun had disappeared over the Pennines, but the sky above Teesside was still bright, with that limpid, watercolour wash that brings an early summer day to a close. The little market town of Yarm was filling with Saturday night revellers. The clatter of heels and babble of youthful voices filled the High Street.

Jaq sat at the window of her flat and ran her hands over the leather-covered strongbox, pausing at the brass latches at either side. The click-click of metal and the faint scent of lavender as the lid began to open conjured up a vivid memory of her mother opening this box.

Angie. Maria dos Anjos Ribeiro da Silva. Cold and distant. Always disapproving. A beautiful, sensitive, highly strung woman knocked off her fragile balance by war, the death of her son, sent into a tailspin by the disgrace her daughter brought on the family, crashing and burning when her husband died. Obstinately living on in catatonic misery for another twenty years.

Jaq blinked, dry-eyed. Where was the grief at her mother's passing? What did she feel? Relief? No, not that. The sorrow ran deep. A dull ache ever-present, a dark river of longing for what could have been, what might have been, snaking back from their separation, merging into their shared past.

Jaq sighed. If not relief then what? Release. Yes, that was it. Angie's pain was gone, and with it Jaq's guilt, dissipating with her mother's last breath.

Jaq opened the strongbox and made a quick, visual inventory. All the cash had gone. Whether Jaq had received everything that remained when she visited, or whether someone had taken it since, she didn't know. Would the nuns steal an old woman's cash? They had cared for her mother for a long time. Why wait until her death to rob her? A venal priest perhaps? She didn't really want to pursue that line of thought. With no idea how much her mother owned in the first place, there was no way to prove if anything was missing. A long court case in Portugal held no appeal. Jaq didn't need money that badly.

She reached in and removed the papers.

The official documents were bound in different-coloured ribbons, little rolls of waxed paper that captured officialdom, bureaucracy, law and order, rights and property.

The first roll she untied contained her mother's birth and death certificates – Maria dos Anjos Couto Roubado Ferreira Ribeiro da Silva. Born Luanda, Angola. Died Lisbon, Portugal.

The second was her mother's marriage certificate, a civil ceremony, to Anton Oleich Sakoshansky, Russian diplomat, political attaché to the Red Army mission in Angola. A marriage of love between ideological opposites, a union that shocked Angie's wealthy parents into disowning their only daughter. Mother-daughter schisms seemed to run in the family.

The third contained the birth certificates of Angie and Anton's children. Jaq unrolled the entry for her brother, Samuel Anton Gaspar Ribeiro da Silva.

There was no death certificate, those niceties tended to get lost in civil wars behind enemy lines.

Outside, an ambulance siren wailed, the flashing blue light glinting and diffracting in the mirror. She closed her eyes and tried to picture Sam, but the images would not come.

Poor Sam.

She found her own birth certificate next: Maria Jaqueline Marta Ribeiro da Silva. A document that had proved useful when she needed a new passport in a hurry, fleeing trouble in Slovenia before rushing headlong into catastrophe in Belarus and Ukraine.

Under the rolls, two jewellery boxes lay in the base of the strongbox. The smaller one held a ring, a clear central stone flanked by a circle of coloured gems. Almost certainly from Angola but she'd never seen her mother wear it. Perhaps it was an engagement ring from the fiancé she rejected, the son of a wealthy family in Luanda. Blood diamonds? The second box was larger and held more familiar things. A pair of smoky quartz earrings, the cut stones sparkling in their elegant settings, a fine silver chain with a crude wooden cross, a carved jade brooch, two simple gold bands, one large, one small. Were these the rings exchanged by her mother and father when they married? Did her father leave his ring with his wife before he went back to war, back to his death at Cuito Cuanavale? Or did someone take it from his corpse and return it to Angie? With a letter perhaps?

Jaq ran her fingers over the silk lining. There were no letters or photographs in the box, but there was something odd. The inside dimensions appeared smaller than the outside, shallower. She put her hand in the box and tapped all round. An echo returned from the bottom of the box. Hollow. A secret compartment? She turned the box upside down and hit it smartly on the base. Nothing moved. She put her hands inside and searched the silk lining for some lever, a mechanism to open the base. *Nada.*

She had a sudden memory of her mother, turning away from her, shielding the precious case behind her bony frame. Closing the box and then opening it again.

Jaq closed the lid. She pushed the clasps away from the handle. Opened it. Empty. She tried again but this time she pushed the clasps towards the handle. A faint *click* from inside the box. When she opened it, the false bottom was ajar.

Heart pounding, she prised it open.

From the secret compartment of her mother's strongbox Jaq extracted three rolls of documents.

She started with the oldest. Woven linen paper, with ragged threads along the edges, unrolled to reveal an engraving of a bull elephant emerging from the jungle, while a steam train crossed a viaduct overhead – bonds in a private rail company in Angola, *Caminhos de Ferro de Luanda*. These documents, which promised to repay the bearer large sums of money, would never be honoured; the company had collapsed long ago.

Most of the roll concerned the railways, but there were other bonds too: land concessions for a coffee plantation with mining rights. All pre-1975.

The second roll contained green engravings on pink parchment, company shares in an iron mine. Probably worthless now. After the 1974 revolution, when Portugal exited its biggest colony with indecent haste, the new Angolan government seized and nationalised private mines into one giant state enterprise – *Ferrangol.*

The last roll was the newest. As Jaq unrolled the glossy blue-white papers her short cry of surprise lengthened into a howl of pain.

Praia de Moçambique, Florianopolis, Brazil

A thin band of light appeared on the horizon, delineating sea from sky. Outside the beach house, dawn was breaking.

Inside the beach house, a man and a woman sat in silence. The man held a gun. The woman was staring at a phone in disbelief.

Jaq spoke first 'Where is Mercúrio?'

'Safe.' The man tapped the barrel of his gun against his thigh. 'For now.'

'What do you want from him?'

'From him? From that worthless beach bum?' He made a fist with his left hand and then opened it. 'Nothing.' His thin lips curved into a half smile. 'But we understand that he means something to you.'

Play it cool. 'He walked out on me a week before Christmas,' she shrugged. 'Why should I care what happens to him now?'

'You're a bad liar,' Crazy Gloves snarled. 'We know exactly what he means to you.'

Unlikely, given that she didn't really know herself.

'You won't stand by and watch him suffer.'

That at least was probably true. She'd never learned to cut her losses. Never been able to let go of those she had once cared for. Or those who depended on her. Not after what happened to Sam.

'Let Mercúrio go.'

'I'll make a deal.' Crazy Gloves leant forward. 'Tell me where the strongbox is, and I'll tell you where we're holding him.' He looked at his watch. 'If you are quick, you might even be in time to save his life.'

Jaq had no idea why this man wanted the safe – he was welcome to the damn thing, welcome to the vile contents – but she could never tell him who she had given it to or where it was right now.

6

Cumbria, England

After closing her mother's strongbox, Jaq barely slept.

As soon as it was light, she collected Aunt Lettie's ancient Land Rover from the garage and set off over the Pennines into Cumbria.

Summer came late to the north of England. The leaves on the ash trees had not long burst out from sticky black buds and retained a pinkish hue. A mixture of shimmering new green and clattering old gold clothed the beech hedges, the verges underneath filled with pink campion and blue speedwell and the horse chestnut trees above still decorated with white flower candles.

Jaq paused at the entrance to the farmhouse kitchen. A kettle whistled on the stove and delicious scents wafted from the open Rayburn oven, acetyl pyridines from the Maillard reaction taking place inside the loaf of freshly baked bread that Emma knelt to test.

'Jaq.' Emma cast off her oven gloves and jumped up, arms open wide. 'At last!'

Emma possessed a special, melting warmth. Human body temperature averages 37 degrees centigrade, or 98.6 Fahrenheit, and yet the woman who married her best friend always felt perceptibly warmer. And soft. So soft. Not fat, just rounded in a way that made Jaq feel like a stick of hard ice in her embrace.

'I was so sorry to hear about your mother.' Emma released Jaq from the hug and took a step back, blue eyes like searchlights.

'Thank you.' Jaq dropped her gaze, blinking away the unexpected prickle of tears.

'Are you OK?'

With anyone else, Jaq would have dissembled. *I'm fine. My mother was in constant pain, suffering from advanced dementia, she didn't know me, didn't want to know me.* But there was something about Emma.

Ben burst into the room.

'Aunty Jaq!' He barrelled towards her on sturdy little legs, his face beaming with excitement. 'Have you brought me a present?'

'Ben, where are your manners?' Emma chided. 'Jaq has had a long journey.'

'But I've got something for her!' Ben rushed to the fireplace and collected a stout forked stick. He turned and stopped, glancing at his mother. 'Why is she sad? Aunty Jaq is never sad.'

Jaq wiped her eyes with the back of her hand. 'I'm not sad any more.' She reached out and took the stick. 'This will make a great catapult.'

Ben nodded. 'That's what Daddy said. He said you'd help me to make the whizziest and dangerousestest slingshot in the world. In the universe. In the whole galaxy.'

Emma handed Jaq a tissue. 'Johan is out kayaking with a corporate group. He'll be back around six.'

Jaq glanced up at the clock. A few hours to kill.

'OK, Ben. Help me to unpack and then we'll get to work.'

Jaq travelled light. Ben pulled her small trolley case, tugging and yanking it over the gravel and Jaq followed with the battered leather safe and two bottles of wine.

'What's that?' Emma asked, ignoring the wine and pointing to the box.

'Some ... um ... legal stuff.'

'You want me to take a look at it?'

Emma held out a hand to take it.

'Not now.' Jaq glanced at Ben. 'Later.'

Too late.

'What's that box for?' Ben let go of the suitcase and the metal trolley handle clattered to the tiled floor.

Jaq shrugged and lifted her mother's safe onto the chair for his inspection. 'It's an old safe. All the way from Africa.'

'What's inside?'

'There's a present for your little sister, for when she grows up.' Jaq took out the jewellery box with the jade brooch. 'And some old papers. Your mummy is going to check something out for me.'

Ben brought out his stick and sized it up against the box.

'Would this keep my whizziest catapult safe?'

'Better than safe.' Jaq opened the lid and removed the papers before showing him how to open the secret compartment.

'Wow!' He did a little dance of joy. 'Is this for me? Can I keep it, can I?'

'Ben, no.' Emma rebuked her son.

Jaq laughed. 'It's OK. Where's the harm? I'd love him to have it.' She handed the empty box to Ben. 'Here, this is for you. Keep this safe safe.'

Praia de Moçambique, Florianopolis, Brazil

Outside the beach house, the garden was coming alive. As the flowers unfurled to meet the early morning sunshine, a pair of tiny hummingbirds, their body feathers iridescent emerald and sapphire, hovered to drink the nectar. A troupe of little monkeys chattered as they groomed one another on the edge of the forest. A female marmoset with white patches on her black fur and rings round her tail ventured into the garden, heading for the passion-fruit tree. At the squawk of a parakeet, her tufted ears twitched, and she scampered back to the others.

Two men entered the garden carrying spades and began digging. Crazy Gloves had given new orders to his sidekicks.

Through the window, Jaq watched in dismay at the inept search for recently buried treasure.

'The strongbox isn't here,' she said.

'Where is it?'

She shook her head. 'I don't have it.'

'That's bad news for Mercúrio.'

Could she distract him long enough to make her escape? Go straight to the police? And if she managed to reach them before this madman stopped her, how would the authorities respond? Brazil was the home of extortion by kidnapping; the disparity in wealth between rich and poor, the inequality of opportunity, encouraged criminal gangs to redistribute wealth using more unconventional routes. The under-resourced local police were at best ineffectual in the face of organised crime. At worst they were complicit. Involving the police in a kidnapping often led to the permanent disappearance of the hostage. Whatever the rights and wrongs of it, whether or not Mercúrio wanted to see her again, she couldn't abandon him.

Play for time.

'I can give you money,' Jaq said. If they agreed to let her go to a bank, she could raise the alarm, enlist the help of his surfing friends.

'I don't want money. I want the strongbox.'

Why? 'It's just a worthless leather-covered metal box.'

'I'll be the judge of worth.'

'All the documents are gone.'

'I have no interest in the contents. Just the box itself.'

'I gave it away.'

'Then get it back.'

She turned her hands, palms upwards and shook her head. 'I can't.'

He pulled a small phone from his top pocket. 'Shall I tell them to throw him into the sea?' he asked.

Jaq bit her lip – perhaps that was his best chance of escape. Mercúrio was in his element in the water, a superb swimmer. As if Crazy Gloves could read her mind, he added. 'Hog tied, in chains.'

'Stop.' She held up a hand in alarm. 'I'll try.'

'I can wait.' He put the phone back in his pocket. 'I'm not so sure about poor Mercúrio.'

'The box is not in Brazil. I'll have to go and get it. How do I get in touch with you?'

'You don't. We'll call you.'

'You have to give me, give him, time. A month.'

'A week,' He stood up. 'Be back here by midday on Christmas Eve.'

Jaq did a quick calculation and shook her head.

'That's only five full days. I don't think I can make it in time.'

'You better hurry, then. Or say goodbye to Mercúrio. This time for good.'

He turned on a squeaky crepe sole and walked out of the front door.

Y 6

Cumbria, England

On the north shore of Lake Coniston, the sun dipped over the western hills hours before dusk. An amber light lit the sky. The peaks glittered with burnished gold. A pillar of white wood-smoke rose from the farmhouse chimney. No wind, just the whizz and splash of projectiles hurled into a lake by a brand-new catapult.

The lights of a car swept over the summit of the winding road, easily identifiable as Johan's by the clatter of kayaks on the trailer behind. Ben tucked the catapult into his waistband and grabbed a handful of stones from the beach.

'Wait till Daddy sees this!' he shouted.

Jaq followed the little boy as he raced up the path towards the farmhouse, slipping on leaf litter and dislodging mossy stones that tumbled back towards the lake. 'Remember, no pointing that weapon at people,' she shouted after him.

Ben swung on the gate as the Land Rover rumbled over the cattle grid and crunched up the gravel drive. Jaq hung back, keeping to the shadows, watching father greet son. Johan assumed a serious expression, but the corners of his mouth twitched as Ben explained the construction minutiae of the catapult, its awesome reach and their plans to construct a trebuchet next. Johan must know that she was waiting in the darkness, she could sense him sensing her, but it wasn't until Ben raced off to collect more stones that he straightened and walked over to the trees.

'Hello, Jaq. It's good to see you.'

He wrapped his arms around her and pulled her close. A warm embrace, solid, reassuring, safe. More than safe. Like coming home. Except this wasn't her home. Jaq pushed him away, feeling hard muscle against the palms of her hands.

'Hello, Johan.'

He caught a wrist before she could back away, his eyes locked on hers.

'I'm sorry about your mum. Whatever the circumstances, it's a tough gig.'

She dropped her eyes and nodded. 'Want a hand with the kayaks?'

They worked well together, always had. No need for words. Johan unstrapped the trailer, and she matched her movements to his, remembering how to adjust for his strength with her technique. A synchronised dance, fluid, responsive: lift and drop, rotate and tip, swing and stack.

Emma waved at them through the farmhouse window, her daughter on one hip. Jaq waved back, smiling. Jade scowled and buried her face in her mother's chest.

Dinner, almost ruined when the cat attempted to make off with the roast chicken, was the usual chaotic family affair. Jaq cleared away and washed the dishes while Emma and Johan read to the children upstairs.

Curled up on the sofa by the fire, Jaq was almost asleep when they reappeared, hand in hand. They separated, Emma to get drinks, Johan to select some music from his vinyl collection.

'Ben is thrilled to bits.' He pulled a black disc from the red and yellow cardboard sleeve and placed it on the turntable. 'He's all fired up with the plans to build a giant catapult.'

Emma uncorked the bottle of *Herdade de Esporão* that Jaq had brought with her and poured two glasses. She handed one glass of ruby-red wine to Jaq, the other to Johan and picked up her own glass of water. She sat on the sofa next to Jaq. 'Will you be able to stay long enough to see it through?'

A wife's warning – don't outstay your welcome? Or a mother's concern – don't raise my child's expectations if you can't finish the project. Or just a lawyer's request for factual information?

'Stay as long as you like,' Johan said, glancing over at his wife who nodded slowly.

'Cheers,' Jaq said.

They clinked glasses.

'Is there a lot to sort out?' Emma asked. 'Your mother's estate, I mean.'

Johan threw a log on the fire. Damp wood hissed and crackled in the flames.

'No.' Jaq said. *And yes, but not in the way Emma meant.* 'My great-aunt dealt with it years ago. The property in Lisbon was sold to set up an annuity to pay for Angie's care. There wasn't much else.' *The costume jewellery. And the papers left to punish me.*

'There were some documents you wanted me to look at?' Emma said.

Johan put a hand on his wife's arm.

'It's just …' Emma shrugged it off. 'Sorry to be a bore, but I have something I need to finish for tomorrow, so if it's not urgent …'

The truth had waited this long, another day wasn't going to make a difference. Part of her was relieved that she didn't have to face up to it right now. She took a long sip of wine.

'It's not urgent,' Jaq said.

Emma placed her glass of water on the table. 'Then, if you two don't mind, I'll be in the study.' She stood up.

Jaq waited until she was gone. 'Everything OK?'

'Emma's busier than ever. She's representing this family of asylum seekers. Parents and two kids. Pretty rough story, they had to get out. A cut-and-dried case, but the UK government won't make a decision, and in the meantime, they can't work.'

'That's insane.'

'I know. Makes me ashamed to be British.'

Johan topped up Jaq's glass from the bottle. They sat without speaking for a while, letting the alto sax fill the void until the record finished.

'I can't forgive my mother.' Jaq's voice was quiet, barely a whisper.

Johan stood up and switched off the amplifier. He came and sat down next to her on the sofa.

'It's not always easy being a parent you know.' He put an arm around her. 'She lived through revolution and war and the death of her son.'

Jaq laid her head on his shoulder. 'She was a hopeless parent, even before Sam died.' Sinking back against his chest, she recoiled at the familiarity. Johan's body was too muscly to be comfortable, too attractive to be safe.

She slipped from the sofa to the sheepskin rug in front of the fire and fed some twigs into the flames, allowing the crackling tension to spark and hiss and flare. Beautiful combustion, but all it left was ash. Let it go.

Johan stretched out on the sofa, as if it had been his intention all along to displace her. 'Not all adults make good parents. And she was ill, wasn't she?' Johan tapped his temple.

Jaq snorted. 'She used that as an excuse.'

Emma appeared at the doorway.

'The fuckers!' she shouted. 'They've issued a deportation order!'

'You're joking!' Johan jumped to his feet and took the phone she held out. 'Christ almighty. And on a Sunday night.'

'It's deliberate. Most people can't get hold of a lawyer in time, and by Monday morning they are already in detention.'

'But most people don't have you as a lawyer,' Johan said.

Emma smiled and hugged him. 'You OK if I go?'

'You want me to come with you? That is,' he glanced over at Jaq, 'If Jaq doesn't mind babysitting.'

Emma shook her head. 'Nothing you can do. You guys stay here. I'll be back as soon as I've lodged the appeal.'

The crunching of gravel and the clatter of wheels over the cattle grid preceded a throaty hum of gear change followed by a low roar as the car climbed the steep pass. Then silence.

If Jaq was going to tell anyone what she'd discovered in the secret compartment of her mother's box, it would be Johan. But it would be safer if Emma was there too.

Johan picked up the bottle, tilted his head, one eyebrow raised in inquiry. Jaq put a hand over her glass and shook her head. He put it down again.

'I'm going to check on the kids,' he said.

Jaq yawned. 'I might be ready to turn in myself.'

Johan nodded. 'You OK with the futon in here.'

'It's perfect.'

'I'll wait up for Emma,' he said. 'I'll be in the study if you need anything.'

What I need from you right now, you are no longer free to give. 'Goodnight, Johan.'

'Night Jaq.'

They didn't embrace.

Florianopolis, Brazil

The sun rose above the sea. Turquoise water lapped against a crescent of white sand bordered by a glossy green fringe of forest. The air washed clean and fresh by last night's rainstorm.

A shaft of sunlight flashed through the east-facing window, the golden baubles on the Christmas tree catching the light. A bead of sweat trickled down between Jaq's breasts. Another hot day. Christmas was a northern festival, designed to bring cheer amid cold and dark. An incongruous celebration in the southern hemisphere, where it fell in the middle of summer. Not that Jaq had ever been a fan of Christmas; all this decoration had been Mercúrio's idea.

She didn't bother to shower. The need for speed, the desire to escape from the beach house – sullied by the visit of Crazy Gloves and his henchmen – took priority. Pausing only to pull on a leather jacket and grab the shoe roll, collect her passport and lock up, she was on the road within a few minutes. Jaq opened the throttle on her motorbike and headed for the airport.

She wasn't entirely surprised to be followed. If the situation had been less serious, she might have smiled at the rent-a-wreck that rattled over the sandy paths behind her. This was a cut-price outfit. Which didn't make it any less dangerous.

The road surface turned to gravel as she left the beach behind, and then tarmacadam as she approached the first small town. Other traffic filtered onto the road, and she was able to take advantage of the bike's speed and superior handling to overtake and put some distance between her and the tail. By the time she reached the dual carriageway, rising from the lagoon into the hills, there was no sign of the beaten-up car that had followed her.

What did they want with the strongbox? It was empty now. What could possibly be so important that they were willing to kidnap an innocent surfer to secure compliance with such a senseless demand? How did they know what he meant to her? What did he mean to her? Was this some sort of test? Less about the strongbox and more about her integrity?

No, she couldn't follow that train of thought, didn't like where it led. Right now, she preferred action to soul searching. Time enough for reflection once Mercúrio was safe.

Santos Dumont airport was still waking up, but the 24-hour covered parking was always open. She drove the bike to the lowest level of the underground car park and chose a corner space. Difficult to spot from the main ramp, but she still manoeuvred the bike into the shadows before rocking it onto the centre stand.

Inside the airport, she could only buy a ticket as far as São Paulo or Rio. She chose the former; the business hub of Brazil had more regular connections to Europe.

The next available flight got in to São Paulo before noon. The international flights left afternoon and evening, South American time, in order to arrive at a civilised time in Europe the next day. Johan could bring the box and meet her somewhere far from the Lake Coniston farmhouse. Ten hours flying time from São Paulo to Lisbon and only three more hours to Manchester. They could meet in Portugal on Jaq's home turf. She could be on her way back the same day with time to spare. Perhaps that was asking too much of Johan, making him travel so far. What about London? Fourteen hours flying time. Heathrow would be easier than Gatwick for anyone travelling from the north. Unless he was coming by car. Christmas weather, Christmas traffic. She could change planes in Frankfurt or Amsterdam and meet him in Manchester. Yes, that might be fairer. Best to speak to him first, then book flights that matched what worked for him.

The kidnappers had Mercúrio's phone, so they knew her number. Could they be tracking her phone? Monitoring her calls? She couldn't take the risk. She'd put Johan and his family in danger once before, she wasn't going to do that again. But she had to get a message to him.

When the first shops opened, she purchased a pay-as-you-go mobile phone from a man dressed as Santa Claus.

Jingle Bells

Jingle Bells

England was four hours ahead. She called Johan on the new phone. No answer. He must be out on the hills, enjoying the fine scenery and appalling reception.

She tried Emma's mobile.

The farmhouse landline.

Nothing but endless ringing bells.

Jingle all the way.

Y 6

Cumbria, England

The lake lay smooth as silk in the early morning summer mist. Jaq dived in from the rocky bluff and gasped as cold water enveloped her. She swam in long, smooth strokes: strong even kicks, elbows high, forearms curling forward, fingertips piercing the water in a superman glide – ten to two, ten to two. As she approached the first island, she stopped to get her bearings. The ripples radiated back towards the farmhouse.

Today was the day to tell them. No more procrastination.

Heavy clouds lowered over the mountains, the dark sky threatening an abrupt end to the early summer warmth, a storm approaching from the west. She turned away and swam into a pool of sunshine.

A warm glow enveloped her skin as she emerged from the lake. The joy of cold water came from the release of dopamine and serotonin to the brain. After the first shock – heart pounding, skin tightening, endocrine system on full alert – came the reward. Like banging your head against a brick wall, lovely when it stops. She wrapped a towel around her head, draped a thicker one over her shoulders and jogged back for a hot shower.

The smell of bacon wafted up the stairs, a sudden ravenous hunger drove her down to the kitchen.

Emma smiled, putting down the carton of eggs to hug her.

Soft. Sunny. Light. Happy. A foil to Johan's hard, dark, brooding reticence. Yin and Yang. Is that what makes a couple work?

'Good swim?' Emma asked.

'Fabulous. And now I'm ravenous.'

Emma pointed to the large silver machine on the counter. A rectangular base under two large, heated discs with long handles. A cross between a grill and a miniature spaceship. 'Waffles OK with you?'

And how. Jaq nodded. 'How did it go last night?'

'Success.' Emma grinned. 'Court orders riddled with errors. I kicked up such a stink that they retracted them.' She broke an egg into a bowl of flour and tossed the shell into the compost bucket. 'I've launched an official complaint.' Crack, slop, crunch – another egg and another. 'Should keep things quiet for a while.'

'They're lucky to have you.'

Emma added milk to the well of eggs and began to stir, little wisps of fine flour rising from the bowl.

'Shouldn't be a question of luck.'

The red light on the front of the waffle machine went out with a clunk as the old-fashioned bimetallic strip broke contact.

Emma poured the creamy batter into a ceramic jug and handed it to Jaq.

'Can you do the waffles while I finish the bacon?'

The handles of the waffle machine were spun from thick wire, wound into a helix, thin at the top and bottom, thick in the middle, the perfect design for heat dissipation. The machine was at 160 degrees centigrade, but the hollow spring handle remained cool to the touch as Jaq lifted the heavy lid from horizontal to right angles. She threw a dod of butter onto the base, using a pastry brush to smooth the melting fat over the dimpled plates, before pouring a test dollop onto the heated pan and closing the lid on its sturdy hinge. Steam began to emerge from the gap between heated discs, lifting the top disk slightly. When the hissing stopped, Jaq opened the lid again and used a knife to lift out a perfect miniature waffle, just as Ben raced into the room and hugged his mum's knees.

'Over here,' Jaq said. 'Quality control, please.'

She blew on the test piece and handed it to the little boy, who gobbled it up before awarding it a thumbs up.

Johan appeared in the doorway, Jade on his shoulders. He ducked as he came into the room and swung her into a high chair.

'Smells delicious!' He smacked his lips and began to set the table. Place mats, glasses, cutlery, napkins.

'Can I help?' Ben dragged a chair over to the waffle station and climbed up.

'I'm relying on you.' Jaq said. 'Remember the toolbox talk?'

Ben nodded. 'It's hot.'

'How hot?'

'Very hot. Dragon fire hot. Hot enough to burn me to a crisp.'

'Good. So, what don't we do?'

'We don't touch the metal.'

'And what else?'

'We keep away from the steam.'

'Excellent.' Jaq lifted the left lid of the waffle iron, added butter and handed him the jug. 'Let's get to work.'

Ben poured a cupful of thick batter onto the heated metal; Jaq closed the left lid and opened the right hand one for him to repeat the process. The first one had petals, extra lobes where batter spilled out of the side, lava flows of yellow gloop bubbling and hissing. The second was a crispy diamond, not quite filling the mould. Before long they had a rhythm going and a stack of half a dozen perfectly circular golden waffles.

The microwave pinged and a little jug of melted butter joined the table along with crispy bacon, maple syrup and a tall cafetière of rich-roast coffee.

Ben chattered all through breakfast, elaborating on his plans for the giant siege weapons that he and Jaq would construct.

Jade rejected the waffle and demanded some cereal. Emma poured a cupful of rice crispies into a bowl and placed it in front of her.

'Jaq, can you give her some milk?' Emma said.

Jaq handed the milk jug to Jade. The baby grasped the handle with a chubby fist.

'Jaq, no!' Johan jumped to his feet.

But he was too late. Jade turned the jug upside down, emptying milk over the cereal, over her chair but most of all over herself. The jug clattered to the floor and smashed into tiny pieces.

Jade began to wail.

'Cheer up.' Emma grabbed Jade, swinging her out of the chair. 'No use crying over spilt milk.'

'I'm so sorry.' Jaq fetched a cloth from the sink while Johan brushed away the shards of pottery. 'I didn't think—'

'Rookie error,' Emma said. 'You don't have kids.'

It was time to set the record straight.

São Paulo, Brazil

The São Paulo traffic was at a standstill. Engines revved and horns blared. The air outside the taxi window had turned a sickly yellow, the morning sun refracted by petrol and diesel fumes. Even biofuels, ethanol made from fermenting sugarcane waste, create pollution when sucked, squeezed, banged and blown through an internal combustion engine.

The flight from Florianopolis had landed in Congonhas airport one hour late. The old regional airport was in the southwest and Jaq cursed herself for rushing onto the first flight. Now she had to cross the sprawling, crowded city of São Paulo to reach Guarulhos International Airport in the northeast.

The taxi driver rolled down his window and directed a stream of invective at the brand-new jeep trying to muscle in from another lane. A blast of heat and fumes entered the battered old taxi.

The northern hemisphere might be shivering through one of the coldest winters on record, but south of the equator it was peak summertime.

São Paulo, with a metropolitan population of 20 million, built on a high plateau beyond the *Serra do Mar*, was 70 kilometres from the sea. Ringed by hills, the city became unbearably stuffy as Brazilian summer arrived, the temperature in December already over 30 degrees.

Paulistas – the natives of São Paulo – were on the move. A lot of them. All shapes and sizes and colours and ages. She stared up at the giant plastic Santa Claus waving at the queue of cars from the roof of a shopping mall. The most populous city in one of the largest countries in the world was Christmas shopping en masse.

Jaq checked her watch. She'd already missed the first flight out.

She took a deep breath, regretting it as she inhaled the fumes and started coughing. There was absolutely nothing she could do about the traffic, so she might as well make use of the time.

She tried Johan again. Still no reply. Where the hell was he? Perhaps he wasn't picking up because he didn't recognise the number. She tapped out a text.

Johan, we need to talk urgently – Jaq

She used her normal phone to call her boss. It didn't matter if anyone listened in to this call.

'Bruno, Jaq here.'

She'd been lucky finding work in Brazil, and her employer, Tecnoproject, seemed remarkably laid back about her hours. However, as her visa sponsor, they had to know when she left the country, or she might be barred from returning.

'Jaq!' He sounded pleased to hear from her. 'How's it going?'

'I'm flying to Europe for a few days. Family business.'

'But you're coming back?' The concern in his voice would have been gratifying if she hadn't had other things to worry about.

'Yes.' Most definitely.

'Fine. Merry Christmas!'

She inspected the other phone. No reply to her text.

The traffic was still barely moving. She checked the time again. Too late for the London flight. The next best option was Teesside via Amsterdam. If the kidnappers knew so much about her, they would already know where she lived. Or find out easily enough.

The moving traffic brought renewed squealing and honking as dozens of cars jostled to move into a single space, each intent on their own progress at the expense of anyone else.

Jaq tried Johan's mobile again.

Johan, where are you?

Y 6

Cumbria, England

The river frothed and boiled, the storm rain rushing from mountain to sea, carrying everything in its path.

Johan led the way in his bright-blue kayak. Jaq followed, ducking as she approached the mossy stone bridge, her body pressed flat against the scratched fibreglass hull, the paddle held firmly against one side of the yellow kayak. With the river in full spate, there was barely clearance for a boat under the centre of the stone arch, let alone for the paddler inside.

Johan was waiting for her on the other side, fighting against the current.

'That was close,' he shouted. 'You okay?'

She gave a thumbs up as she surged past him. Relief and exhilaration snapped to total concentration as she approached the white water. A foaming, boiling cauldron of danger. Follow the eddies. Tip at the swell. Johan was close behind, watching her back, the way he had always done.

As soon as it started raining, it was Johan's idea that they go for a paddle.

'Beats skiing any day,' Johan yelled as they curled into a deep pool.

'Only for wimps who do their sport sitting down!' Jaq retorted.

They flew over the final rapids and raced each other down the broad channel leading to the top of the lake.

Jaq emerged first into the vast expanse of grey water. The view never failed to impress, the lake fringed with ancient woods, wedges of mist clinging to the valleys, and stony outcrops adorning the rugged hills above.

'Did I pass?'

'With flying colours,' Johan said.

They paddled across the lake, side by side.

'I have news,' Johan said.

Jaq glanced at him. 'Good news?'

He nodded. 'Emma's pregnant.'

Of course. That explained the softness in her face and the odd dance around alcohol.

'Congratulations.'

'We wanted to tell you earlier, but, what with your mother and everything …'

Jaq smiled. 'Good news is always welcome.'

They rounded the headland and swung towards the jetty.

'Did I ever tell you the real reason why Gregor and I split up?' Jaq asked.

'Because he was a pompous arse who didn't deserve you?' Johan said.

Jaq struck the surface of the water with the flat of her blade to drench him in cold water. He rocked to avoid it but didn't retaliate.

Jaq and Gregor had married shortly after Johan and Emma. Johan had been his best man at the wedding. Gregor could've chosen any one of his friends from home, from work. Instead, he'd chosen Jaq's best friend. Who happened to be a man. A cruel trick. One of many.

'I told Gregor I didn't want children.'

'And he did?' Johan sounded surprised. 'I thought he already had them.'

'A daughter.' The reluctant bridesmaid at their wedding, a sullen, scowling teenager, now a mother herself.

'Gregor wanted a son.'

At the sight of his frown, she turned away, facing the distant jetty. Church bells rang out across the water.

'It wasn't just that I didn't want to.' Her voice fell to a whisper. 'I couldn't.'

He paddled round to face her. 'It's more common than you know. Emma and I were lucky.' Ben was a honeymoon baby, born nine months after the wedding.

She unstrapped her helmet and shook her wet hair. 'Not that either. Turns out, I never had the option.'

Johan's kayak remained motionless in the water despite the waves lapping against the side. Such deceptive power. His stillness belied a core strength, his stomach muscles countering the rocking waves.

'I don't understand.'

The concern etched on Johan's face caused her to hesitate. But if she didn't tell him, who could she tell?

'When I was at school, in Lisbon, there was a teacher—'

'Yoo hooo!'

Absorbed in her own memories, she hadn't noticed the group of paddlers approaching, a family of two adults and two children, the woman in the double kayak waving her oar at Johan.

'Former pupils,' he groaned from the side of his mouth. 'Sorry Jaq, I'd better go and say hello.' He waved back.

'Sure. We can talk tonight.' Perhaps it was better to wait, safer to tell Emma and Johan together, important that there were no secrets between the three of them. 'I'll see you back at the pier.'

They paddled off in opposite directions.

Guarulhos International Airport, São Paulo, Brazil

The passenger door slammed shut, and the taxi driver saluted as he roared back into the maelstrom of traffic.

Jaq pushed through the revolving door, shivering at the sudden blast of air-conditioning and piped Christmas music.

Deck the halls with boughs of holly
Tra la la la la
la la la la

She draped the motorbike jacket over her bare shoulders and made a beeline for the ticket desk. The easiest option was a return ticket to Teesside via Amsterdam.

As soon as she was through security, she tried Johan's mobile again, then Emma's. No reply. Where were they? She desperately needed to warn them. If Ben still had the strongbox, Johan could bring it somewhere neutral – a safe, anonymous place. Once she had it, she could exchange it for Mercúrio's freedom.

Would they play fair? Men with gloves and guns were not renowned for honouring contracts. Except in Brazil, where kidnapping was rife, almost business as usual; the perpetrators usually gave up their captives if their demands were fulfilled. She had to try. What choice did she have?

In desperation, she dialled the farmhouse landline again. A woman answered, but the voice on the phone was not Emma's.

'Hello,' Jaq said. 'Who is this?'

'This is Beryl, Johan's mother speaking.' The voice was frosty.

'Hello Mrs Smith. It's Jaq speaking, Jaq Silver. Can I speak to Johan?'

'Johan is in the hospital with Emma.'

The hospital.

'Her labour started last night.'

Porra! Why hadn't she remembered Emma's due date? Because she was a rotten friend, so intent on her own mission that she forgot everyone around her. Other people had lives too. So much for the plan that involved Johan riding to the rescue like a knight in shining armour.

'Is she OK?'

'I'm here at the farmhouse with the children, waiting for news.'

Jaq detected a coolness to her voice. Perhaps Johan's mother had never forgiven Jaq for breaking up with her son. Not that his family had been particularly welcoming when Jaq and Johan were dating. But like most mothers, she probably saw her child as perfect. In that they agreed; it was exactly why Jaq had ended the relationship all those years ago, long before he met Emma.

Even if Jaq and Beryl Smith had been best pals, she couldn't ask anything of the family right now. But at least she could establish if Ben still had the strongbox.

'Could I speak to Ben?'

'That would not be convenient.' Mrs Smith's voice had grown several degrees colder. 'We're waiting for news. We need to keep the line free. Now, if you'll excuse me.'

The dial tone told Jaq that Johan's mother had hung up. *Merda.*

This was getting complicated. Should she go and fetch the box herself? Go directly to Coniston? What if she was followed? Would that put Johan's family in danger? Again. Perhaps by the time she arrived in Europe, the new baby would be safely delivered, and Johan would be free to talk. They could hatch a plan, find a way. Maybe she could send a courier to collect the strongbox. And deliver it where? Her flat in Yarm. The kidnappers must already know the address. It was on most of the official documents she possessed.

Jaq checked the departures board. She still had two hours before her flight boarded and she needed to use every second wisely.

The backless, mini-skirted beach dress, motorcycle jacket and flip flops didn't constitute the most comfortable outfit to travel in; she'd freeze on arrival in England. Time to get more suitable clothes and a change of underwear.

There were several lingerie shops, the sort with only three items for sale, most of the shop taken up with video screens of impossibly shapely models showing off their surgically perfect bodies on a catwalk. Not selling underwear so much as selling sex. This was the place travellers bought provocative gifts for others. Gregor, her ex-husband, used to like buying her this kind of stuff, and she didn't mind wearing it. But then their sex life had never been the problem.

She selected three sets of panties – one to wear, one to wash and one spare – and a bra – without looking at the price labels.

At the check-out she gaped at the number that flashed up at the till.

If a problem can be solved by money, it's not a problem.

It was the sort of thing only a rich Edwardian, raised in British India, could say and get away with, but not for the first time did she thank Aunt Lettie for the education. Not just the formal one, but also the pragmatic one. The money she earned as a contract engineer gave her independence and security. Airport shopping was for situations where time was more precious than money.

She swallowed hard and paid up.

In a souvenir shop she picked up three cotton T-shirts, three pairs of socks and a travel bag with a picture of Sugar Loaf Mountain.

There wasn't a whole lot of choice in more substantial covering, but one concession had multiple brands and lay completely empty. Checking the prices in Balúrdio, it was clear why.

'*Oi,*' said the bored shop assistant in welcome. '*Que tal?*'

Jaq flicked through the racks and picked up a pair of designer jeans in her size and a silk shirt a couple of sizes too big. 'Do you have a changing room?'

The assistant showed her to a storage space right at the back, separated from the shop with a curtain. Clearly not many people bothered to try on clothes in Balúrdio. The cubicle was no more than a walk-in cupboard with a mirror, the false ceiling missing and open to the roof space above. But, most importantly, it had a power socket.

She unwrapped the new underwear, more packaging than fabric, and changed quickly. The jeans were lower on the waist than she liked, but the silk shirt covered her exposed midriff and was generous enough that she could wear one of the T-shirts underneath – the whole assembly comfortable enough for travelling.

Jaq opened the shoe roll. She paused for a moment, lost in admiration at Marina's extraordinary technology, a kit to create footwear for any occasion. This was not the time to make use of all the options, including colour-matching, all she needed was something robust and comfortable. Ten minutes later, Jaq was lacing a pair of thick-soled ankle boots.

The old clothes remained behind, stuffed into the plastic bag from the souvenir shop. Jaq stowed the plug, controller, jacks and cables of the shoe roll, grabbed her leather jacket – planes could be cold places on overnight flights – and marched out of the changing room.

The shop had become busier. At the counter, a young woman in a sleeveless summer dress was deliberating over a scarf, trying to negotiate a discount. The shop assistant ignored her to attend to Jaq, collecting her boarding card and the tags from the clothes she had chosen. Over the Tannoy came the announcement that the Miami flight was boarding. When Jaq's first credit card was declined, the other woman became impatient.

'Excuse me, I have a flight to catch.'

Jaq frowned. Everyone in this airport had a flight to catch. But Jaq still had plenty of time, so she stepped aside.

'Can I just pay for this?' The dark-haired woman pushed the scarf forward.

Jaq nodded at the assistant. 'Please, go ahead.'

The woman paid and left.

Jaq's second card worked fine, she completed the transaction and made her way towards the gate. It was only when she looked at the boarding card to check her seat that she realised she had the wrong document. She was not Elena Azevedo, and she was not travelling to Miami at the back of the plane in seat 46D. Only the gate was the same. The sales assistant in Balúrdio must have mixed the boarding cards up. She looked up to see the other passenger already passing through the final security check.

Jaq waved and called out, 'Elena!' but the woman was distracted by a couple of security guards. They'd probably noticed the discrepancy between passport and boarding document and were escorting her somewhere to sort it out.

Jaq returned to the airline desk.

'I'm afraid I need a new boarding card,' she explained the problem and handed over the document she'd been given in error.

'No problem.' The man at the counter tapped a few keys. 'Looks like neither of you are checked in.' Poor Elena, had she missed her flight? 'Here you are.' He handed her a replacement boarding card. 'Have a safe trip.'

As the plane thundered down the runway, the air flowing over the curved profile on the top of the wing moved faster than the air travelling past the underside and the thousand-tonne plane began to lift into the air.

Jaq understood the Bernoulli equation – how an increase in velocity must be balanced by a decrease in pressure, how the shape of the wing caused air to move at different rates top and bottom, with the higher pressure underneath causing an upward lift – and at take-off she often paused to appreciate its elegance in practice.

But today she wasn't thinking about fluid dynamics. She stared down at the city lights as the plane rose higher and higher. Her time in Brazil had passed so quickly. Her seemingly hopeless quest, searching for a needle in a haystack, had brought so many new experiences, fine new friends. And more. So much more.

What was Mercúrio doing right now? Was he safe? Her feelings for him were confusing. Their relationship was not what everyone assumed. Too complex to explain to people she didn't know well. Even though he'd walked out on her, it didn't mean they would never see one another again. Or did it? What if she didn't get back in time? Would Crazy Gloves really kill him?

There was nothing she could do now. Trapped inside this aluminium tube travelling at 500 miles per hour, soaring 10 kilometres above the Atlantic Ocean she had less than a week to save his life.

⎄ 6

Cumbria, England

It was still light after the children had gone to bed, so they took their drinks out to the farmhouse orchard. Johan carried the glasses, Emma the cushions and Jaq followed with the bundle of documents she'd extracted from the strongbox before handing it over to Ben. She set the papers down on a circular garden table.

Cuckoo, cuckoo. A warning? The branches of the quince and medlar trees rustled as little birds took flight. A light breeze fluttered the edges of the paper scrolls.

'These are what you wanted me to look at?' Emma asked.

'Some are not worth your time.' Jaq separated out the older papers. 'But I need your help with these.' Her voice dropped to a whisper as she picked up the glossy blue-white roll.

Emma reached out a hand to take them.

'First I need to explain something.' Jaq took a gulp of wine.

'I'm sorry about earlier.' Johan turned to Emma. 'We were talking out on the lake when Mrs Campbell spotted us.'

Emma twisted her lips. 'One of those women who think they own my husband just because he gave her a few kayaking lessons.'

'Teacher-pupil stuff can get complicated.' Johan turned back to Jaq. 'You started to tell me about one of your teachers at school.'

Jaq closed her eyes. 'Mr Peres.' She couldn't picture him now, but she could remember exactly how he made her feel.

A warm hand on the small of her back guided her towards the darkroom door. At the click of a switch, the door locked behind them, a red light glowing through the darkness. Passing under trailing vines of film, the strips of cellulose acetate brushed against her cheek, her nostrils alive to the aromatic chemicals: ammonia, vinegar and testosterone.

With the passage of time, she could barely believe she was in this scene, barely accept she had let her teacher take her hand, pull her onto his knee as he perched on the single darkroom stool.

It still made her tingle, the memory of his hot breath in her ear, describing his love for her. Asking her if she felt the same.

'Sim,' *she whispered. Yes.*

He wanted to show her how much she meant to him, promising to take it slowly, to be gentle. The way he stroked her long hair, it was only natural that his hands brushed her breasts. His voice deepened as he unbuttoned her school shirt. Her breathing quickened at the unexpected textures: his beard on her breasts, his lips on her nipples, his hands around her waist.

Only when his long fingers strayed under her skirt did she push him away that first time.

How amazed she'd been at his sudden remorse. He stopped at her command. His actions spoke more eloquently than his words, convinced her of his genuine passion. Poor fool that she was.

He told her what she wanted to hear, how much he loved her. If she loved him, he said, if she really loved him, then she must trust him. He would never hurt her. They kissed until she was dizzy and then he begged her to leave before he lost all control. It was the first time she recognised her power, a new and glorious feeling.

The next time they went to the darkroom together, she allowed him to explore further, let his hands squeeze her bare knees, his fingertips glide up her soft inner thighs, until it was she who was pushing herself towards him.

But when he guided her hand to his crotch she pulled away, more disturbed by the unexpected changes in his body than in her own.

The third time, he became angry. Perhaps he had misjudged her, he said. Perhaps she was not ready for true love. He pushed her away, tidied himself up and left the darkroom abruptly, ordering her to wait five minutes to be sure that no one had seen them.

Something changed after that. He wouldn't meet her eyes in lessons. He seemed so forlorn. Heartbroken. She suffered such anguish. How could she have disappointed the man she loved? And who loved her in return. How could something that felt so right ever be wrong?

He waited. Waited until she invited him in. To the darkroom. To her secret, private place. Soon, she was taking the lead, confidently guiding him, discovering pleasure in her body that she had not known existed.

The day it went too far, he claimed that it was her fault, that she was a devil, a minx and temptress. And by then it was too late.

'When I was at school in Lisbon, I fell in love with my chemistry teacher.'

Johan and Emma exchanged glances.

'I became pregnant.'

All this had happened to different a Jaq, a trusting, gullible child she no longer recognised.

'The bastard.' Johan said.

Emma put her water glass on the table. 'You had an abortion?'

Jaq shook her head vigorously. 'Elective abortions weren't permitted in Portugal before 2007, the church made sure of that.'

Emma's hand flew to her mouth. 'You mean you had the baby?'

The birth certificate had been so tightly rolled Jaq had almost missed it under the junk bonds and shares. At first, she'd guessed there must be a sibling she didn't know about. Infant mortality in the Luso-African colonies had been high, even in the twentieth century.

But the paper was newer than the others, the blue-white paper shiny and smooth, the print crystal clear. She had stared at the date. Blinked. Swallowed. The paper rustled in trembling fingers as she read the names. Mother – Maria Jaqueline Marta Ribeiro da Silva. Father – unknown. Child – unnamed.

She'd let the paper fall to her lap and closed her eyes. The pain was visceral, starting in her gut and climbing to her throat. She fought the urge to vomit. Why had her mother kept this? Angie had rejected her only grandson long before he was born, why hang on to the evidence of her daughter's disgrace?

Jaq, convinced her unborn child would be a girl, had toyed with names – Olga or Isabella like the grandmothers she'd never met. She hadn't really considered names for a boy. As it turned out, there wasn't time to name him, let alone christen him. The nuns said it was for the best. God had taken away the fruit of her sin and now she could repent and devote herself to God's work. She hated them then.

Jaq handed the document to Johan.

Emma's eyes narrowed as her husband passed it on to her. He shook his head, almost imperceptibly. No, not even Johan, her best friend, knew her secret. Until now.

Emma scanned it quickly. 'Oh my God, Jaq, what happened to the baby?'

'They told me he died at birth.'

Emma hung her head and a tear dropped onto the table.

'The poor mite.'

'And what about you?' Johan asked.

'I was taken to hospital afterwards.'

Jaq smoothed the medical order, the paper rough against her fingertips, and passed it to Emma.

'I don't understand. What does it say?'

'Compulsory detention on the grounds of diminished mental capacity,' Jaq translated. 'Sterilisation on the grounds of uncontrollable libido.'

Emma gasped. 'You were sterilised?'

'They must have performed the operation in the hospital, on my mother's orders.'

'She didn't tell you?' Johan asked.

Jaq shook her head. 'She barely spoke to me after I told her I was pregnant.'

It still hurt. More than almost anything. The shutting down, shutting out.

'But why?' Emma's mouth was still open in shock. 'Why would anyone sterilise a perfectly healthy girl?'

'I guess in Angie's mind, sexual incontinence was a form of mental illness.'

'You really didn't know?'

Jaq shook her head. 'My Aunt Lettie whisked me away to England.'

'When did you find out?'

'When Gregor and I were trying to have a baby.'

Johan and Emma exchanged glances.

'I never knew you tried.'Emma said. 'I just assumed you never wanted ...' She blushed. 'Jaq, I'm so sorry. We were busy with Ben and ...'

Jaq's expression softened as she put a finger to her lips. 'You were always there for me.' The married couple had moved closer together as she talked, Emma's head resting against Johan's shoulder. 'Both of you. It was me, not you. I was angry. I didn't want to talk. I wasn't ready. I took it out on Gregor, punished him without telling him why.'

'He was hardly blameless.' Emma cried. 'Wasn't he sleeping with his secretary?'

'Our marriage was already on the rocks by then. His affair was the final nail in the coffin.' Jaq sighed. 'It was good in a way, allowed me to vent my fury at something else.'

On to Slovenia and a job in avalanche control. Setting off controlled explosions was wonderfully therapeutic.

Emma shook her head. 'I struggle to understand why a parent would sanction such a thing.'

'My mother was anything but a normal parent.'

'Or that any doctor would carry out such a barbaric instruction.'

Jaq pursed her lips. 'There is no shortage of professionals who believe that women's bodies need to be controlled by others.'

'It's a triple violation.' Johan's voice was low and taut. 'You were groomed by someone you trusted, raped—'

Jaq started to protest but Emma interrupted. 'Coercion into sexual acts where consent cannot be meaningfully given is statutory rape.'

'You lost a baby.' Johan stood up, fists clenched. 'And instead of convicting the abuser, they punished you instead. Ripped away your chance of ever having another child.'

'I started over.'

Emma took her hand. 'You are an extraordinarily strong person, Jaq.'

Jaq squeezed Emma's hand in return. 'I thought I had come to terms with what happened, made my peace, moved on.' She sighed. 'Until I found this.'

The cuckoo called again. Rich, mellow, rounded notes. A master of deception. A bird preparing to lay its egg in a foreign nest and let another species do all the hard work of raising a chick.

Jaq passed them the final papers.

A certificate, signed by the mother superior and counter-signed by Angie. And a receipt for 10,000 escudos.

Her baby hadn't died at birth, he'd been sold for adoption.

Ben appeared at the door of the farmhouse kitchen in his Spider-Man pyjamas, with tousled hair and bare feet.

'Baby crying,' he said.

If his eyes hadn't been drooping with sleep, he might have noticed that Jade was not the only one.

Johan crossed the garden and scooped his son up in his arms, holding him tight.

'Dad! I'm not the baby.' He glanced over at Jaq to see if she'd noticed, but her eyes were closed, her head resting against Emma who had wrapped both her arms around her friend.

Ben struggled in his father's arms. 'Put me down.'

Johan let him slither to the ground and then took his hand. 'Come on, let's see what Jade is up to.'

Ben cast a glance over his shoulder as they moved inside.

'Why do babies cry?' he asked.

'Well, sometimes they are hungry, sometimes they are cold, sometimes they need their nappy changing.' They climbed the stairs together. 'And sometimes they are frightened ...' Johan's voice cracked with emotion. 'Or lonely.'

'Maybe Jade had a bad dream.'

'Maybe she did.'

'But you can tell her a story.'

'That's a great idea. Will you help me?'

In the farmhouse garden, the breath of the two women was so soft now, they might have been sleeping.

Emma spoke first. 'I don't know what to say.'

'There's nothing you can say.' Jaq pulled away from Emma's embrace and reached for a glass on the table. 'You're the first people I've told.' She took a sip of water. 'Finally, it's real.'

'How do you feel?'

'At first it was shock. My life is a lie. I grew up believing that my child died at birth. But he's out there, somewhere.'

'It's a pretty shocking thing to find out.'

'And then it was anger. Anger at my mother.'

'Perhaps she was trying to do what was best for the baby ...'

'You think adoption was best?'

'You were so young, and she was ill ...'

Jaq slammed the glass onto the table. 'Stop defending my mother, OK. She was mad and bad. What sort of mother has her child sterilised? What sort of mother sells, SELLS her grandchild?'

Emma shook her head. 'It's beyond understanding.'

'If she'd really been doing what was best for the baby, she wouldn't have kept all those documents.'

'The adoption papers?'

'And the receipt. Don't forget the receipt. She wanted me to find it. She wanted to punish me.'

It was quiet upstairs. Johan re-appeared with a bottle of whisky.

'Anyone else?'

Jaq pushed her empty water glass forward. 'God, yes.'

'I wish I could.' Emma said.

There was an awkward silence.

'C'mon guys, I'm genuinely happy for you. What happened to me all those years ago doesn't affect my love for you and for Ben and Jade and won't affect my love for your new baby.' She raised her glass. 'It's not a zero-sum game – your blessings are not at my expense.'

Emma started to cry again. 'I just can't imagine it Jaq. Giving birth and then having the baby taken away.'

Jaq put a hand around her shoulder and pulled her close.

'That's because you are a great mother. I'm not sure I would have been. I would have done my best, but I was scared as hell.' She sighed. 'This is hard to admit, but maybe when they told me my baby died, through the devastation and grief there was a glimmer of relief.'

'Jaq, how old were you when …'

'Old enough.' Was her age relevant? She'd been over the age of consent in Portugal. Abuse of power could happen at any age. She took a sip of whisky and then another, welcoming the way it burned her throat.

'My brother was dead. My mother blamed me, plunged in a deep, dark valley of depression, between nervous breakdowns. My father was absent, fighting an unwinnable war in Angola. A teacher at my school was kind to me.'

'You were vulnerable, Jaq,' Emma said.

'I thought we were in love – how naive and stupid can you be?'

'The bastard,' Johan said through gritted teeth. 'I hope you shopped him.'

Jaq shook her head. 'No one would have believed me. He was an inspirational chemistry teacher, a brilliant photographer, the star of both the science and art departments, married with children, a regular churchgoer. It would have been my word against his.' She paused. 'And I still thought I loved him.'

Until she caught him in the darkroom with an even younger girl. And then she initiated his downfall, engineering an accident in the chemistry lab. Her first brush with chemical warfare.

'So, what happened to you?'

'When I couldn't hide the pregnancy any longer, I told my mother and she sent me to a convent. There were other girls there, girls like me. It was awful. I escaped, but my mother sent the police to bring me back.'

Emma let out a roar. 'And they didn't prosecute the father?'

'My teacher? No. I refused to identify him. They'd have found a way to blame me, just like my mother did.'

'Did he know about the adoption?'

'He didn't even know I was pregnant. He'd left the school long before I was sent to the convent.' Her idol turned out to be just another sexual predator, with many 'special' girls. Special because they were vulnerable.

Her substitution of potassium for sodium prior to a demonstration of metal reactivity and the subsequent explosion and fire cost him his eyebrows and his job.

Johan cleared his throat. 'Does he need to be told now?'

'He died long ago.'

'So, the adoption was cooked up between your mother and the nuns?' Emma said.

Johan stood up. 'I am so angry for you.'

'What's done is done,' Jaq said. 'I can't turn back the clock.'

'And now you know,' Emma stretched out a hand and laid it over Jaq's. 'What next?'

'What do you think?' Jaq finished her whisky and set the glass down on the table with a determined thud. 'I'm going to find my son.'

Y 6

Shanghai, China

Frank Good took his place on the podium and stared down at the sea of upturned faces. Close to a thousand people stared back at him, waiting for his welcome speech to start. The Chinese factory workers, bussed in from Nanjing and further afield, formed a sea of blue at the back. The commercial team, who worked in offices wherever the company had business interests, made up the white-shirted middle tier. In the two front rows sat the more colourful visitors, the global leaders of Zagrovyl. Although a few of those from Europe had worn suits, most of the North Americans were informally dressed. The big-bellied men slouched in polo shirts, the single female executive, who held the Mickey-Mouse title of Corporate Integrity, wore a hideous loose dress. The West's days of business primacy were over. The new world order would be forged by the BRIC countries: Brazil, Russia, India and, most powerful of all, China.

It had taken some persuasion to get the Zagrovyl board to hold the annual symposium in Asia instead of the usual North American or European city, but the stellar growth that Frank had presided over in China could no longer be ignored.

Frank stepped up to the microphone and cleared his throat.

'Welcome to Shanghai, ladies and gentlemen.'

His personal assistant was translating tonight. She stepped forward and bobbed her head. 'Ni Hao …'

'I am honoured to open our annual symposium with a challenge.'

He looked around to ensure everyone was listening and to allow Alice to catch up. Why did Mandarin always sound so aggressive?

'My challenge is this – how fast can we move to a zero-carbon business?'

'I enjoyed your speech.'

He turned to appraise the woman standing in front of him. Golden-haired and nicely turned out, she presented a manicured hand and smiled. Her glossy crimson nails matched her lipstick.

'Clara Sousa, from Zagrovyl, Brazil.'

He ignored her outstretched hand and leaned forward to kiss her, on the left cheek and then the right. Her scent was exotic, spicy, a hint of ginger. Her silky hair brushed his cheek and a golden strand caught in his collar stud as she pulled away.

'Frank Good,' he said.

She laughed. 'I know. You're the reason we're all here.'

The swelling was mainly due to pride.

'Your green energy division is breaking all records.'

He acknowledged her praise with a smile.

'The planet's future is definitely in the hands of the BRIC economies,' she continued. 'But I'm afraid I don't share your confidence about Zagrovyl in Brazil.'

He looked around for someone else to talk to. *I agree, but …* What was it about some people, usually women, that made them think that they had the right to contradict him. The *but* brigade. Or butt brigade in her case. She had a remarkably shapely backside. He smirked at his own wit. Perhaps he'd grace her with his company for just a little longer. Long enough to put her right.

'In what way?' he asked.

'Corporate headquarters don't understand how business is done in my country.'

'And how is business done in Brazil?' As if he didn't know. The Western press had just broken a whistle-blower's story. The traitor claimed that his European employer paid millions in fake consulting fees that ended up in the pockets of politicians in Brasilia via giant state enterprises.

'We're a cordial people.' She fluttered her eyelash extensions. 'I don't mean polite and friendly, although that is part of our makeup, but passionate, wholehearted, loyal. We can be cerebral – *cérebro* means brain in Portuguese, but we're more often led by *o coraçao*, the heart, the true root of the word cordial.' She paused to sip her flute of champagne.

'So, it's who you know, not what you know?' Frank said.

'Exactly.' She smiled, showing perfectly straight, white teeth. 'The detached, arms-length, contractual approach,' she continued, 'that cold and sterile separation of the people from the activity, that doesn't work in Brazil.'

'And how should Zagrovyl head office,' he nodded over at the shrew-eyed director of corporate integrity in her hideous frock, 'adapt to a more *cordial* style of business?'

'By leaving us alone. By trusting us to know how to do business in Brazil.' She ran a hand through her hair.

He reappraised her. Was this a useful rebel willing to challenge the shibboleth of corporate puritanism? A fellow traveller in the real, messy world of high finance and fast deals?

The waitress scurried back and stretched up to fill Clara's glass.

'We're a warm people.' Her crimson lips parted slightly. He would bet his bottom dollar that Clara Sousa would not just be warm, but sizzling hot.

From the corner of his eye, he caught sight of Graham Dekker, President of Global Operations, moving towards them.

'Fascinating.' He adjusted his jacket. 'Shall we continue our conversation after dinner?'

Frank didn't wait for her reply as he turned to greet his boss.

Y 6

Lisbon, Portugal

Jaq's search began in Lisbon.

At the top of Rua de Estrela, *Igreja de Nossa Senhora do Desterro*, the Church of Our Lady in Exile, loomed into view. The walls were lined with posters announcing a new series of choral concerts.

Jaq walked slowly past, reading the notices to delay the moment. Tomorrow's early evening concert was dedicated to renaissance polyphony. From Palestrina to the *Magnificat secundi toni* of the less well-known Portuguese composer Manuel Cardoso.

Her footsteps slowed, as if the uneven pavement had turned to sticky molasses under her feet, holding her back. She stared down at the ground. The cobbled mosaic of traditional flinty limestone cubes shone bright and smooth in the morning sunshine, the Jacaranda trees creating little shadowy waves as a light breeze shook the summer leaves. She forced herself to walk the length of the church and face the door of the convent.

The first time she'd passed through the convent gates, more than twenty years ago, she'd had no idea what to expect. Travelling in the car of her mother's lawyer she peered up at the grand arch through tinted windows. Mr Centeno sat beside her, a man as wide as he was tall, but lacking any compensating joviality. He scowled at her from under his homburg hat – why wear a hat in a car? and she recoiled from the stink of stale sweat – why wear a tweed suit in summer? as he informed her that this was her new home, and that it was all for the best.

Angie had stopped speaking to Jaq on being informed of the pregnancy. Communicating with her only child through a lawyer might have seemed melodramatic to an outsider, but it represented something of an improvement in accuracy as the housekeeper – who prepared their meals – had tended to soften the messages from mother to daughter. Jaq had been spending as much time as she could at school and after-school activities, so Angie had often retired for an early night by the time her daughter returned home. Truth be told, Jaq and Angie had been avoiding one another ever since they moved into the large, dimly lit, stuffy flat in Lisbon, an apartment block that had last seen maintenance in the 1970s and had not been redecorated since it was first built 50 years earlier. The shutters remained closed during the day to protect the elaborate French furniture with its heavy gilding, the thick oriental rugs and the privacy of a once wealthy Angolan refugee who found it impossible to adapt to newfound poverty.

'What about school?' Jaq asked the lawyer as the gates closed behind the car.

Mr Centeno glowered at her. 'You're pregnant,' he said.

'It doesn't stop me ...'

'Haven't you embarrassed your family enough?'

As the car came to a halt, a nun came bustling out to meet them. Jaq lowered her head and steeled herself for a new life.

Now Jaq rang the bell and listened as the pad-pad of footsteps was followed by the rasp of a metal shutter. A small window opened in the convent gate and brown eyes regarded the visitor through a slit. A side door creaked open, and Jaq stepped inside.

A silent nun showed her to the office of the mother superior. Dona Mafalda smoothed her grey robes, adjusted the white wimple and rose to meet the visitor, enfolding her in an embrace. Jaq resisted the pressure of a chunky wooden cross and rosary pressing against her, submitting reluctantly to the soft lips aimed at her cheek but landing on her chin.

'It's good to see you again, *menina*.' Child. That's how they saw her. Even now.

The elderly nun pulled back and scanned her face. 'How have you been?'

How had she been? So much had happened since she was last here. Her mother's safe, the secrets it contained. The shock of discovering the extent to which she'd been lied to.

The mother superior mistook her silence for grief. 'It takes time to come to terms with such a loss.'

They'd spoken on the phone, but Dona Mafalda had refused to give her any information, insisting she come in person.

'And losing a mother is—'

Jaq interrupted. 'You know that I am not here to talk about my mother.' She took the papers from her bag and pushed them across the desk.

'I was told that my son died at birth. Now I find out that he was adopted.'

The mother superior glanced at the adoption receipt, paled and picked up a brass bell.

'Perhaps we should take some refreshment.' The high clear tones of the brass bell summoned back the nun who had shown her in.

'Our coffee is not the best, we don't run to a proper machine, but Dona Emília makes a wonderful *carioca de limão*. Will you join me?'

Jaq shrugged, anxious to get this little charade over so they could talk about what mattered.

The hot drink came in china cups, a sliver of lemon peel in hot water, fragrant and refreshing. The office looked different. Gone were the heavy oak bookcases with elaborate carvings, replaced by office-style bookshelves and drawers. The furniture was new too, the dark wood replaced by a lighter, modern laminate. The velvet drapes had been taken down and slatted bamboo blinds fitted in their place. How much else had changed since the old mother superior died? The current incumbent, Dona Mafalda, was not to blame for Jaq's treatment here, except insofar as she represented the management of an institution with a long history of incarcerating women and preventing them from exercising any reproductive control.

When Dona Emília had left and they were alone again, Jaq placed the cup carefully on the saucer. 'I want to know who adopted my son.'

Mafalda looked up at the ceiling. 'I'm not sure we have that information.'

The mother superior made a poor liar.

'I am absolutely sure that you do.'

'Even if we did …' Mafalda blushed and made a steeple with her fingers. 'Are you sure it's a wise course to pursue?'

'I'm sure.'

Mafalda laid a soft hand over hers.

'My child. This has come as a shock to you. But think back to how young you were. The adoption gave you the chance to move on, to make a good life. Your mother did what she thought was best for you.'

Jaq pulled her hand away and laughed, a low bitter laugh. 'She had me sterilised.'

Mafalda's eyes narrowed. 'The church played no part in that. Of that, I can assure you. Sterilisation is a sin. Children are God's gift to the world, no one has the right to interfere with God's divine blessing.'

Perhaps the nuns hadn't known about the surgery, hadn't sanctioned it explicitly. But nor had they intervened to protect a vulnerable child.

'She took money! She sold her own grandchild.'

'You made a terrible mistake.' The mother superior crossed her arms under an ample bosom. 'But God found a way for some good to come from that. The blessing of a newborn baby, a gift to a barren couple desperate to start a family.'

'My son was not God's to give away,' Jaq hissed.

'We are all God's children. Even you, foolish and headstrong.' Her voice grew harder. 'Be realistic. You were naive and unmarried, in no position to look after your own baby. Through adoption, the child found a secure home. We must always think, first and foremost, about the interests of the child.'

'He's an adult now.'

'And what if his adoptive parents didn't tell him he was adopted? They took a newborn baby into their home, into their hearts. Have you thought about how painful it might be for him? Even if you are his birth mother, his real parents are the people who raised him. Why not let it be? Move on.'

'Doesn't the truth matter?'

'What if he doesn't want to have anything to do with what you call the "truth". What if he doesn't want to acknowledge you?'

'I will respect that. He can make his own decisions. If he doesn't want to talk with me, that's fine. But I have to give him the option.'

'And what about his genetic father.'

'His father is dead.'

'You are sure?'

'Absolutely.'

Mafalda sighed. 'It's all in the past. Why rake back over old ground? Why interfere in something that happened over twenty years ago?'

'I want to know who adopted my son.'

'Your son went to good people. What's done is done. What's gone is gone.'

'I can't accept that.'

'You are ignoring my advice?'

'Yes.'

'You are resolved to pursue you own selfish desires, ignoring the feelings of everyone else involved?'

'I have a right to know.'

'Rights, pah! What about obligations? What about humility, atonement and compassion?' The mother superior rose to her feet to indicate that the meeting was over.

▽ 6

Estoril, Portugal

Estoril, with the head office of lawyers *Centeno e Filhas,* was once a separate town. Fifteen kilometres from the centre of Lisbon, a casino and a row of fine mansions towered above the harbour, replacing the humble cottages once occupied by fisherfolk. As Lisbon grew, new housing blocks sprouted along the north shore of the Tagus. The towns of Carcavelos, Estoril and Cascais became part of greater Lisbon, connected by a fast road and a slow train.

Jaq stared out of the window as the suburban train wheezed and clattered out of Cais do Sodré. She had chosen to sit on the river side, but the carriage was empty and she could see up to the gardens of the *Museu de Arte Antiga* on the land side as they trundled past Santos.

The train clunked through Alcantara docks. A cruise liner was just leaving the port, riding high in the water, sending out a mournful hoot of farewell, already suffering *saudades,* that uniquely Portuguese word for the longing felt for a place you are forced to leave.

The train lumbered on to Belém, past Salazar's supererogatory monument to the Discoveries. Across a park with fountains, tour buses had pulled up outside the Manueline Mosteiro dos Jéronimos, waiting to ferry tourists on to the sixteenth-century Torre de Belém. Concrete, stone and marble gleamed, blinding white in the bright sun. The water sparkled as the train rounded the headland at Algés and the river widened. The line between

76

fresh and salt water was a band of darker colour, where the river water met the blue-green sea. The wind and tide created waves, lapping against the shore as the train thundered on to Caxias.

A few palm trees appeared where the old road – the *marginal* – ran beside the train tracks. Once the most dangerous road in Lisbon, rich, young men raced fast cars along a road so close to the sea that waves often crashed onto them.

The silver carriages rattled past Carcavelos and Jaq prepared to get off at São João de Estoril.

She emerged into a leafy oasis of pastel-coloured mansions in lush gardens and struck up the side of a steep hill until she reached the address.

The lawyers' office, *Centeno e Filhas*, stood in the grounds of what had once been a royal palace, long since demolished and returned to the republic.

'*Dottora da Silva, seja bemvida.*'

'Please call me Jaq.'

The lawyer took Jaq's outstretched hand and shook it.

'My name is Carmo. I'm a partner at this firm and I'll be dealing personally with your affairs.' She pointed at an open door that led to a small meeting room with French windows that opened out onto the orchard of the former estate. Jaq took a seat facing the trees, the smell of lemon blossom mixing with fresh coffee as a young man poured beans into a coffee machine.

Carmo waited until her assistant had dispensed their drinks and departed, closing the door behind him.

'I understand you knew my uncle?'

Jaq had called the office to find that Mr Centeno was long retired and that his niece now ran the firm. Carmo could not have been more different from her uncle. Small and slim, she wore a sleeveless linen dress, her shapely legs in low-heeled court shoes. There were no rings on her fingers, but she wore a pair of drop earrings, rainbow colours sparkling through shoulder-length fair hair, expert highlights covering a hint of grey. Her scent, something subtle with hints of vanilla, mingled pleasingly with the notes of citrus wafting in from the orchard.

'He was my mother's lawyer.' Jaq shuddered at the memory. 'I only met him briefly.'

'I am so sorry for your loss,' Carmo said.

Jaq lowered her head.

'How may I help you?'

It was one thing to tell Johan and Emma, the warmth of their farmhouse kitchen and friendship countering the chill of confession. It was quite another to reveal everything to a total stranger. Jaq opened her bag and pulled out a bundle of papers, the older ones from her mother's strongbox.

'My mother left me these.'

Carmo flattened out the ragged, yellowing Angolan Railway bonds and traced the picture of a steam train ascending a precipitous mountain at an impossible gradient.

'Your mother was a *retornada*?' A returnee, the name they applied to the million Portuguese nationals who returned from Portugal's colonies after independence.

'I was born in Africa,' Jaq said. 'As were my mother and grandmother.'

'Me too.' Carmo smiled. 'But we came back before the revolution. What about you?'

Jaq lowered her eyes. 'It's a long story.' And not one she wanted to dwell on right now. She took the other documents, the birth certificate and adoption receipt, and slid them over the desk. She kept back the sterilisation order, there was little point in complicating things further.

Carmo cast her eyes over them and then pounced, suddenly alert. She picked up the birth certificate.

'This is your child?'

'Yes.' Jaq swallowed hard.

'And he was adopted?'

'I didn't know.' The emotion rasped at her throat.

'You discovered this,' Carmo gestured at the document, 'in your mother's papers.' Her eyes opened wide. 'You really didn't know?'

'They told me he died.'

A glass of water and a box of tissues appeared in front of her. Jaq pushed them away angrily.

'I want you to find out what happened to him.'

'That won't be easy,' Carmo said. 'It could be a lengthy and expensive process.'

'Whatever it takes.'

'And stressful.' Carmo opened a drawer, selected a leaflet and pushed it across the desk. 'Here's a voluntary service that offers advice and counselling.'

'Thank you.' Jaq left the leaflet untouched. She didn't need to talk to anyone, what she needed was action.

'The convent won't give you information?'

'Not without a court order, no.'

Carmo nodded slowly.

'Do you have any other leads?'

'Your law firm must have been involved in this,' Jaq said. 'Do you have any records that might identify the adoptive parents?'

'I checked after you called and there is no file on your family.'

'Is there any chance, that Mr Centeno, your uncle, kept a private file?'

'I'm afraid not.' Carmo shook her head. 'We digitised all the old information before moving into this new office.'

'Could I speak with him?' Much as she disliked the prospect of resuming any contact with the lawyer, a foul man party to the incarceration of one child and the theft of another, she would follow any lead available to her.

Carmo shook her head. 'He's very ill.'

'Please.'

'Let me see what I can do.'

Not good enough. Time was of the essence. Jaq strained to remain civil. 'It's important.'

Carmo nodded. 'Who is dealing with your late mother's estate?'

'She bequeathed almost everything to the church.'

'Do you want to contest that?'

'No,' Jaq shook her head. 'I believe that my great-aunt made those arrangements many years ago in return for my mother's care for life.' And even then, the convent had attempted to renege on the deal when Angie's dementia worsened. Never trust a nun.

'You are the only surviving relative?'

'I believe so.'

'And your mother left you nothing?'

Jaq laughed bitterly. 'Just this bombshell.' The evidence that Angie had sold her only grandson. 'In an old leather and steel strongbox with those junk bonds.' She pointed to the documents on the desk. 'And some trinkets.'

'Was your mother of sound mind?'

'Absolutely not.'

'Then you might consider contesting the disposal of assets.' Carmo held up a hand as Jaq started to protest. 'Hear me out. If nothing else, it might be useful leverage to get the adoption information without going to court.'

'I see.' Jaq was warming to this woman.

'With your permission, I'll contact the convent. I won't mention the adoption information request. I'll advise them that you are considering contesting the will. If they have any sense, they will look for a compromise.'

A lateral attack. Sometimes you have to move sideways to make progress. Jaq nodded. 'It's worth a try.'

'Do you have any idea of the value of your late mother's estate?'

'I think her family lost everything in Angola. There was some Lisbon property, but it was donated to the church in trust.'

'I'll need a complete inventory. And an official valuation of any jewellery.' Carmo sighed. 'If the estate is as small as you think, we may not have much of a lever to bring the church authorities to the negotiating table, but we can use Lusitanian bureaucracy to make it as painful as possible.'

'It's how you make a living.'

Carmo threw her head back and laughed. 'Some see it like that, but we lawyers have our uses.'

She flicked through the Angolan railway bonds, ragged woven paper, with prints of trains. The last document in the pile was in better shape, pinkish parchment with a green engraving. 'You have a mixture of originals and copies.' She turned the last document over. 'The original of this one is held in a bank in Luanda.'

'Original or copy, I'm pretty sure they're equally worthless.'

'Probably,' Carmo nodded, then held the document up to the light. The engraving printed onto the pink parchment showed a procession of native men emerging from jungle, bent double from the heavy loads on their backs. 'I have connections in Angola. I'll get these checked out.'

'All I care about is finding my son.'

Carmo put down the documents and met Jaq's eyes.

'I'm with you all the way.'

6

Praia de Guincho, Cascais, Portugal

The wind was picking up, frosting the green swell. White horses, manes streaming in their wake, galloped towards the beach: huge waves rolling and crashing onto golden sand. The early morning surfers were heading in for a late breakfast, and the kitesurfers had started strapping on their harnesses in anticipation of what looked to be the perfect afternoon conditions.

Jaq plunged straight into the water and came up gasping. The sea was cold without a wetsuit, and the force of each wave dislodged a new part of the flimsy bikini she'd picked up at a market stall. Not that she cared. She'd happily swim naked. There were few swimmers on a windy weekday outside of the *época balnear*. But the flags were green, the tide was coming in and she knew this beach. Knew it well enough to avoid the dangerous currents that could sweep you out to sea. Next stop America. She swam just beyond the first break and then parallel to the shore, keeping an eye on her towel covering a small bundle of possessions.

Beyond the wide beach, sand dunes rolled towards the jagged *Serra de Sintra*. The gilded domes of the gothic Pena Palace sparkled in the sunlight, the crazy towers and turrets silhouetted against the bluest of skies. She swam against the rip tide, towards *Cabo de Roca*, the most westerly point in mainland Europe, barely moving against the powerful current. Once she was exhausted, she turned back for the easier swim towards the fort.

As she emerged from the sea, her phone started ringing. By the time she sprinted to her towel and dried her hands, it had stopped. She recognised the number: Carmo, the lawyer from *Centeno e Filhas.*

Jaq dried her hands, pulled the towel over her head and returned the call.

'Any news?'

'Nothing good, I'm afraid. I'm just leaving the convent.'

Jaq adjusted the towel and turned away from the wind. Sharp particles of sand attacked her exposed skin.

'You met with Dona Mafalda?'

'Yes. Interesting character.'

'And?'

'She won't budge.'

Jaq pulled the towel tighter around her. The shivering started somewhere deep inside her. Once started, it was hard to stop.

'Jaq, Jaq, are you still there?'

'Just about.'

'I can hear the sea, where are you?'

'Guincho.'

'Meet me at the Carbon café? The Kitesurf hire place. I'll be there in 30 minutes.'

Jaq threw modesty to the winds, stripped off her wet bikini and dressed as quickly as her damp, shaking limbs would allow. Her shorts seemed to stick over her hips and the T-shirt got tangled in her hair as she wrenched it down. The open weave cotton jumper wasn't much protection against the wind, and the sandstorm stung her bare legs as she ran towards the dunes to find shelter. As soon as she was out of the wind, the sunshine warmed her skin. By the time Carmo pulled up in an open-topped Mercedes, Jaq was calmly sipping a small black coffee at the bar of the kitesurf café.

'*Galão com café da máquina,*' Carmo ordered a coffee and came to sit beside her. 'Have you been surfing?'

'Just swimming.'

'My son's a surfer – well more of a kitesurfer these days – he's probably around here somewhere.'

'Professional?'

Carmo scrunched up her nose. 'In the sense that he does it all the time and occasionally gets prize money, yes. In the sense that he makes a decent living from it, no.'

'But it brings him joy?'

Carmo beamed at her. 'It definitely brings him joy. And joy to his family too.' She took a sip of her coffee. 'Look, I didn't want to say this over the phone.' She looked around to make sure they were alone. 'But there was something odd about my visit to the convent.'

'Odd?'

'Dona Mafalda was charming enough at first. When I served notice that we would contest the will, she seemed surprised but unperturbed. Told us that they would countersue for the cost of your mother's care, which – she claimed – was far more than the income from the assets.'

'She told me the same thing some time ago.' It was the reason Jaq had taken on a series of high-paid but risky contracts. 'And it might be true. I guess the property would be worth a lot more now, a whole block in Lapa, but it was very run down and had sitting tenants when it was donated.' Dona Dolores and her maid on the ground floor, the Santos family with an indeterminate number of children above the flat that Angie and Jaq briefly occupied, an artist's commune in the garret. 'I think it was sold at auction to a developer, but I'm not sure.'

'That rather limits our room for manoeuvre. But there's something else.'

Carmo paused as a surfer moved towards them. His wetsuit was undone to the waist, exposing a T-shirt with the words ECOPTO emblazoned over his broad chest. Jaq followed his progress in the mirror behind the bar, took in the bare feet, athletic body, powerful shoulders, black beard and smooth bald head. He caught her eye and frowned, advancing to stand behind her at the bar. The hairs stood up on the back of her neck and she turned to meet dark eyes that were strangely familiar.

'Was that you swimming earlier?' he asked.

She nodded.

'This beach can be dangerous, you know,' his voice deep and hostile.

She bristled at the aggression. 'I know.'

He reached past her to take a bottle of water, turned and left.

'That was the world kitesurfing champion.' Carmo whispered. 'He runs this place.'

She stood and walked over to the veranda.

Jaq followed, watching as a group of kitesurfers set up on the sand, using the wind to inflate their colourful parachutes, angling their surf boards to speed over the shallows towards the waves.

The bearded man led the way, roaring into the sea, twirling to catch a swell, leaping clear just before it curled and crashed, turning a somersault in the air before landing smoothly in deeper water, waiting for the others to follow.

Something stirred in Jaq's memory, but she pushed it away.

Carmo turned away from the sea. 'Do you have time for lunch?'

Jaq looked up at the clock behind the bar. All the time in the world, and no time at all. 'Here?' Although the swim had made her hungry, the tired-looking croissants, sweaty *pastéis de bacalhau* and limp *rissóis* in a glass case didn't look particularly appealing. And the owner wasn't exactly friendly.

'No. This place serves fuel. I need food and I know a great place nearby.' Carmo placed some notes on the bar and stood up. 'I have something else to tell you.'

The little bistro in Areia wasn't much to look at, but its popularity bode well. Carmo and Jaq had to overshoot some distance to find a space to park the car. The aromas emerging from the kitchen pulled them on as they retraced their steps. Jaq, suddenly hungry, quickened her pace.

Carmo surveyed the packed restaurant. Every table was taken. 'How hungry are you?'

'Ravenous.'

'People are leaving,' She pointed at a group of men in overalls at a table with coffee and balloon glasses of *bagaço*. A waiter was writing their bill on the paper tablecloth using a pencil and they began counting out notes.

'Do you eat seafood?' Carmo asked.

'If I know where it's from.'

Carmo walked over to the waiter and quizzed him before returning to the door. 'Atlantic prawns from North East England, razor clams and mussels from the West Coast of Scotland and *cadelinhas* from Caparica,' she announced. 'All fresh from Cascais market today.'

'You're not suggesting all of that together?'

'Yup,' Carmo smiled. 'This place makes the best *açorda de marisco* in the world. Fancy sharing one?'

'I'll let you decide.'

They waited at the bar. The barista brought them bright yellow *tremoços*, lupin seeds with leathery skin that, when bitten and pressed between thumb and forefinger, released a soft, salty bean.

The whoosh of the coffee machine, clatter of crockery and banter from the departing workers made it impossible to hold a conversation. Jaq popped a couple of *tremoços*, discarding the skins in a clean ashtray, and tried to control her impatience.

The waiter cleared a table, scrunching up the old paper table-cloth and replacing it with a new one, throwing down cutlery and napkins. He beckoned to them and Carmo barked their order as they took their seats. *Açorda de Marisco da casa, agua sem gas, salada mista.*

Once the water arrived, Jaq couldn't hold back her questions any longer. 'So? What happened.'

Carmo returned to the subject of her visit to the convent, going back to where she had left off, the attempted negotiation.

'The mother superior was perfectly polite,' Carmo said. 'I think she's become quite fond of you. She insisted it was in your best interests to leave well alone.'

With friends like Dona Mafalda, who needed enemies. 'Is she still maintaining that they don't have the adoption records?'

'No, we got past that hurdle at least. I suggested that my uncle had kept his own records ...'

Jaq sat up straight. 'He did? You've found something?'

Carmo shook her head. 'I'm sorry Jaq. He remembers very little these days. And, as I said, all the old records were digitised.'

'I'd still like to talk to him.'

'I promise to arrange it.'

'When?'

'The minute he's out of hospital.'

The main course arrived in an earthenware pot.

'Let's eat first, then I'll tell you more.'

The waiter opened the lid, and with great ceremony, broke an egg, discarded the albumen and mixed the yolk into the bubbling liquid. Jaq could smell the garlic and fresh tomato, coriander and bay leaf, lemon zest and yeast from the dry bread used to give body to the seafood stew. They piled their plates and ate in silence for a while. Jaq felt warmth and strength returning to her core. She waited until Carmo had cleared her plate.

Carmo wiped her lips with a napkin. 'When I got to the car, I realised that I'd left my scarf behind.' She pointed to the silk square that she fastened over her hair when the car roof was down. 'I went back for it, only to walk into a veritable commotion.'

'Commotion?'

'A shouting match.'

'What about?'

'I heard your name, so I slipped back into the mother superior's office. There were two other nuns with her, both very elderly, and a younger priest, Father Nuno I think.'

She picked out a large prawn from the pot, and started to peel it, blowing on her fingertips to reduce the heat.

'And?'

'Dona Mafalda was furious with me for "bursting in" as she put it. One of the nuns gathered up a bunch of pictures and stuffed everything back into an envelope.'

Carmo popped the pink crescent of prawn into her mouth.

Pictures? Did the convent have photos of her son?

Carmo took a sip of water. 'I demanded to see what they were hiding.'

'And?'

Carmo shook her head. 'Dona Mafalda told me she'd see me in court.'

'And the envelope?'

'She put it in her desk drawer and locked it.'

Jaq's eyes lit up.

'When was this?'

'This morning. I called you from the car after I left.'

'Do you think the envelope might still be in the drawer?'

'I don't think she'll show anything to us without a court order.'

'And what if I don't ask permission?'

'Jaq … whatever you're thinking …'

'I'm not asking for your permission either.'

'Then the less I know, the better I can help.'

Carmo gave Jaq a lift to Cascais. At the train station, Jaq caught sight of herself in the glass of the ticket booth. If her hair had dried to rats tails after the swim, now, after a fast drive in an open-topped sports car, it resembled a salty haystack. No point in trying to comb it. And no time to wash.

She left the train at Santos station and climbed up through the steep streets of Lapa, stopping to drink from a water fountain in Estrela Park before walking on to the British cemetery.

The arch-top double gates only opened fully for funerals. On the alternate Sunday mornings when there was a service in St George's church, the smaller left-hand gate was left ajar. The rest of the time, the doors were locked closed and entry was restricted. The grey metal intercom had a stern message: by appointment only, Monday to Friday 10 to 12 p.m.

Jaq pressed the buzzer.

There was another way in. A secret tunnel between the basement of the British Hospital and the top corner of the cemetery. The route Jaq had used, any time of night or day, when she escaped to visit Dona Adelina. The person most likely to help her now.

The gate remained obstinately closed. Jaq lent on the buzzer until the intercom crackled to life.

'Quem é?' Adelina might be ancient, but her voice was still strong.

Jaq identified herself. 'I need your help.'

A little hatch appeared in the massive wood door. Steel hinges squealed and Jaq peered through.

Ɏ 6

The British Cemetery, Lisbon, Portugal

As Jaq opened the wicket gate, she paused to greet the ghost of her younger self. A ritual she repeated every time she visited the cemetery, and she'd been coming here for more than two decades.

She stepped through and faced the trees, arms open wide. Sunlight shone through the jacaranda, tinting the path with violet-blue light. The fronds of the tallest palms swished in a light breeze. A cuckoo called. She closed her eyes until she sensed the approach, welcoming the mounting pain, ready to share the burden, lessen the weight on the shoulders of a young girl. A girl whose brother had already died in the war that would kill her father. A girl rejected by everyone else she cared about: her lover, her mother, her teachers, her church, her friends. A girl who had given birth to a baby she thought she didn't want. Until he was taken away from her, along with the possibility of ever having another child. A girl who had been abused and betrayed, imprisoned and robbed, tricked and mutilated. A girl who learned the hard way that the only person she could ever depend upon was herself.

The future had come to teenage Jaq in a moment of clarity. She had escaped to the grave of Nuno Correia, a baby who lived only 15 minutes in 1832. His parents had loved that baby so much, had been so distraught at his passing, they had constructed one of the most beautiful memorials in the whole cemetery, a riot of cherubs, stone birds and animals. This was the place she came for reflection. Her own baby, born in secret, had no grave. The nuns took him away.

Prostrate and weeping beside the grave of the 15-minute baby, she sensed that she was no longer alone. At the rustle of light footsteps on the path, she bit her tongue to quell the howls, pressed her fists into her eye sockets to staunch the flow and turned her face away from the approaching visitor.

The sunlight had warmed her skin, dried her tears and a light wind caressed her hair. Her heartbeat returned to normal. She opened her eyes and glanced back at the path. Empty, nothing but the trees, the deep blue of the jacaranda. As she stood to peer over the headstone, she caught a flash of movement, her own reflection thrown back at her from a mirrored vase. A young girl with a broken heart and a torn body, framed in the glass, distorted and repeated. No one else there. No one but herself. Her multiple future selves.

She bowed her head and absorbed the trill of birdsong, the hum of insects, the swishing leaves, breathing in the scent of jasmine and rose. This was a place of peace and beauty, an oasis of calm. Wherever she went, wherever they sent her, wherever life took her next, she would always return to this place.

She closed her eyes and saw herself walking up the same path, as a young woman, a mature woman, an old woman. Knew that those women were her best chance of survival. And so she parcelled up her pain and handed it to them, her future selves coming to meet her. With each step, with each caress, with each embrace, she grew straighter, stronger, bolder. She walked through the gates determined to start anew.

Jaq let her go, leaning back to close the door with a soft click.

Au-au. At the bark of a little dog, she opened her eyes again and bent to ruffle the curly haired coat of the terrier that lived with the caretaker in a tiny cottage inside the cemetery. She looked up to see Dona Adelina shuffling down the path. She must be over eighty years old now, but the garden looked as beautiful as ever, the graves clean and tidy, a stern matron in total control of both the living and the dead, her faithful canine companion never far from her side.

They embraced and Jaq made her request.

Dona Adelina never asked questions. Married to a coffin maker, she had observed bereavement at close quarters over decades; witnessed the repeated cycles of denial, anger, bargaining, depression and acceptance. She offered silent assistance to those who grieved. For Jaq, there was always water, simple food and a place for the night in the cottage inside the high cemetery walls. And once, when the police came looking for Jaq, Dona Adelina had sent them away. She might not be able to read or write but she remained wise beyond words. And always looked out for Jaq.

Unlike Angie.

Her mother's grave wasn't here, in this beautiful cemetery where bones were left in peace. Did the Catholic nuns ignore the lovely garden under their noses just because it was linked to a Protestant rather than Catholic church? Or because a grave here wasn't an option? Space was short in central Lisbon, for the living and the dead. The nuns had followed their own traditions, burying Angie with a sachet of quick lime in the drab, bare cemetery of Prazeres. Calcium oxide plus water makes calcium hydroxide, killing the bacteria that normally decompose dead flesh, replacing the slow microbial decomposition with a faster chemical process. In three years, they would dig up Angie's bones and place them on a featureless marble shelf, in a booth resembling a left luggage storage depot.

Was her mother finally at peace? Perhaps, for those who believed in God, there really was a life after death. Was Angie reunited with her men at last?

It wasn't the bones that mattered, only the memories.

Lock it down, lock it in.

Focus on the future.

6

Lisbon, Portugal

The towers of the Convent were visible from inside the British Cemetery. Jaq looked up at the spire of St George's church. All she really needed was a rocket belt and she could fly from one to the other.

Don't be ridiculous.

She straightened the nun's habit she'd borrowed. Dona Adelina knew how to procure most things. Friendly with the laundry that took in the washing from the local nurseries, school, convent and hospital, it didn't take long to put together a disguise. The grey gown was loose, even the largest size was a little short, ending above Jaq's ankles rather than trailing along the ground. She had to walk with a stoop, knees bent, to avoid revealing her footwear. The white wimple was stiff and uncomfortable, fastened tight to secure the coif, with a grey veil at the back. Jaq donned the glasses found in a cardigan pocket and not yet claimed from the laundress; the thick black frames and bottle-glass lenses forced her to look down to see her way and helped to hide her face.

The concert at the *Igreja do Convento de Nossa Senhora do Desterro* started at 6 p.m. and the doors to the church would open about half an hour in advance. From inside the church, she could make her way to the tunnel that led to the convent.

The church doors might have opened wide to the public at 5:30 p.m., but the door to the convent tunnel was firmly locked. There was one other way to access it, from the organ loft.

Jaq looked around. The church was empty. She slipped round to the back of it and turned the handle on the organist's door. It was locked too. *Ah catano!* Both locks were old-fashioned and difficult to pick, as she knew from experience, impossible if they were bolted and padlocked on the inside, which was almost certainly the case. The nuns took their security seriously.

She peered up at the gallery that held the organ. A tricky climb, but if she started from the tomb at the wall she gained a couple of metres. The chattering outside grew in volume, people gathering in the sunshine, preparing to enter for the concert.

Now or never.

Jaq walked back to the entrance and closed the church doors. She couldn't find the key to lock them, so she dragged a couple of wooden chairs to wedge against the iron handles. It wouldn't take much effort for those outside to push past, but the faithful were a credible and obedient bunch and were more likely to wait until a priest welcomed them in. She took off the rosary with its clumsy wooden cross and tested it for strength. The cross was nicely filleted with a dovetail joint and also glued, the perfect anchor. The beads were strung on several strands of nylon cord, thin but super strong together. The weakest point was where the nylon cords ran through a brass ring at the top of the cross. She re-tied the cord around the cross to make it stronger, then unwound the long rope belt from her waist, tying one end to the rosary in a bowline – saying a silent thank you to Giovanni, her expert sailing teacher.

She swung the rope around her head until the cross was at the height of the gallery and then flicked it forwards. It took three attempts to catch. The cross slipped sideways between the balustrades and with a twist of her wrist she flipped it lengthways, so it caught between the wooden stanchions. The sacred cross as an anchor. Someone should write a sermon about that. Let's hope it would hold her weight, especially after that blowout lunch of *açorda de marisco*.

She slid off her shoes and climbed up the side of the tomb, standing on tiptoes to catch the trailing rope. She used it to stay upright, concentrating as much of her weight as possible through her feet as they found toe holds in the wall. Half-way up she rested on a window ledge, listening for new noises. Someone was hammering on the door.

She looked back down, too far to give up now.

One last supreme effort was all it needed. Stretching from the ledge to the gallery she was about a foot short. If she jumped she had a chance of making it. And a risk of falling to the stone floor below.

Her heart somersaulted at the scrape of wood on stone. The external door was opening. She was out of time.

Jaq leapt. Her hands made contact with the balcony, her fingertips touching a wooden pillar. As she scrambled for a firmer hold, gravity took over, pulling her down. She grabbed the rope as she fell and swung from the gallery, breathing hard.

Nearly there. Now to pull herself up.

If it had been Johan in this position, he would have used his enormously powerful arms, shoulders and back muscles to lift his own body weight, hand by hand up the rope, catching the wooden balcony and hauling himself over the balustrade. Many of the male athletes she knew found pull-ups relatively easy. Not so for Jaq. Despite all the swimming and kayaking, her real muscle strength was from her core downwards, her leg muscles far better developed than her arms. But strength is not about muscle density, strength is knowing how to use what you have.

Before Aunt Lettie bought the Land Rover, she had a comically underpowered car. On a weekend break in the Lake District, loaded with camping and climbing equipment, the car refused a particularly steep hill. Her aunt simply turned the car round and reversed all the way to the top.

Without losing any height, Jaq turned herself upside down, working a leg up to wedge it between the wooden stanchions, securing herself by hooking her knee around it. The other leg followed and soon she was hanging upside-down from the balcony by her knees.

Now her weight was supported by the balcony, and she could use her stomach muscles to raise herself. The wooden structure groaned, and she felt a slight movement.

She looked down at the floor five metres below. If she fell, her head would smash against the stone slabs, her neck would break, and she would die. The wood creaked again.

Jaq tightened her stomach muscles and swung herself up, grabbing the top of the wooden banister. It was relatively easy to unthread her legs until she stood on tiptoes on the outside of the balcony. With one last push she vaulted over.

Jaq flopped onto the floor of the gallery and looked back down. A gaggle of women, dressed entirely in black, had entered the church. They were turned away from her, bowing and genuflecting towards the altar. Had they spotted her? An upside-down nun hanging from the organ loft. Had anyone raised the alarm? No time to think about that.

Jaq rescued her rosary, muttered the first honest prayer since childhood, untied the rope and wrapped it back around her waist.

The door from the organ loft to the back staircase was locked. All she could do was wait for it to be unlocked, for the nuns to pass through, and hope that they left it open.

The interior was unusual among Lisbon churches in that it was almost plain. Just a frieze of beautiful blue-and-white tiles with Moorish patterns up to eye level, and then smooth white plaster between the pinkish sandstone pillars and arches. No elaborate wooden carvings covered in gold leaf, no life-size painted statues, not even a Madonna and child or a man dying on a cross.

A choir assembled at the front of the church, sixteen men and women. The door to the gallery clicked open and the nuns began to arrive.

Jaq sat in the shadows and waited.

Manuel Cardoso was born in the sixteenth century, a devout Catholic monk and composer who enjoyed the patronage of kings. The choir did great service to the Renaissance music with all its chromatic spice and crunchy dissonance. There was something utterly ethereal about the music. Her heart stopped thumping, her pulse slowed and she felt a slow calm descending.

The choir filed back to their seats and the priest invited the congregation to join him in prayer. The nuns in front of her sank to their knees and bowed their heads. Now was her opportunity.

The door to the back staircase was unguarded. Jaq opened it quietly and slipped through, descending first the wooden stairway from organ loft to church, and then the stone staircase down into the underground passage that linked church and convent. The stone was cold and rough against her bare feet as she hurried through the darkness.

At the far end, she reached a steel door and put her ear to the keyhole, listening. All was quiet in the convent. She tried the handle, it squealed, but moved easily. Scraping the steel door against stone, she cracked it open, a lozenge of light falling onto the stone floor of the tunnel.

She peered round the edge of the door. All clear. It opened silently. She slipped through, and then pushed it closed again. The key had been left in the lock. Excellent. She locked the door and slipped the key into her bra. This might buy some time, give her the distraction she needed. Keeping her head bowed, she climbed the stairs, sticking to the shadows, emerging into the cloisters of the convent. The lights were off in the administration block and the concert had thirty minutes to go.

Jaq had plenty of experience breaking into the mother superior's office.

The first time Jaq had broken in was early on in her imprisonment, before the birth of her baby, when she still imagined she might get help from the education authorities, from her teachers or even from her school friends. She had pursued every avenue to call their attention to her plight.

In the days before mobile phones, the only telephone in the convent was in the office of the mother superior. Security was light if you were already inside the walls. The inhabitants were either God-fearing or nun-fearing. Jaq would have taken her chances against a deity she didn't believe in, but there were some ferocious nuns to be avoided at all costs.

She'd employed a little ingenuity to assist in the break-in. A soft drinks bottle, thrown into the rubbish, provided the perfect lock-picking material – PET, polyethylene terephthalate as she later learned. Cut a rectangle from the cylinder, straighten it out, double it over, pinch the fold, trim the edges and slide between door and jamb. It took a bit of wiggling, but the flimsy office locks were no match for her determination.

It had come as a shock to discover that she was an embarrassment to everyone outside. Only after several break-ins and hopeless phone calls did she come to terms with the fact that her 'confinement' was as much a relief to the pedagogical community as it was to her mother.

One door closed after another.

She decided to break out. That took more ingenuity. The gates, separating virtue inside from depravity outside, had heavy-duty locks and serious guards. The simplest route to freedom was through the church: ironic really. The convent was linked to the church by a tunnel. Stone stairs led down to a basement beneath the convent and a steel door opened into an underground passage. At the other end a wooden staircase led up to two exits. The door directly into the church was used three times a day, for matins, lauds and vespers, also for communion and confession. The other door led to a spiral staircase that opened into the organ loft with a gallery. A community service or a choral concert – the church had particularly lovely acoustics for unaccompanied polyphony – meant that the church doors opened wide to the faithful outside. From the organ gallery, the nuns could observe the congregation below without being seen.

Several failed attempts to walk out through the church doors resulted in additional penance and chores. She was only spared the usual punishments

*of starvation, isolation and beatings because of the advancing, and now
visible, pregnancy.*

*In the end, she left the convent the same way she arrived, in a car with
tinted windows, but this time at the wheel.*

The lights were off in the mother superior's office. Jaq took the
universal key, a rectangle of PET, and used it to open the door. She
padded over to the desk. Could her file still be here?

She held her breath as she tried to open the drawer. Firmly
locked, that was a good sign. The lock might be strong, but it was
only as good as the material that held it. With her Swiss Army
penknife she gouged the barrel from the laminate, taking care
to make a neat job. She pressed the tumblers and opened the
drawer.

Inside was a buff envelope, exactly as Carmo had described. She
opened it quickly, desperate to investigate the contents properly,
but the room was dark and time was running out. All she could
do was to check it was the right dossier. She pulled out the first
photograph and came face to face with her teenage self, side by
side with a boy of about the same age.

In a corner of the office, a high-spec colour photocopier, used
for printing saint's day notices and orders of service, glowed in
standby mode. Jaq copied the documents and photos, laying them
face down on the glass, closing the top, resisting the urge to look.
There'd be time later.

A shout from outside made her duck back down. The service
must have ended. The nuns would be in the tunnel, banging on the
door to the basement, calling attention to the fact that it was locked.
Her time was almost up. She pulled up her gown and stuffed the
photocopies into the waistband of her pants. She returned everything to the envelope and closed the drawer, pushing the lock
barrel back into the wood until she heard it engage. She slipped
from the office, locking the door behind her.

As she'd hoped, the confusion of finding the church door locked and the key missing had drawn everyone to the convent basement. Even the guard was absent from her post. Jaq took the key, warm from her breasts, and laid it on the guards' desk. Then she opened the side door and stepped into the outside world again.

Back in the cemetery, the elderly caretaker had retired for the night. Jaq hung up the key and folded the borrowed clothes carefully. No point in leaving a message, Dona Adelina could not decipher letters, although she could read souls.

The grave of Nuno Correia, the 15-minute baby, lay in darkness. Jaq took the photocopies past the tomb of Henry Fielding, the English novelist, to a place where a gap in the trees let the full moon shine through. She sat for a long time in the silence of the British Cemetery, gazing at the face of her baby son for the first time.

Jaq rarely cried; a river of tears had been lying in wait.

Once she could breathe again, she washed her face with cold water from the irrigation tank. The prospect of returning to a dark, stuffy hotel room held no appeal. Jaq knew where she needed to go. The same place she'd run to when she first escaped from the convent all those years ago.

Back to Guincho beach.

Y 6

Praia de Guincho, Cascais, Portugal

Jaq followed the smell of woodsmoke and found him where she knew he would be waiting, beside a driftwood fire in the dunes behind Café Carbon. She stood in the darkness and watched him for a while. The kitesurfing champion of the world. Of course. It was Xavier all grown up.

He smiled when she stepped into the firelight. 'I wasn't sure you remembered,' he said.

And she hadn't, not until she had looked again at the copy of the police mugshot in the mother superior's drawer. And realised just how young they had been.

'How could I forget?'

She sat down opposite him and studied his face in the firelight. The thick, dark, curly hair was all gone, and his features had hardened, once soft skin now deeply lined by the wind and sun or otherwise covered by a dark beard.

'It's been a long time, Xav.'

'More than twenty years.'

Pregnant Jaq had escaped from the convent driving the priest's car. More than prepared to hotwire it, a skill she had mastered in an Angolan refugee camp, she laughed to find the keys in the ignition. No one checked to see who was behind the tinted windows as the car approached the main exit. The doors swung open, and she sailed out through the gates in the same way she'd arrived – but with a little more control.

The ecclesiastical car had been easier to manoeuvre than the jeeps she'd driven in the guerrilla war, the roads much better, but teenage Jaq had driven slowly and carefully to avoid suspicion. She didn't really have a plan, but after months of imprisonment in the convent, she was thirsting for open spaces: for the ocean. She followed the marginal *as far as it went, then drove the car into the dunes so it could not be seen from the road.*

Xavier had been out with friends from Cascais, smoking weed in a burrow in the warm sand. The shock of being almost run over by a pregnant nun in a stolen car sent most of his friends running for their bikes and scooters, but Xavier hung around, recognising the depth of her trouble.

He stayed with her that first night. Kept watch over her things while she swam. Shared his bottled water. Let her talk. Pointed out the stars when she was tired of weeping. Held her hand until she slept.

Over the next few days, he brought her clothes, food, water, a tent and sleeping bag. And advice, pointing out the hopelessness of her position. She couldn't remain homeless. The summer would soon be over. It would be too cold to live outdoors. He tried to persuade her to return to the convent, for the sake of the baby.

When the police found them, they were much harder on him than on her. One of his friends had shopped them, jealous of the amount of time Xavier was spending with Jaq. The police accused him of fathering her child, although she was already seven months pregnant when she first met him, accused him of raping her, although their friendship was entirely platonic, accused him of stealing the car, refusing to believe that Jaq could drive.

The nuns reluctantly took her back in, ostracising her completely, sentencing her to almost unbroken silence. Back in the convent, the fiery anger that had kept her going began to fade, to dim, until it was almost snuffed out.

Almost, but not quite.

It was the pictures, or one picture in particular, copied from the locked drawer of the convent office, that had jogged Jaq's memory. The police mugshot of Xavier showed him as a young man. He might have changed outwardly, but the dark eyes were unmistakeable.

'I tried to find you again,' she said. 'Before I left Portugal.'

'I was in prison.'

'Because of me?'

'Because of you.'

She sighed. 'You were the only one who tried to help.'

'By the time they let me out, you were gone.'

'I'm sorry, Xav. I didn't know.' She closed her eyes. How selfish she had been. 'My aunt took me to England.'

'What happened to your baby?'

She bowed her head. 'It's a long story.'

He reached into a cool box and drew out two beers, opening one and passing it to her. 'I'm not going anywhere. Are you?'

Jaq passed him everything she had copied from the locked drawer of the mother superior's office. He switched on a torch and lingered over a photograph of Jaq as a schoolgirl. 'What a serious child you were,' he said.

'I didn't have much to be happy about.'

'Your mother?'

'She's dead.'

He didn't offer any false platitudes, moving on to the photograph that showed the two of them, the night they were taken to the police station. Two hopelessly naive teenagers, who expected the adults to believe them, to understand, to take action. Xavier with abundant, curly black hair and rounded face, Jaq gaunt and hollow-eyed, her belly swollen, her head shaved.

'I always thought we'd have made a handsome couple.' He observed her, his brows tightening. 'But you grew some hair.' He ran a hand over his bald scalp. 'And I lost all of mine.'

'It suits you.'

He guffawed. 'You didn't recognise me at first, did you?'

She bowed her head. 'I had other things on my mind.'

'And yet, I knew you the moment I saw you in the water.' His eyes bored into her. 'Of all the beaches in all the world and you have to swim into mine ...'

She drew back from the fire into the shadows, gazing across the beach to the dark hills with Pena Palace on the top, illuminated in colours to highlight its crazy gothic glory, and up to the moon and the stars. This was one place, one time she had been briefly happy. When this gentle man had helped her to stop fighting, to accept the world as it was, not as she wished it to be. Made her pause and feel the baby kicking vigorously inside her. Persuaded her to accept the fact of her pregnancy. A crazy few days when she had enough freedom to choose incarceration. For the sake of the child.

He moved on to the paperwork and frowned. 'Your baby was adopted?'

She told him about the lies, how she'd grown up believing her son had died at birth, the shock of the discovery, and the start of her search.

'What do you know about ...' he returned to the adoption form and squinted at the names ... 'Dr Carlos and Evangelina Costa.'

'A Brazilian-born dentist and his wife with a practice in Lisbon. They're the ones who adopted my son.'

'And what are you going to do now?'

'I'm going to find him.'

Y 6

Lisbon, Portugal

On the application to adopt, Dr Carlos and Evangelina Costa registered their address as Calçada de Carriche, a road in the north of Lisbon beyond Lumiar. Blocks of flats had been rushed up during the white heat of economic confidence as Portugal prepared to join the European Union in 1986. From Odivelas to Telheiras, row after row of tower blocks sprang up. Calçada de Carriche was now a six-lane motorway, one that Jaq had to cross several times before she found the right tower block.

The new housing might have made an appealing destination in the late 1980s, but it was looking a little weary now. The recession of 2008 had hit Portugal hard. A bunch of kids kicked a football around on a patch of scrubby waste-ground littered with broken glass and rubbish. Is this where her son had grown up? What did it matter, so long as he was loved?

She tried the buzzer for flat 80. No reply.

There was a café on the ground floor and Jaq ordered a coffee and a glass of water from the bar.

'Do you know a family in this block by the name of Costa?'

The barman shook his head.

'*Mãe!*' he called out to the kitchen.

An elderly woman shuffled through.

'*Quem é?*'

'This girl,' he used the word *menina,* 'wants to know about the Costas.'

'Rui Costa?'

Jaq swallowed hard. Had Carlos and Evangelina named her son Rui.

'Old man, Rui?' The woman nodded at a group of old men sitting at one of the tables outside.

'No, Carlos and Evangelina,' Jaq said.

The old woman nodded. 'The Brazilian? The dentist?'

A little flutter of excitement. 'Yes.'

'They left years ago. Twenty years or more.'

The spark of hope fizzled out.

'Do you know where they went?' Jaq asked.

'Search me.'

'Do you think their neighbours might know?'

'I doubt it.' The old woman sniffed. 'Snooty pair. Thought themselves too good for the likes of us. Always complaining. Everything was better in Brazil: the climate, the food, the music, the beaches. Annoyed some folk who told them if it was so bloody great where they'd come from, why didn't they just bugger off back. After that, they kept themselves to themselves.'

'And his dental practice?' Jaq asked. 'Any idea where that is?'

'Rui and his mates might remember.' She smiled to reveal teeth that had never received a dentist's care. 'For a brandy.'

Jaq paid for brandy and the barman went outside with the bottle. The men round the table raised their glasses in a toast of thanks.

'Lisbon,' said the barman on his return.

'Which district?'

'They're not sure. Jorge things maybe Estefânia.' He put the bottle back on the shelf and brought out a telephone directory from under the counter. 'It had a funny name, he says. The Golden Tooth. Something like that.' He pushed the directory over to Jaq.

It wasn't hard to find. The Golden Smile. Strange name for a dental practice. Most people wanted dazzling white teeth; gold fillings were a thing of the past. She took a note of the number and the address.

'One more question? Do you remember a child with them? A baby?'

The older woman shook her head.

'No, they were a childless couple.'

Jaq thanked them, paid for another round of drinks and left.

She walked back to the metro stop at Lumiar and took the underground train as far as Marquês de Pombal. From there it was a short walk up to Campo Mártires da Pátria, a lush garden on a hill, right in the heart of the city. She stopped for a moment to gather her thoughts.

There was no reason to worry. It was likely that Carlos and Evangelina had moved house. The flat in Calçada de Carriche would be their first home arriving in Portugal from Brazil. Perhaps their business had been so successful, they were able to move somewhere better, closer to the surgery.

But as she got closer to the practice address, the neighbourhood turned rougher, the buildings more dilapidated. The dental clinic was on the top floor of an old building behind the University Hospital.

Jaq stood in the narrow alleyway and stared up at The Golden Smile. It didn't exactly inspire confidence. The sign was broken and one of the windows boarded up. With a heavy heart Jaq pressed the buzzer. When there was no reply she tried the door. It opened and she climbed the wooden steps. The dental clinic on the top floor appeared long abandoned. She knocked and called out. The door of the flat opposite opened. A man with an impressive moustache stood in the doorway.

'I'm looking for Dr Carlos Costa.'

'The Brazilian? He hasn't been around for years. He sold his business on, but the new dentist hasn't been able to make a success of it either.'

'Do you have any idea where he is now?'

'Costa? He went back, didn't he?'

'To Brazil?'

'Yup.'

'When?'

'Ages ago. The surgery has changed hands a few times since then.'

'Any idea where in Brazil Dr Costa might have gone?'

'Search me.'

'What about the current dentist? Might he know?'

'Well, he might, but it won't be much use to you.'

'Why not.'

He cleared his throat. 'Committed suicide, didn't he.'

Poor man.

'Who else might know Dr Costa?'

'None of the Jonny-come-lately trash around here.' He spat into the corridor. Jaq stepped back.

'What was he like? Dr Costa?'

'Arsehole. Always complaining. Never liked him much. Wife was a bit of all right though.'

Jaq turned and left. She'd heard enough.

She rode the little yellow funicular, Elevador do Lavra, back down to Avenida da Liberdade and walked through the Baixa to the river. She sat on a bench in Praça do Comércio and watched the ferries leave Terreiro do Paço for Barreiro.

A sort of numbness had descended on her. It was a serious blow that the Costa family had left Portugal – a country of 10 million – for Brazil – a country of 200 million. Twenty times the number of people and one hundred times the land mass.

Before she'd left Guincho beach last night, she'd promised to meet Xavier for dinner. The one bright prospect in an otherwise bleak day. As she rode the train back to Cascais she tried to see the positive. She was on the trail, and it was not yet cold. People remembered Carlos and Evangelina even though they'd left Portugal twenty years ago.

A distance had suddenly opened, a gulf of thousands of miles of

Atlantic Ocean between her and her son. The need to formulate a search plan would give her time to think about what she would do when she found him. For find him she would.

Stepping off the tram at Guincho beach, she watched the kitesurfers racing along the bay. Xavier was taking a class and it was late before the last pupils finished. He emerged from the sea, a huge red sun behind him. Not a bad silhouette.

The kiss was unexpected, cold and salty but not unwelcome. At the question in his eyes, she shook her head.

She held his board while he detached the harness and rolled up the kite. They carried everything back to the gear store, Jaq stowing it while he showered. Afterwards they sat on the decking outside Café Carbon, sharing a cold beer as she told him the story of her day.

'And you have no idea where they are now?'

She shook her head.

'All I know is that they moved back to Brazil.'

'What will you do now?'

'What do you think?'

He sighed. 'You're going to Brazil.'

'I have to find him,' she said. 'You understand that.'

'Brazil is a big place.'

'And I'm a resourceful woman.'

'I never doubted that. You're the most single-minded person I've ever met.'

'And that's a bad thing?'

'You certainly take no prisoners.'

'What is that supposed to mean?'

'You'll disappear from my life as fast as you reappeared.' His voice sounded forlorn. 'Perhaps we can make a date for twenty years hence? Or can you just promise to turn up at my funeral?'

Jaq stood up. 'I'm sorry I hurt you, Xav. I'm sorry that you went to prison on my behalf. I didn't know. I couldn't have stopped it even if I had known. No one believed me.'

'I believed you.'

'And look what it cost you.' She couldn't hold back the emotion any longer. Every step she took forward set her further back. The last few days had been an emotional rollercoaster: the cemetery, the convent, the dental surgery and now the realisation this man felt something for her, something that went beyond friendship. Time to leave before she hurt him more. 'It was a mistake coming back.' She started to walk away.

'Wait!'

He moved quickly, blocking her way without touching her. 'Don't go.'

'I have to find him.'

'I know.' He backed away, hands held up in surrender. 'Starting tomorrow. It's too late to do anything tonight.' He gestured back to the table. 'I promised you dinner. Please stay.'

'What's the point, Xav? I'm bad news. I hurt the people I care about. I don't mean to, but I can't seem to help it. I ruined your life once; I'm not doing it again.'

'You know nothing about me, Jaq.' He smiled. 'I've done a fair bit of listening. Willingly. Because I care about you. Maybe you could stop and listen to me too?'

She crumpled. 'You're right.' She sank down into the sand. 'I'm sorry.'

'You didn't ruin my life Jaq. You liberated me. I was a stupid rich kid from Cascais. I could have rolled into the family business. Prison opened my eyes to what mattered.'

The wind had gone out of her sails. 'And what does matter to you, Xav?'

'Many things. Kitesurfing. Café Carbon. The planet we live on. How we keep it safe for the future. Someday I'll tell you more about ECOPTO. But right now, all that matters is you and me.' He held out a hand. 'And our friendship.'

She let him pull her up. They walked side by side back to the deck.

'Hungry?'

'Thirsty.'

'Drinks are in the cooler.'

He bent to light the barbecue.

After dinner they lay in the warm sand and named the stars, the same way they had passed the time all those years ago.

As teenagers they had done no more than hold hands. They were older and wiser now. Jaq could no longer ignore the effect of Xavier's adult body on hers. The way his voice resonated, vibrating something deep inside of her. The scent of aloe vera from the soap he used had not entirely washed away the hints of rubber from his wetsuit and terpenes from the sea. She could still picture him riding the waves, strong and agile.

It seemed the most natural thing in the world to roll over towards him, to cup his face in her hands, to press up against his broad chest, to lower her lips to his.

He responded to her kiss, sweet and slow, but when her hands strayed under his shirt, he groaned and pushed her away.

'No, Jaq,' he said. 'Not like this.'

Her cheeks burned as she rolled away from him.

'I've waited for you this long,' he said. 'I can wait a little longer. Go and do what you have to do. Come back when you're done. I'll be here.'

He put his arms around her then, his chest against her back, holding her close as their breathing slowed, releasing her only as he fell asleep.

She left him before dawn, touching his salty forehead with a sandy kiss, escaping the arms that reached out for her.

Jaq walked across the dunes and didn't look back.

DETONATION MINUS 5

10,000 metres above Cabo de Roca, Portugal

The sun was still rising as the plane from South America reached the westernmost tip of mainland Europe.

Jaq yawned and gazed out of the window, straining to spot the curving sandy bay where Guincho beach nestled in the lee of a rocky outcrop. The frosty Sintra hills glittered in the rosy dawn light, but the coast was blanketed in winter fog.

Summer seemed a long way away. Would things have turned out differently if she'd stayed with Xavier? If she'd conducted her search through Carmo, the lawyer who had been so helpful, who'd reached out to her own personal network in the Portuguese-speaking world?

Look where that had led.

Jaq pulled the thin airline blanket up to her chin and shivered.

Y 5

Luanda, Angola

The Bank of the Holy Ghost ought to be a divinely safe place to keep one's documents. The Angolan headquarters soared over the city, and from Senhor Ferreira's office he could see from São Miguel Fort right across Luanda Bay. Well, he could have if he hadn't been hunched over his computer screen, puzzling through a spreadsheet.

His desk phone rang. 'Ferreira here.'

'Jorge, It's Carmo, Carmo Centeno, from Lisbon.'

'Carmo!' The little of fizz of pleasure made him sit up straight. 'I was hoping you'd call.' Although they'd agreed not to, he'd been struggling to keep to his side of their deal. 'So very sorry to hear of your uncle's illness. How are the family bearing up?'

'Well, thank you.'

She brought him up to date, her husky voice making his ear tingle pleasantly. He reciprocated with his own family news, limited since the divorce and subsequent escape to Angola. His adult children only talked to his ex-wife, and she was in no hurry to share any news. Carmo's sister was married to his ex-brother-in-law, so she probably knew more about his children than he did. Time to change the subject before she judged him harshly. 'And to what do I owe the pleasure of this call?' he asked, hope making his mouth go dry.

'I'm phoning on behalf of a client.'

He struggled to keep the disappointment from his voice, maintaining an even, professional tone. 'I see.'

'My client has inherited some Angolan deeds, but we only have copies.'

'And the originals?'

'Stored at the headquarters of the Banco Espirito Santo.'

'Then I will certainly be able to help you.' He saved his spreadsheet and opened the confidential database. 'What's the name of your client?'

'Dr Jaqueline Silver.'

Ferreira tapped the keyboard. Nothing. 'Would the originals be in her name?'

'In the name of her mother. Maria dos Anjos Ribeiro da Silva. Recently deceased.'

He made a new search. 'Ah, yes. The family were clients. Angolan *retornados* weren't they?'

'Yes. The documents are from before 1974. Would it be possible for you to confirm that you still have them? And if they are of any value?'

'Hmmm, things got a little complicated around 1974.' Revolutions caused mayhem for banks. 'I can certainly check. Do you want to send over the details?'

He promised to phone back once he'd looked into the matter, and no sooner had he put the phone down than a ping announced the arrival of an email. Carmo was nothing if not efficient.

He printed the document and ran his eyes over the details. A poor photocopy, but, with a little effort, most of the information was legible.

The deeds had been issued by an Angolan mining company. Now almost certainly worthless. If the Portuguese Carnation Revolution had been relatively peaceful, it was because the violent battles had played out thousands of miles away in the colonies. The financial and human cost to Portugal of attempting to maintain an empire – Angola, Mozambique, East Timor, Guinea-Bissau, São Tome and Principe – led to a home revolution against the fascist dictator Salazar and his successor Caetano. Seventy-five thousand people died in Angola fighting the war of independence. And when independence came, it came overnight, without structures for governance or any period of transition. Millions were killed or displaced in the civil war that followed.

Ferreira walked to the window and stared out over the booming city. He loosened his collar. Even with the air-conditioning on, it felt unbearably stuffy in his office. The traffic flowed like a river along the bay, but the sky was darkening to the west. A storm brewing.

For anyone else, Ferreira would have sent a junior clerk. But for Carmo, lovely Carmo, he decided to go down to the basement himself. Not that he would admit that he was still in love with her. Easier to tell himself that he needed a break from the financial forecasts that had kept him pinned to his chair for several hours.

Ferreira took the public lift down to the ground floor, before passing through the special security outside the access to the vault. As he descended the marble stairs, he imagined flying back to Lisbon, taking the train to Estoril, stopping at the flower stall to buy a big bouquet, surprising Carmo as she was closing up the office. Suggesting a working dinner. Yes, that would show her how much he valued her as a professional, respected her life choices. How much he was ready to change.

A huge leather-bound ledger held the index, each handwritten entry carefully inscribed in beautiful India-ink copperplate. Ferreira lost himself for a while – his passion for history awakened – but as he turned the pages it saddened him to see how much had changed.

Revolutions happen when politicians stop listening. When people are pushed too far, beyond the point of elasticity, they focus on what must change, not what needs to be preserved. The status quo is no longer an option; institutions stretched to breaking point start to snap. And when they finally shatter, people are wounded by the ricocheting fragments, others by the whiplash. It's a lot easier to destroy than to rebuild.

He refocussed on the task and entered the date, checking the gold watch on his wrist before writing down the time, adding the reference: 2-8-18-32-18-2 and then the name of the client. He debated whether to put the owner's name, but as she was now deceased and he couldn't remember the name of her heir, he wrote Maria de Carmo Centeno in careful, looping longhand. It gave him pleasure to write her name. He stared at it for a while.

The document storage followed a logical pattern. Room 2, Aisle 8, Cabinet 18, Safe 32. Inside the large safe, he ran his fingers over the profile of partition 18-2, the front of a long, slim, shallow drawer. As Ferreira unlocked it, he heard a click, like the bimetallic strip on a kettle breaking contact.

He didn't hear the automated release of the boron compound into the drawer or the fizz as it started to react with the documents inside.

As he pulled the drawer open, a tiny dart shot from the drawer, piercing the skin on his neck. The poison moved quickly through his body, paralysing his diaphragm. He clutched his throat, fighting for air.

The clattering of a teleprinter, deep in the basement, was the last sound that Jorge Ferreira heard as he fell to the floor, fighting to breathe. The last image behind his eyes was of his children, too far away to say goodbye as he was borne heavenward on angel wings.

⅄ 5

Teesside, England

The wind blew the summer rain sideways. The contrast between dawn on a beach in Portugal and dusk in the north of England could not have been more dramatic. Jaq shivered as she stepped off the Manchester Airport train and hurried down the hill to Yarm High Street.

After Aunty Lettie died, Jaq was only ever passing through the Yarm flat, with little incentive to attack the mould creeping up the bathroom tiles or the dust on top of the bookshelves. Cleaning was something that Jaq understood in theory but avoided in practice. There were always more interesting things to be doing. And if you set a high standard, you made a rod for your own back; it soon became a never-ending cycle of dusting and sweeping, vacuuming and scrubbing, wiping and polishing. If you left things alone, kept on top of essential hygiene like kitchen and bathroom surfaces, then the dirt built up to a stable level, where it didn't really get any worse. Daily chores could be carried out weekly, or even monthly, with an extra cosmetic tidy-up before overnight visitors.

The strongest presence here was Letitia.

Jaq's gaze wandered over the collection of Paula Rego tiles on the wall, all birthday and Christmas gifts from her great-aunt.

Each glazed tile was 14 centimetres, 5 inches, square and decorated with simple dark lines on a cream background. With quick, deft strokes the artist had painted a story.

A girl holds an owl aloft. Her hair in bunches with bows, she is dressed in a knee-length frock with puffed sleeves and a pinafore. A tiny bald figure in pyjamas stretches up towards the bird. On the other side sits a dog, tail wagging, body facing away but eyes turned back towards the supplicant. Does the owl represent knowledge? What information is being kept from the imploring child?

Less than a month ago, she'd opened Angie's strongbox.

After the initial shock came anger. Who knew? Who had conspired to deceive and mutilate a child? Nothing about her mother's behaviour surprised her. As for the nuns, they simply disgusted her with their slavish devotion to a set of outdated, patriarchal, misogynistic rules. But Lettie? When her great-aunt had flown from England to rescue her, what did she already know? And what did she find out later? Jaq closed her eyes.

She'd been hiding in the chapel, the only place the nuns left her alone, when the door opened and closed. Brisk footsteps moved down the central aisle, squeaking on the flagstones with more staccato than any nun's slipper glissando. The footsteps stopped right next to her wooden bench.

'Maria Jaqueline?' A woman's voice. An English accent.

Jaq closed her eyes. Didn't this person know that talking in chapel was forbidden?

The stranger sat on the bench and shuffled up until she was almost touching Jaq.

'I'm your Aunt Lettie. Your great-aunt really. Your grandfather – on your mother's side – was my brother.' Jaq had to concentrate on the unfamiliar language, the northern accent, the family history. She had never known either set of grandparents. Her mother's family in Angola broke off all contact with Angie after she married a man they disapproved of.

'I came as soon as I heard.' She extended a hand, tentatively. On the middle finger she wore an unusual ring. A square setting with brightly coloured tiles that shimmered in the dim light.

Jaq murmured something unintelligible.

'Shhh.' A nun appeared out of the darkness and hissed at her, a finger over her lips.

'No, I won't shhh.' Aunt Lettie raised her voice. 'And nor should you. You should have spoken out. Protected this child instead of punishing her.'

The nun gasped and scuttled away,

Jaq stared at her feet. Beside her own cheap slippers, her aunt's trainers looked like colourful boats. She imagined the freedom and comfort shoes like that would give. To be able to run and run, run and never stop.

'Thank you,' Jaq said. She extended her own hand and sighed as her aunt covered it. The older woman's palm was soft and warm. It jolted her even now, to realise that this was the first human contact she'd had, skin to skin, since the birth. The other fallen women were forbidden from mixing, and the nuns maintained a disapproving distance, as if pregnancy were catching. Her mother had not been to see her, not once, since the day she was locked up in this place.

'I've come to offer you a new home.'

Jaq raised her eyes, past the jeans and padded gilet. The face opposite was lined, and the hair was grey, but her aunt dressed, carried herself and spoke like a much younger woman.

'In England. With me. I know you'll need time to think about it …'

A side door opened, and three nuns bustled through, marched up the aisle towards them, tight-lipped, brows wrinkled, gesticulating with fury.

Jaq squeezed her aunt's hand. 'When can we leave?'

They'd come to this flat. From a strict convent in Lisbon, Portugal, to a bohemian flat in Yarm, England. Jaq had almost no memory of the journey, but she remembered her first night: opening the door to the room prepared for her with such thoughtful care, full of books, a stereo and rack of CDs; sitting down for the first meal at a little table looking out over Yarm High Street; talking with the first adult who had ever listened to her, really listened.

No. Lettie hadn't approved of Angie's actions. She loved children, although she never had any herself; no way would she have agreed to the adoption. She believed in female empowerment; no way she would have permitted the sterilisation. She had arrived too late to stop everything; it must have happened too fast.

But did Lettie know after the fact? Decide not to divulge the truth in some misplaced belief that it was for Jaq's own good?

Jaq shook her head. Lettie must have been told the same pack of lies, that Jaq's baby died at birth. Lettie wasn't afraid of the truth, and she could never have sustained that big a cover-up, right up to her death.

What was the use of dwelling on the past? Right now, all that mattered was planning her trip to Brazil and figuring out a way to fund it.

5

Luanda, Angola

It was the security team who found Senhor Jorge Ferreira on the marble floor of the bank vault, lying directly beneath the drawer he had just unlocked.

If the guards had stopped to fully open it and look inside, they might have noticed wisps of steam, then tendrils of smoke. The perborate compound released into the drawer, triggered by the key turning in the lock, reacted with the moisture in the documents, producing hydrogen peroxide, which bleached the ink. As the hydrogen peroxide decomposed to hydrogen and oxygen, the heat of reaction was enough to start a slow fire that steadily burned the pages to ash.

If the guards noticed the faint smell of burning paper, they ignored it, more concerned with the state of their colleague.

The body was still warm, if motionless, but the guards were not trained in CPR and by the time the ambulance arrived, it was too late for Senhor Ferreira.

The paramedics who attended were probably a little too quick to diagnose a heart attack. But then they had probably never heard of batrachotoxin.

Perhaps one or other of them had seen a TV documentary where South American Indians fired venom-tipped arrows from blowpipes to kill their prey. They might even have known that a deadly venom could be scraped from the skin of tiny frogs – golden *Phyllobates terribilis* and multicoloured *Phyllobates bicolor*.

While collection of the batrachotoxin was hard and dangerous work, the effort was ultimately rewarding. A single gram was enough to kill 5,000 adult humans.

But the Angolan paramedics had no direct experience of the jungles of South America. They had been born, trained and now worked in downtown Luanda, a city of six million and rising. They were not looking for the tiny dart that had penetrated so far into the victim's skin that it was quite invisible to any cursory investigation. Nor were they aware of the physiological action of the toxin, how it interfered with the sodium ion channels in the body, distorting the signals to muscles and nerves, paralysing first the diaphragm and ultimately stopping the biggest muscle of all.

All they knew was that Senhor Ferreira's heart had stopped suddenly and – despite their best efforts – irreversibly.

Schiphol Airport, Amsterdam, The Netherlands

The Christmas music began again as the pilot announced that the plane from São Paulo had started its descent into Amsterdam.

Jaq yawned to release the pressure in her ears and reset her watch to local time, four hours ahead. More than 24 hours since the kidnappers had delivered their ultimatum. Time was running out to fetch what they wanted and bring it back to Florianopolis.

And what did they want? A box. A leather-covered steel box that had belonged to her mother. A safe that Jaq had given to a child. She had found one secret compartment. What if there were more? What exactly were they looking for? And why was it so important?

And what if it wasn't what they expected? What if they thought her mother's box contained something that was no longer there? Would they still release Mercúrio?

She'd slept little during the overnight flight from Brazil to Europe. As she queued to leave the plane, the exhaustion began to catch up with her. A dull, grey light shone through the windows, the rain streaming against the glass. She shivered, glad not to have to brave the northern weather just yet. She would remain in the airport and wait for her connecting flight from Amsterdam to Teesside.

Jaq took the opposite direction to the rest of the disembarking crowd. She knew Schiphol airport like the back of her hand. With direct flights from Teesside, it made the perfect international hub, much more convenient than Heathrow, which required four trains:

Heathrow to London Paddington, Paddington to King's Cross, King's Cross to York, York to Yarm. Schiphol was an airport full of interesting nooks and crannies. She found a quiet spot with reclining seats, set an alarm on her phone and stretched out.

Was it only a few months since she'd been here last, preparing for her first trip to Brazil? She'd changed so much since then. What was it Xavier had said before she left him on Guincho beach? That she took no prisoners, was doggedly single-minded. That at least still held true. She had five days to save Mercúrio and she couldn't waste a minute. Sleep wouldn't come, so she walked the length of the airport, up and down each of the long glass corridors.

In the main shopping area, seasonal carols permeated the air. The mournful brass arrangement always made her feel sad. No, not sad, wistful.

Silent Night
Holy Night
All is calm
All is bright

The staff were dressed as Christmas snowmen in white jump-suits with big, black buttons. Little bells tinkled on their felt top hats as they moved to attend to the stream of customers anxious to buy Belgian chocolate, French perfume, Scottish Whisky. Presents for loved ones? She bit her lip and moved away.

She spotted the man lurking near the giant Christmas tree, a tall, thin man with a buzz cut. It wasn't that she recognised him, it was his movement that marked him out. Or lack of it. He had that special sort of stillness that comes with professional training and long experience. He wasn't hiding the fact that Gate D6 was under surveillance. Coincidence? Most of the UK flights left from D6. Inverness, Aberdeen, Glasgow, Newcastle, Teesside – no reason to think he was waiting for her. But some instinct made her careful.

She took a seat at the shiny Heineken bar and ordered a beer she didn't want along with a water. She watched the watcher in the mirror. Was he alone? Part of airport security? Anti-terrorism?

A young woman with shoulder-length dark hair came down the escalator and checked the departure board at the bottom. The watcher stiffened. From an inside pocket he drew out a photograph. He looked at the picture and then looked at the woman. He turned away and spoke into his lapel. As she began to walk towards D6, he started to follow. Jaq held her breath.

'You don't like the beer?' The bartender asked.

'It's a bit early.' Jaq moved her head so she could see the little drama playing out behind her. The woman looked again at her boarding pass, realised she was at the wrong gate, and retraced her steps into the main concourse. Would the watcher follow? No. He returned to his position beside the Christmas tree.

Jaq did a quick calculation. There were three other flights leaving from D6 around the time of the Teesside flight. Each Embraer 100 held up to 50 passengers. If all four flights were full, 200 potential travellers. How many would be female? General population was more or less evenly split, unless you were in China or India where pre-natal sex selection and female infanticide had skewed things. Or in a business hub on an early morning weekday, with most people travelling at company expense. She watched the ebb and flow and made an estimate. One in five. No more than 20 per cent female. So, at a rough estimate, 40 women would be travelling through D6. She watched the watcher. He didn't move when a group of Asian students walked past. Group them into ethnicity. Hmm, the vast majority of travellers were white, although women were better represented in all races than men. At most she could eliminate one in four. That left 30 women like her. He didn't move when a group of students walked past, nor was there so much of a flicker of interest when a grey-haired couple stepped onto the elevator which descended into D6. So, ten will be too young and ten will be too old. That left ten just like her. A dark-haired woman rushed down the concourse, and he was back on his feet. She waited to see what would happen. The watcher spoke into the little metal tulip on his lapel and started to follow.

An airport security guard appeared from nowhere at the top of the escalator and blocked the entry to D6.

They were stopping all dark-haired, white women, neither young nor old travelling from D6. By her estimate it was a one in ten chance they were looking for her. Those were poor odds in anyone's book.

The guard gestured to the woman to step aside. She began to remonstrate, pointing at the time, waving her boarding card. Jaq couldn't hear what she was saying but had been in that position enough times to be able to imagine. *I'm late. I'm going to miss my flight if you don't let me through.* The watcher joined them, a false smile on his face. At his request, she passed him her boarding pass. He checked it and waved for her to proceed. Shaking his head at the security guard, the watcher retreated to his observation post.

A prickle of fear ran through her. It mirrored exactly the scene she had witnessed at Guarulhos Airport before leaving Brazil. Elena Azevedo, the woman from the clothes shop, who had picked up Jaq's boarding card in error, had been detained by security men with army buzzcuts. But in Elena Azevedo's case the boarding card identified her, wrongly, as Jaq Silver. Elena had been taken away. And missed her flight. What had happened to her? And why?

Jaq made a decision. Time to find another route to Britain.

She slid from her bar stool and headed in the opposite direction to gate D6.

DETONATION MINUS 4

Port of Tyne, Newcastle, England

The Amsterdam ferry, *Princess Beatrice*, let out a long, mournful warning as it approached Port of Tyne. In the grey light of morning, Jaq zipped up her leather jacket and stepped out on deck. From the railing, she watched the smaller boats scuttle out of the way.

The winter swells on the North Sea had made for a rough crossing from Amsterdam to Newcastle. She wasn't sea-sick, unlike many of the other passengers, but she'd had little sleep, turning her brain to mush.

Focus. Concentrate.

She was a day behind her original schedule. Abandoning the one-hour Teesside flight and taking a sixteen-hour ferry felt like a crazy decision in retrospect. Had she imagined the scene at the airport? Who could possibly be looking for her?

Crazy Gloves was waiting in Brazil. She still had no idea why he wanted an empty strongbox, but it made no sense for him to send men to detain her. Everything that had happened in Brazil had made her paranoid. Why had she panicked? Jet lag? Too late to do anything about it now.

Jaq rarely looked backwards. Regret used up energy that could be better employed in forward planning. What mattered now was recovering the box and getting back in time to save Mercúrio.

'D'you have a good time?' The man who had joined her at the railing slurred his words. He'd been propping up the bar all night; she could smell the alcohol on his breath. 'I bloody love Amsterdam.'

The men at Amsterdam airport, could they be from Interpol? She'd been arrested by the police before now, but cleared of all wrongdoing. Had someone reopened a case against her? In normal circumstances, she wouldn't be too concerned. She had nothing to hide. But she couldn't afford for them to take her passport away while she proved her innocence, could brook no delay.

The man took her silence for encouragement to continue. 'Bit of last-minute Christmas shopping?' He moved closer. 'Your fella back there?' He nodded in the direction of the passenger accommodation. 'Or are you travelling alone?'

She moved away.

Truth be told, the men at Schiphol didn't look like Interpol detectives. There had been something different about the scene at the airport, more like a military operation than police surveillance. They looked like professionals, not the kind of men who would work for Crazy Gloves and his cut-price outfit. The airport team had been short-haired and disciplined. Crazy Gloves travelled with goons who were long-haired and anarchic.

Did someone else have an interest in the strongbox, her cursed inheritance? If Crazy Gloves and his gang were determined to get their hands on it, was there another team, with much richer resources, equally determined to stop that from happening?

What was the significance of the strongbox in all this?

The ferry let out a long hoot. Jaq shook her head, trying to clear her jet-lagged, sleep-deprived brain. Right now, all that mattered was to recover the wretched leather box from the farmhouse in Coniston and deliver it to Crazy Gloves in Brazil. She would do everything in her power to meet the kidnappers' demands. Who knew if it would be enough?

After all they had been through, she could not let anything bad happen to Mercúrio.

Not again.

In the arrivals lounge of Port of Tyne a stall was selling hot mince pies and mulled wine; the scent of cloves and sugar filled the air.

God rest ye merry gentlemen
Let nothing you dismay

Jaq moved away from the queue to call Johan but it went straight to voicemail. A few minutes later, her phone pinged. A message. Thank God. She scrolled to the text.

Sorry, can't talk now. Complications. About to go into theatre.

Jaq texted back,

Sending love.

Dassssss! The plan no longer involved Johan. Time for a rethink. She called the farmhouse and John's mother answered.

'Yes.'

'Hello, Beryl. I've just heard that Emma's going into theatre. Are you OK?'

'I'm so terribly worried.'

'We all are.' Jaq paused. 'Is there anything I can do?'

'Thank you, dear, but no.'

Perhaps she could send a courier. Someone willing to deliver Christmas presents for the children and pick something up in return.

The tone in the voice at the other end suggested it would be unwise to share the plan, give Beryl an option to refuse. The box had to be collected whether she had permission or not. But how to persuade Ben to give up the precious strongbox? Perhaps he would swap it for something better. What would he want most in the world?

'How are Ben and Emma?'

'They're fine, missing their mum and dad.'

'Could I speak to Ben?'

'He's at school, dear.' Her tone was disapproving, as if Jaq was some sort of monster not to know that it was a school day. 'In fact, you were lucky to catch me. They break up for the Christmas holidays this afternoon, so Bertrand and I are taking them home.'

'To Warrington?'

'Yes. We think it will be easier for everyone.' She sighed. 'We don't know how long ...' A sob escaped her. 'Now if you'll excuse me?'

'Merry Christmas, Beryl. Please send my love and best wishes to Bertrand and the whole family.'

'Pray for them, my dear.'

Jaq moved back into the passport queue. She was through immigration before it occurred to her. Beryl and Bertrand were taking the children away. Johan and Emma were at the hospital. The farmhouse would be empty. Jaq's heart soared. Her first real break in this nightmare. All of her complicated planning had been to ensure that she didn't put her friends in further danger. But if no one was there, she could go and fetch the box herself and to hell with it if she was followed.

Yes, there was a risk that she was revealing where her friends lived, but given how much they already knew about her, given that Johan's address was in her passport as emergency contact, it was a risk she was willing to take. So long as the family weren't at home. Once she had the box out of their house, they would no longer be in danger.

First to lay a trail of breadcrumbs.

Perhaps she was being paranoid, but if she really was being followed, then there were some steps she could take to make it more difficult.

Jaq took a taxi to the train station, where she bought a ticket to Lockerbie using her credit card. The small town hosting a high-security prison was the cheapest destination in Scotland. When the train to Aberdeen slid into to the station, she jumped on board, hid her phone in a luggage rack and jumped out again before the whistle blew. She watched the InterCity125 pull out of the station.

The fastest route to the farmhouse was to hire a car in Newcastle and drive direct to Coniston, but she'd need to use a credit card and that was the easiest thing in the world to trace. Instead, she paid cash for a train ticket to Yarm. Aunt Lettie's ancient Land Rover was still waiting for her in the garage.

The train to Manchester Airport was crowded, and Jaq was glad to get off at Yarm. A Salvation Army band was playing carols outside the town hall, the mournful brass harmonies replaced by upbeat music as she dipped into a coffee shop. It didn't take her long to see that her flat opposite was under surveillance – how many soldiers did this operation have?

Jaq abandoned the order she had paid for and slipped out of the back door and into the alley that ran beside the river and led straight to the garage where the Land Rover was stored. As she turned the key in the ignition and the motor roared to life, the dismay at the extent of the surveillance operation turned to something else: relief that she was not being paranoid, determination that she would prevail, excitement at the prospect of evading her pursuers, however many of them there were.

It was raining hard as she approached the final rise behind Lake Coniston. The west wind soaked up water as it blew over the warm Irish sea, dumping it on the hills where it met the chill from the east. A single-track road wound over the shoulder of the mountain, zigzagging down to a National Trust car park and on to the farmhouse beyond, the only habitation and the end of a dead-end road. Only one way in or out and no other cars visible.

Good.

The only other access was on foot over the mountains or up the lake by boat. The pebbly beach below the farmhouse dropped away to deep water. No motor craft were permitted on the lake, and it was a long paddle or swim to the next launch point.

Jaq continued down the pass. The cattle grid rattled as the car crossed over. She parked the Land Rover in the woods behind the kayaks, hidden from the house.

Johan kept a spare set of keys in the paddle store. She searched for them in vain. Gone. Perhaps his parents had taken the spare keys.

She surveyed the house through the pelting rain. It was an idyllic spot when you could see the lake and the mountains. Usually, a warm light shone out through the windows, smoke curled from the chimney, but as December dusk approached and the mist closed in, the empty farmhouse appeared dark and forbidding, a fortress in the rain.

The box was most likely going to be in Ben's room. She scanned the upstairs windows, one after another. All were closed and probably latched inside. She ran over to the house, splashing through puddles of water, and tried the outer doors in the vain hope that someone had forgotten to lock up. No such luck.

She'd have to break in. The timing sucked. The last thing Johan and Emma needed was to return from hospital to find that someone had busted their locks. How could she do it and make it look like nothing had happened?

Jaq sized up the back door. The distance between the cat flap and the snib was a little longer than her arm, but not by much. Which gave her an idea.

Sprinting back to the woodshed, she found the branch lopper, a long metal pole with a scissor mechanism operated by a string. There was the real deal, and then there was Ben's toy version, made of plastic with no sharp edges and a bendy pole.

It took some practice, and she had to lie on the ground with the rain pelting down onto her upturned face. This was not what Balúrdio had in mind for their designer jeans and silk shirts, and she was glad of the leather jacket protecting her back and shoulders from the sharp, wet gravel. After a few false starts she managed to dislodge the back-door key and retrieve it through the cat flap.

Once inside, the shivering started. Cold and filthy, she didn't want to leave a trail of dirty water through the house. She unlaced her boots, shrugged off her jacket, but her shirt and jeans were dripping as well. Just inside the back door was a laundry with a bathroom and small electric shower. She inspected the clothes drying on a rack. Emma was shorter and rounder than her, even before the latest pregnancy. Johan was a similar height, but he had a man's wider waist and narrower hips. Still, she'd be able to find something from among the clean, dry clothes. She undressed and stepped into the shower.

She hadn't stopped to wash before leaving the beach house almost 48 hours earlier. The hot water streamed over her skin, and she sighed with pleasure.

Outside, a car reached the top of the mountain pass and began the zigzagging descent down the shoulder of the mountain. The rain was even heavier now, and the vehicle moved slowly on the single-track country road.

The car passed a National Trust car park and continued towards the farmhouse.

Cumbria, England

Lost in the pleasure of soap on her skin and hot water cascading through her hair, Jaq heard nothing as the car came over the cattle grid. It was only when the security lights flashed on that she became aware of someone outside.

She stopped the water to listen.

A car door slammed, and footsteps crunched over gravel. They stopped at the front door.

She grabbed a towel and stepped out of the shower.

A key in the lock.

Footsteps in the hall

A gruff voice outside the door.

'Be quick.'

Jaq retreated into the shadows as the door to the laundry opened and the light clicked on.

A little boy stood in a pool of light. She breathed a sigh of relief and stepped forward.

'Ben, it's me. Jaq.' She put a finger to her lips. 'Shhh. Close the door.'

He seemed remarkably unperturbed to find her in his house, naked except for a towel. In an incomprehensible world, one more peculiar example of adult behaviour was not going to trouble a small boy on a mission. He obeyed her instruction and the door latch snicked behind him.

'Hi Aunty Jaq.' He looked around, eyes sparkling. 'Are Mummy and Daddy back too?'

She shook her head.

'The hospital's going to make Mummy better, isn't it?'

'They'll look after her.' She tried to smile.

'Daddy needs to stay with Mummy while she's poorly, so I'm going to Gramp's house.' He pointed at a boot rack. 'But I forgot my wellies.'

'Ben, can you keep a secret?' she whispered.

He thought about it for a moment and then nodded sagely.

'Please, don't tell anyone you saw me here.'

He put a finger to his lips in conspiratorial fellowship. 'Secret.'

'And Ben, you remember the box?'

'The safe box?'

'Yes, where is it.'

'I hidded it.'

'Good boy. Where did you hide it?'

'I know how to open the secret bits.'

The secret compartment at the base of the safe was guaranteed to delight a small boy.

'Clever boy. Is it in your room?'

He shook his heads. 'Granny and Gramps don't like me playing with catapults.'

'They are very wise, it's a serious weapon. Can you tell me where it is?'

'Are you in trouble?'

'A little bit.'

'Is the bad man coming back?'

Her heart contracted. This poor child had almost perished at the hands of one of those bad men. Jaq had saved Ben in the nick of time, diving into the lake as his boat sank into the water. How much did he remember? Enough to be useful.

'The police arrested the bad man who tried to hurt you. He's in jail, far away.' Boris Cimrman was serving out his life sentence in Belarus. 'But I need your help again.'

'I helped you last time, didn't I?'

'You were very brave. Where is the box, Ben?'

He bit his lip, wrestling with the request. Then he brightened. 'Do you need my catapult to fight the bad men?'

'I need the box too,' she said.

'Will you give it back?'

Could she lie to him? Try evasion. 'I'll make you the biggest and best catapult ever.'

'A trebuchet?'

He didn't miss much, little Ben. 'A trebuchet.'

'Deal,' he said and stuck out a hand.

'Deal if you tell me where the box is.'

Footsteps outside.

'Ben, where are you? Have you found everything?'

'Coming, Gramps.'

Ben grabbed his wellington boots from a rack and raced to the door.

'Ben, wait,' Jaq hissed. 'Tell me where the safe is?'

The door handle turned.

'Why is it all wet in here?' Bertrand's voice got louder as the door began to open. Jaq put a finger to her lips and retreated into the shower.

Ben pushed his grandfather back into the hall. 'Had to wash my wellies.'

Oh dear, she had turned the child into an accomplished liar.

'Good boy,' said Bertrand. 'Let's go.'

'Wait, I forgot the light.'

Ben reappeared in the doorway.

'In the woodshed,' he whispered.

The light went off.

Jaq waited until she heard the car pass over the cattle grid and then rumble up the hill. She dried herself and dressed quickly, grabbing the first things that came to hand, a T-shirt, long-sleeved tartan shirt, cotton leggings plus thick socks, a woollen jumper and hat. She gave Ben and his grandfather ten minutes to get over the pass and then she put on her boots and slipped back out into the rain, crossing the farmyard to the woodshed. The padlock was long gone, cut off by the police after Emma had been locked inside by the same man who tried to drown Ben.

Jaq slid the bolt and stepped into the gloom, the fresh smell of rosin filling her nostrils. At first, she couldn't see anything, but as her eyes adjusted to the gloom, she spotted a sharp metal corner behind a stack of logs.

She took the box into the kitchen. It was dark now. Before turning on the lights, she closed the doors, shutters and curtains. The last thing she wanted to do was to advertise her presence. Who knew if there were hidden watchers? She put the box on the farmhouse table.

What was it about this box that was so important? What had she missed?

The leather covering was a little more battered and torn, but it was still recognisably her mother's safe. She opened it to find that Ben had filled it to the brim. The sight of the little boy's most precious things brought tears to her eyes. She sat back, suddenly exhausted.

When had she last eaten? She hadn't been able to face dinner on the ferry, the sea too rough. She'd started a coffee in Yarm this morning but left the cheese toastie uneaten on spotting the man watching her flat.

She stood and opened the fridge. Almost empty except for half a pint of milk and six eggs. Emma usually kept a well-stocked larder; the farmhouse often got cut off in winter. Perhaps everything perishable had gone with the children and animals to Warrington.

Jaq opened the pantry and selected a tin of mixed beans: haricot, borlotti, red kidney, black-eyed and pinto. She drained the liquid and decanted them into a pan, adding a tin of tomatoes. There were more eggs in the cold store, so she added a couple to the bubbling mix and waited until they were poached.

Mercúrio cooked a mean bean stew; her best effort tasted insipid in comparison. Was it the lack of oil, onion, chilli and *chouriço* or her lack of skill? It was so long since she'd cooked for herself. Cooking was something Mercúrio had enjoyed. Hadn't he? She'd contributed in other ways. Hadn't she? They'd worked well together for a while. Hadn't they? So why had they argued? Why had he walked out? If they hadn't fought, if he hadn't left in the middle of the night, then he wouldn't be in the gloved hands of Crazy and his gang. In terrible danger.

She stared at the mess in the pot, her appetite waning as her anxiety returned. Where was Mercúrio right now? Were his kidnappers giving him enough food and water? Did he have somewhere to sleep? Was he safe?

She looked over at the box. What was it about this metal and leather box that was worth a man's life?

A gust of wind made the sleet rattle against the window. She looked out. The white snow of the mountains was descending into the valley. If the weather got much worse, there was a risk that the mountain pass would close. She couldn't afford to get trapped here.

The bean and egg mess was almost edible once dotted with tabasco. Fuel rather than food. It sated her hunger and would release energy slowly. There was a lot still to do.

First she'd clear up, so that there was no trace of her to alarm anyone when they returned. She'd unpack Ben's treasures and leave them in his room. She debated writing a note for Johan and Emma, but decided against it, best to wait until their crisis was resolved. This was not the time to muscle in and add to their troubles.

After washing and drying the dishes, she took the eggshells to the compost heap and the tins to the recycling bin outside. She collected her horrendously expensive wet clothes, stuffed them into a plastic bag and dumped them in the Land Rover. Jaq found a shoebox and unpacked Ben's treasures from her mother's metal and leather safe. The skull of a small animal, some rounded pebbles, a toy soldier with an arm missing, fragments of eggshell wrapped in cotton wool, an antique brass key wrapped in pink tissue, some pretty glass beads: emerald and aquamarine, a length of knotted rope. After transferring the contents, she closed the lid and reversed the latches, heard the internal click and extracted the catapult from the secret drawer. Would Ben mind if she took it as well? It might yet prove useful. She stuffed it into her bag. Feeling her way up the stairs in total darkness, Jaq carried the shoebox to Ben's room and slid it under his bed.

She sat on the floor and briefly closed her eyes. When had she last slept? Was it only two nights ago she had been rudely awakened in Floripa by Crazy Gloves? It felt like an eternity. She'd been unable to sleep on the transatlantic flight from São Paulo to Amsterdam or on the ferry from Amsterdam to Newcastle. The temptation to climb into Ben's little bed was almost overwhelming. And why not? Her return flight was booked for the day after tomorrow, leaving Teesside airport at 6 a.m. She had a full day and two nights to kill. Her Yarm flat was under surveillance so she couldn't go back there. Should she spend the night here? Rest awhile? Leave once it was daylight? It was so tempting.

Jaq shook herself awake. It was wrong to spend any more time here than was strictly necessary. Whoever was watching her might have been tricked into following her ticket to Lockerbie or her phone to Aberdeen, but it wouldn't be long before they realised they had lost her. And then they might start looking for other people she knew and places she frequented. Best to get out of here and find an anonymous hotel that accepted cash. Now she had the box, perhaps she could get a seat on an earlier flight.

Jaq returned to the kitchen, turned off the lights and opened the shutters and curtains. She picked up the strongbox from the table and took one last look back.

Why Crazy Gloves wanted the box, she had no idea. But if it meant saving Mercúrio, she would do whatever she was instructed to do.

Time to fly back to Brazil.

DETONATION MINUS 3

3

Li

Lithium
6.941

Barnard Castle, England

It was after midnight when Jaq arrived at a small hotel outside Barnard Castle.

The Morritt Arms was just large enough that she would not be remembered, just small enough that she could spot anyone following her, and just cheap enough that she could pay with cash. It also had lovely staff, fast internet and great food.

She had one day to kill before her journey back.

The risk in sticking with the booked flight was considerable. What if the buzz-cut tattoo brigade had access to the airline passenger information? An earlier flight would have been ideal; she couldn't risk a later one, couldn't miss the deadline. But the Christmas holidays meant that routes from the UK hubs were packed with skiers going north and sunworshippers going south. There were no alternatives available.

Truth be told, she was more worried about what Crazy Gloves would do to Mercúrio than what the incompetent soldiers might do to her. After all, she'd evaded them three times: at Guarulhos, São Paulo due to someone else's mistake, at Schiphol, Amsterdam due to instinct and in Yarm thanks to experience. Hopefully, they'd tracked her old phone to Scotland and then given up.

Jaq had the strongbox. The booked flight would get her back before the deadline. She could leave the Land Rover at the maintenance workshop in Barnard Castle, out of sight behind Specsavers on the High Street, and get a taxi to the airport.

Now she needed to rest and recharge.

But when she stretched out on the comfortable bed and closed her eyes, images of Mercúrio filled her thoughts and kept her from sleep.

Υ 1

A Beach in Brazil

The first time she saw Mercúrio he was lying on a surfboard. He'd been circling around, just beyond the break ignoring the first few sets, waiting. When a monster wave rolled in from the deep, he paddled harder than the rest of the group and was the only one to catch it as it reared up. He rode it hard and fast, with pure, unadulterated joy.

She watched him from the deck of a beach restaurant.

The waiter followed her gaze.

'D'you surf?'

'A little.'

'Me too.'

'Is there anywhere I could hire a board round here?'

He shook his head. 'But someone will lend you one.' His smile was friendly and open. 'I surf after work. My name's Luis by the way.'

She found herself smiling back. 'Jaq.'

'Come down to the beach tonight.' He nodded towards a stand of palm trees. 'I'll find you what you're looking for.'

If only he knew.

There were thousands of surfers, mainly young men, a few older ones and a handful of women. During the day they spread out, occupying the full length of the beach. At night they gathered together in groups, lit campfires and partied.

It was the music that drew her on. Warm sand between her toes, silken breeze on her skin, the rhythmic crash of waves on the beach as she strolled, parallel to the sea, towards her guesthouse. A lone male voice snaked up towards the dunes. Jaq stopped and cocked an ear as she recognised the closing crescendo of a song by Nirvana. She changed direction, walking up towards the dunes, away from the sea, and stood transfixed. A group of surfers were gathered round a bonfire. The singer stood apart, leaning against a tree, a guitar slung by an embroidered strap over his bare chest, his face in shadow.

A chord sequence she didn't recognise introduced a new song with a slow, haunting melody and catchy chorus.

Tristeza ... amor ... beleza ... pavor .... Saudades ...

Saudades. That untranslatable Portuguese word. A bittersweet emotion familiar to those far from home. For those who have no home. Slaves transported from Angola, their villages burning behind them. Settlers from Portugal, their boats shipwrecked in sight of land. An undefinable mix of melancholy, homesickness, loss and a deep visceral longing.

Jaq stood transfixed until the song came to an end, then turned away to hide the tears. The light was fading fast, but the dunes were dotted with campfires and stars were appearing in the clear sky. A pair of acrobatic shortboarders danced on the waves, their somersaults silhouetted against the surf. A mixed group of men and women were kicking a football around, Jaq made a detour towards the water's edge to avoid their makeshift pitch.

'*Oi, Portuguesa.*' A man detached himself from the goal and waved. In the fading light it took her a moment to recognise Luis, the waiter from the restaurant.

'Hi,' she waved and walked on.

'Wait,' he shouted. 'I found a board for you.'

She stopped and swivelled round. Luis grabbed the hand of a young woman and they sprinted towards her. 'Angel meet Jaq.'

Jaq smiled and exchanged air kisses. Angel was a beautiful

woman, tall and curvy with auburn dreadlocks that clattered with beads.

'Gol!'

A shout from the abandoned goal announced the end of the game. The footballers collected their belongings and headed back along the beach, away from her hotel.

'This way!' Luis pointed after them, towards the dunes. 'C'mon.'

The campfire flames were higher now. The guitar chords just audible between the roar and splash of waves.

'Where are we going?'

But she already knew. Some things were just meant to be.

Jaq kept to the edge of the campfire in the dunes.

Mercúrio, surrounded by admirers, didn't even look at her. She tried not to look at him, but it was easier to concentrate on what others were saying after he strolled away.

She checked out the shortboard, accepted a beer to close the deal, refused another and said her goodbyes.

The sand was still warm. Her feet sank into the soft ripples, making progress slow. She moved diagonally towards the sea where it was firmer underfoot and stood at the water's edge for a moment, watching the swell and break, tension and release.

'Leaving so soon?'

Mercúrio appeared from nowhere, standing beside her, staring out to sea.

'I didn't recognise the song you were singing,' she said.

'"Lithium"?'

'No, the one after it.'

'You liked it?' His voice was hesitant.

'Yes.'

'I wrote it.'

'What's it called?'

'"Saudades".' He turned to face her. 'I wrote it for you.'

DETONATION MINUS 2

Teesside, England

An icy fog had settled over Teesside. Jaq could barely see the entrance to the airport as she waved goodbye to Ahmed, her taxi driver, at five o'clock in the morning. She shivered and zipped up her leather jacket. The metal slider was freezing, and she wished she'd brought gloves.

'Hello, Dr Silver. That was a flying visit, even by your standards.'

Check-in staff were familiar with all the regular passengers. Mandy had been at the airport for as long as Jaq could remember, but right now small talk was the last thing she wanted. She slid her passport across the counter.

'Brazil, eh?' Mandy smiled. 'Weather a bit better?'

Jaq made an effort to smile back. 'It's summer there.' Mandy was only trying to be friendly.

'Christmas on the beach?'

'Maybe …'

'I'm jealous.'

If only you knew …

'Anything to check in?'

Jaq placed her Sugar Loaf Mountain travel bag onto the weighing scales. She lifted the battered leather box by its handle and placed it on the counter. 'I'll take this as my carry-on.' She needed to keep it beside her, keep it safe.

'That's fine. Just to let you know, we're expecting some delay.' Mandy printed and inspected her boarding card. 'But you should have plenty of time to make your connection.'

Schiphol Airport, Amsterdam, The Netherlands

Lars didn't have much difficulty identifying her as the passengers queued to board the transatlantic flight at Schiphol. She was late to the gate and arrived at a sprint, but the fog meant that her next plane wasn't yet on the stand, probably circling high above the North Sea waiting for permission to land. Shoulder-length dark hair. Athletic figure. Not as tall as the brief stated, but then women wore so many different heel heights that it was hard to estimate, and she was in flats today. The giveaway was her hand luggage, and that was all his boss was really interested in.

He moved quickly. His uniform, courtesy of Carnival Fancy Dress, was more suited to a certain sort of nightclub than an airport, the ID-badge photo looked less like him and more like the man he had seduced to get it; the airline staff might have been more suspicious if it hadn't been for Hettie. The golden springer spaniel drew all attention away from him as she trotted obediently at his side.

'Special pre-boarding inspection,' Lars announced. He nudged Hettie with his toe and she began her charm offensive. He lowered his voice. 'Anti-terrorist checks. We've had a tip-off.'

'What do you need?'

'Nothing. Just back me up if there's any argument.'

He turned back to the departure lounge and walked slowly from passenger to passenger, allowing Hettie to sniff each of them.

The woman clutched the leather box to her chest on the first pass. On the second pass he asked her to put it on the ground. He made the signal to Hettie and she went wild, right on queue. Sniffing, pawing and then barking.

The woman looked alarmed.

'Why is he doing that?'

'I'm sorry.' Lars adopted his most conciliatory expression. 'We're going to have to search this.'

'What for, why?'

'Special precautions. The dog is trained to detect certain scents. I'm sure it'll turn out to be nothing.' He ruffled Hettie's head. 'We'll go to the office. Come with me.'

'But my flight ...' She pointed at the queue forming at the gate and raised her voice. 'I need to—'

A member of the airline security staff approached. 'Madam, please go with the officer.' He smiled. 'It's just routine. There's plenty of time.'

He gestured back towards the corridor. 'The sooner we do this, the sooner we'll be finished.'

That at least was true; it didn't take long. They'd told him to be careful, warned him that this one was a lot more dangerous than she looked: fit and clever and had been known to fight. He wondered if she was carrying any weapons. Maybe he should undress her first?

In the room he'd prepared, he ordered Hettie to face away and guard the door. The dog didn't like violence and had been known to defend the wrong person.

'Take off your coat please.'

She looked around the room. It seemed to dawn on her gradually that it was more of a cleaning store than a security interview room.

'Why?'

'So, I can search you.'

'I want a female officer present.'

'Of course.' Lars pretended to speak into his radio. 'My colleague is on her way. In the meantime, please take off your coat and open your bag.'

'Can I make a call?'

He waited until she was distracted, busy extracting her phone with trembling hands, before attacking her from behind. It was quick; he snapped her neck in two rapid moves, held her upright for a few seconds while she twitched. The phone fell to the ground as she went limp. He ground the glass with his foot until it smashed, removed the SIM and kicked the shell into a corner. He stacked her body, still warm, behind the toilet rolls.

Hettie whimpered but remained facing the door.

'Good girl,' he said and ruffled her ears.

He opened the leather box and made a quick inventory. Once the flight pillow and spare clothes had been removed, there was surprisingly little in there. A paperback, a cereal bar, tissues, tampons, some make-up: eyeliner, lipstick, three little pots of mysterious creams. In truth, when you took out all the rubbish stuffed in there, it was more of a shapeless leather bag than a box.

He checked the instructions again. The sinking sensation in his stomach sent him back to the corpse. Her dead eyes bored into his soul as he checked the name on her passport. Jacinta Guedes.

He'd been so sure it was Silver. She'd booked a seat on the Amsterdam to São Paulo flight a week ago and no one else in departures even vaguely fitted her description. He checked the name, paused and then extracted the boarding pass from the same pocket. Right seat, wrong woman. Damn!

He couldn't have missed her. If the dead woman wasn't Silver then she must have taken a different flight. He needed to think carefully.

'C'mon Hettie.'

He opened the door and checked that the coast was clear before slipping out into the service corridor. The golden spaniel followed. He turned and snapped the handle before pushing the door closed. It wouldn't slow them down much, but it should buy a little time. Enough time to get out of the airport and call his boss.

No point hiding anything from the Colonel, he'd find out anyway. That man had eyes and ears everywhere.

There had to be a plan B.

Teesside, England

Jaq paced up and down between the Christmas tree and reindeer-drawn sleigh decorating the departure lounge of Teesside Airport. Battered leather box in hand, she stared out at the plane, a Brazilian Embraer 100, that should have taken her on the first leg of a journey back to Mercúrio. There was no doubt that she'd missed her intended connection, but if she could just make it to Amsterdam, there were later flights that would still get her back before the deadline.

The weak dawn light revealed an ever-thickening fog. *Plenty of time* didn't look so generous now.

A seasoned traveller, delays had never bothered Jaq before. There was always work to do: reports to write, emails to reply to, people to watch or a good book to read. She generally found it easy to switch off, treating travel as a sort of restful limbo where you handed yourself over to the care of others. You were fed and watered at regular intervals and nothing you did or said was going to get you to your destination any faster, so you might as well relax and enjoy the freedom from responsibility. Now, for the first time, she understood how her carefree attitude might have infuriated more anxious passengers.

She approached the only member of airline staff in evidence. 'Any news?'

'Wings still need de-icing.'

Jaq looked around for the single machine that Teesside Airport used to remove the dangerous weight of frozen water.

'What's the problem?' She could do it herself. A bucket of ethylene glycol and a hose and she'd have them clear in no time. At this rate Santa's sleigh would be a quicker route over the North Sea.

Mandy appeared at the security barrier and beckoned to her. 'The flight's going to be cancelled,' she whispered. 'They're about to make an announcement, but if you want to jump the rebooking queue, head out now.'

Porcaria! Jaq returned to the lounge, grabbed her leather jacket and made her way back through security as the Tannoy crackled into life.

'Ladies and Gentlemen, I regret to announce that Flight 1534 to Amsterdam has been cancelled.' An angry roar erupted from the waiting crowd. 'Please collect your luggage and make your way back through security and our staff will book you onto the next available ...'

Jaq grabbed her travel bag from the belt and arrived at the check-in desk just as Mandy took her place behind the counter.

'I've already checked your options. Even if you drive to Newcastle right now, you're not going to make the next Amsterdam connection. But there's another flight to São Paulo from Paris that gets in twelve hours later.'

It was cutting everything very fine. Too fine.

'Any other options?'

A queue was forming behind her.

'Manchester via Frankfurt, but it's not a partner airline, so I can't guarantee a decent seat.'

'What time does it get in?'

Mandy tapped on the keyboard. 'Six hours after you were due to arrive.'

'Can you check connections to Florianopolis?'

The man behind her pushed forward. 'This isn't a bloody travel agency. I need to get on the next flight. I have a very important meeting.'

Jaq resisted the urge to skelp him with metal edge of the leather box.

'And my trip is a question of life or death,' she said.

Mandy turned the computer screen to face her. There was at least one good connection, and even a later one that would get her back ahead of the deadline.

'OK, I'll take the Manchester option.'

Mandy tapped the keys and printed a voucher. 'I can't issue the boarding cards, but you should have time …'

Jaq was already out of the door, phone pressed to her ear. 'Ahmed, I need a ride to Manchester Airport. Are you free?'

'I'll be there in ten minutes.'

He was as good as his word.

'Change of plan?'

'Freezing fog. And something about the de-icing machine.'

Ahmed laughed. 'I hear Bert slept in.'

'Bert?'

'The guy who does the early shift.'

Was Mercúrio's life dependent on a Teesside airport de-icing driver? Jaq clenched her fists. If Bert had appeared before her now, she would happily have throttled him.

At Manchester Airport, her wallet considerably lighter and Ahmed's children's future more secure, Jaq waited in the queue for the check-in. The Christmas decorations and piped music were getting on her nerves.

God rest ye merry gentlemen
Let nothing you dismay …

There was a lot to be dismayed about. She didn't have any

frequent flyer privileges with this airline, which meant going to the back of the economy queue.

The counter staff were dressed as elves.

'Anything to check in?'

'Just the bag.'

'And that?' The check-in man pointed to the leather box.

'This stays with me.'

The elf shook his head. 'I'm afraid it's not the regulation size.' He pointed to a frame at the entrance to the queue. 'All hand luggage needs to fit into that. 55 by 40 by 23. You can try if you like,' his smirk told her that he already knew it wouldn't fit. 'It'll be perfectly safe in the hold.'

'Look you don't understand ...'

'I'm sorry madam, but it's for your own safety.'

Safety? Did he have any idea? And what about Mercúrio's safety? What if the strongbox was lost in transit, delayed? Where was the Christmas spirit?

'Can I speak with your supervisor.'

'Of course, madam. Please just step to the side while I help the other passengers.' The ones who don't make trouble, she thought sourly.

The supervisor was even more elfin and even less sympathetic.

'If you want to take the flight, you must obey the rules.'

'Let me explain—'

The evil elf held up a hand to close down any special pleading. 'Take out anything you need and check it in.' She looked at the battered box with an expression that suggested she had recently swallowed a lemon.

'What about business class?'

'Do you have a business class ticket?'

'No, but I'm prepared to buy one.'

'Then you'll have to take a later flight. We are already fully booked.' She sniffed. 'Now, if you'll excuse me.'

Jaq stamped her foot and threw her head back with a howl of rage. People started to edge away from her. Careful, perhaps the hold was the least bad option. The box was made to last. She had to get on this flight. What choice did she have?

Jaq had passed a luggage shop on her way in. She retraced her steps and found the franchise for a top brand of suitcases. The box was almost a cube, so she had to go for a ridiculously large suitcase to contain it. The cost made her feel nauseous. She closed her eyes, bit her lip, thought of Aunty Lettie and paid up.

She made her way back to the check-in desk, surrendered the box inside the brand-new suitcase and sent up a prayer to Mercury, the god of travel.

Mercury. Mercúrio. The irony was not lost on her.

Jaq was the last passenger to board the plane. The door closed behind her and the safety briefing started the moment she took her seat.

Once the plane was in the air, she flicked through the in-flight magazine, pausing at the familiar face of Brazilian reality TV presenter César. The wildly successful Hélio Television series, *The Missing*, was now available on demand. Entertainment from pain. Jaq closed the magazine and stared out of the window at the rain.

On her way to Brazil for the second time this year. How very different this felt from the first trip, when she had set out so full of hope.

Y 5

Hélio TV Studio, Rio de Janeiro, Brazil

The spotlight stopped at César. He sat on the sofa, ankles crossed, arms by his side and nodded at the clapping audience, making a mental note to remind the sound engineers to digitally enhance the applause, overlay with previous recordings of rapture before the show was broadcast.

'Welcome back.' He smiled so that his newly whitened teeth glinted in the studio lights. 'You are watching *The Missing*!' He flicked a lock of hair from his eyes. 'The show that reunites some families,' he paused to stroke his neatly trimmed beard. 'And drives others apart.'

The audience laughed.

'Tonight, we have an audience with Colonel Cub.'

The music changed, the jaunty theme tune faded and was replaced by a slow drumbeat, almost funereal.

César stood and approached a large screen at the back of the stage. 'Good evening, Colonel.'

The screen lightened to reveal the silhouette of a man. The tempo of the music increased, and the drone of low brass gave it depth.

'Can you hear me?'

The shadow head gave a curt nod.

'Can we tell the audience where you are right now?'

'Classified.' The voice was disguised and came across as

distorted, robotic. The music developed into slow electronic chords.

'What can we tell them?'

'We can tell them about the bones.'

'Bones?'

'I know where to find the bones.'

Now the music was jangling, clashing, packed with uncomfortable dissonance.

'Human graves?'

Again the curt nod.

'Who is buried in these graves?'

'The missing.'

MISSING, boomed the voice.

The studio lights came up to reveal an elderly couple seated on the guest sofa. César returned to his chair and addressed them.

'Gloria and Stefano, welcome.'

They looked at each other and then at the audience, white hair and round eyes, like frightened rabbits caught in headlights.

'Stefano, can you tell us where you're both from.'

'We live in Sampo. I'm retired now, but I was a mechanic.'

'And Gloria?'

'I was a teacher, primary school.'

'Can you tell us what brings you here tonight?'

'It's about our son, Francisco.'

César modulated his voice to sound gentle. 'Tell me about the last time you saw Francisco.'

'When he told us he was dropping out of university.'

'He was a student?'

'Yes.'

'But he failed his exams?'

'No, no.' Gloria rushed to her son's defence. 'He was a brilliant child. Top of his class in everything he did.'

'So why did he decide to leave university?'

'He got caught up in politics, wanted to change the world.'

'I see, and how did that make you feel.'

'Proud,' said Gloria, wiping away a tear.

'Worried,' said Stefano. 'The boy never worked a day in his life.'

Gloria started to protest but Stefano continued. 'His nose was always in a book. He didn't know much about the real world. Perhaps we spoiled him, but he was so bright, so kind, so thoughtful.' His speech faltered. 'So optimistic, so naive.'

'Do you have other children? Did Francisco have brothers, sisters?'

Gloria started to say something, but Stefano interrupted.

'No.'

'But he left home, swapped academia for politics.'

'He said he was going north.'

'Where to?'

'He couldn't say.'

'What was he going north to do?'

'To fight for the rights of workers.'

'And you never saw him again?'

Gloria was weeping again. Stefano put an arm around her. 'We never saw him again.'

César leaned forward. 'When did you last see Francisco?'

Gloria's weeping was too noisy. They'd have to cut some of that. Real tears made faces ugly.

Stefano answered in a wavering voice. 'In 1973.'

'In 1973!' César exclaimed. 'You haven't seen your son for forty years.'

'We know he's dead,' Gloria interrupted. 'We just want to bury him before we die.'

Too soon. They'd have to edit that bit out.

MISSING, boomed the voice.

Cut!

César let the production assistants look after the old dears in the break. The next segment was the video footage of Gloria and Stefano's visit to the clinic last week. A photogenic doctor in a white coat established that they were the genetic parents of Francisco and took samples of their DNA to assist with matching any remains that were found.

Action!

The music restarted and the spotlight found César sitting forward in an armchair.

'Let me recap for you. Gloria and Stefano, a retired mechanic and primary school teacher from São Paulo want to know what happened to their son, Francisco. Their only child disappeared in 1973 when he dropped out of university and went north to change the world.'

'Now some of you out there weren't even born in 1973. A complicated period of modern history, so we've invited an expert along to explain what was going on in Brazil at the time.'

The studio lights came on to reveal a third guest sitting beside the elderly couple on the sofa. A middle-aged man with round specs and a goatee beard.

'Professor Osvaldo, welcome. Tell us what you do.'

'I lecture in history at the State University of Santa Cruz.'

'And what is your specialist area?'

'Modern history of Brazil. The period from 1950 to 1980.'

'With 1973, the time that our guests last saw their son Francisco, slap bang in the middle. What can you tell us about that time?'

Professor Osvaldo launched into his lecture. He might be telegenic, but he was a bit of a windbag. This was prime time TV, not a university seminar. It would have to be cut, but they could use some of it. The bit about Jango could stay; the elected president of Brazil deposed by a military coup had been rehabilitated now the left were back in power in the form of Lula and Dilma. The best part was the most gruesome, the torture techniques employed by the army to make their communist captives talk; the expression on the faces of his elderly guests would play well.

MISSING, boomed the voice.

Cut!

Action!

César stood to address the audience.

'Gloria and Stefano want to know what happened to their son. He joined the communists and went to start a peasant revolution. The military were ordered to neutralise the threat. A vicious guerrilla war ensued. Was Francisco a victim of that war?

'Colonel Cub, are you still with us?'

'Yes,' the voice rasped.

'Can you tell us what you were doing in 1973?'

'I was just a boy. But I saw everything.'

'What did you see?'

'First the students came to our village. They were kind to the children. Then the soldiers came.'

'Were they kind to the children too?'

'We ran away whenever we saw them coming.'

'Why?'

'We saw what they did.'

'And what did they do?'

The laugh was truly chilling. No amount of sound engineering could disguise the pain and madness.

'First they asked questions. About the students. Where had they gone? They did bad things to the people who didn't know or wouldn't tell.'

'Bad things?'

That chilling laugh again. 'Terrible things.'

'And the students?'

'Some of them got ill, in the jungle. They were city kids, unused to our way of life. They came back to the village to get food and medicine.'

'Did you help them?'

'Some did. Most were too afraid.'

'Afraid, why?'

'The soldiers were watching, waiting.'

'Did they attack the village, punish those who had helped the students?'

'Later. First the soldiers followed them.'

'And then?'

'They captured them all.'

'Colonel Cub, did you know Francisco?'

The picture of the smiling, black-bearded young man flashed up onto the screen.

'It was a long time ago, there were hundreds of them, I can't be sure it was him or not.'

'What happened to the students?'

'The soldiers made them talk.' The terrible laugh again. 'And then they killed them.'

Gloria was wailing through hiccups. The sound engineers would have to deal with that.

'And what happened to the ... mortal remains?'

'They buried them in the jungle.'

'And you know where the graves are?'

'I can take you there.'

MISSING, boomed the voice.

Cut!

The video sequence was magnificent. César wasn't sure where it had really been filmed – they didn't have the budget to send a crew to Tocantins – but he had to hand it to the cameraman for creating an atmosphere. Rain lashed down onto a dense jungle canopy. A muddy river roared over a waterfall. A brightly coloured tanager flew into a tree, and a group of monkeys set up a chatter of alarm. The camera panned out to show the convoy of jeeps, white crosses on their roofs, heading deeper into the jungle. The action cut to the dig. The cry of first discovery, the investigators gathering round. The nod of the actor playing the part of a medical examiner confirming, to the camera, that they'd found a mass grave, and the bones were human.

Action!

The studio lights went up and the doctor from the earlier video clip, the one who had taken the elderly couple's DNA joined them and César in the studio.

'Doctor Carlina. Thank you for joining us.'

She waved her dark curls and nodded.

'Can you confirm that you have analysed a sample from the human remains found in the jungle?'

'I can.'

'And can you tell us if any of them are a match?'

The doctor turned to the elderly couple

'I'm so sorry to tell you this.'

César watched the couple closely. What would be worse, he wondered. For them to know that their communist son had been tortured and killed by the military dictatorship or to be left wondering what had happened to him.

'We found a close match between your DNA and the DNA of one of the bodies.'

'Can you be sure?' Gloria sobbed.

Stefano took her hand. 'Is there any chance …?'

The doctor shook her head. 'There is only a thousand to one chance that it is a coincidence.'

César put on his most sympathetic face

'We found Francisco.'

MISSING THEN FOUND.

Church music played, a choir singing a lament.

Gloria's weeping went on far too long. The editors would have to deal with that. But César managed to coax some final words from Stefano.

'Thank you.' He was quite dignified for a mechanic. 'We can bury him now, in the family plot.'

'And you can begin to heal.' César said,

Stefano shook his head. 'We can start to grieve.' He sighed and took his wife's hand, kissing it with extraordinary tenderness. 'We can finally let go.' He bowed his head, as if in prayer. 'It won't be long before we join Francisco.'

Cut!

César addressed the camera. 'Join us next week.'

The theme music began to play.

'A child kidnapped from school in São Paulo. His desperate parents in a race against time. Should they pay the ransom? Should they involve the police? What would you do?'

The music turned percussive and sombre.

'Colonel Cub helps us to find more bodies buried in the jungle. Can our expert medical team match the remains, give closure to the relatives searching for their loved ones?'

Back to the theme music.

'Join me next week for another episode of ...'

THE MISSING.

Y 5

São Paulo, Brazil

São Paulo, or Sampo as the locals called it, came as a surprise. Some viewed the monster megalopolis as a dystopian nightmare, a place stuffed with featureless skyscrapers and motorways, the kind of city you might long to escape from. It turned out to be the kind of city Jaq wanted to burrow into and explore.

She had done her homework before leaving England, carrying out as much research as it was possible to do remotely. Tracking down a Brazilian dentist by the name of Carlos Costa who had once worked in Portugal should be straightforward. After all, how many could there be?

The profession of dentistry started with the rise of sugar consumption in the sixteenth century. As the largest exporter of sugar, with its special tooth-rotting powers, it was hardly surprising that Brazil also became a major producer of qualified dentists.

Jaq's emails to CFO – *Conselho Federal de Odontologia,* the Brazilian Dentists Association – had been a complete waste of time. They declined to give any information on members. A telephone call was a little more productive. After getting bounced around between receptionists she spoke to a young man with a musical voice. He proudly informed her that Brazil produced 17,000 dentists a year from 220 educational institutions. From a quick check of the records, the CFO had 350,000 dentists currently registered with them; he was able to tell her at least ten thousand of those had Carlos and Costa somewhere in their full names. And they had private practices from Porto Alegre in the south to Belém in the north, from Salvador in the east to Manaus in the west. No, he couldn't cross-reference those who had been in Portugal in the time period she specified or were married to an Evangelina, and no, he couldn't provide addresses in Brazil. He suggested she try Facebook or LinkedIn.

Curled up in her sitting room in Yarm, she'd identified potential leads through social media, but after a few telephone calls it became clear that a face-to-face approach would be needed.

Jaq's UK contract agency had found an engineering consultancy based in São Paulo, the largest city and commercial centre of Brazil. Tecnoproject were always looking for technical consultants with experience in the oil industry and offered her a job after a phone interview. A job that would bankroll her travel to and around Brazil.

With a temporary technical expert visa and a one-way ticket to São Paulo, she left summer in England for winter in Brazil.

On the evening of her second day in Brazil, Jaq met her new boss. She recognised the man waiting in the hotel lobby from the photo on the Tecnoproject brochure. Older than his website portrait, grey-haired now, he was as short and wide as he was cheerful. Dressed in loafers, jeans and a polo shirt, he carried a leather bag slung across his chest and sunglasses perched on the top of his head.

She approached him.

'Bruno?'

He extended a hand. 'Dr Silver?'

'Please, call me Jaq.'

'*Encantado.*' They shook hands. 'Are you hungry?' he asked.

Truth was she had been grazing all day, and it was close to midnight in Europe. But when in Rome ...'

'Thirsty,' she said.

'Then I know just the place.'

The rooftop bar commanded a spectacular view over the city. Helicopters whizzed between skyscrapers and ribbons of red taillights crossed streamers of white headlights as they snaked around a looping highway. Her eyes were drawn to the huge park in the middle, a pool of dark stillness in the midst of a bright, bustling city.

A waiter approached to take their drinks order.

'Have you tried a Caipirinha?' Bruno asked. 'I mean a genuine Brazilian one.'

Jaq smiled. 'Not yet.'

While they waited for their drinks, Bruno pointed out the night lights, signposts to the varied districts of the gigantic city.

Two tumblers arrived with chunks of lime swirling amid ice in a mud-coloured liquid.

Bruno raised his glass. 'Cheers!'

Jaq chinked her glass with his.

Sugarcane, *saccharum officinarum,* in all its forms had created this uniquely Brazilian cocktail. The rum was made from cane juice, *garapa*, fermented to produce ethanol, then distilled to *Cachaça* strength. The woody waste from the cane, *bagasse*, was burnt to provide heat and power: steam for distillation and electrical energy to power the freezer to make the ice cubes. Citrus trees provided the sharp and aromatic contrast, and the whole delicious concoction was sweetened with cane sugar.

Brazil in a glass, and possibly the most delicious cocktail she had ever tasted.

They talked easily: about the journey, about Brazil, about Europe, and Bruno ordered snacks.

As she sipped her second cocktail, marvelling at the mega-city sprawling beneath her feet, a little quiver of excitement lifted her spirits. Here she was, in a new country, a new continent, embarking on a quest that was more important to her than anything she'd ever done before. For the first time since she opened her mother's safe, the possibilities seemed more thrilling than the challenges appeared daunting.

Carmo, the Lisbon lawyer, was following up other leads in Angola as well as Brazil. She'd also applied to the courts for disclosure of any records in Portugal. Carlos and Evangelina would have needed visas, residence permits, and the original application would reveal where they had lived before they went to Portugal. When they returned to Brazil, Jaq could only hope they'd gone back to the same place.

She'd made it here, found a good job, a job that would allow her to travel the length and breadth of Brazil. She had a shortlist of a dozen possible dentists, any one of whom might have adopted her child.

She didn't know his name, didn't know where he lived, didn't even know – she swallowed hard – if he was still alive. All she knew were the names of his adoptive parents. From her research she had several possible candidates. It could be any one of them, it could be none of them.

She would visit each one of the dentists on her list until she found the right one. Get to know the place where her son had grown up and figure out what sort of man he had become.

She needed to take this slowly, to judge the right time to approach him. Or – and this hurt to think about, but the mother superior had been right – to confirm he was safe and well and then leave him alone to get on with his life.

Decisions on how to or whether to approach her son could wait. Right now, all she could focus on was finding him.

She was going to take her time for once. Do this right. After all, over twenty years had passed since she'd been forcibly separated from her child. A few more months weren't going to make a difference.

Were they?

¥ 5

Rio de Janeiro, Brazil

In the Rio de Janeiro branch of the Bank of the Holy Spirit an alarm sounded in the basement.

Pedro, the senior clerk, hovered outside the bank manager's office door. He knew that his boss hated being bothered after lunch, making it clear to his senior staff that an undisturbed hour after eating was essential to his health and their wellbeing. A time for strategic, conceptual thinking. If he closed his eyes to aid digestion and reflection it was purely coincidental.

But the incessant stop-start ringing of the mysterious alarm made it impossible for anyone in the bowels of the bank, the thrumming hub of the operation, to continue work.

What concerned Pedro most was that no one had a clue what the alarm meant. There were no armed robbers in the building. The bank had already closed its doors to the public for the morning and would not re-open until after lunch. The security cameras indicated that everything was in its correct position, apart from the agitated junior clerks, dancing around with hands clasped over their ears.

He had checked the procedure manuals, although it was hard to concentrate with the infernal din of the alarm and the intensifying complaints of his staff. There was really no alternative but to alert the boss.

Pedro knocked at the door again, louder this time.

'Come!'

He opened the door far enough to stick his head round.

His boss lay on a sofa, rubbing his eyes. 'This better be important.'

'An alarm.' Pedro explained the dilemma. 'I can't understand what triggered it or how to silence it,' he concluded.

'What does it sound like?'

Pedro opened the door a little wider. The shrill trrringing followed by bursts of silence could be heard even from the director's suite on the upper floor.

'That's the telex machine alert.'

'The telex hasn't operated for years. I'm not even sure where it is.'

The bank manager rose to his feet and walked slowly to the wall safe. 'Wait outside.'

A few minutes later he appeared at the door. 'Here.' He handed Pedro a slim gold key. 'Go and see what's wrong.'

It took Pedro a few minutes to find the cupboard where the telex machine had been hidden, and then his problems just got worse. The noise was bad enough with the cupboard doors closed, deafening once they were unlocked and opened. He could now see an alarm code – 200.592 – but there was no sign of a manual to explain how to respond to it. Alice, the bank manager's new secretary, appeared with headphones covering her ears.

'What's that, then?' She yelled.

'It's a telex machine.'

'What's one of those?'

'Like a telegraph,' he shouted.

She stared at him, slack jawed.

'You know, a way of sending messages over long distances.'

'Like Instagram?'

He sighed. 'A bit like that.'

'What's wrong with it?'

'No idea.'

She leaned across him and flicked a switch. The infernal alarm stopped only to be replaced by a manic clattering as typewriter keys punched a ribbon of paper that began to spool onto the floor.

'Look, it's trying to say something.'

Once it had stopped, Pedro picked up the strip of paper, a thin strip about a centimetre wide and half a metre long. The message was from the main branch of the *Banco Espirito Santo* in Luanda, Angola. He read the message out loud.

Urgent
Storage breach
Mercury Protocol triggered
Urgent
Inform client immediately

Pedro took the message up to the manager's office and knocked at the door. This time a bellow of rage greeted him. His boss came to the door and Pedro handed him the paper tape.

'What do you expect me to do with this?'

'I'm a little lost myself.'

'Send Alice up right now.' He burped, and the smell of garlic was almost overpowering. 'And tell her to bring me a coffee.'

Y 5

São Paulo, Brazil

Jaq took a taxi to her dental appointment. The first Dr Carlos Costa on her list had a clinic in the centre of São Paulo, in the relatively affluent Higienópolis area. The dental surgery occupied the fifth floor of a thirty-storey skyscraper and the lift doors whooshed open to reveal a large, brightly lit reception area filled with modern art and pot plants.

'*Bom dia.*' The receptionist smiled, revealing teeth so white they dazzled. The rest of him was impressive too; this was a man who worked out. He could have sauntered straight out of a model agency catalogue.

'*Bom dia.* I have an appointment with Dr Costa.'

But first, it seemed, she had to run the gamut of the pre-consultation. After providing her credit card details, the first interview was with a cosmetic technician, a languidly beautiful, raven-haired woman who inspected Jaq's gums, her teeth, her tongue and took photographs, which she then doctored on the screen to illustrate what the Smile Solution clinic could do for her, straightening and whitening perfectly healthy teeth. Jaq made non-committal noises, agreeing to look at the brochures and bespoke payment plan and consider the very special offer that was only valid until Carnival.

In the meantime, Raven-hair suggested that Jaq avoided strong coffee and red wine.

In your dreams.

Next stop was with a pair of dental hygienists. One picked and polished and tutted while the other aspirated Jaq's mouth until her jaw began to ache.

It was an hour before she was led into Dr Costa's surgery. A short, thin man with grey hair, his professional profile on LinkedIn was a good match for the man she was looking for. But Dr Costa was not the chatty sort. He had the chair reclined and her mouth clamped open before she'd had a chance to ask the first question.

'What's this?' he exclaimed. He tapped one of the two mercury-amalgam fillings at the back of her mouth. 'Where on earth did you get these done?'

'Anggggaand.' Impossible to articulate while he had his fingers in her mouth.

'England?' He asked. 'On the NHS?'

She nodded. A friendly clinic in Yarm not long after she'd moved in with Aunty Lettie. Years of parental neglect followed by an unplanned pregnancy had taken their toll on her health. It was not just her teeth that had needed attention.

'Oh, the barbarity of socialised dentistry!' he lamented.

At least it was free to everyone under 18.

'Are you pregnant?' He barked.

She shook her head. One thing that she could be absolutely sure of.

'I'm taking some X-rays of your teeth. Let's see just how bad they are.'

Was this the man who had raised her child? Under the bright light she could not feel herself warming to him. He didn't ask permission as he shoved a sensor in her mouth, became curt and irritable with the assistant who came forward with a lead apron. She closed her eyes and hoped that this was the wrong Dr Costa.

'How is Evangelina?' she asked, as he raised the chair to show her the images of her teeth on a backlit screen. 'And your son.'

'Who?'

'Your wife and son.'

'I don't have a son. My wife is called Carlotta.' He frowned and nodded at a group photo on the windowsill behind them: a woman and two pretty little girls. 'Do you know her?'

'Those are your only children?' she asked, filled with relief.

'Yes,' he said, and his hard face softened for a moment.

'Sorry, my mistake.'

He pointed to the X-rays.

'You have strong, healthy teeth.' He wrinkled his nose as if disappointed. 'But those fillings will have to be replaced.'

'Is it urgent?'

'No.' He frowned. 'In any case, if we replace them with white fillings, we may as well whiten your other teeth first.'

She nodded, pretending to agree.

'My assistant will make the appointments.'

Jaq left the building before anyone could detain her.

Y 5

Rio de Janeiro, Brazil

In the Rio de Janeiro branch of the Bank of the Holy Spirit, Pedro's manager shouted and swore at his new secretary, but Alice was as lost as the rest of his staff as to what the hell the telex meant.

Pedro racked his brains. He had been working at the bank for twenty years and had never heard of a *Mercury Protocol*. It was his wife, Maria, delivering a hot lunch, as she did every day, who suggested they call Gloria, the bank manager's old secretary, long retired.

Pedro had to check with his manager first. Gloria had not taken her dismissal well, furious to be replaced by someone who might be younger and prettier but was certainly not so well qualified.

The manager huffed and puffed and ranted and raged. Eventually he saw the sense in the suggestion, but he shut the door before making the call.

'Send a taxi,' he barked after 20 minutes of hard bargaining.

Pedro met Gloria from the taxi and accompanied her to the room where the archive was kept. He suspected that she knew exactly what to look for, but she took her time. It was probably a while since she'd had someone to talk to, so he played along until she gave him the file on the Mercury Protocol and identified the next steps.

Pedro telephoned the *Banco de Espirito Santo* in Luanda, Angola himself. The man at the other end sounded confused, but he provided the verification codes without demur.

Gloria recommended that they wait until lunchtime before

contacting the Colonel. He was always unpredictable, she said, but his morning rages usually softened a little over lunch, although not to leave it too long as once he started drinking, he wouldn't let anyone get a word in edgeways.

The bank manager girded his loins before placing the call.

There was no answer.

'What next?' asked Pedro.

'The phone is often down.' Gloria shook his head. 'The Colonel lives in a remote place.'

'Doesn't he have a mobile?'

'No masts, no satellite dishes, no infrastructure.'

'Then we wait until his landline is fixed?'

'Too urgent.' The bank manager shook his head. 'Someone will have to go and deliver the message in person.'

With a sinking feeling Pedro realised that all eyes were on him.

Y 5

São José dos Campos, Brazil

Jaq's first week in São Paulo consisted of flat hunting, dentist chasing and visa bureaucracy.

The apartment options were discouraging. If she wasn't careful, most of her disposable salary would be spent on rent. She couldn't stay indefinitely in a hotel at Tecnoproject's expense but might have to rethink the luxury of a place close to work. She'd have to find a flat further away from the office on Avenida Paulista.

The dental appointments were dispiriting. The second Dr Costa on the list was a more cheerful fellow than the first, but unmarried without children. The third must have exaggerated his LinkedIn profile as he was far too young to have been practising in Portugal twenty odd years ago. Both admired the health of her teeth and gums, lamented the barbarity of British dentistry and proposed expensive remedial treatment, which she neither needed nor wanted.

The red tape involved in regularising her work situation – a temporary technical expert visa arranged in London – was made bearable by a friendly *despachante*, whose sole job was to help foreigners jump the ever-increasing hurdles placed between them and useful economic activity.

Not that Bruno seemed to be in any rush. He was waiting for the next tranche of work to come in from the Cuperoil refinery in Curitiba and suggested she familiarise herself with the process safety reports in the meantime: mechanical integrity inspections, hazard and operability studies and layers of protection analysis.

It was only when she complained that she'd been there a week and still hadn't done anything useful that Bruno arranged for Jaq to go on her first external meeting with an experienced sales engineer.

Marco picked her up at the hotel and they drove out along the Dutra highway. Their destination, São José do Campos, lay between São Paulo and Rio de Janeiro in the Paraíba Valley, and Marco used the journey time for a bit of mansplaining.

'The thing to remember,' he lectured her, 'is that in Brazil it's rude to arrive early, to set an agenda or to try and get down to business too soon.'

Cordial. That's what she'd read. In the sense that business in Brazil was all about heart. In a society moved by the heart, the cordial man prizes personal connections over impersonal institutions. She drifted off as Marco explained the importance of social interaction, tuning back in when he began a history lecture.

'The Jesuits founded the settlement of São José do Campos. It was disguised as a cattle ranch.'

'Disguising what?'

'A *redução*, a mission. The Jesuits gave refuge to native Brazilians. In the sixteenth century the new settlers were looking for workers, but they weren't so keen on paying them. The Guaranis, the local tribe when the Portuguese arrived here, took refuge in the mission.'

A more compassionate colonialism for those who didn't mind a heavy dose of Catholicism. Better than slavery. Or was it?

'They came for safety, equality and education.'

'And for music?' The only part of the convent experience that Jaq remembered with any pleasure was the choral concerts.

'And for music. The intention may have been pure, but the Jesuits carried European disease – measles, flu, smallpox. The locals lacked immunity, 90 per cent of them died.'

'Ninety per cent? That's terrifying.'

'And for those who survived, the healthy ones who gained immunity, it was just a matter of time. The slave hunters of São Paulo, the *Bandeirantes*, watched and waited. All the hard work of travelling miles on unpaved roads, hacking through vegetation, avoiding poisonous snakes and insects, injury, disease and armed resistance in order to capture a handful of natives was being done by others, an all-you-can-eat buffet opening on their doorstep. Before long the raids started, and the poorly defended mission collapsed.'

'Poor Guarani.'

As the car sped past fields, Marco went on to explain that after the enslavement of the remaining Guaranis and expulsion of the Jesuit founders, São José do Campos became a centre of agriculture, growing first cotton and then coffee in the nineteenth century, reinventing itself in the twentieth century as a health retreat, packed with hospitals and sanatoria for tuberculosis sufferers. When streptomycin came along, a cure for TB that didn't involve fresh air, São José do Campos became the centre of the Brazilian aerospace industry: success through change.

'And, when the national Brazilian aerospace company unveiled its first plane, who was it named after?'

'Guarani?'

'Nope,' He shook his head. 'The flag-waving slave hunters! The *Bandeirante*, a turboprop passenger aircraft, EMB 110, was launched by Embraer in 1968.'

'And Embraer is based here in São José dos Campos?'

'Yes, along with Boeing and Airbus. All three companies have research centres in the same technology park. *Parque Tecnológico de São José dos Campos.*'

'An all-you-can-eat buffet right on Tecnoproject's doorstep?'

'You catch on fast.' He winked. 'You'll do all right.'

They turned at a sign announcing Aérex and drove into the visitor's car park. Jaq stared up at a wide, modern office block topped by a curved roof in the form of an aeroplane wing.

'This visit is a long shot. I'm not sure why Bruno suggested you come along.' He glanced at her sidways. 'I'm an old friend of the technical director, so just keep quiet and follow my lead.'

The woman who welcomed them would have been arresting in any circumstances, but what struck Jaq most was the warmth she radiated. After a brief exchange with Marco, she turned her full attention onto Jaq.

'Welcome!' Marina had a deep, rich voice. 'So how is a *Portuguesa* liking Brazil?'

'It's fascinating,' Jaq replied. 'Though I think I might like Caipirinhas more than is good for me.'

'*Beleza!* Marina's grin, perfect white teeth in a wide mouth, lit up the room. 'You've discovered our sugarcane rum? *Cachaça* packs the best punch, but you know you can make them with sake or vodka instead? Sakerinha or Caipiroska.'

'Now why did no one mention that before?'

Marina laughed. 'Where are you living?'

'A hotel right now. I'm looking for an apartment I can afford.'

Marina sympathised over Jaq's search for accommodation in São Paulo, suggesting areas of the city that Jaq hadn't considered so far.

Marco interrupted, turning the conversation back to news of old college friends.

'We were at university together,' he explained. 'Back when Marina was a—'

Marina clapped her hands and stood up.

'My next meeting has been cancelled.' She smiled at Jaq. 'Would you like a tour of the facility?'

The Aérex complex, a new-technology test centre for all the large aerospace companies in the technology park, stretched out behind the glass and steel office block with a series of hangars, workshops and test bays.

They were just leaving the hypersonic wind tunnel when Marina turned to Jaq.

'The next section is for prototypes. I can't take you too close, restricted access, but there's a viewing platform.'

They climbed to a glass-walled corridor and paused above the prototype hangar. Inside was an aircraft that looked as if two gliders had been stuck together, twin-bodied, like a flying catamaran, with a tank in the middle and immensely wide wings on either side.

'Zero emission. Powered by a hydrogen fuel cell.'

Marco stepped in between Jaq and Marina. 'Have you flown her yet?'

'Hoping for a chance once the ground tests are complete.'

'You're a test pilot?' Jaq tried to picture Marina in a pilot's uniform. It was difficult to imagine, but she couldn't quite say why.

'I learned to fly before I could drive.'

'Sponsored through university by the Brazilian Air Force.' Marco added. 'In the days when …'

He tailed off as Marina shot him a look.

'And I had a commission for seven years after that,' she said.

'You flew Air Force planes?' Jaq asked.

'Occasionally, though I was employed as a design engineer, not a pilot.' She smiled. 'In the military, you get to test out your own designs.'

'Is this one of your designs?'

Marina smiled. 'Teamwork.'

'Where is the hydrogen stored?' Jaq asked.

Marina indicated the tank in the middle of the double-bodied plane.

'And the bulk hydrogen, for refuelling?'

Marina pointed to the corner of the hangar.

'Have you thought about ventilation?' Jaq asked. 'I used to work with explosives,' she added.

'Interesting.' Marina looked at her closely. 'What sort of explosives?'

'Most sorts. I worked in a research centre in the Alps for a while.' Beautiful Slovenia, how she missed it. 'We set off controlled avalanches to keep the ski slopes safe.'

'Any experience with hydrogen?'

'Lots.' Her very first explosion in fact. Potassium metal and water gives hydrogen gas and … BOOM! 'It's not easy to handle, but so long as you follow the design codes and keep everything in the open air, it dissipates quickly.'

'Hmm. Come with me.'

Marina led them down metal stairs at the side of the hangar and out onto scrubland at the back.

'We're working on an expansion project, a zero-carbon test centre – hydrogen fuel cells, oxygen generators, solar panels, wind turbines, fuel additives.'

Marco's eyes lit up. 'Will you need some project support?'

Marina ignored him. 'I wanted to put the new hydrogen tanks out there,' Marina pointed to an empty field. Her fingernails were manicured and enamelled in pearlescent pink. 'The engine test centre will be inside an acoustic enclosure, here.' She swivelled on her heels and pointed to a small area of scrubland. 'And this area will be for the fuel cells.'

'That sounds a sensible plan.'

'But the new engineer wants to put the cryogenic tanks inside to reduce the cost of keeping them cool.'

Jaq shook her head. 'It's hard to detect a leak, and if the hydrogen accumulates, it takes very little energy to set off a serious explosion. Like the Muskingum River disaster in 2007.'

'I guess it's not too late to reconsider the layout.' Marina clicked her tongue against her teeth. 'Could you come along to a project meeting?'

'Is there anything else that Tecnoproject could help with?' Marco asked.

'Until your colleague here pointed out the obvious, I hadn't thought of bringing in anyone from the outside.'

'We have good people.' Marco said. 'I can vouch for them.'

'Send some CVs and I'll consider it.' She pointed down the corridor towards the female toilets. 'Jaq, do you want to freshen up?'

Marina waited until they were standing side by side, washing their hands in adjacent basins. 'I might need your expertise on a completely different project.' She met Jaq's eyes in the mirror. 'Apart from Aérex, I have other business interests.'

Why the sudden caginess?

'It would involve a trip to the south of Brazil.'

The perfect excuse to visit the southern dentists on her list.

'I'd have to check with—'

Marina shook her head. 'Don't mention this to Marco. I'll call Bruno direct.'

Back in the car, Marco growled as he pulled out of the car park.

'That's the first time Marina's even considered bringing in design contractors.'

Jaq waited for congratulations or a thank-you, but when it didn't come she glanced sideways at Marco. 'That's a good thing, right?'

Marco went through a red light and then braked sharply as a car sped across the junction. 'I've been trying to get people in there for ever.' He scowled. 'Along you come on your first day and make it look easy.'

He put on the radio and turned up the volume until the music was as loud as his brooding silence.

♈ 4

Tocantins, Brazil

The bank clerk from Rio took off his Panama hat and waved it at
the cloud of flies. Pedro wiped the sweat from his forehead with
a spotted handkerchief. *Porra*, but it was hot out here. The boat,
a long canoe with an outboard motor, afforded no shelter. On the
first stretch of river, the boat created its own breeze, but as they
wound their way into ever smaller, shallower tributaries, the speed
dropped to match the frequency of soundings; a bag of sand on
a rope, dropped into the water from the prow, was all that stood
between safe passage and shipwreck.

The water broiled, brown and opaque, except for the occasional,
terrifying flash of an alligator eye or slithering coil of a water
cobra.

Why had he come? He was not a young man, nor a brave one.
His health was delicate at the best of times. He took great care
with his diet to avoid the gastric flare-ups that had plagued him
since childhood. Why hadn't he refused when the bank manager
ordered him to deliver the message in person? He could have
assigned it to one of the junior clerks.

But Pedro had never travelled further north than Teresópolis.
Like many *Cariocas* he had a mixed ancestry. His surname was
Italian, and his grandfather came from Sicily, escaping the hell
of the sulphur mines in search of a better life. He'd married a
local girl. Pedro's caramel-coloured skin hinted at non-European
blood, perhaps native Tupi, more likely a descendent of slaves

shipped from Africa to work on the sugar plantations before they were freed in the nineteenth century. His parents had been born in the centre of Brazil, escaping to the city as soon as they were able and never looking back. He wished he'd shown more interest in their stories when they were still alive. Now he was curious to see their part of the country. And even more curious to meet Colonel Cub.

The boat slowed as they approached the waterfall. One of the crew picked up a gun and fired a shot into the undergrowth of the left bank. A black caiman, six metres long from the tip of its huge reptile jaw to the end of a sinuous tail, scurried on tiny legs and splashed into the water, followed by a smaller alligator. The predators swam past the boat, partially submerged, but through the ripples he could make out black scaly skin with a band of silver-grey. Their teeth were designed to grab, holding a man down until he drowned and then storing him in an underwater larder, letting him rot a little before tearing off meal-sized chunks. Smaller prey could be swallowed whole.

Pedro shivered. He'd hoped to see pink river dolphins, manatees, giant otters and turtles, but so far it was just flies, alligators, snakes and more flies. He slapped another insect from his mouth, and it fell to the deck of the boat, red with his blood.

The boat pulled up at a muddy beach.

'This is as far as I take you.'

Pedro swallowed hard.

The boatman pointed 'See the path? Just keep climbing. You can't go wrong.'

Pedro wiped the sweat from his eyes and stared at the sandstone cliffs rising above the river valley into dense jungle. He began to tremble.

'No. You promised to guide me. All the way.'

The man cleared his throat and spat into the river. Something rose in the water to catch the phlegm and Pedro put a hand over his mouth as nausea threatened to overwhelm him.

'We stay with the boat.'

Pedro sat down. He had grown up in the city, worked his whole life as a bank clerk. He possessed no survival skills.

'I'm not going alone.'

The boatman pulled a gun from his belt and pointed it at him.

'Get out!' he barked. 'The Colonel is expecting you.'

☿ 4

Sapiranga, Vale dos Sinos, Rio Grande do Sul, Brazil

Jaq emerged from the regional airport of Porto Alegre where a driver was waiting for her, displaying a card with 'Dr Silver – Tecnoproject' and underneath the stylish logo of the company Transform.

Bruno had been vague about Marina's requirements, asking Jaq only if she'd be willing to fly to Porto Alegre in the south and spend five days in Sapiranga, a town nearby. As the Curitiba safety study work still hadn't come through, and there were further delays at the Cuperoil refineries in São Paulo and Salvador, Jaq didn't feel she had an option to refuse. And once her boss agreed that she could add a weekend of personal time to the mission it seemed the perfect opportunity.

But why all the secrecy? All Bruno would tell her was that Marina was involved with a newly formed spin-off from her family's venerable shoe company, with its only factory in the far south of Brazil.

It took a while for Jaq's luggage to arrive. She preferred to travel light, but when visiting one of the premier fashion brands in Brazil, she'd packed for all eventualities.

As they left the airport, the rain started. It grew heavier as they drove out of the city, great grey sheets lashing the car. Jaq could see nothing of the countryside, and the drops of water drumming onto the car roof and splashing up from the road made it difficult to hold a conversation. The rain eased as they approached Sapiranga.

'Paulo suggested I show you the hotel before we go to the factory.'

'Paulo?'

'Oh, I'm sorry. I always forget he calls himself Marina now.' The driver shook his head. 'I've known him since he was born.'

So, Marina was born a man.

The driver wrinkled his nose as the car drew up outside a featureless concrete block.

'We don't have many hotel options; this is the best of a bad bunch. Is it OK?'

'All I need is a shower and a bed.'

'I'll wait here while you check in.'

It was a short drive from the hotel to the factory. Outside the rather grim industrial town, the landscape opened up into suburbs of generous houses: German-style chalets and Italian classical villas set in landscaped gardens. The driver turned off the main road and drove up an avenue of young trees. Automatic gates opened to reveal a vast emerald-green lawn. In the centre, on the top of a slight hill, stood an ultramodern block, a riot of glass and brightly painted concrete, unexpected curves and sharp angles, the company name and logo Transform illuminated with coloured neon lights.

Marina – immaculately turned out in a cream linen skirt suit, pink blouse and matching stilettoes – came down the steps to meet her.

'*Bemvindo!*'

'Quite some place you have here.'

'My great-great grandparents started the business.' Marina led the way to her office on the top floor, with a spectacular view over the river valley.

'Right here?'

'They started up in the town. My grandparents bought this

land to expand, but the business got into difficulties in the 1980s, a time of hyperinflation in Brazil, and it remained moribund for years.'

A young man arrived with coffee and water and Marina waited until he had left.

'Then low-cost products from China and India threatened to put us out of business. My parents made beautiful, high-quality shoes here, but they didn't move with the times. Until recently, work practices had hardly changed since the nineteenth century.'

'But now you're making changes?'

Marina took a sip of coffee and patted her lips with a napkin.

'My parents wanted a son to take over the business.' She glanced sideways at Jaq. 'They're getting a daughter instead. We fell out over it for a while. But, finally, I agreed to set up the new unit.'

Transform. 'So now you're the boss of the family shoe company, in addition to your full-time job in São Paulo.'

'Just the Chief Concept Officer here.' Marina smiled. 'I leave the day-to-day running to professional managers.'

'And how can I help?'

'I want you to come to this with an open mind.'

'I'll try.'

'Here's the concept. The universal shoe for the travelling woman. Women need different shoes for different activities. And they need shoes that fit properly. We provide a multipurpose shoe that transforms, depending on the occasion.'

Jaq frowned. It was a great idea. Most of her check-in luggage had been taken up by shoes: safety boots for the factory tour, brogues for meetings, trainers for running and slingbacks for the evening; that many shoes wouldn't fit into a carry-on. But multi-purpose footwear, the shoe that tried to be all things to all people, usually ended up being good for nothing. Too dull for dancing, too weak for walking – lowest common denominator. Where was Marina going with this?

'What's your shoe size?'

'Size six in the UK, thirty-nine in Europe.'

Marina consulted a chart. 'Thirty-six in Brazil.'

Marina opened a drawer and pulled out a cylinder, about the size of a gift box for a bottle of malt whisky. She placed it on the table, opened the lid and pulled out a roll of fabric, tied with a ribbon.

'All you need is a flat surface and an electric socket.'

She loosened the coloured ribbon and spread out the contents. The roll of thin backing fabric had multiple compartments sewn on, and inside each pocket was a different shoe part.

'Let's say you want to go to the Festival of Roses tomorrow night, and you need some drop-dead gorgeous bright red shoes.'

'Is there a festival of roses?'

'Oh, yes. You've come at just the right time.' Marina opened one of the fabric pockets. 'We select the heel first. Choose a height in inches between one and six.'

'Let's not go crazy.' Jaq rarely wore high heels. 'I still need to walk.'

'And dance! Start with two inches then?'

'OK.'

Marina pulled out a left heel and then a right one.

'What shape of heel do you prefer? Needlepoint stiletto, elegant court, block and chunky or wide and flared?'

'Court.'

Marina twisted a knob at the base of each heel, until the bottom diameter was smaller than the top. She reached back into the roll and pressed a couple of heel caps onto each base.

'Next we need the outsole, the part that connects heel and toe to the ground.'

She pulled out two pieces of thick, leathery fabric and handed one to Jaq. 'Feel it.'

The material was about five millimetres thick, but soft and flexible. On one side it had a series of raised channels, made of a harder material.

'The heel slots in here.' Marina demonstrated with one heel and passed the other to Jaq to copy. 'And now you need to add the coulter and toe cap.'

Marina passed Jaq a curved piece of fabric for the heel and a pointed piece for the toe. Each had its own raised channels and grooves that slotted snugly into the corresponding profile in the outsole, elegantly designed so that a toe pushing forward or heel pushing back would only increase the stability.

'And now the welt, toe puff and the side uppers.'

Jaq watched Marina and then repeated the construction process.

'A bit of filler for comfort and then the inner sole. The top is in contact with your foot, so it needs to be soft and breathable. The base needs to be spongy and mould itself to your skin. I like to use calfskin or kid leather backed with natural cork.' She handed Jaq a cork sole and a soft leather one and Jaq slipped one, then the other, into place.

'Nearly there.'

Marina held up the shoe and shook it, it wobbled.

'Could you dance in that?'

Jaq bit her lip. Was Marina insane? The object in her hand was like a shoe made of jelly. Even if it would stand her weight without collapsing, which she doubted, it lacked any rigidity against lateral movement, a recipe for a broken ankle.

'Now comes the clever bit. The controller.'

Marina pulled out a tiny box from the fabric roll. It was the size of a mobile phone with a couple of raised knobs and switches, a USB connector and two probes. She turned the wobbly shoe upside down and pressed the pointed end of one of the probes into the heel cap, and then connected the controller using a USB cable to a socket on her desk.

She set a timer and then pressed a switch. The shoe began to move, subtly at first, shrinking, straightening, tightening.

'It's much better if you do this part with your foot inside the shoe, but just to demonstrate.'

'What's happening?'

'We use a shape memory composite to construct the shoe. I call it "Polymemory" – a crosslinked polyurethane matrix with about 2 per cent carbon. All it takes is a small electric current to induce physical crosslinking of the embedded carbon nanotube network to give room-temperature rigidity.'

The controller emitted a little beep and Marina unplugged the shoe, handing it to Jaq. The previously wobbly shoe was now perfectly rigid; what had looked like a crude assembly of parts was now a smooth continuum.

'That's amazing.'

'Try doing the other one on your foot?'

Jaq took off one safety boot and sock and slipped the wobbly shoe onto her foot. She connected the controller probe to the heel. The shoe began to rise, to strengthen, to close around her foot. Not too tight.

After the beep, Jaq removed the probe and stood up, took a step, swivelled and turned. 'Perfect fit!'

'Not perfect no. We prefer to take a cast of each foot and then we can make a shoe kit that is unique and bespoke for each client. Now, what about colour?'

'Colour?'

Marina plugged the controller back into the shoe on the desk and pressed a toggle switch. Then she rotated the dial slowly. A faint hum permeated the office.

Jaq gasped as the outer surface of the shoe went from matt black to an intense, almost velvety red.

'I must be dreaming.' She rubbed her eyes. 'I don't believe what I'm seeing. How on earth does that work?'

'Colour is an optical illusion. The outer layer of the composite is a nano material inspired by bird feathers. Feathers have micro-structures with special optical properties. Millions of tiny filaments, called barbules, can enhance colour. We use sound waves to shake the surface, altering the frequency to bring the differently shaped filaments up to the light.'

'The default state is matt black, vertically angled, strap-shaped barbules that minimise light reflectance. But if we shake those out of the way with sound waves, we can bring forward the dihedral barbules that give out a lovely, rich red. And if I keep going,' she turned the knob and the shoe colour brightened to a pillar-box red and then orange. 'We can cover the full spectrum.'

'How on earth did you discover this?'

'I was inspired by the Brazilian tanager, *Ramphocelus bresilius*, a lovely little bird that changes colour to attract a mate.' As she turned the knob, the colour changed to yellow-gold, emerald-green, navy blue and then shades of purple. 'We're still working on brown to cream.'

'May I?'

Jaq took the shoe from her foot and plugged in the controller, watching with renewed amazement as the newly built shoe changed colour.

'Of course, it's best to colour them together. That way you get exactly the same shade. For the stiffness, the timer ensures equal rigidity. But colour matching is an art.'

'How much does the shoe kit cost?' Jaq already knew she wanted one of these, needed it.

'Oh, it's expensive. Too expensive to commercialise just yet. But the shoes are reusable. We're testing one pair that have already been constructed and dismantled a hundred times.'

'Dismantled?'

'Yes. A travelling shoe is no good unless it can be packed flat.'

Jaq stroked the shoe. 'You can undo this?'

'All you need is heat to break up the physical network of carbon nanotubes. We've wired in a resistance filament to provide just that.'

Marina turned the colour controller back to its default position, the shoe fading to matt back. She removed the needle-shaped jack from the heel of the shoe and slid it under the toe. She flicked another toggle swich and turned up the dial. The shoe began to wilt.

'Don't touch it yet, it can get quite hot. Give it a few minutes.'

'Complete elastic recovery?'

'Yes, thanks to the structure of the polymemory it returns to its original shape.'

Marina turned on a desk fan to cool the first shoe and repeated the heating process with the second shoe.

'Should be OK now.'

Jaq picked up the first shoe, still warm to the touch. She unlocked each of the pieces, sliding them through their grooves and laid them out on the desk. Marina returned each to its designated pocket.

'There's only one problem with the prototype.'

'And that is?'

'And that is where I need your help.' She rolled up the shoe kit and retied the cylinder with the ribbon. 'It's the reason I asked you to come here.'

'I'm all ears.'

'The polymemory, the fabric the shoes are made from …'

Jaq waited as Marina stowed the shoe roll back in its drawer.

'It has a habit of exploding.'

Y 4

Tocantins, Brazil

The bank clerk watched helplessly as the boat disappeared round a bend in the river. As the thrum of the outboard motor receded, the noises of the jungle took over. The incessant high-pitched whine of insects and chatter of birds almost masked an ominous rustling from the undergrowth. Almost, but not quite.

Pedro shivered, despite the heat. He was a long way from Rio, two thousand kilometres to be exact, walking alone and unprotected beside a tributary that fed the river Tocantins. Movement in the water suggested that the alligators were restless. Hungry. He took a deep breath and set off up the sandy path. At first it snaked away from the river, but it doubled back and climbed, zigzagging up the side of the waterfall. When he reached the first clearing, he stopped to marvel at the sight: a series of rapids, frothing and tumbling over rocks as far as the eye could see.

He'd been walking for about an hour when the smell of woodsmoke quickened his pace. Fear gave way to euphoria. He was nearly there. He could deliver his message, call the boat back and get out of this terrifying wilderness. He would never travel outside the city again.

Lost in thought, he didn't hear them sneaking up behind him until he was surrounded. The men were dressed in army fatigues. The camouflage kit didn't look like standard issue, it hung loose and ragged from the wiry frames of the soldiers.

'*Bom dia.*' He took off his hat and made a small bow. 'I'm looking for Colonel Cub.'

A young soldier beckoned. 'Come.'

Pedro struggled to keep pace with the men. Were they guiding him or capturing him? The young man had run ahead, the other soldiers hadn't spoken a word, only pointing and nudging. Their silence was unnerving, it made the noises of the jungle even louder, but with the constant screeching and twig-snapping rustling from the undergrowth, he was glad of their guns. The path climbed steeply between sandstone cliffs and suddenly there were more soldiers, a few small huts at the side of the path, a vegetable patch here, a goat tethered there. The path turned sharply and passed between sandstone cliffs.

Emerging into a clearing, the soldiers halted as the ground fell away. They pushed Pedro forward until he was standing on the lip of a quarry.

Pedro looked down and his eyes opened wide.

Y 4

Sapiranga, Vale dos Sinos, Rio Grande do Sul, Brazil

In the office of the Sapiranga shoe factory, Jaq stared at Marina open-mouthed.

'You mean to say, you have just shown me the most magnificent shoes, the solution to every travelling woman's dilemma, and now you are telling me that if I dance in them, they will literally go ...' She splayed her fingers and mouthed the word BOOM!

Marina laughed at her shocked expression. 'No, no, not while they are being worn.'

'So, when you say, the shoes keep exploding ... what exactly do you mean?'

'Come, let me show you the pilot plant.'

Jaq put her safety boots back on, wriggled into a hi-vis gilet and donned a hard hat. The production area stretched out behind the office block: a windowless shed with a corrugated iron roof, breeze-block walls and no obvious entrance.

Marina led the way, touching a pass to a black box in the wall. A green light flashed, and a section of the wall slid to one side to let them in.

The space felt larger inside, brightly lit and laid out in a grid pattern, with a workstation at each of 12 stages. The chatter of cutting and sewing machines faded as they climbed the stairs to enter the first control room through a double airlock. Marina greeted the two workers by name, a man and a woman in orange overalls who sat at computers. She introduced Jaq as a visiting safety expert.

Marina took Jaq to a large glass window with a view of the factory floor below. 'This is where we make the polymemory.'

'It's basically polyurethane, right?' Jaq thought back to her days as a lecturer at Teesside University. 'Polyols and isocyanates.'

'A chemical cocktail that must be handled with extreme care.' Marina pointed to the small tanks and reactors. 'Minimum inventory, just-in-time production, careful control of stabilisers.'

She pointed to a second area.

'Next we make the carbon nanotubes. We're trying out a few different processes: electric arc, laser, plasma, electrolysis. Most promising so far is chemical vapour deposition.'

They left the control room and returned to the factory floor. The whir of high-speed rollers became louder as they moved forward.

'The spinning section is here. It's a dry-jet process.'

'Where you re-dissolve the polymemory, extrude it through tiny holes?'

'Exactly. The spinnerets are heated, and we remove most of the solvent in the air gap as the polymemory fibres emerge. Of course, we condense and reuse all the solvent.' Marina pointed to a large refrigeration plant. 'It's a closed system with almost no waste.'

Jaq looked up at line after line of gossamer-thin filaments running the length of the building. 'And the spinning process is to stretch the polymer threads?'

'Yes. The fibres enter a coagulation bath.' Marina pointed to a black rectangular tank. 'The rate at which we pull the fibres as they cool allows us to orient the molecules in the yarn to give it the strength we need.'

'And you make everything yourself?'

'This is research-scale equipment, just a pilot plant. But it gives us complete control of the recipe, the additives, the fibre diameter and strength, the final performance of the polymemory.'

The clatter of a loom grew louder as they approached the weaving section. Spools of fibres were combined in the right proportion and woven into a deceptively soft fabric that would harden when connected to an electric current.

Marina explained how they adjusted the weave for different parts of the shoe, adding copper filaments for the heating cycle or nano-barbules for the colour effect and then led Jaq to the cutting section where a computer-directed knife cut out the pieces of the shoe to a precise program.

At the very end of the assembly line, the various pieces were tested, assembled and packed into rolls.

They left the factory floor and entered what looked like a small gym.

'Would you like to see how we make the moulds?'

'Sure.'

'Bare feet please.'

Jaq took off her safety boots and socks.

'Now hop onto this running machine.'

A series of laser beams played across her feet as she moved one in front of the other.

'I'm going to increase the speed. Just stop me when it is no longer comfortable.'

Jaq increased her pace to keep still, jogging and then running flat out.

'Excellent, most people don't make it to eleven.'

The belt began to slow.

'Now for the dance floor. Marina directed Jaq to a circle. Can you throw some shapes?'

'Do I have to?'

'Here, this may help.'

Marina flicked a switch and the 7/8 rhythm of a bossa nova filled the room.

Jaq's hips began to sway and then her feet were moving, almost against her will.

'Nice,' said Marina and joined her, sashaying around the room.

'And finally, just stand here.'

Jaq stepped onto a raised platform with a handrail, like a conductor's lectern.

'Hold on please.'

Jaq grabbed the bar, just before the ground under her feet began to give way, the flat plate liquefying into a soft, gelatinous substance that wrapped itself round and between her toes, oozing over her feet and up to her ankles.

'Ten, nine …' Marina counted down, 'two, one, zero. Now, extract your feet.'

With a slurping, popping sound Jaq extracted first her left and then her right foot, leaving holes where her feet had been, perfect three-dimensional negatives.

'And finally, the foot jacuzzi.'

Jaq placed her feet in a warm bath. The bubbles tickled.

Marina handed her a towel.

'Take as long as you like. The alginate jelly mould takes a few minutes to cure. We make the casts, copies of your feet, with a sort of plaster of Paris, and then adjust for movement using the information from the lasers.' She handed Jaq a thick, fluffy towel. 'And with all that digital information, we can make a bespoke shoe kit, just for you.'

Jaq dried her feet and put her safety boots back on. They passed into the store where the plaster casts were kept. Shelf upon shelf of lifelike plaster feet, big ones, little ones, wide ones, narrow ones, feet with bunions, feet with fallen arches. Jaq shivered at the thought of her own feet joining this museum.

'All very impressive. But I haven't spotted any explosions.'

'Let's grab a coffee and I can tell you more.'

The canteen opened out onto a garden of roses. Marina showed her how to operate the coffee machine and Jaq followed her lead. They took their cups outside to a table in a secluded arbour.

'The explosions happen during the heating cycle, the dismantling.' Marina explained.

'How does the heating work?' Jaq asked.

'We thread a filament of copper wire into some layers of the memory polymer, they clip together to form a network linked to a socket in the toe piece. With the forward current, through the heel, we crosslink the carbon nanotubes to stiffen. When we "reverse" the current ...' She formed quotation marks round reverse with her index fingers, '... sending it through the toe, it passes through the copper network and heats up the adjacent layers enough to break the carbon nanotube crosslinking.'

Marina took a sip of coffee.

'Unfortunately, when it gets too hot, the polymer starts to decompose, releasing free radicals that set off a chain reaction and ...'

'Boom!' Jaq said.

'It's quite safe so long as you use the control box correctly.'

'What if someone were to bypass it, plugging it directly into the mains?' Jaq asked.

'Then you'd have exactly 3.3432 minutes to detonation.' Marina pursed her lips. 'We've measured the worst-case energy release, and while it's unlikely to kill anyone directly, it could cause some nasty injuries.'

'Or start a fire?'

'Precisely. So, we're looking at additional controls, but that means adding complexity and complexity adds bulk.'

'Instead of adding controls, why not fix the problem at source, find another way to heat?'

'We tried microwave heating, before we came up with the copper filaments, but it was much worse. The time between softening and decomposing was only a few seconds. We wrecked dozens of microwaves when prototyping.'

'What about hot water?'

'Domestic hot water isn't warm enough, even boiling water from a kettle won't do it. You have to get above 120 degrees centigrade to start the softening.'

'Steam at pressure then, an autoclave or a bottle steriliser?'

'If it's for travellers, it has to be something you would find in an average hotel room.'

'Let me give it some thought.' Jaq finished her coffee.

Marina checked her watch. 'I have some family business to attend to, but we could meet for dinner near your hotel?'

Jaq nodded. 'Perfect.'

An idea was already beginning to form.

Y 4

Tocantins, Brazil

The Colonel's headquarters resembled an overgrown adventure playground. The structure supported by stilts in the middle of the quarry had been built with local materials – wood, twine, thatch, leaves and clay, an exuberant castle of multiple circular towers, each with a thatched conical roof and a wooden balcony running the full circumference. One tower was connected to the next tower by a V-shaped rope-bridge of knotted twine. The collapsed remains of earlier constructions suggested that a new tower was built every few years, each one more elaborate than the last, with the oldest left to rot.

If the construction was flimsy, the position was strong.

High in the jungle, it was a long winding climb. The path zigzagged beside a river, climbing to a plateau from where it plummeted in a series of waterfalls and rapids. The navigable portion of the river was not far, at least as the condor flies. From a hide in the sandstone cliff, a soldier monitored everything that moved on the river far below. The great curves and sweeps meant ten miles of water had to be travelled for every mile of progress.

A sandstone bluff formed a natural, easily defendable gate and the old quarry formed a dry moat around the main fortress.

Pedro, the Rio bank clerk, teetered on the edge of the quarry, avoiding physical contact with the soldiers who crowded round him. It was a long way down. Had they brought him here to kill him?

He started at a sudden noise, almost losing his footing. With a whirring and creaking, a wooden bridge began to extend from the castle. It stopped about two metres from where Pedro stood, open-mouthed.

A man appeared at the other end, deep in shadow. A deep voice boomed out of the tower.

'Who are you and what do you want.'

'I have a message for Colonel Cub.'

'Who is the message from.'

'From the *Banco de Espirito Santo*.'

'And what does the message say?'

Was this the Colonel speaking? On this, at least, Pedro's instructions were clear.

'I'm to deliver the message in person.'

The shadow made a dismissive gesture and barked an order. Pedro heard the snick of a safety catch being released on a pistol and a rifle barrel pressed into his back, pushing him forward towards the edge of the quarry.

'It's a long way down,' said the shadow. 'The fall might not kill you instantly, but by the time you hit the bottom, you won't be in any state to deliver any messages.' He laughed. 'You choose. We shoot you and it ends fast. We push you into the quarry and leave you to die slowly, or you give me the message and I decide whether to let you live to meet the Colonel.'

Pedro's legs were shaking so hard he could barely stand. A warm stream of urine ran down his leg.

'I'm waiting.'

Pedro's voice came out in a whisper. 'The Mercury Protocol has been triggered.'

With a grinding of metal gears, the wooden bridge extended the last few metres and made contact with the stone circumference of the quarry. The shadow stepped out into the light to reveal a tall, muscular man, dressed in dark combat trousers and boots. His skin was the colour and sheen of ripe *jaboticaba*, his well-developed bare chest oiled and glossy. He walked over the bridge and stood in front of the bank clerk from Rio. The gun barrel disappeared from Pedro's back and the soldiers began to laugh.

'Greetings.'

The bare-chested man saluted, and Pedro made a feeble attempt to copy, turning the gesture into a wave at the last minute.

'How was your journey?'

'I'm not used to travelling.'

'I can see that. Well, you're here now.' The man's eyes travelled down to the damp patch on his trousers. 'And it looks as if you could use a wash. Come with me.'

He gestured for Pedro to follow him across the moat and into the complex, the bridge bouncing and swaying as they progressed.

The inside of the fortress was even more extraordinary than the outside. Open slits let in natural light, and flowering plants grew up the inside of packed-earth walls, a luxuriant dynamic wallpaper. A curved wooden staircase ran between several floors. Perfumed candles burned in alcoves, giving off a delicate scent of lily.

The man clapped his hands and a boy appeared.

'Make our guest welcome.'

The youth bowed his head and gestured for Pedro to follow. He led the way across a rope bridge to the guest tower, a little tree house, simply furnished with wooden furniture. The boy pushed aside a curtain of vines and indicated a balcony.

A central water tower collected rainwater and when the boy pulled a twine lever, a clear stream cascaded down a half-pipe to a shower head.

Pedro was shaking hard now. He collapsed onto a wooden stool on the balcony. Before he had a chance to protest the boy knelt in from of him to remove his shoes and socks. Pedro's fingers fumbled with the buttons on his shirt, but they were suddenly fat and clumsy. The boy stood and gently pushed his hands away. Pedro allowed himself to be undressed, turning his head away at the smell of his piss-soaked trousers.

The boy waited to see that Pedro had everything he needed and then retreated.

'The Colonel will see you on his return.'

Pedro stood naked in the shower, the fat drops of rainwater washing away his grime and shame and tears, waiting for the trembling to stop.

Y 4

Sapiranga, Vale dos Sinos, Rio Grande do Sul, Brazil

The double doors of the *churrascaria* led into a vast hall, heaving with movement. The smell of grilled meat filled the air, the babble of voices echoing off the smooth plastered walls. Most of the tables were occupied, but a waiter rushed forward to clear a space for Marina and Jaq.

'It's not normally this busy.' Marina was wearing a close-fitting, long-sleeved emerald dress with perfectly colour-matched high-heeled shoes. Jaq was glad she'd made an effort to dress up too, although her sweater dress and slingbacks made her look positively dull in comparison to her host. 'But everyone is getting ready for the Festival of Roses tomorrow.'

A waitress arrived with a tray of beers and took their order.

'Cheers!' Jaq raised her glass.

'*Saúde!*'

Marina picked up a coloured disc from her place setting. 'Do you know how a *churrasco* works?'

'Not yet.'

'You help yourself to a starter,' she gestured at the buffet in the middle. 'Then you turn this to green.' She flipped the disc. 'They bring you the barbecued stuff. All you can eat.'

Jaq watched the roving waiters with skewers of meat. They manoeuvred between tables, stopping to carve a few slices onto a diners' plate before moving on.

'When you've had enough …' Marina flipped the disc back to red.

The central buffet groaned under the weight of fresh produce: lettuce, rocket, endive, chicory, tomatoes, peppers, artichokes, olives, potato salad, as well as cold meats, cheeses and pescatarian alternatives, sashimi and sushi.

Jaq followed Marina, assembling a mixed salad on a small plate before returning to the table.

'I had an idea,' Jaq said. 'For a different way of heating the shoes. It's not as elegant as your copper filaments, but it might work.'

'I'm listening.'

'Most hotel rooms have a hairdryer.' Even her simple room in Sapiranga had a small one in the drawer. 'The air flows over an electrical element and comes out between 120 and 160 degrees Celsius. Would that be enough to soften your shoes?'

Marina nodded. 'It's worth a try.'

The meat started to arrive, first a slab of beef, then a leg of pork, a shoulder of lamb, a chicken kebab. They were silent for a while as they tried one thing after another.

'I have a surprise for you tomorrow,' Marina said.

'The Festival of Roses?'

'That's not until the evening. Can you keep the whole day free?'

'Sure.'

'I'm going to show you my other project. I'm working on belts as well as shoes.'

'More polymemory?' Jaq frowned. 'How is that going to transform a belt.'

'Wait until tomorrow.' Marina winked. 'I don't want to spoil the surprise.'

A waiter brought a tray of sliced meat. Marina helped herself to another gargantuan portion, then paused and put half back.

'I'm sorry I was late tonight. Family stuff. The usual arguments about who's going to be where at Christmas.'

Jaq twisted her mouth. 'I'm not a big fan of Christmas. I prefer to spend it by myself.'

'Me too. That's what the argument was about. I'll be there for the kids, but that's it.'

'You have children?' Why did that surprise her?

'I have two beautiful daughters.'

'And they live here?' Jaq asked.

'With my ex-wife.' Marina dropped her eyes. 'I was their biological father.'

Jaq knew that Marina was waiting for her response. 'So now they have two mothers,' Jaq said. 'Lucky them.'

Marina looked up, eyes shining, and Jaq sensed the relief in her eyes. 'The children are fantastic. It's my siblings and parents who are the most challenging.' Marina sighed.

Jaq put down her fork down and focussed her full attention on the woman in front of her.

'How so?'

'They think I am suffering a mental breakdown.'

'Are you?'

'What do you think?'

'You seem pretty together to me,' Jaq smiled. 'For a mad inventor, that is.'

Perhaps she'd gone too far. 'Are you OK?'

Marina grinned. 'I was so glad to get away tonight. So looking forward to this.' She indicated the noisy hall, gearing up for festival dancing. 'But enough about me. My driver tells me you want to visit a dentist. You have pain?'

'Heartache, not toothache,' Jaq said.

'I could introduce you to my orthodontist back in São Paulo.'

Jaq shook her head. 'It's not what you think.'

A dessert trolley arrived, and Jaq used the interruption to gather her thoughts. 'I came to Brazil to look for someone.'

Marina paused, spoon poised between plate and mouth. 'I'm intrigued.'

'When I was very young, an unmarried teenager, I had a baby.'

Marina put down her spoon.

'My mother arranged for him to be adopted.' Jaq kept her voice level. There was no need for Marina to know everything. 'A Brazilian dentist and his wife. I'm trying to trace them.'

'How far have you got?'

Jaq told her the little she knew about Carlos Costa and Evangelina.

'You don't know the child's name?'

Jaq shook her head.

'You poor thing.' Marina placed a hand over hers. 'Can I help?'

'Yes, perhaps. You seem to know everyone. And everyone seems to trust you.'

'Does Marco know about this quest? Or Bruno? Anyone at Tecnoproject?'

Jaq shook her head.

'It's complicated. I don't want my employer to think that I'm too distracted to do a job of work.'

Marina leaned back.

'Brazil is a place that works on who you know, on trust and connections. You need to use all your contacts. And maybe you should go to the press ...'

'No.'

'Why not? You've nothing to be ashamed of?'

'It's not shame for myself.' Jaq tested that for a moment. Of course, in hindsight she felt embarrassed by her foolishness in falling in love with a teacher, for her gullibility in believing it was reciprocated, her total ignorance about the facts of life. But despite the nuns, her mother, the roly-poly stinky lawyer, Jaq had never felt shame over her pregnancy, over giving birth, only sorrow that she had never met her son. And that was what had to change. 'I'm ashamed of what my mother did, but she's dead now.'

'There's a Hélio TV show. *Os Desaparecidos. The Missing.* It's incredibly popular, audience of millions. Their success rate is almost 100 per cent.'

The reality TV show that was on screens everywhere? 'No.' It was the last thing she wanted.

'I know the presenter, César. Maybe he'd put you on the show.'

It sounded like the worst idea anyone had ever had. 'No. I don't think so.'

'You could at least talk to him, to his researchers. Find out how they do it, how they make the connections, track people down.' Marina smiled gently. 'I'll be in Rio anyway next month. We could have dinner with César. No obligation, just listen.'

⅄ 4

Tocantins, Brazil

Pedro had to wait for his audience with the Colonel. His clothes were not returned to him, instead he was given a white cotton kaftan, along with a hearty meal.

However tedious he'd found his work at the bank, however much he'd disliked his manager, he would give anything to return to that daily routine.

In the Colonel's headquarters, Pedro had the freedom of the guest quarters, but there was no TV or radio, not even any books. He asked to make a phone call, to reassure his wife, advise his colleagues of his delayed return, but the best they could offer was a pen and paper, thick ivory parchment, a fountain pen and an ink pot. He spent the evening writing to Maria, a long cheerful missive so as not to offend his host or alarm his wife, although he suspected the letter would never be posted.

Pedro was falling asleep when the summons came. The boy who had been attending to him led the way to the vast dining tower, lit by flickering candles.

From the darkness, a pale man emerged to shake his hand. It was difficult to guess his age. His hair was white, his sallow skin was deeply lined, and he was so thin that Pedro could make out his ribs under the fine white robe. He had a slight tremor and his movements, which he kept to the minimum, appeared awkward or painful. He looked more like a ghost than an army officer. Except for the eyes. The eyes gleamed with a strange fire.

The soldier pulled out chairs so that Pedro and the Colonel were seated opposite each other, with the width rather than the length of the table between them.

The usual bean stew was accompanied by thick steaks of beef that had been overcooked and were tough to chew. Pedro noticed that the Colonel barely touched his food.

'What do you know about the Mercury Protocol?' the Colonel asked.

Pedro shrugged. 'Nothing.'

'And yet you came all this way to deliver a message.'

Pedro moved his head, down then up in a gesture of respect. 'You are a very important client for the bank.'

Colonel Cub snorted.

'How is the guest accommodation?'

'Very comfortable, but my wife and colleagues will be getting anxious. I really should be returning home.'

'But you've only just arrived!'

'And now I must leave, sir.'

'You don't like this place?'

'Oh, I like it very much, and if my wife were here with me ...'

'You don't like my company?'

'I didn't mean that, sir.'

'Well, well, little man. Perhaps you are right. You've come a long way to deliver an important message.'

'Thank you, sir.'

'And as soon as you give me all the information I need, I'd be happy to bid you farewell.'

'All the information?'

'Your name, little man?'

'Camargo. My name is Pedro Camargo.'

'Pedro, Pedro.' The Colonel's voice took on a gentle, caressing tone. 'Are you very brave or just very stupid?'

Pedro lowered his eyes. There was no right response to that sort of insult.

'I have your name. Now I want the other names.'

Names? What names? Pedro looked up in alarm.

'You will understand that I can't share any confidential information …'

'Can't or won't?'

The ice in the Colonel's voice chilled Pedro to the bone. He dug his fingernails into the palm of his left hand.

'The bank treats all client information with the utmost respect.' The pain helped him to keep the fear out of his voice. 'You wouldn't like it if we divulged private information about your account.'

The Colonel smiled. 'You're quite right.'

Pedro's body slumped with relief.

The Colonel barked an order and Pedro felt heavy hands descending onto his shoulders, pushing him further down. He yelped, swivelling his head to identify his attacker, the bare-chested giant who had received his message on the first day.

'We wouldn't like that,' the Colonel said. 'We wouldn't like it at all.' He stood and walked round the table until he was directly in front of Pedro. 'In fact, if we were even to suspect that the bank had shared any of our private information …'

In response to a further nod, the guard slid his hands down Pedro's shaking arms, grasping his captive's wrists, pushing him forward and wrenching his hands up behind his back.

'Then the consequences would be very …' Pedro screamed as the rotator cuff muscles and tendons in his right shoulder began to tear. 'Very painful.'

'I swear …' Pedro cried, twisting to the left.

'What do you swear, little man?' The pressure stopped.

'Your privacy is safe in our bank.'

'But it's not, you see,' the Colonel hissed. 'Someone tried to access documents in your bank in Angola. Tried to steal what belongs to us. No one is safe, least of all you, little man, until we have their name.' He nodded. 'All their names.'

When the pressure started again, Pedro could no longer think straight. He'd have given them every name he'd ever known just to make the pain stop. At the sickening pop of his left shoulder dislocating, he began to retch.

As the pressure on the right shoulder increased, he escaped into unconsciousness.

☿ 4

São Paulo, Brazil

A car passed through the deserted streets in Sapiranga. The remnants of last night's festivities were still in evidence. The Festival of Roses had been the perfect end to an extraordinary day.

Marina had lent her visitor a car and a driver for this final day in the south: the most practical way of travelling several hundred miles to visit three dentists.

Jaq had already decided to stop pretending to be a patient. A new approach was needed.

At the first stop, just outside Criciúma, inside a dingy, dirty building, she didn't make it past reception.

'I was wondering,' Jaq kept her lips closed now when she smiled, 'if you could help me to track down an old family friend.' A little misleading, she'd never met him herself, but it seemed a fair description of someone who had care of her son. 'Carlos Costa. A Brazilian dentist who worked in Portugal for a while. Married to Evangelina. With a son now in his twenties. Would you know how I could get in touch again?'

The dental nurse who doubled as receptionist gave a disinterested shrug. 'Dr Costa doesn't work here any more,' she said. 'He moved up north.'

There were stains on the sleeve of her uniform, patches of dried blood, which made Jaq glad she didn't have to undergo treatment here.

'Do you have his new address?'

The receptionist didn't even pretend to search for the information.

'No.'

'Would anyone else here know how to find him.'

'No.'

The next stop, in the centre of Rio Grande, was a little more constructive, in that at least she met a Dr Costa. An elderly man, she quickly established that he was not the dentist who had adopted her son, but at least he took her contact details and promised to ask around.

At the final appointment, in Porto Alegre, the Dr Costa she was looking for had long retired, but the receptionist gave her the name of a practice in São Paulo where his only son, a man in his forties, now worked. A dental practice she'd already visited and dismissed.

On the evening flight from Porto Alegre back to São Paulo, Jaq stared down at the twinkling lights of multiple towns and cities far below, stretching out as far as the eye could see. She'd always known it wouldn't be easy finding her son in a country so vast and so populous.

But was it even possible?

Y 4

Tocantins, Brazil

Pedro awoke in agony. He was back in his cell, lying on his stomach, head hanging over the side of the bed above a tin basin. He groaned as the fire across his back sent flames licking at his useless shoulders.

The boy's thin legs emerged from the shadows and advanced towards him.

'Don't touch me!' Pedro screamed.

The boy ignored him, bending down to remove the basin, replacing it with a glass. He inserted a long straw, guiding it to Pedro's lips, tipping the glass slowly to administer some sweet, syrupy drink.

Within minutes, Pedro's ears began to buzz, and the room started to spin. He fought against another bout of nausea; whatever medicine he'd been given, he preferred to keep it down if it alleviated the agony for even an instant. He tried to ignore the gentle hands of the boy who was undressing him, dipping a cloth into warm water and dabbing it onto his skin.

In his drugged state, the sensation of the boy climbing onto his back was not entirely unpleasant. His son, Luis, had liked to slip into the bed with Pedro and Maria, snuggling in between them in the early hours of the morning. Pedro could never get back to sleep, terrified that one of them might roll over and crush the child, lost in wonder at the fragile beauty of the sleeping toddler. A grown man now, they didn't see Luis as much as Maria would like. A tear strayed from his eyes. Would he ever see his wife or son again?

His arms lay useless at his sides, so he was unable to resist when the boy slipped a wad of cotton between his teeth and tied a gag over his mouth.

'Quick, quick,' the boy whispered.

When the pain came, it was worse than anything that had gone before. Pedro bit down on the cotton as the boy took one shoulder and then the other, yanking them forward so that each ball of bone returned to its socket.

The boy released the gag and dismounted. With surprising strength, he flipped Pedro onto his back, pulling his arms forward now and checking the shoulders for rotation.

Pedro roared with pain, but when he saw the Colonel's face looming above his bed, his screams turned to sobs.

Would this nightmare never end?

Pedro closed his eyes as a chair scraped across the floor.

'I hear you have been unwell,' the Colonel said. There was no trace of irony in his soft voice.

'We take the comfort of our guests very seriously,' the Colonel continued. 'As you can see, we have an expert doctor.'

Pedro felt the light touch of the boy's hand on his brow and heard a murmured exchange in a language he didn't understand.

'I'm told you have a fever.' The Colonel made a tutting noise with his tongue. 'Fortunately, we may have the right medicine to make you better.' He coughed. 'There's just the small matter of payment.'

Pedro's eyes flew open. Seriously? This madman was going to torture him and then make him pay for treatment?

'I don't have any money with me.' Pedro said. 'But if you let me go, I can send some.'

'Oh, I wasn't thinking of money. What I need right now is information,'

'Information?'

'Names.'

However terrible his situation, what sort of man would he be if he escaped from this horror by condemning someone else? A stranger.

'I don't know any names.'

'Then, you'll have to be more careful.'

Pedro bit his lip, trying to control an urge to let out a manic laugh.

'You mentioned how much nicer it would be to be here with your family. I'm sure we could arrange that.'

Empty threats.

'If Maria received news that you were gravely ill, I'm sure she would rush to your side.'

Clearly, they didn't know Maria. Her rushing days were over. Maria would never leave Rio. The Colonel was just guessing. After all, Maria was the single most popular name in Brazil. The next sentence made his heart sink.

'Or perhaps she'd send a message to Luis. To tell him that you've been injured in an accident and that he must come here immediately?'

So, they knew everything. However much he wanted to protect a stranger, would he really sacrifice his son? Condemn him to this hell?

'Did you know that Xica's pregnant?'

Was the Colonel bluffing? How could this man know more about his daughter-in-law than he did?

'Of course, it's still very early, and pregnancies don't always proceed as planned. All it takes is a minor illness, a fall. It would be such a shame if anything happened to her. To your unborn grandchild.' He made a slow tutting noise.

'Alternatively, you could complete your mission and go home to them. There's no doubt that the bank would want you to obey every request of their most important client. You would be doing no more than your duty. After all, I doubt that the scoundrels who attempted to access our information, to steal our property were even clients of the bank.'

'What is it that you want?'

'Just the names. Who opened the secure storage in the bank in Luanda?'

Pedro sighed. This name he could give up without fear of consequence.

'It was a bank employee, Jorge Ferreira.'

'And now he's dead?'

How could they possibly know that?

'Yes, he's dead.'

'And his client?'

A Lisbon lawyer, thousands of miles away in Portugal, safe in fortress Europe, protected by a police force that upheld the law, by an army that took its orders from the government rather than the other way round. Surely a lawyer in a civilised country would be safe from this nutter?

The Colonel brought his face closer. 'The name of his client, Pedro, my dear little man.'

Pedro squeezed his eyes shut and prayed for forgiveness.

'Centeno,' he whispered. 'Carmo Centeno.'

☿ 4

Estoril, Portugal

The news about Jorge Ferreira finally reached Carmo Centeno through her sister. Luisa called three times while she was in a meeting. When the conference finished, Carmo took her phone off silent mode, checked the missed calls and rang her sister back.

'Is everything OK?'

'Did you hear about Jorge?'

'Jorge who?'

'Our sister-in-law's ex brother-in-law.'

It took Carmo a moment to follow the thorniest branch of the family tree. 'Ferreira? What about him? I was speaking to him just recently. Actually, he owes me a call.'

'Forget that. He's dead.'

'Dead? *Santos!* What happened?'

'No one's very clear. He was at work. A sudden heart attack.'

'*Meu Deus*. How old was he?'

'In his forties. Shocking isn't it. I guess moving to Angola was more stressful than we realised.'

Carmo put down the phone and closed her eyes. She remembered the warmth in Jorge Ferreira's voice as he promised to call back, perhaps meet up. A single tear escaped from her left eye and rolled down her cheek.

After the call had finished, she wiped her face, saved the file she'd been working on and closed the office for the day.

Carmo drove past Guincho and up into the hills, leaving the car at the side of the road and climbing through the forest until she reached the little chapel hidden among the jagged stones, great boulders of granite that protected this place from tourists and the west wind.

She sat for a while, eyes closed, not praying but remembering the man who first brought her to this place. The tall trees rustled in the breeze, the scent of sun-warmed pine and burnt-sugar succulent filling her senses.

Jorge called the Serra da Sintra the mountains of the moon. He'd known this nature reserve like the back of his hand, every path and peak, every nook and cranny, every secluded spot where lovers could meet far from the prying eyes of their families.

A sob escaped her. If only they'd been braver. Jorge was ready to leave his wife, his children for her, but she hadn't been prepared to make the same commitment. He'd taken the transfer to Angola to give her time.

Now their time had run out.

Carmo climbed to the viewpoint and waited until the granite boulders began to glow pink. The sun hovered above the sea, a pair of kitesurfers, performing impossible acrobatics, cast long shadows far below.

She didn't want to be alone any more.

When she reached the kitesurfing café on Guincho beach, her son was still in his wetsuit, a bottle of beer in one hand, a phone in the other. The owner of Café Carbon was there too, standing under the outdoor shower, his hairy chest and black beard smoothed by the torrent of water.

Christiano put down the phone and raised his beer, condensation dipping from the glass.

'*Mãe*,' he grinned at her. 'Fancy a beer?'

She shook her head.

'You free for dinner?' she asked.

'Maybe,' he said. 'I was heading out with Xavier.'

'He's welcome to join us.'

'At home?'

She nodded.

As the car swept into the drive, Carmo noticed that the office lights were on. Strange. She'd definitely turned everything off before she locked up. And no one else had a key. She drove into the courtyard but remained in the car until she heard the roar of Xavier's jeep on the hill, followed by the crunch of gravel as he turned up the drive.

Christiano's bare feet emerged from the passenger door, he jumped out, still in his wetsuit.

'What's for dinner, *Mãe?*'

Carmo put a finger to her lips and pointed to the office.

'I think someone's broken in,' she whispered.

Xavier appeared at her side, fully dressed in canvas shoes, jeans and a T-shirt with ECOPTO emblazoned across the chest. 'Want me to take a look?'

She nodded.

He moved swiftly over the flagstones and stopped beside a window, peering in through the glass.

He turned back. 'Call the police.'

Frankfurt Airport, Germany

The Christmas decorations in Frankfurt airport were a little more restrained than Manchester, and the carols piped through the intercom more familiar. The scent of warm gingerbread filled the transfer corridor, a young woman in a traditional *dirndl* handing out little cookies in the shape of Christmas trees with piped icing decoration.

Jaq refused the cellophane-wrapped gift and moved swiftly through security, scanning the illuminated screens for her flight to São Paulo, heart sinking as she registered the delay.

Through the glass wall of the international departures lounge, thick flurries of snow twirled in the wind, silvery-white against a pewter sky. It had been clear and icy in Teesside, dull and wet in Manchester. Where had this snowstorm appeared from? What if transatlantic flights were cancelled because of the weather? Her options were limited now; the airline had her box. Somewhere in the bowels of this airport, Mercúrio's passport to freedom was travelling across subterranean conveyors towards the plane resting on the runway.

Her phone pinged. A text from Johan.

Baby Chloe arrived safely this morning. Mother and baby fine. Father exhausted.

She texted back her congratulations and then spotted a free

computer outside an internet café. She grabbed a coffee and logged in, ordering chocolates for Emma and a cigar for Johan. She spent a bit of time looking for catapults, rejecting the adult hunting models in favour of a picture book with detailed diagrams of siege weapons and instructions on how to build a scale-model trebuchet. She clicked the gift wrap option and composed a note.

Ben, thank you for helping me and lending me your catapult. When I get back, let's build something bigger and better! See you soon. Jaq.

She was about to log off when a thought occurred to her. Whatever happened to Elena Azevedo, the woman who picked up the wrong boarding pass at Guarulhos Airport?

Her search produced an instant news result, one that brought a chill to her bones. Elena was dead. Murdered. The body of the young woman, aged 29, had been discovered in a waste bin in the Cumbica industrial estate of São Paulo. She'd last been seen hailing a taxi to take her to Guarulhos Airport on her way to visit her boyfriend in Miami. The police were looking for the taxi driver.

Jaq swallowed hard and was about to look for more information when a *Breaking News* item flashed onto the screen. *Murder at Schiphol Airport*, the headline screamed, along with a picture of a woman about her age, with dark, shoulder-length hair, discovered with a broken neck in a cleaners' storeroom in Schiphol Airport. Jacinta Guedes had been due to travel home to Brazil for Christmas. A last-minute booking on the very flight that Jaq had missed. She sat staring into space as her session on the computer timed out, roused from paralysis by the clatter of the departure board as it refreshed, the split flaps of the electro-mechanical Pragotron announcing that the delayed flight to São Paulo was now boarding.

Jaq glanced over her shoulder as she moved towards the departure gate. No one behind her. No one running to the gate to stop her. As she passed through the final security check and walked down the covered gangplank to the plane, the catatonia of denial gave way to a shiver of fear.

Why would someone want to kill her? It couldn't be Crazy Gloves; he could have shot her in the beach house. No, he needed her alive, at least until she brought the strongbox to him. So, who were the buzz-cut tattooed soldier boys? Had they detained and killed innocent Elena Azevedo, just because she had a boarding card in the name of Jaq Silver? And what about poor Jacinta Guedes who'd snapped up the vacant seat on a plane that Jaq had missed?

Had she overlooked something important? Was all this trouble connected to the empty strongbox that was stowed below her in the hold of this plane? Or was there some connection with her work in Brazil?

She settled into her seat and buckled up.

Twelve hours of thinking time.

Jaq took out her notebook and began to work back over her time in Brazil, starting from the day when everything started to go wrong.

⅄ 4

São Paulo, Brazil

The São Paulo hotel swimming pool wasn't really large enough for proper exercise, but at least the lack of heating kept other guests out of the water. After a day in the office, Jaq was glad of the opportunity to stretch her limbs a little by swimming in a figure of eight.

As she pulled herself from the pool, she noticed a missed WhatsApp call from the Lisbon lawyer. Had Carmo managed to use her connections to find a new lead?

Jaq dried her hands, wrapped her hair in a towel and dialled.

'Any progress with the dentist?' she asked.

'I have other news, bad news.'

'I'm listening.' Jaq gathered up her things and began to walk towards the elevator.

'My friend in Angola ...'

Jaq entered the empty lift and pressed the button for the seventh floor. Nothing happened, so she waved her room card against a sensor and pressed again. The doors began to close. Through a gap in the door a tattoo-covered arm appeared, followed by a shoulder. Jaq pressed the door open button and a man in army fatigues pushed his way in.

'Com liçença.'

Jaq was suddenly aware of her near nakedness. 'I'll call you back in a minute.' She cut the call and dropped her head so that the turban opened. Catching the falling towel, she wrapped it round her hips. In the elevator mirror she caught his grin and gave him her coldest stare.

'Don't worry, *moça*. Just admiring the view,' he said.

Moça. Girl. Infantilise then harass.

Two could play at that game.

She looked him up and down. Boring beefcake, from his buzz-cut to the tight short-sleeved olive T-shirt, through the wide leather belt with an odd-shaped buckle, baggy camouflage trousers and black ankle boots with dark-green laces, then slowly back up. 'Not much to see from here, *moço*,' she said.

He took a step back. When the lift stopped at the fifth floor a young couple peered in.

'*Descendo?*' Going down?

Jaq let them enter. She'd rather not be alone with angry beefcake. Before the doors could close again, he pushed past and hurried out.

When the lift started rising, the young woman tutted in irritation.

Jaq shrugged her shoulders in apology. '*Desculpe.*' She pointed at the up arrow. '*Só um minutinho.*'

At the seventh floor, Jaq escaped from the lift, the carpet soft against her bare feet.

Inside her room she locked the door and called Carmo back.

'Sorry, I lost you in the lift.' Along with my temper. 'Look don't bother your friend with the Angola connection. I don't think the papers were worth—'

Carmo interrupted her. 'He's dead.'

'Dead? Who?'

'Jorge Ferreira. My friend in Angola.'

'How?'

'At work. A heart attack they think.'

'Carmo, I'm so sorry—'

'He was my age.'

Was she crying? Jaq wished she could send a hug through the ether.

'Poor guy.'

'It happened just after I called him. He went to the bank vault to look for the originals of your documents.' Carmo's voice was recovering its strength. 'When they found him, he was dead, and the originals were gone.'

'Gone?' Jaq sank onto the unmade bed. 'You think his death was connected to my documents?'

'The bank claim it was coincidence. They insist that he was alone in the vault, that no one else went in or out, that the file must have already been empty.'

'You think that's likely?'

'It gets worse.' Carmo voice was hesitant. 'There was a break-in at my office last night.'

'You think it's connected.'

'The police don't think so. They think it was just the usual petty theft, but …'

'But?'

'They took my laptop and a few paper files. They didn't take the TV or my gold watch and earrings, which were in an unlocked drawer.

'Maybe they were disturbed?'

'I don't think so. I was out when it happened. And your file was one of the ones they took.'

Jaq thought back to the documents she'd left with Carmo when they met in Estoril. The only originals she'd handed over were the worthless share certificates and mining concessions. The birth certificate and adoption form had been scanned and returned to her.

'Your laptop files are encrypted, right?' Jaq asked. 'And backed up?'

'Of course.' Carmo sighed. 'Let's hope that's enough.'

4

Tocantins, Brazil

Pedro was suffering from the worst pain imaginable. Not the dislocation of his shoulders, which had been agony enough, nor the crude manipulation that had returned the head of the humerus to its place in the glenoid fossa (as the bare-chested soldier explained later, displaying a terrifying amount of medical knowledge for a torturer), but the torment of knowing that he had sentenced someone else to persecution, or even death. All in vain. The Colonel had broken his promise. The madman had no intention of releasing him. Pedro's family: Maria, Luis, Xica and his unborn grandchild were in as much danger as they had ever been.

And all for what?

The Colonel seemed in a cheerful mood, happy to have Pedro wheeled in at dinner time, having him served even though he could still not use his arms and sit there with them dangling uselessly at his sides while his captor ate.

'Good evening, little man.' He welcomed his prisoner as if he was a long-lost friend. 'And how are we today?'

Pedro had learned to reply to these enquiries with equivocal murmurs. 'Fine.' Any hint of protest met with fury and threats.

'Good, good,' the Colonel beamed.

'The name you gave me.' He paused and looked up. 'Centeno, wasn't it? Very interesting. Very interesting indeed.'

He put down his knife and fork and reached for his mug of

hot milk and rum. Despite his hunger, the smell made Pedro feel nauseous.

'My people went to take a look. Just a lawyer doing their job, you might think? Well not at all, my little man, my poor little, gullible fool. Not at all. Turns out the Lisbon lawyers were in league with our great enemy.'

Pedro murmured something non-committal.

'So, tell me, little man. What exactly is the bank's connection to the Ribeiro da Silva family?'

It was a common enough name. Pedro couldn't think of any significant clients in the Rio branch of *Banco Espirito Santo* by that name, any high-worth customers he dealt with personally, but it didn't mean there weren't any.

'I don't know, sir.'

'Is the name Silver familiar to you?'

'No, sir.'

The Colonel nodded to the soldier. Pedro screamed, even before the hammer came crashing down onto his kneecap.

'You're sure of that, Pedro?'

'Whatever you want. I'll say whatever you want.'

'Oh, no, that would never do, we don't like liars, do we?'

Pedro tried to protect his other knee with the result that his hand took the brunt of the next hammer blow.

'Shhh, now.' The Colonel waved away the noise. 'Such a fuss, such a terrible fuss, and all perfectly avoidable.'

The guard stuffed a rag into his mouth; Pedro began to gag.

'Of course, Carmo Centeno will have to pay, but there is time enough for that. It wouldn't do to close down their dirty little operation too soon, wouldn't do at all.'

Pedro bowed his head. Through his pain he formulated a prayer. A forlorn wish to end this nightmare, even if it meant his death. He didn't want to live long enough to be responsible for a European lawyer's death.

'If we tighten the net too quickly, a little fish might wriggle out and escape.' He chortled. 'And sometimes, the little fish, the Silver fish, turn out to be more troublesome than we thought.'

Pedro raised his eyes to meet those of the Colonel, silently pleading with him.

'Don't you worry. We have operatives everywhere. My men know exactly where Jaq Silver is. No security. She's been careless.'

The Colonel nodded at the bare-chested torturer who handed him the hammer.

'Very careless indeed.'

Y 3

São Paulo, Brazil

It took less than a week for to Jaq complete the design review at Aérex. Rather than commute from São Paulo, she checked out of her hotel and moved into the guest accommodation on the base.

Under her guidance, the team of in-house engineers worked through S&M concepts of process safety – simplify, substitute, minimise, moderate, mitigate. The final team recommendations looked like simple common sense, but simplicity takes wisdom, sense is rarely common and some things are only blindingly obvious with hindsight.

Marina, not long returned from Sapiranga, approached her before the final presentation.

'I hear good things.'

'Your engineering team is great.'

'Handpicked.' Marina beamed. 'Are you still looking for an apartment in São Paulo?' she asked.

'Yes.'

'I might be able to help. One of my friends is working abroad. If you don't mind moving out when he needs it, it could be a short-term solution.'

'What sort of rent would he be looking for?'

'Peppercorn. Just enough to cover the bills.'

'That sounds promising.'

'I'll check if there is transport available. If you're free, we could go and see it after work.'

Jaq wasn't expecting the transport to be aerial, but as the helicopter crossed the Dutra highway with nose-to-tail traffic all the way in to the smog-bound city, she was immensely glad of the option.

Marina piloted the helicopter with calm assurance, taking a loop to show Jaq the long valley of the river Paraíba do Sul, fed by streams from the Serra da Mantiqueira to the west and the Serra do Mar to the east, a mountain range that ran the length of Brazil, rising steeply from the sea to form a weather barrier protecting the high plains.

They flew over the port of Santos, the busiest maritime port in South America, and along the coast, over a long procession of container vessels and supertankers queuing for their turn to enter Baía de Santos. The sun glinted on the railway tracks as trains, each a kilometre long, passed each other going in opposite directions.

'What are the trains carrying?' Jaq asked.

The sleeve of Marina's jacket fell back as she flicked an overhead switch to hand the controls to the co-pilot. A single tattoo decorated her forearm.

'Mainly raw materials for export,' Marina said. 'Iron ore, soy beans, sugar, crude oil.'

'And imports?'

'Manufactured goods. And clever engineers from Europe.'

Jaq grinned at her.

The helicopter headed north, towards the city.

A pink skyscraper towered above the Jardim Europa district of São Paulo, a building so fancy it had its own helipad. They landed and Marina made an arrangement with the co-pilot.

'He'll pick us up later.' She waved as the helicopter took off again. 'Come, the flat is on the tenth floor.'

They called the elevator and, once inside, Marina stared into a camera and then punched in a code. The lift doors opened into the apartment itself, an open-plan living and dining room with a galley kitchen. Picture windows, floor to ceiling, looked out over the city. The walls were covered in framed paintings, reproductions of masterpieces by Miró, Picasso and others.

'Once you're inside, no one else can use the lift to gain entry unless you admit them.' Marina pointed to the illuminated red light, a lock symbol over the lift door. 'You can only unlock it from the inside.'

Jaq padded across the polished wood floor and opened the door into the bedroom and en suite. The apartment block was part of a gated community, and directly below Jaq could see a generously sized pool surrounded by a pretty garden.

'Wow, this is amazing.'

'It's yours until Carnival, if you want it.'

This was a millionaire's flat, not the sort of place a jobbing contract engineer could expect to live in.

'You sure I can afford this?'

'Better that it's not left empty. All you need to do is cover the running costs.'

'It's perfect. But shouldn't I talk to your friend?'

'Trust me, he'll be delighted. And there's an old motorbike in the underground garage. Keys there.' Marina pointed to a wooden bowl with a set of keys and fobs. 'The elevator takes you straight down to the basement.' She pressed a switch and the red locked symbol changed to a green key. The lift doors opened.

'I'm stunned.'

'You can move in tonight if you like.'

'Really?'

This was almost too good to be true.

'There are a few formalities; you'll need to give security a retinal print, but I can sort the rest out and send for your stuff.'

Once Jaq was settled in, Marina took her on a tour of the pool, gym, gardens and café. They ordered coffee and sat in the shade of a large magnolia tree.

'You know it's not safe to walk about outside the compound?'

Jaq peered through the iron railings. 'It seems so peaceful.'

'This is one of the better districts, but the obvious affluence attracts criminals like flies. Don't walk anywhere. Never take public transport. Drive or get an official taxi. And if you get stopped, if someone pulls a gun on you, don't resist. They have nothing to lose and they'll shoot you in the blink of an eye. Just give them everything. Best to have a dummy wallet with some cash that you're prepared to hand over. Don't wear your best jewellery or expensive watches.'

'Marina, do I look like someone who wears expensive jewellery and watches?'

'You epitomise feminine grace, without adornment, Jaq.' There was a tinge of sadness in her voice. Before Jaq could think of how to reply, she'd clapped her hands together. 'I don't know about you, but I think it might be cocktail time.'

'I take it you're not flying the chopper tonight?'

'I'll leave that to my co-pilot. Do you like Japanese food?'

'Sure.'

The concierge arranged a taxi to take them to the restaurant. Marina insisted they take a detour via Tecnoproject so Jaq could see how easy the commute would be.

They drank sake with the sashimi.

'May I ask you about your tattoo?'

'This one?' Marina rolled up her sleeve. 'I had all the others removed, but this serves as a reminder.'

'A reminder of what?'

'Of my Army days.'

'I thought you served in the Air Force.'

'In Brazil, the Air Force counts as part of the Army. Brazil is so vast, we're often called upon to transport men, provide air cover.'

'When was the last war. 1945?'

Marina laughed. 'Our wars tend to be civil wars.'

'Have you ever seen a tattoo of a snake with a pipe in its mouth?'

Marina frowned. 'That was the insignia of FEB, the Brazil

expeditionary force. They were criticised for avoiding conflict. *"Mais fácil uma cobra fumar um cachimbo, do que a FEB embarcar para o combate."'*

'You're more likely to see a snake smoking a pipe than FEB fighting?'

'Exactly, but unfair. Brazil was the only South American country to send troops to support the allies in the Second World War. FEB adopted the insignia of a smoking cobra and now *a cobra vai fumar* means that a fight is inevitable.'

'I see.'

'Unfortunately, there are some nutjob paramilitary groups who've adopted that brand. Why do you ask?'

Jaq thought back to the man in the lift. 'It's nothing.'

Marina checked her phone then signalled to the waiter to bring the bill. 'I have to go.'

Y 3

São Paulo, Brazil

Jaq settled easily into her new accommodation with its clean lines and panoramic view, climate control, gym and pool. If she hadn't been so frustrated at the lack of progress in the search for her son, she might have accepted this new life of luxury with pleasure.

Instead, she spent long hours at the Tecnoproject office reviewing the safety studies for oil refineries, swam, ate dinner and collapsed into bed – waking in the early hours of the morning.

Perhaps Carmo was making better progress.

Portugal was four hours ahead. Jaq called her lawyer.

'How are you doing?'

'Better, thanks.'

'Any news on what happened to ...' Jaq wished she could remember his name, 'your friend in Angola?'

Carmo let out a long sigh. 'I spoke to Jorge Ferreira's boss at the bank. The autopsy confirmed a sudden heart attack.' There was a pause, the rustle of a paper tissue, the sniff of someone trying not to cry. 'He was alone in the bank registry when he collapsed. By the time the paramedics got to him, there was nothing they could do.'

'I'm so sorry.'

'The bank have no records of ever holding your original documents. they claim that Ferreira was looking in the wrong place.'

'So, his death was unrelated.' Jaq felt a surge of relief and then a tide of guilt. 'Are you OK?'

'I'm taking some time out.'

Disappointing, but inevitable. 'I completely understand.'

'Time out to focus on your case.' There was a new, sharper tone to Carmo's voice. 'I don't buy the coincidence theory, so I went to see my uncle in hospital.'

Jaq sat up straight. Could roly-poly stinky lawyer finally do something useful?

'He didn't make much sense.'

Jaq's shoulders sank.

'But something he said, sent me back to the archive.'

'And?'

'You remember we searched for anything related to your mother or her family and came up with nothing.'

Jaq pressed the button on the coffee machine. 'So?'

'We were looking under Ribeiro da Silva.'

A light flashed to tell her that the grounds needed emptying. 'And?' She pulled out the drawer and tipped it into the bin, rinsing it out before slotting it back.

'Jaq, what was your father's name?'

'Anton Oleich Sakoshansky.'

'Sakoshansky.' Carmo repeated the name. 'That's what my uncle said. That's where we found it.'

'Found what?'

'A note in the digital archive, under Sakoshansky, not Silva. Dated 1988. I'm sending you a copy now.'

A message pinged and Jaq opened the image: a letter from a lawyers' office in Salvador de Bahia, with a brief handwritten message.

Dear Mr Centeno, Thank you for your letter of the above referenced date. We confirm that we are still in possession of the item you refer to. However, we received strict instructions from our client and are unable to discuss or enter into further correspondence during the lifetime of Maria dos Anjos Sakoshansky.

'I don't understand.'

'Nor do I.'

Jaq pressed the button again. This time it was coffee that needed replenishing.

'Carmo, I am so sorry about your friend, but how is this helping me to find my son?' She didn't need distractions right now.

'Aren't you a little bit curious?'

'Nope.' Jaq cut open a bag of coffee beans and poured them into the top of the machine. 'So far everything my mother's side of the family has left for me turns out to be emotional stink bombs or grenades.'

'But you're in Brazil, aren't you? I thought you could follow it up?'

Jaq pressed the button only to be told that the coffee machine was low on water. She'd never come across a more needy kitchen appliance.

'If I happen to be in Salvador, sure.' An unlikely destination. There were no Carlos Costas on her list with practices in Salvador.

'What if I call the lawyer direct,' Carmo asked. 'See if I can find out some more?'

'Knock yourself out.'

Jaq drank her coffee and took the elevator down to the garden for an early-morning swim. She threw her phone onto a lounger and covered it with a towel before she took off her dress. Diving into the cool water, she began her workout.

A noise at the fence attracted her attention. A metal object being dragged across the bars.

'Oi, *moça*. Remember me?'

The sun had not long risen, but the motion-sensitive security light clicked into life, illuminating the hammer held by a tattooed arm poking through the fence. Even without the smoking snake, she recognised the voice, the nasal whine of the leering beefcake from the hotel lift.

One of the security guards came running from the office.

'*Oi!* You! Clear off.'

Jaq carried on swimming and by the time she'd completed 50 lengths both men were gone.

She dried herself, slipped the dress over her wet swimsuit and walked over towards the office.

'*Bom dia.*'

'Hi. Did you get a good look at the man outside the fence?'

The guard tapped his keyboard and brought up a picture. Just as she thought, the man from the hotel lift. What was he doing here?

'Have you seen him before?'

The guard squinted at the screen, forwarded it a few frames then back again. 'Maybe, maybe not. This town is full of crazies. Did he bother you?'

'Not really.' Was that true?

'If I see him again, I'll call the police.'

It should have reassured her, but somehow it didn't.

A headache threatened as she reached the office: the lights too bright, the chatter too noisy.

The clicking of wheels passing over the floor tiles made her look up. Bruno was touring the open plan office, stopping to speak to each of the engineers at their workstations, his small suitcase following behind. He was looking smarter than usual, the tasselled loafers, chinos and polo shirts replaced by polished brogues, a well-cut suit, shirt and tie.

He approached her desk last.

'How's it going?'

Jaq bit her lip. There was still no sign of the promised work from Cuperoil. How long would her boss be willing to pay her if she wasn't doing any chargeable work? Perhaps now was not the time to confess.

'Fine,' she smiled.

'You can bring me up to speed when I get back.' He turned. *'Bom trabalho!'* Bruno addressed the whole room.

'Boa viagem!' the engineers replied.

After he left, Jaq put her head in her hands. This was all hopeless. She'd made a mistake coming here, taking this job. Wasting time in an office when she should be out on the road, knocking on the door of every dental surgery in Brazil until she found her son.

Marco sat on her desk, two coffees in hand. They'd hardly exchanged two words since the first visit to Aérex 'You look like you need this.' He handed her one.

Jaq thanked him and took a sip. 'I just don't feel as if I'm doing anything.'

Marco's laugh was as bitter as the coffee. 'Says the engineer with the highest billable hours in Tecnoproject!'

She stared at him. Apart from the visit to Marina in Sapiranga and the work for Aérex, she'd done nothing. Less than a fortnight's billable work in the two months she'd been in Brazil. Either he was mistaken or deliberately goading her.

She refused to rise to the bait. 'I'd like to do more.'

'You're thinking like a European. Business in Brazil is slow,' he moved his hand like a snake, 'and sinuous. One person does all the hard work, visits a customer regularly for years and then one of the other engineers gets the contract.'

She glanced up at him. Was he still sore about the visit to Aérex? Perhaps it was best to address this head-on.

'You'd been visiting Marina for years. Did you mind?'

His smile didn't reach his eyes. 'It's all about teamwork. And Marina is a very special client. How's the flat by the way?'

So Marco knew about the flat. She'd checked the arrangement with Bruno before she accepted, in case there was a potential conflict of interest.

'Fine.' Best not to sound over enthusiastic.

He brought his face closer to hers. 'What's he getting in return?' He ran his tongue over his top lip.

She stood up. Took a step back. 'It's just a favour between friends.'

'He's found you the finest flat in São Paulo and you think he wants nothing in return?'

Jaq blushed. 'I haven't even met him.'

'I'm talking about Paulo.'

'Marina,' Jaq corrected.

Marco laughed. 'You need to learn how we do business in Latin America.' He glanced around the room. 'You could be a little nicer to me, you know. We should help one another out. How about a drink tonight and I'll explain how?' He made a lewd gesture, thrusting his hips towards her. 'You scratch my back, I'll scratch yours.'

Marco was advancing when Rosario entered the room. Jaq took the opportunity to grab her bag and flee.

Back in the flat, she stood in the shower for a long time, trying to wash the memory from her skin. Why had she run away? Why hadn't she punched him? Kneed him in the groin? Spat in his face? Or at the very least screamed the roof down and reported him? The sudden switch from bitterness to such a crude sexual advance had taken her by surprise. He wouldn't have dared try that while Bruno was in the office.

Had Marco made similar advances to other women at work, or only the ones he disliked? That part of the whole episode made her feel sick. Marco wasn't flirting, he wasn't asking her out because he liked her, he was using sexual threat to belittle and scare.

Bruno and Marco were good friends. How would her boss react when she told him? What if this, coupled with a lack of work from Cuperoil, led to termination of her employment?

Not that she cared about the job itself. But her visa depended on Tecnoproject. Could she continue to travel around Brazil without their sponsorship?

There was only one person in Brazil whose advice she trusted.

♼ 3

Rio de Janeiro, Brazil

The first glimpse of some cities makes a person catch their breath. Then there are those that punch you in the gut and take your wind clean away. Rio de Janeiro was one of them.

Jaq pinched herself as the flight from São Paulo banked over a sheltered bay ringed by absurd pointy mountains. The sea was azure blue, the mountains emerald green and the sandy beaches, where the two met, shone pure gold.

It was not until she opened the curtains of her hotel room and stepped out onto the balcony overlooking Copacabana beach, followed the line of surf, the waves crashing onto the beach, the tinkle of sand, that she was able to believe what she was seeing. Possibly the most beautiful city on earth.

After her encounter with Marco, Jaq decided to refocus on the real reason for coming to Brazil. She wasn't here to design nitrogen propulsion systems or reduce Cuperoil's carbon footprint. Her principal objective was not to improve the safety of hydrogen-powered planes or to fix exploding shoes; she was in Brazil to find her son.

There was a Rio de Janeiro dentist on her list. Marina was visiting friends in town. She could kill two birds with one stone. Visit Dr Carlos Costa in Rio and follow up Marina's suggestion to meet an expert in tracking down missing persons.

Before leaving São Paulo, she'd called Bruno and he'd approved a couple of days personal leave.

'You've been working too hard,' he said. 'Take some downtime to recharge your batteries.'

She thought it best not to mention her planned meeting with Marina. Aérex was after all a key client of Tecnoproject. At what point did the professional and personal become blurred?

In any case, she wasn't only here for Marina. Her first task was a visit to the dental clinic. She took the metro to the Alfonso Pena station and walked the rest of the way to the private hospital it operated from.

'Bom dia.'

'Dr Carlos Costa, please.'

'Do you have an appointment?'

'Yes.'

The receptionist clicked on her computer keyboard and pointed at a row of chairs. *'Só um minutinho.'*

Jaq took a seat as the receptionist continued her phone call. She looked around the empty waiting room. On the wall were portraits of the consultants. She stood and inspected each one, heart sinking as she came to Dr Carlos Takayamo Costa. There was no doubting the Japanese heritage in his eyes and hair. She thought back to the passport-sized photos of Carlos and Evangelina in the convent files. This was definitely not her man. Another wasted day.

Back in her hotel room, the room phone rang.

Marina's deep voice caressed her ear. 'Good journey?'

'Smooth.'

'How's the room?'

'Beautiful view.'

'It's even better from the pool. I'm here with César. Meet you on the rooftop?'

The top floor of the hotel was given over to a generously sized swimming pool and outdoor cocktail bar. Jaq paused as she exited the lift to admire the dizzying vista, following the shoreline past

Copacabana and Ipanema to the extraordinary rocky outcrops beyond.

Marina was perched on a bar stool, lost in conversation with the bare-chested barman. Dressed to kill, hair piled into a bun, long diamante earrings sparkling in the sunshine, a halter-neck satin evening dress and ivory heels, Marina made everyone around her look drab. Jaq smoothed down her plain shift dress and adjusted her sandal straps before walking round the pool to embrace her.

'Jaq, this is César.'

Jaq had barely noticed Marina's companion, a middle-aged man in jeans and a polo shirt, long hair in a ponytail, neatly trimmed beard and thick square glasses. He held a small glass of beer in his hand.

'*Encantado.*' He took her outstretched hand and kissed it. '*Beleza.*' His thin, wet lips rested a little too long.

'You were right about the view.' Jaq pulled her hand away to address Marina. 'It's glorious up here.'

'What are you drinking?' Marina signalled to the bartender.

Jaq ordered a Caipiroska and settled onto a bar stool.

'Is this your first time in Rio?' César asked.

'Yes.'

'Sugar Loaf Mountain.' César pointed to the iconic peak, bathed in pink light as the sun began to set. 'It's definitely worth the cable-car ride to the top.' He turned and pointed away from the beach to Rio's other famous landmark, the huge white statue of Christ the Redeemer, arms open wide. 'Unlike a trip up Corcovado, which is just one long queue.'

The drinks arrived and they clinked glasses. 'Beyond beautiful.' Jaq took a sip.

'And ugly in equal measure.' Marina sipped a cocktail that mirrored the sunset: grenadine, orange juices and tequila. 'The *favelas* are among the most violent, most deprived places in the world.'

'And full of the most fascinating stories.' César said.

'Tell Jaq about your show,' Marina prompted.

'Which one?'

There was something about César that made Jaq uncomfortable, but she couldn't quite put her finger on why. Was his self-regarding arrogance hiding something else?

'*The Missing*.'

César puffed up his chest. 'Well, it all started with the *Araguaia* martyrs. But we moved on to other cases.'

'The *Araguaia* martyrs?' Jaq asked.

'How much do you know about Brazil's history?'

César didn't wait for her answer before ploughing on.

'There was a military coup in 1964. The democratically elected President, João Goulart, we all call him Jango, was replaced by a military dictatorship that ruled until 1985. The army had a habit of "disappearing" those who disagreed with them.' He waved his beer glass. 'There was a particularly aggressive period from 1968 to 1973 when they targeted communists. Their bodies were never found.'

'So, *The Missing* is about what happened to those who died?'

'Initially. But we moved on to other stories, those with happier endings.'

'Jaq, tell César your story,' Marina urged.

César held up a hand. 'I need to eat first. Have you booked anything?'

'Not yet.'

'I can probably get us a table at Oro.'

'Really?' Marina looked impressed.

César made a call.

'They can fit us in early. Is 8 p.m. OK? It's not far.'

'Perfect.'

'I'll meet you there.'

Marina watched him leave, phone glued to his ear. 'He's a good journalist,' she said by way of apology.

A taxi took them along the seafront. A wide boulevard ran between the beach and the finest buildings in Rio. Jaq had wanted to walk, but Marina claimed it was too dangerous.

'I thought Leblon was one of the better neighbourhoods,' Jaq said.

'Affluent means dangerous. There are armed gangs up there,' Marina pointed to the twinkling lights of the favelas. 'And they come down to the wealthiest spots to hunt.'

How could people live with such inequality? What pleasure could there be in wealth if you had to shut yourself away to enjoy it. Wouldn't a fairer world be a more enjoyable one? For everyone?

The restaurant was a couple of blocks back from the beach. César was already waiting, phone still glued to his ear. He reminded Jaq of Gregor, her cheating ex-husband, perhaps that was why she had taken such a dislike to him.

The food was delicious. After the blow-out of the *churrasco*, it was refreshing to be served tiny quantities of simple food, every plate bursting with flavour. The richer you were, the less you ate. Those who did hard, manual work needed fuel. Those who travelled by car and lifted only phones, laptops and cocktail glasses ate for entertainment.

'So, Jaq,' Cesar waited until the last course. 'Marina tells me you are looking for a relative.'

Jaq glanced at Marina to check how much she had told César. Marina gave an imperceptible shake of the head.

'A baby adopted in Portugal, brought to Brazil.'

'Do you have a photo?'

'Only as a baby.' Jaq pulled out the photocopy of the photograph she had found in the convent and handed it to César.

He repressed a shudder, sighed and handed it back to her.'

'And you think he made it to adulthood?' he muttered.

'Pardon?' She was getting angry.

'I'm sorry, I'd love to help, but there needs to be something that grabs the public. Why would anyone bother getting in touch otherwise? Without a hook, the story is just too distressingly ordinary. And the chances of success are vanishingly small.'

He folded his napkin.

'Tell you what, though, if you do find him, I'd be happy to have you both on the show. We can always recreate the search. Add a bit of drama, human interest.' He leaned across and kissed Marina. 'Got to fly. Film crew waiting.'

He took Jaq's hand. 'Good luck.'

She pulled it away before he could kiss it. 'Thanks.' For nothing, she thought bitterly.

Marina shook her head. 'I'm sorry. It's my fault.'

The waiter brought the bill. Marina opened it and her disgust deepened. 'He didn't even pay his share. I'd forgotten what a prick that man is.'

'I'll get this.'

'No chance,' Marina smiled. 'I brought you here on this wild goose chase. You're my guest.'

'He is right, though.' Jaq sighed. 'It's hopeless.'

Marina took her hand. 'Don't,' she said. 'You're stronger than this. Come dancing with me.' She checked her watch, rose gold encrusted with zircon crystals that sparkled in the candlelight. 'It's too early for Miroir, but we can cruise a couple of the smaller clubs first.'

Jaq shook her head. 'Not tonight. I should get some sleep.'

Marina pursed her lips in disappointment.

'You're in Rio for the first time.'

'But I'm not here to enjoy myself. I'm here to search for my son.'

Marina opened her arms wide. 'This city is a melting pot. Rio at night is where everyone meets: town and country, young and old, rich and poor. If you are to have any chance of understanding my country, you need to experience this city at night.'

She had a point.

Y 3

São Paulo, Brazil

Oskar received his orders straight from Colonel Cub.

The building security was tighter here than in most places. The rich knew how to look after their own. Fortunately, his time in signals had equipped him with all the necessary skills and an inexhaustible supply of ex-military mates looking for cash jobs with no questions asked. He chose one of the younger ones, Leon, because Oskar had trained him, and he was easy on the eye. People in authority tended to trust the younger ones when it came to digital stuff. If only they knew.

Oskar shot out two of the security cameras with a rifle. It would only have taken two bullets if the damn parrots hadn't gotten in the way.

Leon drove and Oskar hid under a blanket in the back of the RIMPO van, just in case security had taken a picture last time he tried to attract the target's attention. Sure enough, the van was stopped at the gate.

'Bom dia.'

Oskar lay in the dark, heart pumping in anticipation.

'Hi,' Leon said. 'We just picked up a fault message from the security system.'

'Not from here.' The security guard sounded irritated. 'I didn't call anyone out.'

'It's automatic with system 2000. Can you check if there's a problem with ...' Leon pretended to check his notes. 'East six and seven.'

The boy was smooth. Inside the van, Oskar smiled. He'd been trained by a master.

'*Porra!* You're right.' The guard was back. 'Two cameras out.'

The idling engine made the metal floor vibrate. It was hot in the van and there must be a hole in the exhaust; it stank of diesel fumes in here. Oskar coughed.

'Wait.' The guard slapped the side of the van. 'What's in the back?'

Leon switched off the ignition and Oskar could hear the cab door open and close. Two sets of footsteps approached the rear doors.

Under the blanket, Oskar lay completely still as the back door creaked open. He tried not to sneeze as lush garden scents replaced stale diesel fumes.

'Tools and spares.' Leon said. 'Here, this is for you.'

He took a bottle of *Cachaça* from his jacket pocket and handed it to the guard.

The security guard was no different from any other, under-valued and underpaid. 'OK. Drive on.'

As the van trundled through the security gate, Oskar let out the sneeze he had been holding back. If the guard heard, he said nothing.

Once they were inside the compound, disabling the security system was easy. Electricians the world over run internal wires to be invisible to their wealthy clients, people who inhabit a bubble of illusion where services are delivered by magic. But all good tradesmen leave external access for future maintenance.

Leon took care of the cameras. In the old days methods had been cruder. A polaroid picture taken at the right angle and then attached to a selfie stick a few centimetres from a static lens. The cameras that swivelled and zoomed, operated from the security guard's office, took a little more ingenuity, but the right arrangement of mirrors provided blind spots that weren't too obvious unless you were looking closely. Oskar was an expert at that. But these days no art was required. His assistant simply swapped out the cameras with devices that could be controlled from outside, streaming in images that looked perfectly normal.

Once the cameras were doctored – repeating old footage in an endless 24-hour loop – Leon banged on the side of the van and Oskar slipped out. The easy part was done.

'Thanks, mate.' Oskar handed him the rest of the money, a wad of cash.

'Shall I wait for you?'

Oskar shook his head. The external security was now in his control, but it took expertise to hack the interlocks and alarms to individual flats. Oskar preferred to work alone.

'Clean up here and then take the van back to the depot,' he said.

Once he'd gained access to the target's flat, what was the hurry? There was nothing to say he couldn't take his time. Enjoy a bit of luxury living. Wait for her to come home from a hard day's work. He grinned as he imagined the surprise on her pretty face. Shock, anger, followed by fear. He would tie her up while he introduced himself. Until she understood the compact. Then they could get to know each other better. Ensure she showed him some proper respect before he got the hammers out and finished her off.

'I may be some time.' He licked his lips.

By the time the RIMPO van left, Leon at the wheel, Oskar was already at the door of a flat owned by Walter Salgado and recently loaned to Dr Jaq Silver.

Y 3

Shanghai, China

Frank picked up the receiver and stretched out in his leather chair, gazing out at the Shanghai skyline. The sky was dark and a night-time lightshow played out across the skyscrapers on the opposite side of the river.

'Carla,' he said. 'What an unexpected pleasure.'

In truth, he hadn't recognised the name. It was his secretary, ever sensitive to hierarchy, who reminded him that the caller was the general manager of the Zagrovyl operation in Brazil and that Frank had spent time with her during the annual global conference in Shanghai.

Spent time with her. What was his secretary implying? Was she prying into his private life? A thought struck him that made him smile. Was lovely Alice jealous? Did she want Frank in her bed? It wasn't such a bad idea. A cleaner and cheaper option than many.

'How have you been?' he continued.

'Everything is good.' Carla's husky voice, her exotic accent reminded him what a pleasurable time they had spent together. The Brazilian had curves in places that Alice could only dream of. 'And you? How's the project?'

Was she being polite, or did she have some ulterior motive? The extraction of rare earth metals from the treasure trove that Frank had identified was proving more challenging and expensive than his board paper had predicted. Trust the head-office engineers to swan in late with a myriad of unnecessary environmental and safety concerns.

'It's going really well.' That was partly true. The very hint that Zagrovyl had access to large reserves of neodymium and dysprosium outside China's borders had been enough to lower rare-earth market prices. In reality he didn't have to extract a thing. Ignoring engineering advice was one of his favourite tactics. He could just sit on the asset for a while and let the markets do the rest.

'I wanted to ask you a question.'

'Ask away.'

'Do you know an engineer by the name of Dr Jaq Silver?'

Frank's blood turned to ice. It was a name he'd hoped never to hear again.

'What about her?'

'One of our contractors has proposed her for the project in Manaus. She's based in Brazil now.'

Careful. 'Have you met her?'

'Not yet. Her CV came in through Tecnoproject. I saw that she once worked for your division in Teesside.'

His eye was twitching, his chest tightening, his pulse racing. He opened the drawer and shook six tablets from the vial, swallowing them with a gulp of water.

'I fired her,' he said.

'Ah, so best to steer clear?'

Best to keep a million miles away. The tablets worked fast. His breath was coming more easily and with it a sort of clarity. Keep your friends close and your enemies closer.

'No, not at all.' He had to clench his trembling hands into fists to continue. 'She's a perfectly competent engineer. It was a purely commercial decision to close a business. I ran into her again a couple of times.' Anger coursed through him at the memories. It was because of her he needed these blasted tablets, because of her that Sophie was in prison, because of her he had so much unfinished business. Perhaps it was time for a little closure. 'Any idea why she's moved to Brazil?'

'Not a clue.' Carla's voice grew warm and playful. 'Why would anyone want to visit a country with over seven thousand kilometres of golden beaches, delicious cocktails, great food, samba and sunshine?'

'You do make it sound rather appealing.'

'Frank, when are you coming to visit me?'

'I wish I could, but work is so demanding—'

'What about New Year? Or for Carnival in February? Winter in China means summer in Brazil. I have a beach house and you already know how much I love to party.'

He heard a faint buzz on the line. Was Alice listening in?

'I know how much you love to fuck,' he said, articulating the last word with crystal clear diction.

The buzzing stopped abruptly. He smiled as he imagined Alice blushing.

'I liked fucking you, Frank,' Carla whispered. 'I'd love to do it again,' she chuckled, 'and again and again and again and oh …' she tailed off with a low moan and his hand moved to his crotch, unzipping the fly.

'Tell me what you're wearing.'

'I'm at work, Frank. In my best business suit.'

'High heels? Tight skirt? Silk top? Fitted jacket?'

'You see me, Frank.'

'Unbutton your blouse,' he ordered.

She sighed. 'I have to go to a meeting, Frank.'

His disappointment was mixed with irritation.

'You're in Brazil. You're the boss. You can be late.' And unbuttoned. A lovely image.

'Group board meeting.' She sounded genuinely sorry. 'Americans don't do late.'

Or unbuttoned. He guessed she was telling the truth. His quarterly review was early tomorrow, and the Americans worked from west to east, finishing their day as China woke up.

'Do me a favour?' she asked.

Aha, now they were coming to the real reason for her call.

'Add a mention of Brazil in your rare-earth resource report for the board? I want them to sanction some money for an acquisition.'

'I thought your radical environmentalists had put a stop to extraction in Brazil.'

'I know how to handle Ecobrium.'

'Then send me the papers, and I'll take a look.'

'Thank you, Frank. Come and spend some time with me when you can.'

It really wasn't such a bad idea. 'If you do me a favour in return.'

'Name it.'

'See if you can find out what Dr Jaqueline Silver is really doing in Brazil.'

'Of course, Frank.'

'But don't mention my name.'

'I won't. Bye, Frank.'

'Bye, Carla.'

He put the desk phone back in its charging station and sat back in his chair.

Not even the mention of Jaq Silver had diminished his tumescence. He pressed the intercom.

'Alice,' he ordered. 'Come here at once.'

Y 3

Rio de Janeiro to São Paulo, Brazil

Jaq woke in the Rio hotel room to the ping of a message. She called Carmo back on WhatsApp.

'What's new?'

'I called him.'

'Called who?'

'The lawyer in Salvador.'

Jaq suppressed a yawn.

'You listening?'

'Go on.'

'Apparently the Brazilian law firm represented your grandmother, Isabella Ribeiro da Silva, in some business transaction. They wouldn't speak to me, but they said they'd talk to you.'

Jaq had four grandparents she'd never met. Two born and wed in Russia, one born in India who married the other born in Angola. She had absolutely no interest in any of her grandparents' business dealings and many more important things to do than talk to a lawyer in Salvador de Bahia.

On the other hand, the Lisbon lawyer had gone above and beyond their professional relationship to help her and had lost a friend in the process. She wanted to know why. Perhaps Jaq owed it to Carmo to follow up this lead.

Jaq called Bruno.

'I don't want to go back into the Sampo office,' she said. 'Not until you're back.'

He sucked his teeth. 'Is there a problem?'

'Marco,' she said.

'Oh.' He sighed, but it was resignation rather than surprise. 'I see.' But did he? And if he knew that Marco was inclined to misbehave, then why had he allowed it? Perhaps because it only affected the women in the office? Or only the women Marco disliked. 'Leave it with me. I'll deal with it.'

'Do you have any work for me up north? Isn't it about time I visited some oil refineries?'

'I might have something for you with your old employer, Zagrovyl.' Jaq shuddered.

Bruno continued. 'I bumped into the general manager, Carla Sousa, in Brasilia. She's planning to build a factory in Manaus.'

'Too far north.' No need to tell him that she would never, under any circumstances, work for Zagrovyl again. 'I was wondering if there's anything for me in Bahia.'

Bruno laughed. 'You need an excuse to visit some beaches?'

She played along. 'And that.'

'There's the Cuperoil refinery. We have a resident Tecnoproject engineer based in Salvador. I guess a visit would do no harm.'

What did he mean, do no harm? Hadn't Bruno employed her to work for Cuperoil? How could she do useful work without a visit?

'Sounds perfect.'

'OK. I'll speak to Thiago. When can you get there?'

Should she fly straight from Rio to Salvador?

Jaq opened her suitcase. Summer dresses, bikini, shorts and sandals. No long-sleeved shirts or trousers. And more importantly, no safety boots.

'Day after tomorrow?' she offered.

She'd have to go back to her flat in São Paulo.

Safety first.

As Jaq waited in the airport lounge, a familiar face appeared on the large TV screen.

César looked different on screen. At the rooftop bar, in the fancy restaurant, he seemed to melt into the background. On screen, he came alive. He was both the centre of attention and very definitely in control.

'When was the last time you saw your father, Yuko?' César's tanned face filled the screen.

The camera switched to a middle-aged woman, seated on the sofa opposite the TV presenter.

'Over thirty years ago,' she replied. 'I went to school one morning but when I came home, he was gone.'

'He vanished?'

'My mother said he went north to find work.'

'But he never came back?'

The camera panned out to show the studio backdrop, a huge neon sign spelling *Os Desparacidos – The Missing –* and underneath it a woman who was crying.

'Yuko, thirty years is a long time.' César pursed his lips and shook his head. 'Why is it that you are trying to find him now?'

'My mother is ill. She's been calling out for him. She says that there is something she needs to tell him, only him,' Yuko dabbed a handkerchief at her eyes, 'before she dies.'

The *aaahh* from the crowd seemed to go on forever.

'And what is it that your mother wants to say to him?'

Yuko shook her head. 'She won't tell me, only him.'

César made a steeple with his fingers.

'Your mother was too ill to come to the studio, so we sent a crew to her bedside.'

Yuko opened her mouth in surprise as the huge screen behind César's head lit up to reveal an elderly woman lying in a hospital bed, a withered hand clutching the bed sheet.

Had the daughter really not known? Surely she would have had to tell the Hélio TV crew where her mother was being cared for, to arrange permission to film. And the light looked wrong. There was something strangely artificial about the whole scene.

The audience didn't appear to share Jaq's misgivings, the applause reached a crescendo. What were they clapping for?

'Mrs Nakamura, good evening and welcome to ... *The Missing.*'

A blast of music, the theme tune, was accompanied by a dancing light show.

The old woman looked around, confused. 'Hello, who is this?'

'My name is César. I'm with your daughter Yuko.'

'Yuko? Where are you?'

'I'm here, *Mīra.*'

'Yuko tells us that you have a message for her father.'

'Her father is long gone.' A tear escaped from a corner of the old woman's eye and ran over her cheek. 'I made him go.'

Yuko lowered her head. Her glossy black hair swayed from side to side.

'Why did you make him go, Nakamura, *san.*'

'He knows,' she said.

'And what would you say to him today?'

'It's no use,' she said. 'He's lost.'

'Ladies and gentlemen, how many Brazilians have the surname Nakamura?'

A low murmur from the audience.

'There are one-and-a-half million Brazilians of Japanese descent, and Nakamura is in the top-ten surnames. There are tens of thousands of people with the name Nakamura in São Paulo alone.'

Easy to find then, compared to Costa. There were four million people with that name in Brazil.

On the screen, César sprang to his feet. 'And yet we found him.'

Good teeth. As they glinted pearly white under the studio lights, the applause gathered momentum, rising from polite to rapturous. The audience was real, the cameras panned over the adoring crowd, all shapes and sizes, races and colours, but Jaq had a feeling the soundtrack was fake.

The show broke for an advertising break. Jaq took a bottle of water from the fridge and poured it into a glass. César's reality TV show was strangely fascinating.

The adverts dragged on and her eyelids were beginning to droop when the theme music to *The Missing* started up again. The lights did their mad dance and César appeared on screen.

'Good evening and welcome to *The Missing!*' César opened his arms wide. 'The show that reunites some families,' he paused to stroke his neatly trimmed beard. 'And drives others apart.'

The audience laughed.

'Tonight, we have an audience with Colonel Cub. But first, let's return to our special guests.'

The camera zoomed in to the woman seated on the sofa, clutching a handkerchief.

'Thirty years ago, Yuko Nakamura kissed her father goodbye and went to school. When she came home, her father was gone.'

The audience let out a loud *Oooohhh*.

'Yuko was told that her father had gone north to look for work. He never came back.'

Aaahhhh.

'Until now!'

An elderly man appeared on the huge screen behind the presenter.

The woman seated on the sofa sprang to her feet. A hand flew to her mouth, but it wasn't fast enough to muffle the cry that escaped her lips.

'Nakamura *san*, welcome.' César stood and bowed with exaggerated respect.

The old man bowed stiffly.

'Your wife is waiting for you.'

The camera pulled back to show the old man outside a door.

The door opened and the camera followed him as he shuffled forward, into the hospital room where his wife lay dying.

MISSING came the voiceover, *THEN FOUND*, and the familiar music soared.

Jaq stood up. Her flight to São Paulo was boarding.

♆ 3

São Paulo, Brazil

At the shift handover, the security guard forgot to relay the message about the visit from RIMPO surveillance. Too busy concealing the bottle of *Cachaça* the technician had gifted him, he preferred to avoid awkward questions.

Fortunately for the security of the inhabitants of a luxury complex in Jardim Europa, São Paulo, the day-shift guard was a more diligent employee than his night-shift colleague. A former policeman, Chico was unusual in that he took his duties seriously.

He locked up the cabin and did his early morning rounds.

A parcel had arrived for Dr Silver. She might speak funny, with a strange Portuguese accent, but she was always polite, unlike some of the others around here. He telephoned her flat, but there was no reply, so he checked the logbook. She was travelling again. He put the parcel in the post room and returned to his desk.

The phone rang.

That was odd, the call was from Walter's flat, the one Dr Silver was staying in. Perhaps the system had failed to register when she checked back in. He picked up the receiver.

'Security.'

'Where is she?'

The male voice was slurred, thick with sleep or something else, he couldn't be sure.

'Where's who?'

'Silver.'

274

'Who's speaking?'

'Her guest.'

'Mr ...?'

'Pesadelo.' The man gave a laugh, and the line went dead.

Chico retrieved the parcel and locked up the office. He walked to the main door of the apartment complex. Even the security guards couldn't enter without invitation. His finger was poised on the buzzer for the tenth-floor flat when he noticed something strange. No light on the lock. He pushed at the door. It shouldn't open, but it did.

Chico called the police.

After they arrested the naked man in Dr Silver's flat, and before the real contractor came out to reset the security system, Chico arranged for the apartment to be cleaned from top to toe, the sheets and towels changed and her liquor cabinet restocked.

He was just in time.

Shortly after lunchtime, not long after the cleaners had finished, a taxi drew up outside the gatehouse. Chico stepped forward to open the car door.

'*Boa tarde*, Chico.'

'Dr Silver, welcome back. Can I help you with your luggage?'

She picked up a small carry-on. 'I'm fine, but thanks for asking.'

He walked with her to the main entrance.

'Dr Silver, I thought you should know.' He swallowed, his mouth suddenly dry. 'There was an attempted break-in to your apartment block.'

He'd seriously considered not telling her, but the flat was now so clean, she couldn't fail to notice. Dr Silver neither employed a cleaner, nor did she do any housework herself. Whether she'd left the flat in disarray, or whether the intruder had caused the mess, he had no way of knowing.'

Her face paled. 'When?'

'This morning. I called the police immediately and they caught the robber red-handed. Nothing was taken, but I took the liberty of arranging a complete clean.'

'Thank you.' She nodded, colour returning to her cheeks. 'Have they identified the burglar?'

He couldn't bring himself to tell her that the man she'd spotted rattling the fence had been found lying in wait in her apartment.

'No one known to us,' he lied.

She stared at him, wide-eyed, then looked around. Was she wondering how the intruder had managed to get past all the security? He preferred not to answer that question. Or was she worrying that he might come back?

On that point, he hastened to reassure her. 'I know some guys at the police station. You won't have any trouble from him again.'

He'd made sure of that. Or at least, his friends at the station would.

Otherwise, Dr Silver and, more importantly, Walter Salgado and the other residents, would never feel safe again.

10,000 Metres above Salvador de Bahia, Brazil

The huge aluminium bird made landfall somewhere over Recife and turned south towards São Paulo.

The cabin crew handed out little Christmas gifts, sparkling boxes with coloured ribbons containing a single Christmas tree decoration.

From her seat inside the plane, Jaq stared down at the coast of Brazil as daylight faded, the turquoise sea, white beaches and green palm trees gradually replaced by the lights of the cities and towns and the cars that travelled between them.

A flare from a floating oil platform sent tongues of orange flame up into the darkening sky.

Oil.

The rich countries of the world had prospered thanks to access to fossil fuels. Heat and light, transport and power, fertiliser and food, medicines and health, advanced materials and wealth. Was it fair that the developing world should now be chastised for exploiting its natural resources?

By working as a consultant for the oil industry, was she somehow complicit in an impending global catastrophe?

Or was it the way she lived her life that did the damage? Taking a plane, driving a car, using an air-conditioner in summer and central heating in winter, recharging her phone, creating the demand in the first place? Was the only solution to go back to a simpler way of life, living by the seasons, eating only what you grew by your own efforts, on your own land, never travelling beyond your birth village?

Or was there a middle way? If there was, it was up to the scientists and engineers of the world to find it. And find it soon.

Her work had always been focussed on improving safety and efficiency, making better use of precious resources. Banning fossil fuels would only work if every world government acted in unison, otherwise some would prosper in the short term at the expense of others. Greenhouse gases and the weather don't respect national boundaries.

But how long before wind and solar energy, heat pumps and batteries provided a realistic baseload at the scale needed for a new electric economy?

What about green hydrogen? Not as a source of energy, but a vector. On sunny, windy days, the excess electrical energy could be used to electrolyse water. On windless nights, the hydrogen produced by electrolysis would be released to supply the missing power.

Buy why hydrogen, that difficult and dangerous gas. There must be other energy-hungry chemical reactions that could mop up surplus power from renewables and release it on demand?

Or was the solution to be found in biology? The battery in our bodies. ATP to ADP. Adenosine triphosphate to diphosphate with energy released, recharged and reversed when we eat.

Necessity is the mother of invention.

There's the world as it is, and the world as you wish it to be. How do you manage the transition? Cross your arms and complain. Or roll up your sleeves and help.

Jaq had always preferred action.

But her actions always seemed to lead to trouble.

From her window she searched for the city lights of Salvador de Bahia 10,000 metres below.

And shuddered at the memory.

♈ 3

Salvador de Bahia, Brazil

Summer air flowed like warm silk over Jaq's bare arms as she paused to admire the view. A curved bay, sheltered by low hills, was alive with ships heading for the brightly lit port.

The first colonial capital of Brazil, founded in the sixteenth century by the Portuguese, towered above the beautiful Bay of All Saints. The north-eastern city was noticeably warmer than São Paulo, but with a breeze coming in from the sea it was a pleasant temperature.

A steep cliff separated the lower commercial part of the city from the upper residential part. The passenger lift, *Elevador Lacerda*, brought her up to the Pelourinho, the oldest part of the city.

The Tecnoproject engineer, Thiago, had arranged to meet her in the centre.

'Do you know what *pelourinho* means?' he'd asked on the phone.

Jaq shuddered. 'Pillory?'

'Whipping post.' He said. 'You can't miss it. I'll meet you there.'

She left the viewpoint and strode up the steep cobbled streets, past brightly painted houses and ornate churches. It was like being transported back to sixteenth-century Lisbon, but now illuminated by floodlights and with the glorious technicolour of modern paint.

The narrow plaza was wedge-shaped, with a church blocking the far end, cloisters at either side, behind which stood souvenir shops, hotels and restaurants.

In the centre of the Square of Piety the original whipping post had been replaced by a tall stone cross mounted on a plinth. This was the place where African slaves were once brought for public punishment.

Once upon a time, agriculture depended on human muscle.

Of the five million slaves brought from the African continent to Brazil, three million came through Salvador. How many had been tortured here?

It made Jaq sick to think of it and she was glad when she spotted Thiago and they could move away.

The larger cathedral square was buzzing with activity. The beat of drums came from all four corners, insistent, thudding. A group of young men with loose white trousers and bare chests began a *capoeira* demonstration, a graceful mix of gymnastics and stylised combat.

A woman in traditional dress, a strange mix of Afro-Islamic and Baroque, approached them with a tray of street food. Petticoats swayed as she weaved her way between Jaq and Thiago. She wore a layered headscarf, a white-lace bodice with round yoke and short puffed sleeves, draped over a voluminous ankle-length skirt, cinched at the waist, bulked by petticoats and a crinoline-style wire frame underneath. Her necklaces and bangles clattered as she swayed. There were others dressed like her: white-lace bodice, dramatic against dark skin, colourful headscarf, skirt and jewellery. The women resembled gorgeous birds of paradise.

'You want to try *acarajé*?'

Thiago led her to a stall.

'It's a mix of black-eyed peas, shrimp and spices formed into balls and fried in palm oil. Or over here they steam instead of fry, that's *abará*.'

'I'll try the steamed one.'

He placed his order and handed it to her.

It tasted good, as outdoor food does. They wandered through the crowds looking for a bar with outdoor seating.

'When do you want to visit the refinery?' he asked.

'Day after tomorrow?' she suggested.

'Perfect,' he said. 'That gives me time to make arrangements. Any questions about Cuperoil?'

Jaq racked her brains to think of something that made it look like she was even vaguely interested in anything except avoiding Mario and visiting her grandmother's lawyer.

The following morning Jaq walked to the lawyer's office. The address that Carmo had sent was in the lower commercial district, between the passenger terminal and the container port.

The building housing Castanho e Nogueira e Advogados Associados had seen better days. A grand façade with stone columns and lintels framing pastel-pink stucco, the paint was peeling and the plaster crumbling. Dark green vegetation grew from the gutters and a flowering vine had wrapped itself around the cables strung between buildings, the telephone and power lines sagging with the weight of vegetation.

As she approached, Jaq slowed her brisk pace. It felt hotter down here, more humid, even early in the morning. Did she really want to go poking around in her grandmother's affairs?

Jaq took a deep breath and rang the bell. She was admitted into a reception area, all clean modern lines and fierce air conditioning. She walked across the veined marble floor and shivered in front of a smoke glass partition.

'*Bom dia.*'

'*Bom djeeya.*'

The Brazilian accent was different here, more nasal and singsong. Jaq introduced herself and asked to speak to Advogado Castanho.

The young woman took her details and motioned for her to sit on a cream leather sofa. A pile of glossy magazines sat on the low wooden table. Jaq picked the top one up and flicked. Not much content, mainly real estate adverts. All shapes and sizes of luxury villas in Praia de Forte, a beach resort just up the coast. Some with shared pools, others with their own pool, all with access to beautiful beaches and the vast South Atlantic Ocean.

The receptionist brought a small black coffee and a glass of iced water.

'I'm sorry, could you give me your name again?'

'Dr Jaqueline Silver.'

'I don't have any record of an appointment.'

'A lawyer in Lisbon contacted you. My grandmother's family had business with this firm.'

'I see. What was your lawyer's name?'

'Carmo Centeno.'

'And your grandmother's name?'

'Isabella Ribeiro da Silva.'

'Of course.' She smiled. 'Please wait here.'

Jaq checked her phone for messages, clicking onto an email from the helpful elderly dentist in Rio Grande.

'Hi – There's a Dr Carlos Costa who had a practice in Criciúma. He set up a business in Bahia. I'll let you know if I find out more.'

If he did, she was in the right place to follow up. Jaq remembered the filthy room in Criciúma and hoped that this was not the lead she'd been looking for.

Something caught her eye and she turned to look out of the window.

A woman was hauling a cart piled high with cardboard, bent almost double with the effort. The rudimentary barrow looked heavy and, judging by the squeaking wheels, inefficient. She stopped outside the window, turned and called back. A barefoot child a little older than Ben, perhaps six or seven, scampered towards his mother. He was almost invisible under his load of plastic. Each empty bottle was secured with string around the neck. The containers were threaded together so he could carry hundreds. They bobbed like sad balloons, except there was no helium inside to lessen the load. As he drew level, his mother dealt him a vicious slap and then resumed her journey.

'Mr Castanho will see you now.' The receptionist beckoned to Jaq. 'Follow me.'

On a stained-glass window, half-way up the elegant stone staircase, the central pane displayed the scales of justice. Jaq ran her hand over the curved teak handrail, contemplating the scenes of commerce on the side panels: pixelated jewelled glass with lines of lead depicting ships and markets, plantations and courts, wealthy merchants and noblemen. She thought about the woman and child outside. Did the world have to be so unequal?

The receptionist tapped her elegant, pointed shoe at the top of the stairs, and Jaq ran up the last flight. She was shown into a room so large it dwarfed the elderly man who sat at a mahogany desk. He stood as she entered, although it was clearly an effort. A spasm of pain passed across his wrinkled face and his back remained bent as he extended a withered hand across the green baize.

She shook his hand, warm and paper-light.

'How extraordinary,' he said. 'You look just like her.'

'Like who?'

'Isabella. She was your grandmother, no?'

'Yes.' Jaq took a step back. 'You knew her?'

'She was a client, back in the early seventies. I was just an apprentice then, but she made a great impression on me.'

His eyes burned into her. 'She must have been about your age when I met her.'

Jaq had no idea. This was the closest she'd come to her own family history.

'Perhaps.'

He sighed as he sank into his chair. 'Such a tragedy.'

'I don't know much about what happened.' Jaq took a seat at the other side of the desk. 'My grandparents were estranged from my mother.' And her mother was estranged from everyone else, including her own daughter and the grandson she sold.

'I understand that your mother died recently.'

'Yes.'

'I am sorry for your loss.'

Jaq gritted her teeth. 'Thank you.'

'I remember your grandparents well. They were planning to leave Angola. Settle here in Brazil.'

He knew more about her family history than she did. She murmured something noncommittal.

'We did a lot of work in preparation. Everything was ready, but something delayed their departure.'

A revolution followed by a civil war? Jaq cleared her throat. 'I have a letter that you wrote to my mother's lawyer.' She handed him the sheet of paper Carmo had sent. His lips moved as he read it, then he summarised aloud.

'*We confirm that we are still in possession of the item … strict instructions from our client … unable to discuss … during the lifetime of Maria dos Anjos …*'

'What can you tell me about it?' Jaq asked.

He put the sheet of paper down on the desk and steepled his bony fingers. 'You want to know if your grandmother left something for you, no?'

In a nutshell. 'Yes.'

'First, there are formalities to be observed.'

Jaq repressed an inner sigh.

'You have your mother's death certificate?'

'Not with me.'

'I'm afraid I will need certified copies in triplicate.'

Jaq left the lawyer's office and walked along the shore. The traffic thundered along a busy road above her as she crossed concrete wharves, then rocks and finally sand. The city beaches were too crowded for her thoughts, so she continued to the rocky peninsula of Bonfim where a white fort – *Nossa Senhora do Monte Serrat* – guarded the entry to the bay.

Jaq called Carmo and explained what had happened. 'Bloody bureaucracy,' she added.

'I'll get copies certified and send them express delivery. How long are you in Salvador for?'

'A few days. Depends on work.'

'I'll see what I can do.'

Jaq clambered up the grassy hillside until she found a private spot, shaded by a tree, then sat down and stared out to sea.

☿ 3

Salvador de Bahia, Brazil

The petrochemical complex was barely visible from Salvador, only at night did a flickering orange glow from behind the hills reveal its location.

Close up, in daylight, the first oil refinery to be built in Brazil still looked impressive six decades on. If you like that sort of thing. And Jaq did. At least in the sense that she could look at each one of those slim silver towers, with their spiky crowns and helical bracelets, and imagine the months of calculation that had gone into determining the diameter, the height, the internal design. Each of those distillation columns, and she counted a dozen as Thiago drove over the brow of the hill and began the descent towards the complex, separated useful products from the thick, black liquid extracted from under the sea.

Thiago left Jaq at the security cabin to undergo a safety induction.

'I'll come back for you in 30 minutes.'

'What if I don't pass the exam?'

He scowled. 'You'll resit it until you do.'

Along with a crew of scaffolders, wiry men with broad shoulders and thick necks, Jaq watched the induction video on a small TV in a cramped room.

Built at the estuary of the Mataripe river, on a farm that had once grown bananas, the development of the first oil refinery in Brazil was driven by the discovery of oil off the coast of Bahia.

Capable of processing 50,000 cubic metres of oil per day, that's 200 Olympic-sized swimming pools or 2 supertankers or a third of a million barrels per day. Each of the hundreds of product tanks and storage spheres held gas, petrol, diesel, jet fuel, wax and tar.

Fuel that went into cars and trains and trucks and ships, powering international trade, allowing sugar and soy and mangoes and papaya from Brazil to reach supermarkets in Teesside, the tropical fruit continuing to ripen under a methane blanket to arrive at peak sweetness.

Food-grade waxes, crosslinked paraffins, to be used in chewing gum and chocolate, lipstick and skin cream, to be sprayed onto the skin of lemons and limes, apples and pears, locking in the moisture to keep the fruit fresh.

Special oils, straight chain paraffins, to be used to make biodegradable detergents and medicines.

Asphalt for roads, lubricants for machines.

The sun's energy from millions of years ago, captured by plants, transformed by microbes into the basic building blocks of life on earth.

The age of oil was almost over, its time fast running out. As the earth warmed the young would pay for the carelessness of their forebears, the developing nations would pay for the avarice of the developed, the poor would pay for the self-indulgence of the rich. It was ever thus.

Jaq completed the induction exam. She received her contractor pass and collected her personal protective equipment – boiler suit, hard hat, safety boots, googles, ear defenders – and stepped through the turnstile to the factory, sitting on a low wall as she waited for Thiago.

All around were the purrs and sighs, groans and wheezes, booming ship's horns and shrieking alarms of the huge complex. Petrochemicals give off a special smell, each oil refinery subtly different. The top notes, at best spicy, at worst sulphurous, sharp scents that make your eyes water, the middle dominated by hot metal from rust-laden condensing steam, the low notes of treacle and tar. Jaq took a deep breath and committed the olfactory chromatograph to memory.

♆ 3

Tocantins, Brazil

At the sound of a key in the lock, Pedro shrank back into the corner of his cell. The rough sandstone walls pierced the ragged kaftan and grazed his skin: a foretaste of the pain to come. There were no shadows to hide in – his prison always pitch-black or fluorescent bright. He'd been moved from the guest hut to this damp, windowless cell, a pallet of coarse straw for sleeping and a metal pail for ablutions.

Gone was the comfortable guest room with writing desk, reading lamps and ladderback chair. Gone was the wide wooden bed with sprung mattress, ironed cotton sheets and goose-down pillows. Gone was the rainforest shower in a flower-filled courtyard with a private toilet.

The last thing he remembered was the savage hammer attack administered by the Colonel. He'd been beaten half to death. If only they'd finished the job. What else would convince the madman that he had no more secrets to reveal, no one else to betray?

The door opened.

'Time for a little talk.'

Pedro closed his eyes, as if the fact he couldn't see the soldiers meant they couldn't see him. Like a child playing hide and seek by putting their hands over their eyes. The way his son Luis used to play.

Oh, Luis. Oh, Maria. Would he ever see them again?

He cried out as rough hands seized his arms and dragged him upright. A soldier's boot caught the metal pail and kicked it over. The stench of his own defecation made him gag, but he would willingly have put up with it to be allowed to stay in the cell. To avoid what he knew was coming next.

The interrogations followed the same pattern, the Colonel, stuck somewhere in the 1970s, seeing conspiracy and rebellion, betrayal and treachery in every action. And inaction.

'Who sent you?'

The Banco Espirito Santo.

'Who are you spying for?'

I'm not spying. I came to deliver a message from the Banco Espirito Santo.

'Who else knows you are here?'

My colleagues at the Banco Espirito Santo.

'Are you a communist?'

No.

'Are you working for the communists?'

No. I'm a banker.

'Do you know what we do to communists, like you?'

The torture was usually administered by others, and there appeared to be an endless stream of willing volunteers, but the invention came from the Colonel.

'What did you tell Silver?'

It was no use protesting that he had nothing to tell. He'd tried that and been beaten unconscious.

'Why is Silver in Brazil?'

The Colonel seemed to think that Silver was the client of the lawyer Centeno. How reliable the Colonel's military intelligence operation was, Pedro had no way of knowing.

'Why has Silver gone to Salvador?'

If he didn't know who Silver was, how was he supposed to guess her travel itinerary? An equally pointless line of protest, as he knew to his cost when they asked him about São Paulo or Sapiranga or Rio any of the other places she had visited.

'Why is she meeting with a lawyer from Castanho e Nogueira?'

He didn't know who Silver was, why she was visiting the places she travelled to or what she wanted with a lawyer in Salvador.

But whatever he said, it seemed to make no difference to the Colonel.

Y 3

Salvador de Bahia, Brazil

The rooftop terrace of the hotel overlooked a busy port. Jaq
lingered, observing the activity far below.

Modern shipping is a marvel. For a fraction of the price of a
letter, when measured in cost per unit weight, goods are moved
across the globe. Soya beans and iron ore to China, sugar and
coffee to North America,

It was a relief to be out of the office, away from Marco. And at
least here, she could be useful while she searched. She'd started
her visit in the biofuel section, where ethanol derived from bagasse
– sugarcane waste – was dehydrated and blended with gasoline. All
cars in Brazil were designed to run on ethanol in varying mixes
from 25 to 100 per cent.

She would visit the hydrogen section next week. Thiago had
identified several areas of concern where he wanted her support.
The refinery used hydrogen at high temperature and pressure
to desulphurise crude oil and break the carbon-carbon bonds of
heavier products to make lighter fuels to power the jets criss-
crossing the sky.

She'd worked up a proposal for a full safety audit and had
already sent the first draft to Bruno by the time Carmo called
to say that the notarised documents sent from Lisbon had been
received by the ancient, fussy lawyer in Salvador.

Jaq phoned to make an appointment and walked through the
centre of town, taking the *elevador* down to the commercial district.

She kept an eye open for the thin woman and barefoot child who recycled cardboard and plastic, but there was no sign of them today, only men driving trucks.

The elderly lawyer greeted her warmly. If anything, he looked even frailer than before. His hands shook as he pulled the documents from her file. Carmo – as good as her word – had sent the notarised originals of the death certificates in triplicate.

'Well, everything appears to be in order?'

He squinted up at her through thick glasses.

'Can you confirm that you are Maria Jaqueline Marta Ribeiro da Silva, the daughter of Maria dos Anjos Ribeiro da Silva?'

'Yes.'

'And that your father was Anton Oleich Sakoshansky.'

'Yes.'

'There were other children?'

'My brother Sam. He died.' *And if you ask me for his death certificate, so help me the next one to be produced will be yours.*

He opened his desk drawer and drew out an envelope.

'Then, I think, this must be for you.'

He pushed the envelope across the table. Thick cream parchment with text in dramatic curling ink.

'It was deposited with our firm in 1973 by Isabella Ribeiro da Silva.'

Jaq ran a finger over the writing. *Not to be opened before the death of Maria do Anjos Sakoshansky. Deliver to any surviving issue.*

There was so much venom in those words, it made her sick to her stomach. Angie had not changed her name on marriage, most Portuguese women kept their maiden names, unless they were marrying up, and that was certainly not seen to be the case when an aristocratic Angolan heiress ran off with a penniless Russian spy.

By using her husband's name, Sakoshansky, her grandparents made Angie's status clear. She was no longer a Ribeiro da Silva in their eyes. She had disgraced them; they had disinherited her.

But it was the word *issue* that pained her most. Sam had already been born in 1973. They must have known they had a grandson. And even if they had cut off all contact with Angie, surely they would care about Sam? Or was there some gene in the Ribeiro da Silva DNA that made them incapable of normal human emotion? *Issue.* Not son or daughter, not child, not grandchild, not even descendent. *Issue.* Like a waste product. Spawn of the devil.

And any message to be delivered to Angie's children was to wait until after the mother's death. Too late for Sam. How obstinate, how pig-headed, how unspeakably cruel.

Jaq swallowed at the ache in her throat.

'Please open it.'

Jaq stared at the letter, reluctant to touch it. 'Here? Now?'

The lawyer handed her an elaborate silver letter opener.

Jaq slit the envelope and drew out a small circular jewellery box, a handwritten letter and an official document. She handed the document to the lawyer and unfolded the parchment of the letter. The same curling writing transcribed a poem.

Valeu a pena? Tudo vale a pena
Se a alma não é pequena.
Confie primeiro no espírito santo
Com anel, nome e número do canto
Desmonte a caixa com gaveta falsa
A chave para o oriente, esconde na alça
As mapas poente, cobre entre aço e couro
Mas tenha cuidado, nem tudo que brilha é ouro
Deus ao mar o perigo e o abysmo deu,
Mas nelle é que espelhou o céu.

Jaq recognised the first couplet from a book they had studied at school in Lisbon. Fernando Pessoa, one of the greatest Portuguese poets, wrote a long, mystical epic called *The Message*.

This stanza translated loosely as:

Was it worth it? Everything is worthwhile
If the spirit is versatile …

And so on.

What sort of message was this?

The lawyer held up the legal document she had passed to him and cleared his throat.

'This leaves me a little perplexed.'

You and me both.

'The document concerns the purchase of land in Brazil. It's a contract that sets out the extent of the rights, and they are unusual, extensive.'

'In what way?'

'They seem to include control over mining rights. Very irregular. Only Brazilian citizens or companies incorporated under Brazilian laws, with headquarters and management offices in the country, are allowed to mine in Brazil, and there is a strict licensing scheme. What lies under the earth normally belongs to the state, not to the landowner.'

'So, my grandmother tried to buy a mine, but you lawyers messed it up and it's actually worthless?'

'Not exactly worthless. It gives the owner the right to veto any mining activity.' He cleared his throat. 'The legality would be for the court to decide. But in any case, we are missing the most important parts, the original deeds and the land schedules.'

'I don't understand.'

'The proof of ownership and the location: coordinates, a map, anything to specify exactly what land the contract covers. Brazil is a big country; we need to know where the mine is.'

'And the deeds and schedules are not included?'

'The lawyer handed Jaq the contract and she skim-read the first page, then stopped. This had been a problem of hers in the past, ignoring the fine print.

'Can I take this away to look at it.'

'It's yours.'

'Did your firm act for my grandmother?'

'Yes.'

'So, if she bought land in Brazil, won't you have a record of the transaction?'

'I will certainly look through our records.'

These ones probably not digitised.

'But there is no guarantee that your grandmother didn't sell part or all of the land through another agency.'

'Is there no land registry?'

'Yes, but that alone doesn't confer proof of ownership. The original deeds and schedules must be presented. They must have been kept separate for a reason. What is inside the box?'

Jaq opened the jewellery box. Inside was a gold ring.

She held it up to the light. There was a symbol and a number on the inside. A hallmark? *Nem tudo que reluz é ouro.* All that glitters is not gold. Well, this looked like gold. About two grams of it. Hardly a fortune.

In other circumstances it might have been amusing, this Kafkaesque rigmarole. A poem, a contract and a ring. How was this helping her to find her son? What a waste of time. As Jaq stood up to leave, she remembered the message from the friendly dentist in Porto Alegre.

'Do you happen to know a dentist by the name of Carlos Costa?'

'How did you know?'

'Know what?'

'That he was here, asking about Isabella's bequest.'

Jaq froze, suddenly alert. 'What do you mean?'

'A man came here last week. Making wild claims.'

'Can you be more specific?'

'Well, he knew that your mother was dead. Claimed that she'd made promises to him.'

'What sort of promises?'

'Claimed she owed him something.'

'What did you tell him?'

'Nothing.' He smiled. 'He didn't have the right paperwork.'

Her heart beat faster. Was it possible, could it be?

'Can you tell me more about him?'

'He's not a client. I sent him away.'

Her voice trembled. 'A young man? In his twenties?'

He shook his head. 'No. In his sixties. Lives up the coast, near Praia de Forte.'

'Do you have a contact number?'

'Let me see if I still have his details.'

He shuffled slowly through a stack of business cards on his desk, pulled one out and stared at it for a moment.

'Yes, this is him, the retired dentist.'

After all the fruitless searching, was it really possible?

He handed her the card.

Dr Carlos Costa.

3

Salvador de Bahia, Brazil

Praia de Forte was only a short drive up the coast from Salvador. Jaq took the rental car Tecnoproject had arranged. The road was smooth and straight, and it felt liberating to put her foot down. Relatively guilt-free as well; the flex car ran on whichever fuel was cheapest, from 100 per cent alcohol straight from the sugar factory to a mix of anhydrous ethanol plus petrol – the kind they made in the Cuperoil refinery. The only way to tell the difference was the frequency of refuelling.

All her searching, all those visits to dentist after dentist and in the end it was a fussy old lawyer, the one she'd only visited to pacify Carmo, who came up trumps. Now excitement was mixed with trepidation.

On her left lay the Atlantic rainforest, on her right shallow lagoons and shape-shifting sand-dunes with the occasional glimpse of the impossibly blue South Atlantic Ocean. She passed signs for wild animal crossings, arial trapezes for giant sloths to traverse the highway without being squashed by the trucks thundering up and down the main north-south access road.

She'd called the number for the elusive Carlos Costa before she left Salvador. He spoke with a cultured accent, an easy drawl.

'*Oi.*'

'*Bom dia.*' She paused. 'Am I speaking with Dr Carlos Costa?'

'Yes, who is this?'

If he recognised her name, what questions would he ask. Might he refuse to see her? She didn't want to explain on the phone.

'I'm calling from Castanho e Nogueira e Advogados Associados.' Not a word of a lie, she was still in the building. 'I wondered if we might arrange a meeting?'

'Aha, so old man Castanho has reconsidered, has he.' She could hear a smile in his voice. 'He'd better come here.'

'This afternoon?'

'Four p.m. He knows the address?'

'Aí-Pixuna, Praia de Forte.' She read out the address from the card.

'That's right.' He gave some additional instructions.

The beach resort was a pretty little village, packed with well-heeled tourists escaping from the stuffy cities. Despite following the complicated directions, it took her a little while to locate Aí-Pixuna, a gated community some miles north of the town. The main road ran parallel to the shore for a while and then turned inland to re-join the highway. She turned right onto a cobbled street. Between the private road and the sea lay a vast number of private estates. The first were condominiums, flats grouped around a pool. As she drove further they became more secluded, the flats turning to terraces, the terraces to small villas, the villas to mansions. She reached the end of the road and stopped at a high fence, rolling down the car window as a guard in a bright pink uniform stepped out of the security cabin.

'*Oi!*' The greeting sounded more like a growl.

'*Bom dia.* I'm here to visit Carlos Costa.'

The guard checked a logbook.

'Is he expecting you?'

'Yes.'

'Your name.'

She handed him the lawyer's business card. He stared at the name, then stared at her.

'Wait a minute.'

The guard picked up the phone.

Beyond him, behind secure fencing, lay a lush, landscaped garden and a row of six modern palaces facing the sea. Carlos Costa was obviously not short of a bob or two. Despite his early difficulties in Portugal, dentistry must have paid off in the end.

'I'm sorry.' The guard came out of his office and handed back the card. 'There's no reply.'

'Are you sure?' She hadn't come this far to give up now. 'I spoke to him this morning.'

He shrugged. 'Nothing I can do.'

Jaq tried the mobile number on his card, the one she'd used to make the appointment, but there was no answer.

A van approached the security fence from inside the compound. The guard turned away to unlock the gate and the vehicle drove through. The pickaxe logo and company name RIMPO emblazoned on its side looked vaguely familiar. The van driver turned his head away as he passed.

Jaq edged her car forward, but the guard was too fast. He closed the gate and locked it before returning to his cabin.

Jaq got out of the car and tapped on the window. The guard opened it with a sigh.

'Perhaps he's gone for a walk on the beach?' His private beach. 'Can I come in and wait?'

The gateman shook his head. 'No one comes in without a guest pass. Only the residents can approve them. Strict instructions.'

If she couldn't reach him by land, she'd have to try the sea route. Jaq drove back back towards the town searching for a way to access the beach. The public footpath was well hidden, grudgingly respecting the letter, if not the spirit of the law. It was a long, hot walk from the road to the sea. Not everyone had the luxury of living on the beach and those who did had no desire to share it with the public.

The beach, fringed with coconut palms, stretched for miles in either direction. She tried walking in their shade, but the white sand in between shadows burned through her thin sandals, so she took them off, changed into her swimsuit and walked through the cooler shallows, the waves lapping at her ankles.

It was harder to identify the Aí-Pixuna complex and the dentist's house from the beach, and she made a few false incursions. It was further than she remembered, and it would soon be getting dark.

Had she overshot? She stopped to survey the beach ahead when she spotted a flash of pink in the distance, a security guard patrolling the beach in the same distinctive uniform as the gateman.

She hid her bag in the sand behind a rocky ledge and waited until the guard was walking the other way before plunging into the water. She swam round the rocks, dived under the surface, emerging behind a catamaran tied to a jetty.

Dr Carlos Costa's house was even more impressive from the sea. An elaborate wood-clad box, two storeys high with a rooftop pool. At ground level a teak deck led to French windows and the main living space.

The security guard had vanished into a small hut at the far end of the beach, so she took the opportunity to race across the sand. Leaping onto the decking, she grabbed a clean towel from one of the loungers, drying herself and then wrapping it round her hips. She checked that the room was empty before testing the French window. It opened easily, and she slid the glass panels apart until the gap was wide enough to slip through.

A sitting room ran the full width of the house: white marble floor, white walls, white leather sofas, white sheepskin rugs. The only splash of colour inside came from a dozen turquoise scatter cushions and an emerald-green pot holding a pale lemon spray of orchid. A picture window looked out over the sea and stretched as far as the dining area, which had its own window at right angles, looking north up the beach. A door connected the dining area to a small kitchen, all white again and, by the look of it, only for show. The glass doors of the fridges revealed a cigar humidifier, a white-wine fridge, a beer and soda-can fridge and an ice maker. A professional kitchen was partly concealed behind the mirrored panel. This second kitchen would be where food was really prepared, and it connected via a utility room, larder and laundry to a side entrance. Was this how the servants accessed the house? The show kitchen opened into the main entrance hall with a grand staircase lit by a central chandelier hanging on a long chain. A door from the hall led back into the bright-white living space. Jaq had done a complete tour of the ground floor and there was no sign of life.

She backed up and called up the stairs. No reply. Within a few steps she could see that she had come to the right place. It was completely sterile downstairs; Carlos Costa kept more personal stuff upstairs. Starting with the staircase, the walls were lined with framed pictures. His graduation certificate from the dental school was the first of a whole wall of history: a photo of the Golden Smile, his dental clinic in Estefania, Lisbon, in better days; another of the Dazzling Smile, his clinic in Salvador; satellite clinics in Aracaju, Recife, Fortaleza. Pictures of him graduating, on holiday, alone in New York, Florida, San Francisco, Shanghai. In company on a yacht, his arm around the waist of a young, blonde woman who looked nothing like Evangelina. Pictures of the same mismatched couple astride an elephant, in Thailand, the age gap – twenty or thirty years? – even starker. A wedding photo, the tall blonde and the rotund dentist, dated and signed with the names Carlos and Áurea Costa. What happened to his first wife, Evangelina? And, more importantly, what happened to the baby they adopted from a convent in Lisbon? What happened to Jaq's son?

There were more photos of Carlos and the blonde on the landing. The stairs continued to the rooftop, illuminated through a skylight by the last rosy light of the day as the sun approached the horizon. Jaq remained on the first floor. The door to the master bedroom was ajar, revealing the same spectacular view as the living room downstairs. There were more bedrooms, all with en-suite bathrooms and walk-in wardrobes. There was even a room dedicated to footwear, each box labelled with a photo of the shoe inside. She estimated three hundred pairs, all combinations of style and colour and heel heights. Marina's minimalist shoe roll might not be for everyone.

The last room she came to was a study. She called out and knocked on the door, which swung open to reveal a man's bare foot. Heart racing, she pushed the door fully open.

Carlos Costa had never been a beautiful man. Even in his graduation photo, in his mid-twenties prime, he appeared prematurely middle-aged: thinning hair combed over a bald pate, a large nose over thin lips, sallow skin the colour and patina of skimmed milk. As he grew older, his weak chin vanished into waves of jowls; his belly grew and his shoulders sagged. Not a physically attractive man, but at least he'd had a face.

All that remained of Carlos Costa lay slumped in an office chair. The bullet hole in the back of his head had splattered his brains over the computer screen in front of him. Shards of skull and teeth had flown like darts, now embedded in the corkboard behind the computer. A single eyeball remained intact, quivering on the keyboard in a pool of its own jelly.

Jaq gagged, retreating with a hand over her mouth to stop herself vomiting.

Her first thought was to run for the security guard. Down the stairs, her hand already reaching for the front door, something gave her pause.

She'd made an appointment under false pretences, implying that she represented a legal firm that Carlos had recently approached. A firm handling a bequest from her grandmother. A bequest that was being challenged by the man who lay dead in front of her. How was she going to explain her presence here? When it came out that Carlos had adopted her son and then, by the look of things, abandoned him, would that not be motive enough to detain her? She was a foreigner in a country where guns were easy to come by and law enforcement was not renowned for its interest in the truth.

She retraced her steps and forced herself to look again. The death was recent, a couple of hours at most. The blood still red, the haemoglobin not yet fully de-oxidised. There was nothing she could do for Carlos Costa now.

A sudden draught made her whip round. A woman dressed in a gauzy Grecian robe, open to reveal a white bikini, stood at the top of the stairs leading to the rooftop pool.

In one hand she held a cocktail coupe, in the other a pearl-handled pistol.

Y 3

Salvador de Bahia, Brazil

The tall blonde in a white bikini descended the staircase of the beach-front mansion, gold heels clacking on the marble treads, pointing a gun at Jaq.

'You're late.' She made a pantomime of looking at her watch and sucking her teeth. 'Even by Brazilian standards.'

Jaq recognised the woman from the wedding photos on the walls. The newest wife of recently deceased Carlos Costa.

'You must be Áurea.'

'Careful.' The blonde waved the gun at her. 'Stay back.'

The hand on the gun was steady, this woman had killed before.

'You were meant to arrive at four o'clock.' Áurea's voice was low and slow. 'I'd grown tired of waiting.'

'What happened here?'

'You shot my husband.'

Jaq's mouth went dry. 'No—'

'The local police are not very thorough, but you are a terrible housebreaker. Did you know that bare feet leave traces that are even easier to identify than fingerprints?'

'Why would I shoot a man I don't even know?'

'What are the usual motives? The four Ls. Lust, Love, Loathing and Loot.' Áurea took another step. 'Did you love my husband? Did he spurn you? No, I don't think so. He never turned down an opportunity for infidelity.' She took a sip of her drink, her pale-blue eyes never leaving Jaq's. 'Lust? Perhaps he attacked you? Forced himself on you? Did you shoot him in self-defence?'

Humour her. Keep her talking.

'The bullet's in the back of his head,' Jaq said. 'Hardly a defensive wound, more like a cold-blooded assassination.'

'If you say so.' The blonde nodded. 'Loathing then?'

Jaq looked around for something to defend herself with. 'Did you loathe your husband?'

'My former husband. I don't think he's coming back, do you?' Her eyes glittered and her laugh was brittle as glass. 'No, I didn't loathe him. He was a weak man. Sometimes I pitied him, most of the time I just despised him.'

Play along. 'Loot, then?'

'Yes, I think that's the one the police will find easiest to understand. A robbery gone wrong. You broke in and killed him. I tried to defend my husband, so you came for me, and I was forced to shoot you in self-defence.'

'I see.' Jaq evaluated her escape routes. She wasn't leaving until she got what she'd come for. 'Tell me, what happened to Evangelina?'

'Who?'

'His first wife.'

'He divorced her years ago, after his business took off. She was holding him back.'

'And the son they adopted in Portugal?'

'First I heard of it.'

It. Jaq clenched her jaw, containing the rising anger.

'They adopted a baby in Portugal.' Her baby.

'You'd have to ask the ex-wife.'

'Where is she now?'

The woman shrugged. 'What does it matter?'

As her fury boiled over, Jaq stepped forward.

Áurea raised the gun.

Jaq stopped and shrugged. 'You plan to frame me for what you did?' Since I'm going to die anyway, why don't you tell me what really happened here?'

'Carlos promised me something he couldn't deliver.'

Jaq made a guess. 'A gold mine?'

Áurea scowled. 'How did you know?'

Jaq edged towards the stairs, sliding her feet over the smooth marble.

'Was that a reason to kill him?'

The woman with the gun threw her head back and laughed.

'I didn't kill him. You did. And now you'll attack me, and I'll have to kill you.'

Fight or flight? Sometimes, attack was the only possible form of defence. But bare feet could run faster than high heeled sandals and a moving target is harder to hit than a stationary one.

In one smooth movement, Jaq unwrapped the towel from her hips, threw it at Áurea's face and dived to the side, vaulting over the banister. Catching hold of the chandelier chain, she swung herself over to the next flight of stairs and dropped down.

She heard Áurea curse as the cocktail glass flew from her hand and smashed, then the whizz and crack of bullets as the woman fired blindly. Heels clicked on marble, then slid and fell. Given how many shoes Áurea had to choose from, those golden sandals had been a poor choice this morning. Screams of pain and rage followed Jaq as she reached the hall and ducked into the sitting room. By the time Áurea was on her feet again, Jaq was out onto the decking.

Áurea was on the balcony now, calling to the security guard. Jaq dropped to the sand and slithered under the decking. The guard came running, his feet just above her head as he crossed the decking and entered the house.

Bullets hit the sand as Jaq zig-zagged across the wide beach, splashed into the water and swam away.

It was almost dark now, a sprinkling of stars freckling the sky. Jaq was out of range of Áurea's pistol, but the danger wasn't over yet. There were armed security guards all along the beach.

She plunged through the waves, a fast front crawl with short, rapid strokes, swimming away from the beach. Once she passed the rocky outcrop, she glanced back. No sign of activity in front of the Costa mansion. No floodlights, men or dogs.

Jaq continued parallel to the shore, swimming breaststroke now, staying low, gliding through the water to minimise detection.

Áurea must have sounded the alarm by now, alerted the police. Jaq didn't have long.

Once she was opposite her bag, she swam underwater. When it was too shallow even for breaststroke, she found her footing in firm sand and broke into a run, crouching low and ducking behind the rocks to retrieve her bag.

She needed to get far away from the scene of the crime without drawing attention to herself. Single women don't usually go walking on beaches after dark. Best to make it look like a run.

Jaq made it back to the parked car in record time.

After so many weeks of searching for Dr Costa it was time to maximise the distance between them.

Y 3

Salvador de Bahia, Brazil

Back in her hotel in Salvador, Jaq took a long, hot shower until the shivering had almost stopped. She stood on the balcony looking out at the container vessels unloading but seeing nothing. What had happened to her son? She'd pinned all her hopes on finding Dr Carlos Costa. And now she'd found him, why were there no family pictures in his house, no trace of the child he'd adopted? Her child. It was not as if she could ask the dentist. He was dead. And she was about to be accused of his murder.

She'd left fingerprints and footprints all over the crime scene. The victim's phone would have her number as the last person to call, with a phone message identifying her as someone visiting that day. Jaq had first attempted to gain entry round about the time that Carlos had been shot. If Áurea wanted to frame her, the security guard would corroborate the story.

What had she been thinking? Why had she been so stupid? How long did she have before the police arrested her? It was her word against Mrs Áurea Costa's. A foreigner against a wealthy Brazilian homeowner. Perhaps she should go to the British Embassy? Perhaps she should turn herself in.

But Áurea had meant to kill her first. It was much easier to frame the dead than the living; the dead couldn't provide an alternate version of events. Perhaps Áurea would reconsider that plan, find another to blame.

And what if Jaq came forward as a witness? All the evidence

pointed to Áurea as the murderer, but she had not actually confessed to the act. How sure could Jaq be?

A wave of exhaustion washed over her, and she climbed into bed.

In the morning, Jaq went down for breakfast. The reception staff had gathered round the television. Jaq caught a glimpse of the beach north of Praia de Forte and joined them.

The local news had seized hold of the story. Carlos Costa's murder was headline news. But they were calling it a triple murder. Who else had perished?

On screen, a Hélio TV crew in a helicopter flew over the luxury mansion, hovering over a group of policemen standing on the rooftop garden. All eyes were on the woman in the pool. A woman with gold heels and white bikini, her gauzy robe billowing out around her as she floated face down in the water.

Áurea was dead?

The reporter's voice rose above the whirring. 'Police have confirmed that they are investigating the murder of three people in the exclusive gated community of Aí-Pixuna. The identities of the victims have not yet been confirmed, but neighbours called the police after hearing screams from the luxury mansion of Carlos Costa, a highly respected businessman who owns a chain of dental practices across Bahia. Unconfirmed reports suggest that Carlos and his wife, Áurea, perished along with a security guard from the night-shift beach patrol.'

Photos of the supposed victims flashed onto the screen, a well-built man in pink security uniform, the swimwear model and the retired dentist.

The picture cut to the mayor of Praia del Forte

'I am deeply shocked by the reports of an incident in Aí-Pixuna. Praia de Forte is one of the safest places in Brazil. Let's not jump to any conclusions. I suggest we allow the police to do their work. The safety of our residents is paramount, and I can assure you that I will do everything in my power to protect our homeowners and visitors.'

The camera switched to footage of a woman walking between two policemen, an apron covering her face, hurrying away from the property towards a police car.

'A domestic employee returned from a day off to discover the carnage early this morning. It was her screams that caused the neighbours to call the police. She was overheard to report no sign of forced entry or robbery. Neighbours mentioned a blossoming "friendship" between the young wife and security guard and there is mounting speculation that the crime may have been a domestic incident, the unfortunate consequence of a love triangle among the super-rich.'

Relief washed over her, quickly replaced by shame. If they decided it was a love triangle, would they look no further? Ignore the traces of Jaq's visit.

What had happened after Jaq swam away? Áurea didn't show any sign of remorse, nor did her death look like suicide. And what of the security guard? He was patrolling as she arrived. When she ran from Áurea, Jaq had expected to encounter him again on the beach. But he had not re-appeared. When had he been killed?

Whatever happened next, it had taught Jaq one lesson. She was out of her depth. Investigating alone had nearly cost her her life, or at least her freedom. There was absolutely no sign of her son in Carlos Costa's life. Now her only hope was to track down his first wife.

In order to find her son, first she had to find Evangelina.

Jaq was late leaving for the refinery. She'd arranged to meet Thiago at the Naphtha Hydroheater. She tried his number but there was no reply. He must have left his phone locked up in the office. Mobile phones had lithium batteries, which were potential sources of ignition, and not allowed near equipment handling flammable materials.

She was still five kilometres away when she saw a flash of light followed by a fireball expanding above the hill. She stopped the car, put her hands over her ears and waited for the noise of the explosion.

3

Salvador de Bahia, Brazil

Light travels faster than sound. Five seconds after the first flash of light came a whipcrack that rent the air, followed by a roar.

Jaq accelerated towards the refinery, arriving behind the first emergency vehicles with their blue lights flashing and sirens wailing. The fire was gaining strength now, black smoke billowing above orange flames.

The security guards refused to let her in, and she had to hover anxiously outside as the factory staff streamed out to the muster points. Where was Thiago?

From a distance, it looked as if the first explosion had involved hydrogen. The shimmering red fireball had burned cleanly, without smoke, and lasted only seconds.

Had Thiago been in the hydrogen section?

Whatever damage the hydrogen explosion had caused, other oil products had been released, and the fire brigade were now struggling to control the blaze.

The press had arrived too, cameras clicking and whirring, a Hélio News helicopter banked overhead.

The first ambulance screamed out through the gates, and anxious crowds surged forward.

Where was Thiago? Jaq scanned the mustering workers with increasing anxiety. She called Bruno.

'There's been an explosion in the Cuperoil refinery.'

'Are you OK?'

'Yes, but …' her voice faltered. 'I don't know about Thiago.'

'What don't you know about Thiago?'

A familiar voice made her spin round. Thiago was standing right behind her. She hugged him hard and then handed him the phone.

'Yes … Yes … Naptha Hydroheater,' he said in answer to Bruno's questions. 'Jaq and I were incredibly lucky. We were due to visit this morning. Thank God she was late.'

Y 2

Salvador de Bahia, Brazil

The memorial for the two workers killed in the blast at the Cuperoil factory was held on the same day as the funeral of Dr Carlos and Mrs Áurea Costa.

Thiago attended the former, Jaq, the latter.

The hearse drove slowly, followed by a procession of mourners and musicians, the slow drum beat and melancholy brass swelling as they weaved through the streets of Salvador to the cathedral.

Inside the church, a priest conducted a mass for their souls. Jaq waited outside, watching the people coming and going.

She'd taken a risk coming here. What if the gateman was in attendance, would he recognise her? And what if he did? As far as anyone was concerned, she had tried to visit on the day Dr Costa died. It wouldn't be unreasonable to assume that she had been a friend or colleague, completely natural for her to attend his funeral.

But what if the police were also here? What if the security cameras had captured her second visit, swimming in from the sea and entering the house from the beach side? What if they had looked at the CCTV tapes and identified her? What if they were watching and waiting, photographing the funeral guests, waiting to make their arrest?

She'd hoped to be inconspicuous, dressed in a simple black dress, with a headscarf and dark glasses, but many of the mourners were in white.

Why was she taking the risk at all? What did she hope for? That Evangelina would attend the funeral of her first husband? That her son would come too? Would she even recognise either of them if they did?

The family groups were easy to identify. Áurea's sisters were all tall and fair, none quite as stunning as the woman who had died, but recognisably related. As was the silver-haired man who supported Áurea's mother, a woman beside herself with grief.

Could Jaq have done more? Could she have prevented the tragedy? If she had gone for help as soon as she had arrived to find Carlos dead? The guilt was limited. After all, Áurea had been intent on framing her, had even tried to kill her.

The family of Carlos Costa was more extensive. Brothers, sister, cousins, some very young children and one elderly lady. His mother perhaps, or an aunt?

Another group must be the practice staff and clients. Dentists, hygienists, patients. A couple approached to offer their condolences to the family, but the reception was frosty. Others observed and kept their distance.

Jaq recognised the cook from the TV news. The woman who had discovered the bodies was with a group of men and women who were probably the other staff at the gated complex. She turned away in case the gateman was with them.

She sat on a low wall outside the church, listening to the service through the open doors, chanting followed by singing and finally the congregation disgorged into the sunlight, forming a corridor through which the two flower-covered coffins were carried.

Jaq followed.

After the interment in a cemetery on the edge of town, the mourners were invited to a reception. Jaq milled among the guests, seeking out the older members of Carlos's family, those who might remember his first wife. She listened to the introductions, figured out the connections, biding her time until she could approach

Carlos Costa's aunt, a severe-looking woman pushing a man in a wheelchair.

'Dona Avela, my sincere condolences.'

The woman sniffed and looked down her nose. 'And you are?'

Jaq introduced herself as a family friend from their time in Portugal.

'That was decades ago.' She frowned. 'You're far too young to have known my nephew then.'

'It was through my mother.'

'And you came all the way from Europe? For the funeral?'

'No, I'm working in Brazil.'

'I see.'

'Did you know Evangelina?'

She looked around and lowered her voice. 'His first wife? Yes, such a pity.'

Áurea's family were on the other side of the room, but Jaq lowered her voice as well. 'A pity? About the divorce?'

'Oh no, they weren't right for one another. But it was a pity about the accident.'

'The accident?'

'You didn't know?'

'We lost touch.'

'She was killed in a traffic accident.'

'When?'

'Oh, years ago. Not long after the divorce.'

'What happened to their son?'

'Carlos had no children.'

'But they adopted a child in Portugal.'

'I said – Carlos had no children.' She moved away.

Jaq wanted to bring out the adoption certificate, wave it under her nose, force her to read it, make her see that Carlos and Evangelina had taken responsibility for a baby, and then what? If the boy had stayed with Evangelina after the divorce, what had happened to him after her death? Had Evangelina's family taken him in?

She approached another guest, and another.

'Madame, I think you should leave.' The husband of one of Áurea's sisters approached her and took her arm. 'This is the funeral of Carlos and Áurea. It is not the time or the place to be talking about others.'

Jaq didn't wait to be told twice.

Ψ 2

Salvador de Bahia, Brazil

The funeral of the security guard, Nelson Santos, was an altogether more exuberant affair. The mourners, dressed in white were joined by musicians and drummers and a *capoeira* dance group.

Jaq passed through the crowds, trying to find someone who might have worked for the dentist when he was still married to his first wife. People were friendly, eager to help, and she was passed from one group to another, introductions made, contacts facilitated, until she found an elderly woman who was willing to talk.

'Poor Evangelina. She was a troubled woman.'

'Troubled, why?

'She was an orphan herself.'

Jaq's heart sank. So, who had taken in her son? 'Was there any family at all?'

'Not that I know of. She married for stability. I think they were genuinely fond of one another, Carlos and Evangelina, in the early days at least. But the move to Portugal didn't go well, put a lot of strain on the marriage. And when he became rich, he wanted a different sort of wife. I heard that Evangelina was heartbroken, and she never really got over the divorce.'

'And their son?'

'I don't think they were able to have children.'

'But they adopted …'

'First I've heard of it. But then I didn't see much of them after they married.'

'Do you think one of her friends might know?'

'I'm sorry, I have no idea.' The woman took her hand. 'I see you are distressed, my child. Searching for answers. You should talk to Taísa.'

'Taísa? Did she know Evangelina?'

'Taísa knows everyone and everything. Come.'

The funeral procession reached the *Escola Olodum,* home of a social project, and the old woman pointed.

A child stood beside an external stair. He waved, then started to descend. At the basement door, he turned and called to her, but she couldn't hear what he was saying over the percussion coming from inside the building.

'Do you see someone?'

'Yes.'

'Then go. Taísa is waiting.'

Jaq followed the child to the basement. The beat was louder now, insistent. A thin, white drape blocked her way; behind it soft lights flickered and dark shadows moved. Her heartbeat quickened to match the rhythm of the drumming, and something pulled her on.

Jaq pulled the curtain aside.

A woman knelt on the floor in front of a double drum. She wore the elaborate white-lace dress of a priestess. Beside her, candles lit a makeshift altar. Behind a row of small skulls, bleached white and filled with fruit and flowers, stood a statue of a woman and child. The Virgin Mary was robed in blue with a crown of flowers, her face turned towards the plump infant who sat in the crook of her arm, staring out. Both were black-skinned. Above them a carved tribal mask with slanted eyes and grinning mouth was adorned with a head-dress of coloured feathers. Under each one, clay pots and wooden platters were filled with offerings, bunches of bananas, pineapple, coconuts, seashells.

The woman looked up. 'Welcome,' she said. 'I knew you'd come.'

Jaq looked around for the others, the shadows she had seen dancing in the candlelight, but the room was empty. Where had the child gone? She stepped forward and scanned the room, searching for another passageway, an exit, a hiding place, but there was none. The hairs on the back of her neck stood up. Had she imagined the child?

'Are you Taísa?'

'I am.'

'Did you know Evangelina Costa?'

'Please, come closer.' Emilia gestured for her to approach the altar. 'Take off your shoes.'

Jaq followed the instruction.

'Be seated.'

Jaq dropped to the floor and sat cross-legged in front of Taísa. At the sound of a treble voice behind her, Jaq jumped and spun round. There was no one there.

'What troubles you, my dear?'

'I thought I heard something.'

'What did you hear?'

'Someone calling to me.'

'And did you recognise the voice?'

Only from dreams. 'No.'

'What did the voice say.'

'It was a child, asking for help. I thought I saw a boy coming down the stairs.' She rubbed her eyes. 'Where did he go?'

'It is your *orixá* calling to you.'

'My *orixá*?'

'Your link to the spiritual world.'

'I'm more interested in the physical world.'

'Every living person is connected to one of the ancestor gods, your spirit teacher protects you and controls your destiny.'

'I prefer the idea of free will, that I control my own destiny.'

'That is why your *axé* is so low. Your connection to the spiritual force of the universe is weak.'

'Non-existent.'

'We will see what the shells say, the *jogo dos búzios* cannot lie.'

Taísa took a sip from a silver goblet.

'You have lost something precious.'

Her eyes rolled back until only the whites were visible.

'But you won't find it here.'

The drumming began again – where was it coming from?

'He is searching for you.'

Taísa moaned and swayed in time to the rhythm.

'You are searching for him.'

She rattled the shells and chattered her teeth.

'You are both in the wrong place.'

Her head jerked and her eyes snapped back

'Go home.'

Go home. What had Taísa the priestess meant by that? Home to Angola, the place of her birth? Home to Lisbon, where her mother was buried? Home to Yarm, where she'd found refuge and a brief period of happiness? Or home to the millionaire's flat with a helipad and outdoor swimming pool in São Paulo? No, that one at least was definitely not home.

She shook herself. Why was she even thinking about this? Taísa was a charlatan, just another crafty hustler who separated gullible tourists from their money with promises of easy answers. It was all just a spectacle, the drumming and the dancing, the incense and candlelight, the mash-up of Portuguese Catholic and West African Yoruba religions to create *Candomblé*, a dance in honour of the gods.

A dance, that was all it was.

2

Rio de Janeiro, Brazil

From the top of Sugar Loaf Mountain, the whole of Rio de Janeiro stretched out, shimmering in the heat. On three sides, fingers of sea caressed the improbably shaped hills, leaving a narrow strip for the city to cling to between jungle and ocean.

Jaq couldn't settle. It had been Marina's idea to come here, riding the cable car up to the summit and walking down, side by side. Marina didn't ask any questions, just waited until Jaq was ready to talk.

'People died in Salvador, and I don't know why.'

'The dentist's love triangle?' Marina asked. 'I saw the news and wondered. A bit too much of a coincidence that you were in Salvador looking for a Dr Carlos Costa, and a Dr Carlos Costa winds up dead.'

Jaq told Marina what had happened. The unexpected lead from the lawyer, the visit to the home of the man who had adopted her son, only to find the dentist with his brains blown out and her narrow escape from the new wife who had probably killed him.

'Carlos Costa was already dead when I arrived,' Jaq said. 'But by failing to raise the alarm immediately, I let another two people die.'

'One of whom had tried to kill you.'

Jaq shook her head. 'That's no excuse ...'

'What do you think happened to the second wife and her lover?'

Jaq opened her palms heavenward. 'I saw the guard run into the house, he and Áurea were alive and well when I left.'

'More importantly, there was no sign, no trace of your son?'

'Not even a photo.'

'Nor any information about the first wife?'

'Nothing in the house. But I went to the funeral of the security guard, and they told me that Evangelina had died.'

Should she mention the other two? The men burned to death in the Cuperoil refinery explosion? Initial investigation pointed to hydrogen embrittlement of carbon steel, a slow, insidious rot that had been going on for years, an accident waiting to happen. Just chance that she had been due to visit the area at the time of the accident? Or a deliberate attempt to kill her? Either way she'd had a lucky escape, arriving late because of her visit to Praia de Forte and the carnage there.

Marina ran a hand through her hair.

'One thing I don't understand. Why did Dr Costa go to your lawyer in the first place? Was it just coincidence?'

'No.' Jaq stood and stretched. 'The lawyer said he knew about my mother's death and believed he was owed something.'

'Which brings us to the package your grandmother left for you. You still haven't told me what you found.'

Jaq handed her the gold ring. Marina held it up to catch the sunlight.

'What does the engraving mean?'

'Is it a hallmark?'

Marina shook her head. 'Looks more like a symbol followed by numbers.'

Jaq took the ring back.

On the inside surface, what she had taken for a hallmark looked, on closer inspection, to be a chemical symbol, like the Linnean pictogram for female – a circle with a plus sign underneath, but this one had a shallow U on top, adding a pair of horns.

'It might be the ancient alchemical symbol for Mercury, the messenger,' Jaq said. 'There was a poem as well, one of the cantos from Fernando Pessoa's *Mensagem*.

'So there's a message in this ring?' Marina asked.

'All that glitters is not gold,' Jaq quoted.

'Do you want me to get an analysis done? I can use the mass spectrometer at work?'

'Yes.' Jaq handed her the ring. 'The land my grandmother bought had mining rights.'

'Do you think your grandmother left you a gold mine?'

Jaq sighed. 'I couldn't care less.'

'But other people might.'

And then Jaq knew what she had to do.

Guarulhos International Airport, São Paulo, Brazil

They weren't going to make the same mistake twice. With more people on the payroll at Guarulhos, men and women, there would be no errors this time.

Her flight was due in at 8 p.m.

Oskar was ready for her. Payback time. He'd lost his job because of her, been beaten up by the police because of her. Maybe he had broken into her apartment block in São Paulo, but how was he to know it was Fort Knox? How was he to know that the security guard had cousins in the police force?

It wasn't as if the Colonel had done any better without him.

Compared to the usual security jobs, accosting the druggies with nothing to gain by going quietly, detaining men carrying concealed weapons with nothing to lose from using them, they'd probably thought that capturing her would be a walk in the park.

But they'd reckoned wrong. A twisty one, she was.

Five days ago, they'd missed the opportunity to nab her before she left Brazil, grabbing a girl who looked a bit like her after a mix-up with boarding passes. They'd had to silence Elena Azevedo and now it was all over the news.

Then the idiots had missed Jaq Silver in Europe, twice. Four days ago on her way in, and earlier today on her way out. The Amsterdam contact had taken a passenger carrying a leather box, the safe they had to destroy before Ecobrium got their hands on it. Turned out it wasn't the right box or the right woman. Curtains for her. He didn't give much for the Amsterdam soldier's future with RIMPO either.

If Oskar had been involved, that would never have happened. He could have given a positive identification. That's why they'd brought him back in. If you want a job done right, give it to a smoking cobra.

They'd confirmed that she'd left Frankfurt. A scan of the passport – Dr Jaq Silver – triggered the alarm. They couldn't afford another cock-up, so they'd asked Oskar to re-join the team. There was plenty of footage of her in Frankfurt airport. He replayed the video on the computer screen and smiled.

She looked like she hadn't slept in a while, but he'd seen her at closer quarters than most. Yes, he confirmed, it was definitely Silver who had boarded the Frankfurt to São Paulo flight. There was only one place that flight could go. And once it landed, this was the only way out of the airport.

They had her now.

So many senseless deaths she'd have to pay for.

And pay for it, she would.

He'd make sure of that.

2

Rio de Janeiro, Brazil

Hélio TV, the studio where César worked was in the Curicica area of Rio. It felt like a different city, as if she had scratched the surface to find something foetid, something dark and menacing underneath.

'Jaq, what a lovely surprise!'

César beamed at her, as if she was his best friend. She kept her hands to her sides and they air-kissed.

'How's your search going?'

She brought him up to date. The adoptive father and mother both dead and nobody knew anything about the child.

'Do you know how many street children there are in Brazil?'

He didn't wait for her reply.

'Some estimates put it as high as eight million.'

Jaq felt sick.

'I was hoping that one of the mother's friends might have taken him in.'

'What do you have to go on?'

'Documents and photos at the time of adoption.'

César shook his head. 'Hundreds of thousands of people go missing in Brazil every year. And only a fraction of cases are reported.'

He stroked his goatee beard.

'Most people are too frightened of the police to file a report.

In any case, some of the disappearances are at the hands of the authorities.'

Jaq interrupted him.

'I found something that might be of interest to you.'

She brought out the document from the lawyer. Assuming César didn't read the fine print, he was not to know that the contract was useless on its own.

'It turns out that the person I'm looking for stands to inherit a gold mine.'

César's eyes gleamed. 'In Brazil?' he said.

'Yes.'

'And the person you are looking for is related to you?'

She met his eyes. 'He's my son.'

'And your son is missing.'

'Yes.'

César stroked his beard. 'Let me make a few calls.'

Y 2

Rio de Janeiro, Brazil

César's first call was to RIMPO.

'A gold mine you say?'

'I thought the Colonel should know.'

'Who is this person making such an outlandish claim'

'A woman by the name of Jaq Silver.' César explained. 'Searching for her son.'

'Silver, eh?' The man at the other end of the phone laughed. 'Well, well, what a small world. The Colonel has been ... interested in Silver ever since she arrived in Brazil.'

The way he paused before the word *interested* made César shiver. Colonel Cub and his first-hand knowledge of the Araguaia missing had been central to the success of the pilot episode, the reason the series was bought by Hélio TV. But it was César who had turned it into a runaway success – twelve million viewers for the last live episode of *The Missing*. How could he free himself from this Faustian bargain?

'What should I do? Send her away?'

'No. You were right to come to us.'

'I'm not sure she even cares about the gold. She's only interested in finding her son.'

'Hmmm. I have an idea.'

'I'm listening.'

'What if you go ahead? Put her on the show and then find the son for her?'

'Find, as in?'

'What you often do. Place someone convincing in the role.'

'What are you implying?'

'Oh, come on, César. I wasn't born yesterday.' His tone softened. 'TV is entertainment, not reality, and you do know a lot of fine actors.'

'What if I do?'

'We'd be very, very grateful if you would … control this story.'

'To what end?'

'To relieve Silver of the ownership documents. We'll pay handsomely.'

'So, I find someone that fits the description of the missing son, introduce them and then what?'

'Make clear that his job is to get the documents and pass them on to us.'

'And if he goes rogue, decides to keep the gold mine for himself?'

'We'll expose him as a fraud.' He sighed. 'Surely I don't have to tell you how to do your job César. When you audition, you will choose someone who can be … managed.'

'And what if the real son appears out of the woodwork?'

'We kill him.'

Guarulhos International Airport, São Paulo, Brazil

Jaq was last to disembark from the Frankfurt plane into the arrivals hall at Guarulhos International Airport. She followed the other passengers past a giant Santa Claus and his animatronic reindeers, joining a queue for Brazilian immigration that snaked around the arrival lounge.

She paused to turn on her phone, and a series of texts pinged, each one a poison dart of bad news.

The dread washed over her like a freezing shower. Her hold luggage, the leather box that was the key to Mercúrio's release, had missed the connection in Frankfurt. The airline apologised for the inconvenience. Inconvenience? Mercúrio's life depended on her getting it back in time.

A man behind her coughed in irritation. The queue was moving forward, she hurried to catch up.

Another ping. An update on her luggage. It was on the next flight. Arriving in a few hours. She checked the time, momentarily confused by the four hours she'd gained travelling west.

As she approached a turn, the queue doubling back on itself, a security official moved the tape to create a new lane. It led to an additional counter that was just opening. She put her phone in her pocket, took out her documents and was about to move forward when she saw him.

Beefcake. The man with the smoking cobra tattoo.

He was leaning against the wall, right at the back, behind passport control. There was no mistaking the soldier from the lift in the Ibirapuera hotel, the one who'd harassed her while she was swimming in the garden of her apartment block.

Jaq dropped down to one knee, turning her face away, pretending to tie a shoelace.

She crouched low and pushed her way back through the queue, finding a toilet and locking herself inside.

Porcaria de merda. What to do?

She called Marina.

'Jaq! I was wondering where you'd got to.'

'Where are you?'

'At work.'

'Which one?' Shoes or planes?

'Aérex.'

Planes then.

'I'm at Guarulhos.' São José dos Campos was only 70 kilometres away.'

'Coming or going?'

Good question. Neither right now. 'Look I wouldn't ask, but ...'

'Ask away.'

'I need a lift.'

'Sure, where to?'

'Florianopolis.'

Marina laughed. 'That's quite an ask!'

'Do you have a plane?'

'Well, there's that lovely hydrogen prototype in the test hangar. I've been longing to try that out.'

'Would it get us to Florianopolis?'

'Sure.'

'Can you pick me up in Guarulhos?'

'Busiest airport in Latin America? Might be tricky getting a flight plan approved. Can you get a taxi to bring you here?'

'I can't risk it.'

'You in trouble?'

'Big trouble.'

'Leave it with me.'

2

Rio de Janeiro, Brazil

The production assistant took Jaq to one side.

'Are you sure you want to do this?'

'I'm sure.'

'You know that Brazil is full of crazies, deluded people who will try anything for a few seconds of fame?'

Not just Brazil. 'Yes.'

'And desperately poor people who would pretend to be anyone you want them to be for the promise of a few coins, not to mention a whole gold mine.'

'I know.'

'And violent criminals who would kill for less.'

'I know.'

'You run the risk of attracting the wrong sort of attention.'

'I don't care. All I care is that it attracts his attention.' *If he's still alive.*

'If you find him, would you do a DNA test?'

'Yes.'

'Don't use your full name. You're Maria de Jaqueline, right?'

'Just Jaq.'

'OK, don't mention your surname.'

'If you say so.'

'OK, let's go.'

Guarulhos International Airport, São Paulo, Brazil

Jaq opened the door back onto the concourse and then closed it again. The soldiers, men and women, were prowling now. If they knew which flight she was on, they must have realised that she wasn't coming through immigration. The toilets were an obvious place to find her.

If she was to get out of international arrivals, she needed to make it harder for them to spot her. There wasn't anything in her bag that would constitute a disguise. She still had cash; she could buy something. But how to get past them to the shops?

Thank God for false ceilings.

Standing on the toilet seat, she stretched up and punched through the polystyrene square. It crumpled easily. She used the water pipes to climb up into the service void. The panels weren't load bearing, but if she used the supporting structure for the air-conditioning vents, she had a good chance of remaining undetected.

Time for a bit of clothes shopping.

She crawled to the other side of arrivals and dropped through the missing ceiling panel into the changing room of Balúrdio.

It had always astonished her that such eye-wateringly expensive shops in airports ever sold anything, but she was fast turning into their best customer.

The sales assistant was too bored to notice her, busy with her phone. Jaq picked out a summer dress and returned to the cubicle.

Through a chink between changing room curtains, she spotted Beefcake and his gang of thugs. She held her breath, heart pounding, but he walked past.

The phone rang.

'Marina?'

'Life is never dull with you, Jaq Silver. I have a slot for five o'clock tomorrow morning. That good enough for you?'

The flight with her delayed luggage was due in at 4 a.m.

'Perfect.'

'We have to be in and out in 30 minutes.'

It was cutting it fine if the box was late. Time to face that hurdle if it arose.

'Where do I go?'

'Private terminal. JewelJet. I'll text you the details.'

'Can you tell them to expect me?'

'Sure, you heading over there now?'

'Soon. Can you big me up a bit? I might need them to unpick a little problem for me.'

'No need. They're the premium service. This is costing an arm and a leg—'

'I'll pay you back.'

'I'll make sure you do. And Jaq …'

'Yes.'

'Just go easy on the complimentary champagne, OK. I need a sober co-pilot.'

Jaq prepared to leave the way she had arrived. She left the old clothes – Emma's shirt, leggings and socks – on the chair, along with enough cash to cover the cost of the overpriced dress; she had no desire to get some poorly paid shop assistant fired.

The Sugar Loaf Mountain bag contained the very minimum she needed, passport, wallet, phone, shoe roll and Ben's catapult. In the absence of handy climbing pipes, it took all her strength to pull herself back up into the ceiling void, swinging her legs up first and then using her core to raise her torso. She crawled towards the exit only to find that a solid wall separated international arrivals from the rest of the airport.

She dropped back down into the Balúrdio changing room and peered into the shop. Beefcake was standing in the centre of the airport duty free shopping area, right under the arrivals board. A new dress was unlikely to be disguise enough to slip past him.

'Pssst.'

She finally managed to attract the shop assistant's attention.

'Can I pay you?'

'Come to the till.'

'I can't.' She nodded towards the crowded concourse.

'Don't want your husband spotting you spending his money, eh?'

The assumption that she must be spending someone else's money always infuriated her. But now was not the time to argue. The assistant took the pile of cash she proffered, rang it through the till and brought back her change and receipt.

Jaq pushed the change back to her. 'And this.'

She scooped up a heavy necklace from the sale rack, alternating glass and metal beads bigger than marbles.

Ammunition.

'I can't let him see me.'

The assistant's eyes opened wide. She only saw two customers a day and this little drama was better than a soap opera.

'I need your help.' Jaq nodded towards the concourse. 'Is there another way out?'

'Follow me ...'

Y 2

Hélio TV Studio, Rio de Janeiro, Brazil

The spotlight followed César as he made his way into the TV studio and stood in front of the sofa. The applause swelled, mixed with whistles and cheers of welcome.

'Good evening.' He acknowledged the studio audience before focussing on the camera. 'And welcome to *The Missing*!' He flicked a lock of hair from his eyes. 'The show that reunites some families,' he stroked his neatly trimmed beard. 'And drives others apart.'

The audience roared with laughter as if he'd made the joke for the first time.

'First on the show tonight, we have a young lady who has come a long way in search of a pot of gold. Ladies and Gentlemen, please put your hands together and welcome … Jaq!'

Marina had insisted that Jaq dressed up for the occasion. She'd brought Jaq her own Transform shoe roll and then taken her shopping, choosing a sleeveless button-down jumpsuit that showed off arms toned from swimming, cinched at the waist with a wide gold belt. César welcomed her with open arms, kissing one cheek and then the other. He pointed to the sofa opposite.

'Now Jaq, tell us. Where are you from?'

Angola, via Moscow, Lisbon and Teesside. They'd been through this in rehearsal and the producer suggested that she stuck to one to avoid confusion.'

'I came to Brazil from Europe.' It was a reasonable compromise.

'So, Jaq. How do you like Brazil?'

'I like it very much.'

'Beaches, *churrasco*, Caipirinhas?'

The audience laughed.

'All of those, but most of all the people. So warm and friendly.'

There was a murmur of appreciation.

'And what brings you here tonight, Jaq?'

'I am looking for a child who was adopted in Portugal and brought to Brazil.'

'Whoa!' César reeled back in exaggerated surprise. 'Hold on a minute. We hear a lot about Brazilian children being adopted and taken from our country, but rarely the other way around.'

'Well, it's a long story.'

'And we like a good story, don't we ladies and gentlemen.'

The crowd clapped and cheered.

'But help me here, Jaq. The child was adopted more than twenty years ago. So, we're looking for a young man.'

'That's right.'

'And what is his name?'

'I don't know.'

'You don't know?'

Jaq shook her head. This was going to be the hardest bit. She raised her head and looked straight into the camera. 'They took him away before I could name him.'

'Who took him away, Jaq?'

'The nuns in the convent.'

'And why were you and this unnamed child in a convent, Jaq?'

'It's where they sent the unmarried mothers.'

'Were you an unmarried mother, Jaq?'

'I was.' She raised her head and her eyes flashed. 'I am.'

'And you gave your baby up for adoption?'

'I did not.' There was real anger in her voice. 'They told me he was dead.'

A gasp from the crowd, and then a murmur of sympathy.

'So, they took your baby away, arranged for his adoption and told you he had died.'

She didn't trust herself to speak so she nodded.

'And when did you find out that he wasn't dead.'

'Four months, three days and five hours ago.'

There was a ripple of appreciation, then a round of applause.

'And how did you find out?'

'My mother died.'

There was a sigh of commiseration.

'She left some papers in an old leather strongbox.' Jaq paused, the memory still raw. 'That's where I found the adoption certificate.'

'Who adopted your son, Jaq?'

'Evangelina Costa.'

Marina had advised her to keep Carlos Costa out of the picture. It wouldn't do to have the police reopen the investigation into the fatal love triangle at Praia de Forte.

'And what else did you find, Jaq?'

'A bequest from my grandmother.'

'And what was in that bequest?'

Jaq crossed her legs, showing off the elegant shoes that perfectly matched the shimmering belt.

'A gold mine.'

The audience cheered.

'A gold mine in Brazil?'

'Yes.'

'Now Jaq, are you a Brazilian citizen?'

'I am not.'

'And am I right in saying that, under Brazilian law, only a Brazilian citizen can own a mine?'

'That's right.'

'And is your son, name unknown, a Brazilian citizen?'

'I would assume so.'

'So, if he's out there, would you say, Jaq,' he grinned at the audience, 'that this is a golden opportunity?'

Jaq stared directly at the camera.

'Please get in touch.'

Guarulhos International Airport, São Paulo, Brazil

The goods elevator, where the overpriced merchandise for Balúrdio was transported from storeroom to boutique, had an exit onto a zigzag-shaped service corridor that ran directly under the shops, connecting the duty-free area to the main concourse where the general public waited for arriving passengers.

Jaq kept to the shadows, back against the wall, peering round each corner as she made her way towards the exit. She came to the same security wall that extended up into the ventilation ducting. A double door was the only connection between the two areas, before and after immigration, with a security checkpoint on the other side.

She peered through the glass panel.

There were two men on the other side. One was seated. He looked like a normal security guard, the sort who checked the papers of the workers who brought supplies into the duty-free shops.

The other was standing, alert, poised for action. He looked like a soldier, short hair, muscles and tattoos, with a pistol in a holster belt and an automatic rifle slung over his chest.

Two against one. Time to bring out her deadliest weapon.

Jaq reached into the Sugar Loaf Mountain bag and pulled out Ben's catapult, stuffing the long end of the Y into the belt of her dress. She bit the nylon cord from the necklace around her neck and caught the beads as they tumbled into her hands. She filled the side pocket of the bag, reserving the four sharpest and heaviest stones.

It was now or never.

In a swift movement she pushed the door open with her back, swung round, dropping to one knee. First she took out the security camera, shattering the lense with a single missile. Glass showered down onto the security guard and he began to cry out.

'Stop!'

The soldier rushed towards her, making it even easier to find her target. The second bead hit him square on the Adam's apple, slowing his progress as he found himself unable to breathe. His pistol clattered to the floor as his hands flew to his throat. The third missile hit him square on the side of his forehead as he twisted and fell to the ground.

Jaq kicked away the pistol and aimed the catapult at the security guard.

'I don't want no trouble!' He put his hands up in the air.

She stretched the catapult elastic.

'No, please.' He was sweating. 'I won't say anything, I promise.'

She looked at him through narrowed eyes, dropping to the ground to listen to the soldier. He was breathing, but he would be unconscious for some time. She felt inside his pockets and removed his phone. Then she released the strap on his automatic rifle and unclipped the ammunition.

'Please don't shoot me.'

'I don't want to hurt you,' Jaq said. 'But I can't leave anyone here to raise the alarm.'

He nodded at a door behind him. 'Lock us in the storeroom.'

She nodded. 'Open it.'

He took out a key and unlocked a windowless room with a sink, a stack of plastic chairs and a rack of cleaning equipment.

'Move him in.'

The security guard huffed and puffed as he dragged the comatose soldier into the cleaning cupboard. He remained inside, visibly trembling.

'Give me your phone.'

He obliged.

'You didn't see what happened, OK?'

Jaq locked the door.

♒ 2

Hélio TV Studio, Rio de Janeiro, Brazil

The final piece was delivered straight to camera.

Action!

'My name is Jaq, and I am looking for my son.'

The photograph from the convent filled the screen, the picture of a baby with birth date below.

'My son was adopted at birth by Evangelina Costa in Lisbon, Portugal. The family returned to Brazil.'

A photo of Evangelina.

'My son stands to inherit a gold mine.'

The screen panned to the contract for the Brazilian mine.

'Anyone who has any information about him please contact ...'

The deep voice boomed out:

The Missing

Cut!

Guarulhos International Airport, São Paulo, Brazil

Outside the office of the private jet service, Jaq straightened up and assumed her most patrician manner.

She'd disposed of the pistol, rifle, cupboard key and phones in a series of industrial dumpsters in the service corridors before emerging into the atrium of the airport. There were soldiers everywhere and she'd mingled with the crowds, taking a round-about route to the terminal where JewelJet operated.

'Good evening.' A smiling steward opened the door.

'Silver, Jaq Silver.' She offered her passport, but he waved it away.

'Welcome Dr Silver, we've been expecting you.'

'My luggage is coming in on the next flight.' She showed him her phone with the lost property message. 'Can I ask them to deliver it here?'

'Oh, don't worry about that, we'll go and fetch it.'

Thank heavens for private jets and the privilege of the super-rich.

The desk clerk typed the flight details into his computer.

'I can track the flight. We'll send someone out to the tarmac to fetch your luggage as soon as the plane lands. Much faster. Do you have the tag?'

She handed him the boarding card with the luggage tag on the back.

'Can you describe it?'

'Even better.' She handed him the guarantee card attached to the receipt with a picture of the large, hard-shelled silver case.

He took the details, printed a form and handed it to her with a pen.

'Are you happy for us to collect it on your behalf?'

'Delighted.'

'Then just sign here.'

'Now, Dr Silver, you have a few hours before your private jet arrives. Would you like to wash or sleep or eat?'

'All of the above.'

'What would you like to eat?'

'What can you offer?'

'Whatever you like.'

'Miso soup. Sashimi.'

'Can I get you some champagne?'

Reluctantly. 'No.'

'And my colleague does a great massage, if you're interested.'

The tall, dark man at the bar looked up and waved.

Very interested. But no time for distractions.

The sleep cubicle was simple, but perfectly functional. She ate, took a shower, wrapped herself in a bathrobe and slipped between ironed cotton sheets.

DETONATION MINUS 1

Guarulhos International Airport, São Paulo, Brazil

Christmas Eve

Jaq was woken by a knock at the door. It took her a moment to remember where she was.

'Sorry to disturb you, Dr Silver. You asked to be woken at 4:30 a.m.'

'Thank you.'

She washed and dressed quickly, collecting a hot coffee from the smiling steward.

'Your jet has been cleared for take-off from São José dos Campos. It should be landing on time.'

'Any sign of my luggage?'

'Not yet. The international flights come in on a different runway. I believe it's circling, waiting for a landing slot. I'll let you know as soon as it's on the ground.'

'I can't leave without it.'

'Don't worry.'

Don't worry? A man's life depended on her luggage arriving on time.

She retreated back to the cubicle to change her shoes, taking time to colour-match with the new dress. It was the kind of thing Marina would notice. By the time she had finished it was almost 5 a.m.

'Dr Silver, your jet is coming in to land.'

'And my luggage?'

'We've sent someone to fetch it.'

Jaq walked to the window and followed the progress of the light in the sky. Marina brought the wheels down smoothly and Jaq admired the way she handled the beautiful prototype plane. As soon as it was on the ground, Jaq headed out to the tarmac. The cockpit opened and Marina's long legs emerged.

'Hello, girlfriend,' she said.

'Hello, girlfriend.'

'Are you ready to roll?' Marina ducked under the wing to unlock the passenger door. 'Your nozzle redesign worked a treat. I've brought a new belt with me—'

Marina turned to see that Jaq hadn't moved.

'What's wrong?'

'We can't leave yet.'

Having come this far, there was no point continuing without the strongbox. How else was she to save Mercúrio?

'Marina, follow me. I need to show you something first.'

It was thanks to Marina that she'd found him. César's programme provoked thousands of replies. The production team had sifted through them, rejecting the crazies and the villains, getting independent corroboration of birth date, or blood type, until they'd narrowed it down to just one man.

The producer called her at work.

'I think we've found him,' she said. 'A young man claims to have been adopted at birth by Evangelina Costa in Lisbon, Portugal.

'He doesn't remember much about his early life. The family returned to Salvador, Brazil, before he was three. He attended an international primary school. I've checked the records and he was definitely a pupil.

'After his parents separated, he says he stayed with his adoptive mother. He knew her birth date and the fact she was an orphan. He doesn't remember his adoptive father, apparently it upset Evangelina too much to talk about him.

'After Evangelina's fatal car accident, he was sent to the Pius X orphanage in Salvador. But he wasn't happy there and ran away as a teenager. We've checked the orphanage records and the story checks out.

'He's 22 years old. A surfer and musician. His name is Mercúrio.'

When the email came through with his picture, she'd brought her phone down to the garden. It felt as if the walls of the flat were closing in on her, the rented space suddenly too white, too bright, too sterile. She curled up under the big fig tree and listened to the frogs and crickets. In the fading light she stared at her phone, trying to compare the photo of a baby stolen from his teenage mother with the photo of the young man he'd become.

She stared at the picture. Her son was alive. He was healthy. So why did it make her feel so uneasy, so conflicted? Because she'd expected an 'Aha!' moment, instant recognition? Expected to see something of her brother in his features?

It was true that his lips were full and soft, like her own, but his nose was straight and wide, missing the turned-up tip of her brother's. His eyes were brown, fringed with long, dark lashes, not blue like Sam's, nor green like hers.

Jaq could no longer conjure up a clear image of Mr Peres, unable to remember much about her chemistry teacher's appearance. He'd been neither tall nor short, fat nor thin. His hair had been straight, mousy brown, and his skin was paler than hers. He'd seemed so beautiful at the time. She could remember his touch, his smell, the noises he made from wanting her, wanting the girl whom no one else wanted, loving her when no one else did. The scents she associated with him were those of the darkroom, the place where he took full advantage of her stupid, childish crush. Just an unremarkable, middle-aged man, powerful and despicable. Her memories were so clouded with anger now that she preferred not to resurrect them.

She looked from the baby photo to the adult photo and back. Was Mercúrio really the same person? Why should she doubt it?

He was certainly a beautiful man, a son any mother would be proud to call her own.

Now, in the executive lounge of a private airline, Jaq brought a third picture and showed it to Marina: Jaq and Mercúrio with surfboards, standing side by side on the beach.

'This is my son.'

Marina's hand flew to her mouth. 'You found him.'

'Thanks to you. I'd been searching for months.' What a fool. In a country of two hundred million, what were the chances? 'You were right about César and his show. Someone saw the appeal on *The Missing*. Recognised the story. Persuaded Mercúrio to watch it too. He came forward. César's team checked out his story. It matched perfectly.'

'So, you agreed to meet him?'

'Yes.'

She'd borrowed an old motorbike from the garage of her São Paulo flat and ridden down the coast until she found the beach he surfed, anxious that their reunion should be on his terms, in his world, surrounded by his friends. At first she hung back, watching and waiting, but the surfing crowd were friendly, found her a board, invited her in.

'I watched him surf, listened to him sing.'

Mercúrio must have recognised her from the TV show, *The Missing*, because he initiated the first contact. *Leaving so soon? I wrote this song for you.*

Marina's eyes shone.

'Did you know, at once, that he was your son?'

Jaq shook her head.

'I'll admit I remained suspicious.' There had been so many dashed hopes, blind alleys, false leads.

'I wanted us to do a DNA test, but he insisted we take it slowly, get to know one another first. It was his idea that we should spend Christmas together. So he could tell me his story, and I could tell him mine. He thought it would make things easier for us. But it wasn't easy, Marina. Maybe I was too late. The things that had happened to him ... as a child ... had ... damaged him so much. It wasn't easy for us to talk rationally, there was so much emotion, so much anger. The only time we were really good together was when we were surfing. He was in his element on the water. I loved to watch that, be part of it.'

Marina put an arm around Jaq and pulled her closer.

'I thought he was beginning to trust me. But then we had an argument, a terrible argument.' Was it really only a few days ago? It seemed like an eternity, 'He walked out on me. I let him go.'

Jaq laid her head against Marina's shoulder.

'That same night, men broke into my house. Told me they had taken Mercúrio, were holding him hostage. That unless I bring the ransom by noon on Christmas eve, by noon today, they will ...' Jaq faltered.

Marina gasped.

'Unless I get there in time, they will kill him,' Jaq finished.

'What's the ransom?'

'A strongbox that belonged to my mother.'

Marina looked around 'Where is it?'

'On its way.'

Marina looked up at the clock on the wall. 'Jaq, we have to leave in the next ten minutes or I'll miss our slot.'

'He's in danger, real danger.' Jaq's voice broke. 'I failed Mercúrio before. I can't fail him again.'

A man appeared in the doorway with a large suitcase.

'Dr Silver, is this the one?'

Jaq jumped to her feet, relief flooding through. 'Oh, thank you. Thank you so much.'

Marina wrinkled her nose. 'We're flying an experimental plane. I can't be sure that massive *porcaria* is going to fit.'

Jaq clicked the locks, opened the shell and pulled out the leather safe. 'What about this?'

Marina nodded. 'You ready?'

'As ready as I'll ever be.'

'Let's go rescue your boy!'

Florianopolis, Brazil

Jaq opened the door of the bungalow. Crazy Gloves had told her to be here at noon. Marina had landed them on the beach with a few hours to spare. Jaq had told her to hide the plane, stay out of sight. They couldn't risk spooking the kidnappers.

Inside the beach house, there were things that needed doing. The beds were still unmade, the kitchen pans unwashed, everywhere the signs of a hurried exit.

If Mercúrio was returned safely to her, she would gladly play house: sweep and dust, wipe and rinse, strip and wash the sheets, hanging them out to dry in the sea breeze.

If Mercúrio was safe, she wouldn't insist on the test that had caused the argument. They could take their time. Build trust again. Whether he was her son or not, Mercúrio was already a damaged man. And now she had complicated his life by drawing him into her world. Into danger. Please God, let them not have hurt him.

Jaq couldn't bear to remain inside. She took a chair to the veranda and stared out to sea.

Florianopolis, Brazil

On their last day together, they'd bought surf clams at the market and Mercúrio offered to cook. She left him to it, laying the table with a fresh white cloth and silverware.

She slipped into the kitchen to get the wine from the fridge. White for a change. He was talking to someone on his phone, so she took it back to the dining room. She used the sharp blade of her Swiss Army penknife to remove the lead seal before she snapped it closed and extracted the corkscrew, inserting the metal tip into the soft seal. Alentejan cork, formed from the bark of a Quercus suber. Had the cork come from Portugal? Or did cork oaks grow in Latin America too? Suddenly curious, she picked up her phone to search for the answer and noticed a text from Marina with a question about the new geometry of the nitrogen propulsion nozzles.

'Why are you ignoring me?'

She looked up, surprised at the tone of his voice.

'Am I your son or your slave?'

Where was all this coming from?

'Dinner's ready.'

She turned off her phone and laid it on the tablecloth.

'Can I help?'

He flounced back into the kitchen. 'It's a bit late for that.'

She bit her lip and poured the wine. What had got into him? A kitchen disaster? Not by the look or smell of the steaming dish of spaghetti alle vongole he slammed onto the table, a little halo of parsley and clam juice forming around the plate on the white tablecloth.

'I cook for you and you just take it for granted.'

'I'm sorry.' She bent her head to catch the aroma of garlic and wine and surf clams. 'Mmmm. This smells delicious.'

They ate in near silence, the clatter of his fork against the plate building with tension until he threw it down.

'I won't do the test.'

Aha, so that was what this was about. The appointment at the genetic laboratory in Floripa tomorrow.

'I see.'

He scrunched his eyes tight shut. 'You should trust me.' His voice was ragged with hurt.

'It's not a question of trust. Neither of us knows the truth.'

'And you think science holds the answers? You think love can be manufactured in a test tube?'

'I think love is something that grows with time.'

'And I think it should be instant. We recognise our own. When it's right, you just know.' He stood up. 'By asking me to take the test, you're telling me you don't feel anything for me. You don't love me.'

Love. She sighed. How to argue rationally about something that was, at heart, completely irrational. Was it love that had sent her on this wild goose chase? This needle in a haystack search? Or duty? Duty was easier to understand, more impersonal. You didn't have to love someone to feel duty-bound to help them, you just had to believe in a set of rules, take responsibility.

'Perhaps it's you. Perhaps you are incapable of love.'

How to answer that? It would only heighten his anguish to relate all the times she'd loved – truly, madly, deeply. But falling in love didn't require you to switch off your reason. Well briefly perhaps. A smile tickled the corner of her lips and she had to fight to suppress it. What was wrong with her? Now was not the time.

Perhaps he was right. Perhaps her feelings for those men had been lust rather than love. Perhaps the type of love he was seeking – the love of a mother for a child – was beyond her.

'Perhaps.'

How many children did she know? Ben, the son of her best friend, impressed her with his curiosity and courage. She barely knew Jade, his little sister. And much as she found them charming in small doses, it was always a relief when they went to bed and she had Johan to herself. Johan and Emma. How many times had they interrupted a conversation to jump up and see to their children? There was no question who came first. There was no doubting the love. The bond between her friends and their children was in a different league to anything she had ever experienced. And how could it be otherwise? The selfish gene. The children shared their parents DNA. Was it so simple? So mechanistic? What some called love, others recognised for what it really was, the drive to procreate, to nurture and protect a tiny copy of oneself, to bring some meaning to life, and death. To achieve the immortality of your genes. And yet she felt fiercely protective towards baby Lily, the granddaughter of Gregor, her ex-husband, a child with none of Jaq's genes, born with all the cards stacked against her. Where was the evolutionary benefit in that?

'All that stuff about believing I died as a baby. Not knowing that I'd been adopted. That was just lies, wasn't it?'

She clenched her fists. Inside the body of a man there was a wounded child who needed to be heard. Do not react. Let him have his say.

'Blaming your mother, blaming the nuns. Blaming everyone except yourself.'

She gritted her teeth.

'Is it because we don't look the same? Are you ashamed of me?'

A step too far. 'Don't be ridiculous.'

'Oh, I'm not only unlovable, but now I'm ridiculous as well!' He slammed down the glass. 'Anything else you want to get out there? Maybe the fact that I didn't finish school, haven't been to university, haven't got a dozen degrees, like my mother.' He brought his face close now. 'And do you want to know why? Why I haven't stuck with anything?' His eyes shone with tears. 'Because none of the adults in my life ever stuck with me.' He turned away to hide the tears. 'My own birth mother abandoned me.'

'Mercúrio stop it.'

'Stop it? Who are you to tell me what to do? I never asked for you to find me. What right have you to burst into my life and then doubt me? If I'm not enough for you, then I'll leave right now.'

She tried to reason with him, but it was too late.

'All I'm asking is that we do this one test, together.'

'And all I'm asking is that you look into your heart.'

Florianopolis, Brazil

'Maria Jaqueline Marta Ribeiro da Silva.'

Crazy Gloves arrived at noon, right on time.

She hadn't seen his approach. He must have left his car on the road. She hadn't heard him enter. The front door was bolted; his lock-picking skills had improved since the first night he broke in, six days ago.

In the bright noon sun, he looked smaller, less threatening than he had appeared in the middle of the night. He wore the same crepe-soled shoes, long trousers and ironed shirt with a light jacket, despite the midday heat. A medium-sized man with a fair complexion, thinning hair and a long, lugubrious face.

As she observed him, he stepped through the door from the house to the veranda and took a seat beside her, the jacket opening to show the gun in its holster.

'Where is Mercúrio?' she asked.

'Secure.'

'Is he OK?'

'That depends on you. Do you have the box?'

'I do.'

'Good. Bring it to me.'

'Not until I speak to Mercúrio'

'Very well.' He pulled out his phone and dialled. 'Bring Mercúrio to the phone.' He handed the slim rose-gold device to her, and she put it to her ear.

'Let go of me!'

Jaq sighed with relief at the unmistakable sound of Mercúrio's fury in all its familiarity. He was alive. If they both got out of this mess, she would never ask for proof again, she would accept him any way he chose.

'Mercúrio are you OK?'

'*Mãe?*'

How strange to hear those words. Angie had refused to be addressed that way. But Jaq was not her mother. She accepted her responsibilities. Embraced them.

'Yes,' she whispered.

'Get me out of here,' he sobbed. 'Please.'

'Where are you?'

'Enough!' Crazy gloves grabbed the phone from her hand. 'There's not much time left. The sooner you give me the box, the better your chance of rescuing your son.'

Jaq started at him. 'How did you know?'

He smiled, a lizard smile that didn't reach his cold, hard eyes.

'You're wasting time.'

Jaq stood and unlocked the deckchair store. It had seemed like the safest place. She pulled out her mother's battered leather safe.

'Is this what you wanted?'

His eyes gleamed.

'Why?'

'You ask too many questions.' He moved towards her, hand outstretched to take the box.

She dropped it back into the store and locked it again.

'First release Mercúrio.'

'Get out of the way.'

'We had a deal. I kept my side of it.'

He pulled out a gun. 'I could just shoot you.'

'Yes,' she said. 'You could. But you won't. You don't need to. Release Mercúrio and you'll never see either of us again.'

He pressed redial and spoke into the phone. 'Call me in five minutes. If I answer, unlock the chains and let him go.' He fixed her with a cool gaze. 'If there is no reply, weigh him down and throw him overboard.' He sat back down in his chair.

'You bastard.'

'Bring me the box.'

'Where is he? On a boat?'

He looked at his watch. 'You have four minutes and fifty seconds.'

What bargaining power did she have left? If she didn't give him the box, Mercúrio was to be drowned. Unless the order was countermanded in time. 'In exchange for your phone.'

He shrugged and handed it over. She checked the time. Four minutes and thirty seconds since his call.

The impasse broken, she unlocked the store and pulled out the leather safe, placing it on the wooden floor beside his deckchair.

He opened the box. First the conventional way – running his hands inside to find it empty. He closed it and turned the latch the opposite way, unlocking the secret compartment. How did he know all this?

He closed the box again and turned away from her, twisted the handle one way then another. She moved position to try and see what he was doing.

Four minutes

From his sock, he extracted a short knife in a leather sheath. The sharp blade glinted in the sunlight as he withdrew it. He turned the box upside down, the carry handle dangling between his legs. With slow and careful movements, he eased the knife into the leather at each corner, making small diagonal cuts, pushing the knife between leather and steel, probing.

Three minutes

'What are you looking for?'

He gave a grunt of satisfaction. Whatever it was, he had found it. He made long, neat cuts in the leather along each of the four bottom edges and then two diagonal cuts. Peeling away the four triangular flaps of leather, he exposed the metal base of the box. Along each side ran an L-shaped piece of metal, the short leg screwed to the base plate and the long leg tucked up under the leather that covered the sides. He took out a small screwdriver and released the reinforcing channels to reveal an opening. The steel walls were double-sided, the inner edge welded to the base, the sides welded together to halfway up and then each side folded outward from the top, bending back over itself to leave a thin gap.

Two minutes.

Crazy Gloves turned the box right way up and tapped it firmly on the lid. Out of the gap a square sheet of metal emerged. A slim copper plate only a fraction smaller than the dimensions of the box. It caught the light as he pulled it out and held it up, the lines of engraving firm and clear. The writing was in the same style as the mine deeds. Here was the missing schedule, part of the fabric of the box itself.

'Is that all you wanted?' she asked.

It would have been a lot easier if he'd told her. Instead of dragging the damn box around she could have couriered over an engraved copper plate with a fraction of the effort.

'Not quite,' he said.

One minute.

He slid the knife into each of the other three sides, carefully at first and then confidently until another three copper plates emerged, these ones engraved on both sides, swirling wavy lines that made patterns. These must be the maps, topological and geological maps.

2 seconds.

Florianopolis, Brazil

The phone rang exactly five minutes after Crazy Gloves told the kidnappers to call. He had what he wanted; now he could instruct his accomplice to release Mercúrio.

Jaq held his phone out to him.

He shook his head and stood up, engraved copper plates under his arm, the strongbox in one hand, the gun in the other.

'Take the phone,' she said.

'No, you keep it,' he said.

She accepted the call and put it on speakerphone.

'Boss, is that you?'

He said nothing, drawing a finger over his lips.

'Tell them you are OK,' she hissed.

He put a hand to his throat and made exaggerated choking noises.

Jaq put the phone to her mouth. 'Everything is OK,' Jaq said. 'You can let Mercúrio go.'

The disembodied voice chuckled. 'I need to hear that from the boss.'

Crazy Gloves was leaving. Jaq rushed after him as he stepped into the house, thrusting the phone at him.

He took one of the dining-room chairs and threw it to the ground. *Thud!* He leaned against the dresser, shaking it so that plates and cups and glasses tumbled to the floor. *Crash!*

'Boss, are you OK?'

Jaq pressed a button to turn off speakerphone. 'He's fine.'

'Then let me speak to him. Or Mercúrio goes over the side.'

She could hear the clink of metal chains, the slosh of water against a boat hull, the distant crash of waves.

'Untie me,' she could hear him pleading. 'Let me go.'

Crazy Gloves was opening the front door. 'Speak to them,' she yelled at his retreating back.

Mercúrio was shouting in the background.

'No, no – don't kill me!'

She sprinted until she was in front of Crazy Gloves, thrusting the phone at him.

'Tell them to let Mercúrio go.'

He took the phone and cut the call.

The line went dead.

Florianopolis, Brazil

She tried to stop Crazy Gloves, ran after him, but desperation made her weak. When he hit out at her, the metal corner of the strongbox connected with her shoulder and she went down like a house of cards. Lying on the sandy path outside the beach house, she groaned as he drove away.

How could she have let him escape? He had the maps, she didn't have Mercúrio. Would they carry out their threat? Throw Mercúrio overboard? Was he fighting for his life, drowning as they spoke?

Crash, swirl, gush and splash.

It came to her suddenly. The noises in the background. Birdsong meant that the boat couldn't be too far from shore. Then the crash, swirl, gush and splash. First waves hitting a reef, *crash,* the force of the wave pushing the water into underground caverns, *swirl,* creating geysers as the water under the rocky shelf found a way up, springing up like fountains through sink holes, *gush.* The jets of water rising tens of metres into the air and then falling back onto rock, *splash.* There were two places she could think of that sounded like that. One was Boca do Inferno near Cascais in Portugal, the other was at the southern tip of the Isla de Santa Catarina, near Praia de Naufragados. Shipwreck beach. One she and Mercúrio had surfed a few times. It was remote, the road stopped several miles north, and it was a long, tricky hike on foot. But easily accessible by sea.

Or by air.

Jaq raced down to the beach to where Marina was sitting in the sand, back against the tail fin of the plane, staring out to sea.

'Success?'

Jaq shook her head. 'That bastard double-crossed me. He took the box, but he didn't release Mercúrio.'

She hit her forehead with the palm of her hand.

'But I think I know where Mercúrio is. Can we fly?'

Marina jumped into the cockpit. At the touch of a single button the plane sprang to life.

A red light flashed. She tapped the fuel gauge. 'We're low on hydrogen. I'll need to refuel at Floripa airport.'

'There's no time.'

'How far is it?'

'Not far.' Jaq showed her on the flight computer.

'I've never flown on reserve before. I can't promise anything.'

'Please? It's a matter of life or death.'

Marina's mouth tightened. 'I'll give it my best shot.'

The plane taxied across the beach, gaining speed near the shallows as the damp sand became firmer, then lifted into the air. As they banked, Jaq looked down at the beach house, almost hidden in its own lush garden. Once they were level again, they flew south, towards the tip of the long island.

'There!'

The boat was hard to miss. An old trawler, heading out to sea: a pile of junk spruced up with a coat of paint, the Ecobrium logo and new name – *Tartaruga* – emblazoned on the side.

Marina spoke through headphones. 'Jaq, we have to turn back now. Even if you wanted to land, the sea is too rough, the beaches are too short and narrow. I've borrowed a fifty-million-dollar prototype, I can't afford to lose it.'

Jaq grabbed the binoculars.

'I can't see who's on board.' Pray that they hadn't carried out their threat. Pray that Mercúrio was still safe.

'We'll refuel and fly back.'

'There's no time.'

If they'd thrown him out of the boat, how long could he last? He was a strong swimmer.

Untie me!

If his hands had been bound, he'd have to adapt his stroke. Tied in front, he might just be able to swim, a sort of half-butterfly, lifting his head between strokes to breathe. Tied behind, he'd have to float on his back and use his legs, making it hard to steer the right course. Jaq scanned the surface of the sea. If they'd tied his legs as well, then he stood little chance.

Clink.

And if they used metal chains instead of rope, he had no chance at all.

'They're heading out to sea. I have to stop them.'

'And how are you going to do that?'

'Can you fly low and slow enough so I can jump out?'

'You're mad.'

'I'm determined. You drop me, go and refuel.'

Marina shook her head.

Jaq put a hand on her forearm. 'I'm doing what I have to do.'

A look passed between them. If anyone could understand, Marina would. She moved the joystick down.

'Where?'

'Over there.' Jaq pointed just ahead of the boat.

'Parachute?'

'Check.'

'Life jacket?'

'Check.'

'Belt?'

Check.

'Weapon?'

Jaq tapped her head. 'This is all I need.'

'You're completely mad.'

Jaq unclipped her seat belt and opened the door. 'Wish me luck.'

The physics of jumping from a plane are interesting. There are two things happening at once. The vertical acceleration due to the force of gravity, pulling you downwards, and the horizonal deceleration as you lose the thrust of the plane engines. The trajectory is a rather lovely parabola. Your forward speed decreases as your downward speed increases. If you hit the water at terminal velocity, about 140 miles per hour, you're almost certainly going to die. Just the sudden deceleration, your organs continuing to travel inside your body as the skin outside comes to a sudden stop, will cause such massive trauma that your insides are macerated as you hit the water.

Which is why you need a parachute. On release, the lightweight nylon fabric billows out, increasing resistance, slowing you down.

But a parachute needs time to deploy; it only works if the height is right. Too low and you've reached terminal velocity before it is fully open.

Trying to hit a moving target from a low-flying plane is difficult enough with guns, almost impossible with a human missile. Even the smallest conventional plane has to travel above 50km/hr to remain airborne. So, when you jump out of a moving plane, you are travelling at the same speed. Without your own jet engines, you begin to slow down as soon as you leave.

But this was no conventional plane, and Marina was as skilled a pilot as you could wish for. More importantly, Jaq had her own power in the shape of a Transform-Aérex joint-venture rocket belt.

Jaq had spent the day before the Festival of Roses learning how to fly. Marina was an expert teacher.

The rocket belt was a gilet, a sleeveless waistcoat, made of the same polymemory used for the shoes, a superfine mix of polyurethane and carbon fibre, with the addition of two small rocket thrusters.

Hydrogen peroxide – H_2O_2 – is a pale-blue liquid that boils at

150 degrees centigrade. It decomposes in the presence of light or metals to form oxygen, water and heat.

When the hydrogen peroxide is combined with pressurised liquid nitrogen and a catalyst, the chemical reaction generates superheated steam shooting out of twin rocket nozzles at 1,300 degrees Fahrenheit (704.4 degrees Celsius).

And the catalyst?

Silver, of course.

South Atlantic Ocean, Brazil

An old fishing trawler with the words *Tartaruga* emblazoned across the side chugged out to sea from the southern tip of Santa Catarina Island. Something hovered above the boat. A bird? No, too long and thin, like a dandelion seed, narrow at the bottom and umbrella shaped at the top. A tethered kite? No, it moved independently of the boat and there was almost no wind. A woman was descending from an aeroplane with a parachute and rocket belt.

Jaq touched down on the roof of the wheelhouse. The plane circled overhead and then sped away.

She caught the straps as the parachute billowed down, unclipping herself before it could drag her away.

Had they seen her? She lay flat on the roof of the boat and listened.

Noises down below suggested two men. One was directly below, steering the ship. The other was aft, in the mess room.

Was Mercúrio still on board? Imprisoned somewhere on the boat? She let herself down from the roof and crept round the deck. The man in the wheelhouse had his back to her, but she recognised the skipper. Definitely one of the men who had broken into her beach house seven days ago with Crazy Gloves.

Another of the goons, the one who had rampaged through her possessions in search of the box, was in the mess room, stretched out on a hammock, a beer in his hand.

Where would they keep Mercúrio imprisoned?

She crept down the stairs to the lower deck and found a private cabin, which also served as an office, packed with high-specification computer equipment. This must be where Crazy Gloves worked and slept. The heads, where a bathroom would normally be, had been converted into a small laboratory, packed with surprisingly sophisticated equipment. She found the crew sleeping quarters – empty, the engine room – noisy, the shared facilities – smelly, and a locked storeroom.

She put her ear to the keyhole.

Silence.

'Mercúrio,' she whispered.

Nothing.

She tried knocking.

No response.

The lock wasn't hard to pick, it took less than three minutes. Three minutes wasted. Mercúrio was gone.

She dropped to her knees at the sight of his things. The last clothes she'd seen him in. A blue Floripa surf T-shirt had been cut from neck to hem, the white shorts ripped down each leg, his canvas shoes stained with something that looked like blood and his wraparound laser sunglasses snapped right between the eyes. Set into the wall was an iron ring, worn to shiny roughness where chains had recently rubbed against it. Had they held him here in the dark? Brought him the phone to plead for his life? When had he realised it was hopeless? When had it become clear that, whatever she did, they would throw him overboard anyway? When had they cut off his clothes to make identification more difficult? Had he even realised how hard she'd tried? Or did he think she'd abandoned him?

Again.

The anger took her by storm.

She returned to the heads, took off her shoes and and set the timer on her belt to 200 seconds.

The *Tartaruga* wasn't going anywhere.

Jaq unrolled a cable, plugged the double-headed jack into the toes of her shoes and the other end directly into the mains.

Go!

150 seconds.

The skipper's mouth fell open as she emerged on deck.

'What the hell? How did you get here?'

'Where is he?' Jaq demanded.

'Where's who?'

Where's Mercúrio?

He laughed. 'You really don't get it do you?'

'What have you done with him?'

'Exactly what we promised.'

120 seconds.

'But I gave you what you wanted. The deal was that you would release him.'

'And we did.'

A glimmer of hope. Perhaps it wasn't too late.

'You let him go?'

'He's no use to us now.' He laughed. 'We threw him overboard.'

She looked out across the waves.

Mercúrio was a strong swimmer. How close were they to shore when they chucked him overboard? A mile? Five miles? Tough, but depending on currents, not impossible?

'When?'

'About an hour ago.'

90 seconds.

'Where?'

'About seven kilometres down.'

The second man emerged from his hammock, gun in hand.

'I reckon he's reached the bottom of the sea by now.' He dangled a pair of handcuffs attached by a short chain to leg irons. 'We dressed him in these. Care to join him?'

60 seconds and the point of no return.

In the laboratory below deck, current was flowing through the copper wires of the faulty polymemory. Without the control box, it would quickly get very hot indeed. The boat laboratory was a disgrace, a disaster waiting to happen: compressed gases, organic solvents, oxidising reagents.

Jaq stepped backward, her bare feet sliding across the decking.

Keep them talking.

40 seconds.

'Why?' she asked. 'What is *Ecóbrium?*'

She pronounced it with the stress on the second syllable, like opprobrium.

'Ecobriúm,' he corrected her, the stress at the end. 'Ecologia Brasil Ruim.'

'What does that mean?'

20 seconds.

'It means the world is a mess, thanks to people like you.'

'And what do you plan to do about it?'

The skipper shrugged. 'We just follow the boss's instructions.'

The boss. Crazy Gloves.

5 seconds.

'Where is your boss?'

'One step ahead of you.'

Less than a second before the first explosion, due exactly 3.3432 minutes after connecting the toe of the polymemory shoe to an electric socket, the rocket belt powered up, lifting her into the air before the secondary explosion ripped through the boat. The shockwave sent her tumbling towards the sea. She didn't fight it, using the energy of the blast, turning a full backward somersault to right herself and level out without hitting the water. She remained low, skimming just above the crests of the waves as she put her head down, stretched her body horizontal and headed for shore.

South Atlantic Ocean, Brazil

Marina's rocket belt was a prototype, designed for spectacular, short flights. The balance of weight and elegance was firmly on the side of minimum encumbrance, never designed with long-distance escape in mind.

The top speed of 120 kilometres per hour gave the worst fuel efficiency. Accelerating clear of the blast wave had burned into the reserve, only a few minutes of flight left unless power was minimised; she had to preserve every drop of fuel.

It wasn't just the rocket belt that was running on empty. Her anger had started to build when she found the horrible conditions Mercúrio had been held in while she'd raced to collect the strongbox. These men had never intended to honour the deal. They'd laughed as they boasted of murdering her son and the rage had boiled over, epinephrine and cortisol surging into her blood-stream. Fight or flight? For once Jaq had stayed to fight.

Now the adrenaline rush was fading, her heartbeat slowing, her dilated pupils returning to normal, blood sugar falling, nervous exhaustion setting in.

She closed her eyes and the image of the cut, bloodied clothing burned into her retina. The fact that it was cut with such surgical precision was almost worse than if it had been torn. Mercúrio had been chained, unable to fight. Abandoned in a hot, windowless cell. How he must have suffered, chained in that dank little cupboard, listening to the sea on the other side of the ship's hull.

The left engine on the rocket belt began to stutter, making the flight unstable. She adjusted her velocity to a stately 50km/hr and tipped herself in order to favour the left side. Now was not the time to give way to despair. Stop thinking about the prison, the chains, the horror of Mercúrio's drowning as he struggled against the weight of metal dragging him down. Time for grief later. Her focus had to be on survival. How else could she avenge him? Think of the last happy time.

Jaq opened her eyes as she skimmed close to the surface of the water. She followed the Atlantic rollers as they surged across the sea and made a supreme effort to picture Mercúrio on top of, rather than underneath, those waves. Remembering the last time they'd been truly happy, the last time they'd surfed together, twelve days before Christmas.

They'd been out most of the day on the water. She'd caught a few spectacular waves, the last one without heeding his advice, his warning that it was too big for her, yelling at her to dive. The deep ocean swell met an offshore wind, whipping the breakers up into great walls of turquoise glass. She'd popped up on the wave as it turned over on itself, riding through a crystal tunnel, crouching low, working up and down the leading edge of a wave that went on for ever.

Had she imagined something approaching pride in Mercúrio's eyes? He grinned as he applauded her. Perhaps he was ready to open up, to talk to her about what was really going on behind his troubled brow. It was only out here on the waves that they were comfortable, in tune with one another.

She'd left first, exhausted by the day, hungry, hopeful they might talk over dinner. But he'd stayed out late and she ate alone. When he came home he smelt of campfires and marijuana. She was up early to write up the safety studies that were paying for this beach-house sojourn. She kept busy. He slept late and partied later. After that one perfect day, he started avoiding her. Until the argument.

They'd parted in anger. She'd always known it might be too late, promised herself that if he'd told her to go away, to leave him alone, then she would respect that.

Now it was too late.

He had no future, no life.

She'd never intended that her son should die for her.

Poor Mercúrio.

A tear fell to join his watery grave.

Praia de Moçambique, Florianopolis, Brazil

The light was fading, but after Jaq's spectacular barrel, Mercúrio was determined to catch one last wave.

Jaq shook her head. 'I'm heading in.'

He watched as she jogged across the sand, surfboard under one arm. Fit for her age. Fit for any age. It was increasingly uncomfortable, spending so much time with her. The sea was the easiest place to hide. Together but apart. Action, not words. She was patient, he had to grant her that, and her surfing had improved by leaps and bounds.

After a disappointing set, he gave up and paddled towards the shore. Instead of turning right towards the beach house, he turned left, towards a campfire. Most of the guys were playing football further down the beach, leaving Angel to tend the fire. She smiled up at him through dark eyes.

Taking a bottle from the cooler, he sank onto the sand beside her. She licked the long edge of a cigarette paper, rolled up the joint and lit it, taking a long puff before passing it to him. It was good stuff, strong stuff. Either that or he'd been out on the waves too long. He took a sip of beer to stop the earth spinning.

'Is she your girlfriend?'

'Who?'

Angel nodded towards the palm trees that protected the beach house from the southerly winds.

'Jaq?' He laughed. 'No.'

'What then?'

His shoulders slumped. 'She thinks she's my mum.'

Angel's jaw dropped to reveal a perfect set of teeth. 'For real?' She stared at him with dilated pupils so deep he would drown unless he looked away.

'What do you think?'

'She doesn't look that much older than you.'

'Teenage pregnancy. They took the baby away for adoption.'

'And that baby was you?'

He took a long puff.

'No.' It felt good to tell the truth for once. 'I was hired by a Hélio TV show to pretend to be her son.'

'You were adopted?'

'Nope. Mum alive and kicking in Salvador and Dad drunk and comatose in Brasilia. I'm two years older than Jaq's son, but I was the best fit for the job.'

'Is Mercúrio even your real name?'

He shook his head. 'The TV company invented a completely new identity for me.'

'They gave you the same name as her son?'

'No one knows what name the adoption agency gave her son. He could be called anything.'

'I don't get it? Why would you pretend?'

'I'm an actor.' He shrugged. 'Pretending is my job.'

'On screen, perhaps. This is different.'

'And when was I last on screen?' *Surf Rescue Squad* had shown two years ago and the bastard scriptwriters of *Love on the Beach* had killed off his character, his big break, before series two. 'I have debts. I borrowed from the wrong people ...' He hung his head. 'I need the money.'

'Is she in on it? This Hélio TV scam?'

'No.'

'Does she suspect?'

'I don't think so,' he shrugged.

'So what do they want?'

'Who?'

'Your employers.'

'She inherited a gold mine. They want it.'

'Don't you feel bad? Tricking her?'

'Not at first.' He sighed. 'It's just a job.'

'And now?'

'She's not what I expected. I kinda like her.'

'Who wouldn't like a lady with a gold mine, right?'

'I don't think she cares about it that much, and nor do I.'

Angel moved closer. 'But other people do.'

'Yes, that's why they hired me.'

'Who?'

'You don't want to know.'

'I can guess. That creepy game show host. From *The Missing*. What's his name? César?'

'He's just a bit player in all this. No, his orders come from above. From the Colonel.'

'Colonel Cub? Champion of the *garimpeiros*? What does he want?'

'Proof. Maps, deeds.'

'Do you have them?'

'I will soon.'

'What then?'

'I hand everything over.' He shrugged. 'They get the gold mine and I get paid.'

'Do you really think they'll let you go?' She snapped her fingers. 'Just like that.'

'Why not?'

'What if you talk?'

'Who's going to believe me?' He drew back, his eyes suddenly wide. '*Merda*, that stuff is strong. I've said too much.'

She laughed. 'You're safe with me.' Then her smile disappeared, and a new light shone in her eyes. 'I want mining stopped. All mining, but especially the *garimpeiro* stuff. It's an environmental disaster.'

'You're making me feel worse.'

'I could make you feel better.'

He raised an eyebrow and leaned forward, his lips brushing hers.

'Babaca!' She scuttled backwards in the sand, then held up her hands, sandy palms facing towards him. 'What is it with you guys? You know I'm with Luis.'

'Sorry,' he grunted.

'I want you to meet someone. Ever heard of Ecobrium?'

'The environmental extremists?'

'Radical activists.' She looked around and dropped her voice. 'I could introduce you to the boss. Raimundo Elias. He's amazing, inspirational.'

'What's the point?' Mercúrio hung his head. 'I'm in too deep now. The only way out is to hand the deeds over.' He slammed a fist into the sand, a spray of fine particles catching the firelight. 'I wish I'd never taken this job.'

'What if you hand them over to Ecobrium instead?'

'You don't understand. I can't get out now; they'd kill me.'

'Not if Ecobrium kill you instead.'

'What are you saying?' It was his turn to shuffle back. He stared at her. 'Who have you been talking to, Angel?'

'I don't mean for real.' Her lips twisted. 'I mean, Ecobrium stage a kidnap. Your "mum",' she made air quotes with her fingers, 'brings us the deeds. We stop the mining and let you go.'

'That's not going to work. If I don't deliver, whatever the reason, the Colonel will have me killed.'

'So, we fake your death.'

'That seems hard on Jaq.'

'Who are you more afraid of?' There was a mocking quality to her voice. 'Your mum or the Colonel?'

'She's not my mother.'

'Then there's your answer.'

South Atlantic Ocean, Brazil

The coast, the hills of Santa Catarina Island that stuck out from the Brazilian mainland, was still no more than a line on the horizon. Jaq had covered less than half the distance to shore when the left engine of the jet pack juddered to a halt. She switched fuel lines, sending everything to the right side and tried flying sideways, the way Marina had taught her on the day of the Festival of Roses.

Jaq had designed some control improvements: improved tuning to reduce the yaw and pitch, aileron deflection to dampen the roll, dusting out some Fourier transforms to model propulsion and resize the nitrogen nozzles.

Better, but still not perfect.

It wasn't long before the right-hand rocket started spluttering and shaking. It took every muscle in her body to remain level. She couldn't drop her speed any further and remain airborne.

The shoreline wasn't getting any closer, and she was completely exhausted by the time she dropped into the sea.

At the shock of cool water, a surge of energy returned. She trod water as she unclipped the belt, shrugged off the rocket harness and let it sink to the depths. Another expensive prototype lost; she hoped Marina would forgive her.

The sea stretched out around her in all directions, the waves roughened by the wind, visibility worsening as darkness fell.

In a few hours, it would be Christmas Day. Ever since her brother died, she'd chosen to spend Christmas alone. It had taken a supreme effort to agree to Mercúrio's suggestion that they spend the day together. And now he was gone and she was more alone than ever. Alone in the middle of the South Atlantic Ocean.

Was she close now to where they'd thrown him overboard? How long had he been able to stay afloat? Bound with steel manacles, he wouldn't have struggled for long. The thought of his last, desperate minutes, a man so completely at home in the sea, unable to save himself, made her cry out and start to gag.

Stop. Get a grip. Lock it down. Lock it in. What's done is done and can't be undone. The time for grief is when you are safe.

Safe? What use was safe? When had she ever cared for her own safety? Was that the problem? Was it her recklessness that hurt the people around her? Were people killed because they got too close to her?

What about Marina?

Jaq stared up into the sky, willing the elegant twin-bodied glider-plane to drop from the clouds and land on the water.

How long did it take to fuel a hydrogen-powered plane? In a regional airport that had probably never heard of such a thing.

The hydrogen supply pressure would have to be above 700 bar to fill the fuel tank, about the same pressure you'd experience at the bottom of the sea, 7 kilometres down. And hydrogen was a tiny molecule, adept at passing through microscopic cracks and crevices. Would they even have the right fittings for hydrogen? A traditional cone and thread might leak. A double ferrule with extra grip would do better but would they have it in the right materials? The most abundant chemical element in the universe, hydrogen was also highly reactive, embrittling carbon-steel to the point of rapid failure.

As the victims of the Cuperoil explosion experienced to their cost.

That was the trouble with new technology, it might work fine in a lab, or a technology-centre wind tunnel where no expense was spared, but the practicalities kicked in outside of the research environment and into the cost-sensitive real world.

If Marina couldn't fuel in Florianopolis she'd have to ditch the plane. After all, where would she find a spare hydrogen tank on

Christmas Eve? Jaq had landed safely on the ship; her friend would have no way of knowing that Jaq had blown it up.

Marina had promised to spend Christmas Day with her children. No one else knew where Jaq was.

What if Marina wasn't coming back?

Cumbria, England

Christmas Day

Ben woke very early. Normally he'd tiptoe into Mummy and Daddy's room and climb up into the big bed. Depending on which side he chose for the ascent, one of them sometimes woke up. If it was Mummy, she would give him a kiss and send him back to his bed, but then she'd get up. Daddy made grumpy noises but opened his arms for a snuggle, and sometimes he fell asleep again before remembering that Ben wasn't meant to sleep in their bed any more.

But he couldn't go into their room this morning, because Mummy was <u>so</u> tired now she'd got a new baby, and the baby had to sleep with Mummy because she was very, very new and needed Mummy <u>all the time</u>, which didn't seem very fair to him, but Daddy told him to be a good big brother and he was trying very hard to be the best big brother in the world.

Baby Chloe didn't seem that keen on having a big brother, or a sister or even a daddy for that matter, although all three of them were fascinated by her. She was so small and round and bald. He didn't think baby Chloe much liked anyone except Mummy, though it was difficult to tell because she didn't really do much. When she wasn't sleeping or crying or having her nappy changed, she was making little snuffling noises and bashing her nose against Mummy's chest.

His other little sister, ginormous compared to baby Chloe, usually slept through the night. Unless she had a nightmare, in which case Ben heard her first because they slept in the same room, although soon he was going to get a bedroom all to himself. If he stroked Jade's hand and told her a story, she would stop crying and go back to sleep.

His new baby sister, Chloe, didn't like his stories. Maybe they were too grown up for a baby. He liked to include some action and adventure, like the time he saved Aunty Jaq from the bad man.

He was a bit cross with his aunty – she wasn't a real aunty but Daddy told him to call her that – not because she'd taken his things, after all she'd helped him to make the catapult and the safe really belonged to her, although she had given it to him, hadn't she? And it wasn't very nice to give someone something and then take it back. Daddy told him he'd been dreaming when he mentioned coming home with Gramps to get his wellies and seeing Aunty Jaq in the shower, which made him quite cross because he had kept his promise not to tell anyone for <u>ages</u> and when it had just slipped out no one even believed him.

Aunty Jaq had sent him a Christmas present. It was under the tree, wrapped in one of those funny bags with a ribbon round the neck. He'd had a good feel of it when no one was looking. Didn't feel much like a new catapult and it was definitely the wrong size for a safe.

He wouldn't mind a brand-new catapult, but he didn't want a new safe. He wanted the old one back. He was dying to show Aunty Jaq the other hiding place he'd found. Not the secret drawer in the base, that was really, really, really obvious once you knew the trick with the brass thingummies. She might be clever, but he bet she hadn't found the hidey-hole in the handle – or the things inside it. She'd be so proud of him when he showed her.

He was still a bit worried about the shape of the present she'd sent. He hoped it wasn't a book. Why were grown-ups so keen on giving books? Books were boring. Although he liked it when

Daddy read to him, and Daddy liked it too. Really the grown-ups should be giving all the book presents to Daddy.

At the sound of baby Chloe starting to wail – for such a little thing she didn't half make a racket – Ben sprang out of bed. New babies were good for one thing at least, waking up the grown-ups nice and early.

He sprinted into the corridor and yelled at the top of his voice. 'MERRY CHRISTMAS EVERYONE!'

South Atlantic Ocean

For once, Jaq didn't want to spend Christmas Day alone. Adrift at sea, miles from land, she longed for someone, anyone to come and save her.

The water was cold out here, far from the sun-warmed shallows. How long could she last?

If this had been England, she would already be dead. When someone fell from an oil rig in the North Sea in December, you had only minutes to get them out. Even in the sea around Portugal, the body's fuel, and with it your ability to stay warm, would run out after a few hours. But this was Christmas in Brazil. Approaching high summer. Close to shore the water temperature was above 20 degrees, you could survive indefinitely in that. Cooler out here. When had she last eaten? Miso soup and sashimi in the luxury lounge of JewelJet at Guarulhos Airport. If only she'd chosen pasta or bean stew, any other slow-release carbohydrate. The best way to conserve energy now was to keep still and wait for rescue.

Who was she kidding? No one was coming. The only way to save herself was to swim. But she was hungry and thirsty and a long way from shore. It was dark; she didn't even know in which direction land lay.

It would be so much easier to let go.

Jaq didn't believe in heaven, or hell for that matter, which was just as well, given how many men she'd killed. Neither Sam nor Mercúrio, nor anyone else she loved, were floating on angel wings, waiting above the clouds to greet her with a fanfare of harps, lutes and trumpets.

No, when she drowned, her lungs would fill with water. It would be desperately painful for a few minutes, then it would all be over.

Finito.

Full stop.

The sky was black, no stars and no moon. She thought she heard a faint noise, a splash in the distance, but it must be the wind rising.

She was in the middle of the South Atlantic, miles from land.

Cold.

Alone.

She was alone because they'd taken her son from her.

Again.

A faint band of light appeared on the horizon. Christmas Day dawning. A day that Mercúrio would never see.

And then the anger returned.

The first time she lost him, she'd been helpless, a child who was lied to, a child who had no choice but to accept what she was told.

This time she had seen him with her own eyes. Fought to save him.

Failed.

Time to take control. Time to identify the people who'd hurt those she cared about. And stop them before they could cause more harm.

It was time to let go of cerebral Jaq, reasonable Jaq, the thoughtful engineer who tried to see both sides of every argument, to help those around her.

The old Jaq Silver had to go.

No more Ms Nice Gal.

She would avenge Mercúrio's death. Everyone who had played a part, however big or small, was going to pay and God help anyone who got in her way.

The sun rises in the east. Land lay to the west. Jaq gritted her teeth and turned away from the faint band of light. Rolling onto her stomach, she lowered a tearstained cheek into the water and raised her right elbow high, throwing her cupped hand forward for the longest, strongest stroke.

Jaq kicked her feet and started the long, cold swim towards vengeance.

Author's Notes

Polymemory

Many years ago, I carried out research into liquid crystal polymers. Recent correspondence with my academic supervisor, Prof Malcolm Mackley, led us to the design of a material to make Marina's shoes turn rigid and then soft again.

Polymemory material has shape memory on initial distortion because of the embedded (conducting) carbon nanotube (CNT) network (2 per cent carbon nanotube in a lightly crosslinked polyurethane (PU) matrix). 12v across the material excites physical crosslinking of the embedded CNT network and provides semi-permanent room-temperature rigidity. Subsequent heating results in break-up of physical network and elastic recovery due to the PU elasticity returning the material to its original shape.

While polymemory doesn't yet exist, it's just a matter of time.

Colour

I was captivated by a *Forbes* Science article by *@grrlscientist* explaining a Dakota E. McCoy 2020 paper on bird plumage.

The tanager (Ramphocelus bresilius) is a frugivorous bird that lives in Brazil. Using scanning electron microscopy (SEM), finite-difference time-domain (FDTD) optical modelling, liquid chromatography–mass spectrometry (LC-MS), and spectropho-tometry, scientists found that male and female feathers had similar colour chemistry (carotenoids), but only male feathers had elaborate microstructures that allow them to amplify colour appearance before mating. Expanded barbs enhance colour saturation (for the same amount of pigment) by increasing the transmission of optical power through the feather. Dihedral barbules (vertically angled, strap-shaped barbules) reduce total reflectance to generate 'super black' plumage. Dihedral barbules paired with red carotenoid pigment produce 'velvet red' plumage.

https://www.forbes.com/sites/grrlscientist/2020/09/29/brilliant-superred-feathers-are-created-by-more-than-just-pigments/#79f7177e33ae

'Microstructures amplify carotenoid plumage signals in colorful tanagers',

https://www.biorxiv.org/content/10.1101/799783v3.full

Adelina Pires MBE was the caretaker at The British Cemetery, Lisbon. Born near Viseu in 1910, the year that Portugal was declared a Republic, she was sent out to work as a child. A newly married couple took her to Lisbon as a household servant, but she became unemployed when her *patrões* were sent to Angola. She found work at the Anglican Church of St George's in Lisbon, cleaning the church, weeding the cemetery and opening the gate for visitors. She married Pedro, the coffin-maker, in 1937 and moved into a cottage inside the cemetery, where she lived for the rest of her long life.

Adelina never learned to read or write but could tell you exactly who was buried where amongst the many graves, never forgot a face and continued working into her 100th year.

Festival of Roses
The annual flower festival in Sapiranga, Brazil, takes place in November to mark the start of summer in the Southern Hemisphere, not September as described in the book.

Araguaia Guerrilla War
After the military dictatorship took control of Brazil in 1964, a group of communists fled from the cities to the jungle of the Araguaia river basin, in what is now the state of Tocantins. The

communist guerrillas attempted to recruit the rural population to fight a people's war, copying a model of resistance that was successful during the Chinese civil war and the Cuban revolution.

From 1972 to 1975, military forces were sent to eliminate the resistance, employing extraordinary levels of brutality to wipe out both the guerrillas and any locals suspected of harbouring them. They used chemical weapons and torture, summary execution and unmarked burials.

Since 1982, the families of Júlia Gomes Lund and other missing people have been fighting for an investigation into the disappearances and deaths and the right to recover the bodies of their loved ones.

In 2015, the Inter-American Commission on Human Rights concluded that the State of Brazil had violated the Inter-American Convention to Prevent and Punish Torture and ordered that documents relating to the Araguaia Guerrilla War be declassified.

At the time of writing, the bereaved families were still waiting for the Brazilian government to comply with the judgment.

Acknowledgements

Many thanks

To Pamela Erskine (1933–2020), my wonderful mother-in-law, an inspirational grandmother and passionate librarian who shared her love of books freely.

To Prof Malcolm Mackley who designed the potential new material, polymemory.

To Dr Devorah Bennu (GrrlScientist) for alerting me to microbarbules.

To Matt Willis (http://navalairhistory.com/ and http://airandseastories.com/) for his expertise in aviation generously shared.

To my brother Graham Macleod for simulator flying all my routes in real time and my sister Helen Macleod for cheering me on.

To Mark Dufty for invaluable assistance with geology and mining regulations.

All mistakes are my own.

To the northern crime syndicate: Judith O'Reilly, Rob Parker, Adam Peacock, Chris McGeorge, Robert Scragg and Trevor Wood – thank you for welcoming me in to your supportive and riotous criminal fraternity.

To my wise and patient beta readers: Dr Lorraine Wilson (author of *This Is Our Undoing*), Jane Shufflebotham (aka Jane Jesmond, author of *On the Edge*), Barry Hatton (British foreign correspondent in Lisbon and author of *The Portuguese: A Modern History* and *Queen of the Sea: A History of Lisbon*) and – always first among equals – Marjory Flynn.

To my indefatigable agent Juliet Mushens, her insightful assistant Kiya Evans and everyone at Mushens Entertainment.

To my samba-dancing editor at Point Blank, Jenny Parrott, perceptive cha-cha-cha assistant Molly Scull, my condor-eyed copy editor, Francine Brody, and the fabulous conga team at Oneworld.

To my Erskine family, I couldn't do any of this without you: surf boys Andrew and Joseph, lifeguard Jonathan; with special thanks to my brilliant nonagenarian father-in-law, Andrew Erskine, who reads everything and misses nothing.

About the Author

Fiona Erskine is a professional engineer based in Teesside, although her work has taken her around the world. As a female engineer, she has often been the lone representative of her gender in board meetings, cargo ships and night-time factories, and her fiction offers a fascinating insight into this traditionally male world. She is the author of *The Chemical Detective* and *The Chemical Reaction*. *The Chemical Detective* was shortlisted for the Specsavers Debut Crime Novel Award. Her second thriller in the Jaq Silver series, *The Chemical Reaction*, was shortlisted for the Staunch Prize.